MW01257886

STATE OF RETRIBUTION

FIRST FAMILY SERIES, BOOK 9

MARIE FORCE

State of Retribution
First Family Series, Book 9
By: Marie Force

Published by HTJB, Inc.
Copyright 2025. HTJB, Inc.
Cover design by Kristina Brinton and Ashley Lopez
Cover photography by Regina Wamba
Models: Robert John and Ellie Dulac
Print Layout: E-book Formatting Fairies
ISBN: 978-1966871064

HTJB, Inc.
PO Box 370
Portsmouth, RI 02871 USA
author@marieforce.com

The First Family Series

Book 1: State of Affairs
Book 2: State of Grace
Book 3: State of the Union
Book 4: State of Shock
Book 5: State of Denial
Book 6: State of Bliss
Book 7: State of Suspense
Book 8: State of Alert
Book 9: State of Retribution
Book 10: State of Preservation

More new books are always in the works. For the most up-to-date list of what's available from the First Family Series, go to *marieforce.com/firstfamily*

CHAPTER ONE

Surrounded by Secret Service agents, President Nick Cappuano and First Lady Samantha Holland Cappuano were hustled through a ground-level door to an area of the White House she'd never seen before. Codes were punched in by agents who were as serious as they'd ever been.

"What's this about, Brant?" Nick asked his lead agent, John Brantley Jr.

"I'm not sure yet, sir. We were given orders to get you and the first lady to a secure location, so that's what we're doing."

"The kids." Sam looked over her shoulder as they were rushed toward an elevator. "My sisters..."

"They're right behind us," her lead agent, Vernon Rogers, said.

"Where? I don't see them."

"Keep moving," Vernon said. "I promise they're being well cared for."

Sam had full faith in him and the other agents, but whatever terrorist threat had been levied against the annual Easter Egg Roll on the South Lawn of the White House had the agents behaving in a way she'd seen only one other time—

when someone had thrown tomatoes at her and Nick when they were out to dinner in Dewey Beach.

The elevator conveyed them several floors down to an area she hadn't known existed.

"Have you been down here?" she asked Nick.

"Only once, when I was made aware of where it was in case I ever needed to get here on my own."

Sam wanted to ask where his detail would be if he were on his own, but she probably didn't want to know the answer to that question. She felt sick with fear and sweaty with nerves over when their children would be brought to them.

"Felt wrong leaving the kids," Nick said.

"It's not like we were given a choice."

"Still."

"I know."

He put an arm around her and led her to a sofa while the agents worked secure phones in the room. "Have a seat. I'll see if I can get you some water or something."

"All I want is my kids and my sisters and their kids and the others." Everyone they loved had attended the event, and now she and Nick were safely tucked away while who knew what was happening to their hundreds of guests.

Nick was huddled with his agents, his face tense, which did nothing to calm her nerves. And where was the rest of his team? Why weren't they here with him figuring out what was happening and what they were going to do about it?

A few more minutes passed before she couldn't take it anymore. She got up and crossed the room to where he was conferring with the agents. "Where are my children and the others?"

"We're confirming their locations right now, ma'am," Brant said, his tone and expression grave.

"You don't know where they are?" Sam was on the verge of shrieking and didn't care who was listening.

Vernon put a hand on her arm, which instantly had the

effect of calming her. But only slightly. "We're working on figuring out what's going on. The kids are with their details, who'll keep them safe."

"I want them with me."

"I understand."

"Do you?" She blinked back tears. "I want my children with me. *Right now.*"

Vernon activated a radio microphone. "FLOTUS wants the kids brought to them immediately, over."

"Add that POTUS wants them, too," Nick said.

"Make that POTUS and FLOTUS requesting, over."

Vernon listened for a minute. "They're not authorized to be in this space. That's the hangup."

"I authorize them and the rest of our family to be in this room." Nick's tone offered no room for negotiation. "As of this second."

Sam would've found that ridiculously sexy if she hadn't been scared out of her mind.

Vernon pressed the button. "POTUS authorizes immediate access, over." After a pause, he said, "They're coming down now."

Sam's knees were weak and her stomach queasy as she focused on breathing.

As if he knew she needed the support, Nick put an arm around her.

She leaned into him. "Thank you."

"I'm sorry about this."

"It's certainly not your fault—or theirs," she said of their dedicated agents. "Do you know what happened?"

"Drones were spotted entering the National Capital Region's Special Flight Rules Area, which is the restricted airspace within thirty miles of DCA."

Sam recognized the code for Ronald Reagan Washington National Airport.

"Unmanned aircraft, like drones, aren't allowed within a

fifteen-mile inner radius ring without FAA authorization. A dozen drones breached the inner ring and were thought to be headed for the White House."

Sam's mouth had gone dry as she listened to his explanation. "For what purpose?" she asked softly.

"They're still trying to ascertain the type of drone and what the intentions were. The drones were shot down by military planes dispatched from Joint Base Andrews. A team has been sent to retrieve them so we can figure out who sent them and why."

He hesitated, only for a second, but she saw it.

"What else?"

"That's all I know."

"Don't lie to me."

"Samantha..."

"Tell me the truth."

He sighed. "It's being treated as a potential assassination attempt."

Thankfully, he was standing right next to her and moved fast to grab her when her knees gave out. He moved them to chairs. "Breathe, Samantha. Everyone is okay. Whatever's happening was thwarted. Everything worked the way it was supposed to."

She focused on the comforting sound of his voice as she tried to force air into unreceptive lungs. Her chest felt as if it was caught in a vise that was squeezing her tighter by the second.

Someone had launched drones with the intent of *assassinating* her husband.

"Sam, talk to me."

"Where're the kids?"

"They're coming now. We need to be ready for them so we don't scare them any more than they already are."

That did the trick to snap her out of the weird state she'd slipped into after hearing the dreaded word *assassination*. She took a series of deep breaths and fought through the panic that would stay with her long after today. That someone had gone so far as to launch weapons aiming for them... It was the stuff of nightmares.

The door opened, and Scotty pushed the twins in ahead of him.

They ran for her and Nick, who caught them up in tearful hugs.

Aubrey sobbed as she clung to Sam.

Scotty rubbed Alden's back as the boy hugged Nick. Their fourteen-year-old wore a tense expression, which meant he'd heard rumblings about what'd happened—and what *could've* happened.

Sam reached out her hand to him, and he took it, giving it a squeeze.

"Everything is all right, guys," Nick said.

The door opened again, admitting the twins' older brother, Elijah, and his wife, Candace, Sam's sisters and their children.

Sam scooped Aubrey into her arms as she stood to greet the others on legs that were still wobbly from the shock.

Her sisters hugged her and Aubrey.

"That was fun," Tracy said with her trademark sarcasm.

"I'm so sorry, everyone," Nick said. "I hate that our good time was interrupted by nonsense."

"It's okay, Uncle Nick," their niece, Abby, said. "I got to keep my eggs, so it was still fun."

"I'm glad to hear that, sweetie," Nick said, forcing a smile for the child's sake.

Eli took Aubrey from Sam, who'd begun to realize how heavy the little girl had gotten since the last time she'd lifted her. Their Littles were growing up fast, a thought that depressed her. She wanted to keep them young and innocent forever, so they'd never understand words like *assassination* or *terrorist attack*.

Sam turned to Scotty and hugged him tightly. "Are you all right?"

"As long as you guys are, I'm good."

"Did you see my dad's family anywhere?" Nick asked Tracy and Sam's other sister, Angela.

"They were escorted to their car and allowed to leave the grounds, along with most of the other guests," Angela said.

"That's good," Nick said, sounding relieved.

Brant came over to him. "Mr. President, you're needed in the Situation Room. The others are free to return to the residence, but we're asking the first family to remain indoors for now."

"I have to go to work," Sam said.

"That's not going to be possible today, ma'am," Brant said. "We need all available resources here until we have more information about what happened."

Sam didn't like being told she couldn't do something, but she wasn't about to make their jobs any more difficult than they already were. Besides, after the shock of the day's events, she wanted—and needed—to be with her kids.

"I'm sorry." Nick kissed her cheek. "I'll find you guys as soon as I can."

"We're fine. Do what you need to."

After Nick departed for the Situation Room, the agents escorted Sam and the others to the second-floor residence via the elevator that opened into the hallway where they lived. They trooped off the elevator like survivors of the apocalypse, a thought that would've made Sam laugh at her own theatrics under other circumstances.

Nothing about this was funny.

They ended up in the third-floor conservatory, their favorite place to gather. The twins climbed onto Sam's lap, and she wrapped her arms around them while Scotty sat next to her. That they wanted to be close to her made her thankful she'd been unable to leave for work. She was still somewhat new to this motherhood gig and to realizing there was nowhere else she should be than with her children after what had occurred today.

She felt ashamed for even wanting to go to work, but the impulse was hardwired into her at this point. When her phone rang, she worked around the twins to dig it out of her jacket pocket. She wasn't surprised to see the name of her partner, Detective Freddie Cruz, on the screen.

"Hey."

"Hey yourself. Are you okay?"

"I've been better. What're you hearing?"

"I'm not sure I should tell you."

"I already know what they think the goal was." When Eli gestured for the twins to come see him, Sam released them, thankful she could talk more freely to her best friend with the Littles across the room and out of earshot.

"It's unbelievable."

"Thank goodness everything worked the way it's supposed to."

"For sure. But still…"

"Yeah. I hear you."

"What can I do for you?"

"Hold down the fort there. The Secret Service has asked us to stay here. Tell Gonzo, too," she said of her sergeant, Tommy "Gonzo" Gonzales.

"I will."

"Anything going on?"

"A homicide in Southeast. We're on it. Don't worry about anything." Since she'd been signed out for the Easter weekend, Gonzo would've gotten the call on that.

"What? Me worry?"

"I can't imagine how you must be feeling."

"I know it goes with the job and all that, but when it's your own husband…"

"I'm sorry. It's unbelievable."

"Everyone is okay. We're just trying to keep calm over here and stay focused on the kids. What was supposed to have been a fun day sure as hell got messed up."

"It's all over the news."

"Are they using the A word?"

"Yes. They've got national security experts on talking about all the various implications and who might've done it. They're listing some of the more notorious terrorist groups, but so far, no one has claimed responsibility."

It was daunting to think the whole world was talking about —and speculating about—the thwarted assassination of the U.S. president, who also happened to be Sam's husband. "I'm sure I'll hear about it later. Keep me posted on the new case."

"I will. Hang in there."

"I'm hanging. Talk to you later."

Sam closed her phone and released another deep sigh.

"What's the A word?" Scotty asked.

Shit.

"I thought you were talking to Tracy."

"I was multitasking."

Sam laughed and immediately felt better, the way she often did around him. "Nothing to worry about."

"Sure it is. Tell me."

"What did you hear?"

"That there were drones where they shouldn't be, and it's being treated as some sort of possible attack."

"That's right."

"So the A word is attack, then?"

Sam wanted so badly to lie to him, to protect him, but five minutes on his phone would reveal the truth. She'd rather he hear it from her. "In this case, it stands for 'assassination.'" She and Scotty had declared that a swear word when Nick first became president.

"So, like, they were coming for Dad?"

"We don't know that for sure, but that's the theory."

He stared out the big windows at the city they called home.

"What're you thinking?"

"At times like this, it's better not to think."

Smiling, Sam wrapped an arm around him and kissed the top of his head. "I love you so, *so* much, and you're just what I need right now. Thank you for that."

"You and Dad are just what I need all the time. Thank you for *that*."

"Being your parents is the greatest pleasure and privilege of our lives."

CHAPTER TWO

The reports were surreal. Fourteen drones had been recovered, equipped with semiautomatic weapons that, had the drones made it through the robust layers of security, could've killed scores of people gathered for a fun and joyful event at the White House. Everyone Nick loved might've been killed in the effort to get to him.

No one had claimed responsibility as of yet, and the investigation was in the earliest stages. His intelligence team was working as fast as they could to gather data and trace the origin of the devices.

From his vantage point at the head of the table, Nick eyed the others. Teresa Howard, the National Security Advisor he'd inherited from President Nelson, and Defense Secretary Tobias Jennings, also inherited. Nick liked and trusted them and planned to retain them in their roles going forward.

Admiral Forrest Malin, the new chair of the Joint Chiefs of Staff, replacing General Michael Wilson, who, along with other members of the Joint Chiefs, had betrayed Nick—and the Constitution—so flagrantly.

Grace Crowley, acting head of the National Intelligence Agency, whose permanent appointment was pending before the Senate. She was one of the people retired Senator Graham O'Connor, Nick's friend and mentor, had recommended.

They were in the process of putting together their own team, mostly from Graham's deep stable of contacts and trusted allies.

Vice President Gretchen Henderson, Nick's choice to fill the role he'd vacated after he was promoted, was asking all the right questions and demanding fast action from subordinates. She and her teenage children had been on the South Lawn during the Egg Roll, and she was clearly rattled by the day's events and the understanding of what could've happened.

Hours after being hustled off the South Lawn, they still had no idea where the drones had come from. It was easy to lose track of time in the windowless Situation Room under the glow of fluorescent lights.

"The first two that were recovered have no identifying marks," FBI Director Sally Monroe said. Nelson had appointed her to a ten-year term following the murder of the previous director, Troy Hamilton. "No brand-name components or serial numbers. It's possible they were homemade."

"And still no claim of responsibility?" Secret Service Director Ambrose Pierce asked.

"Nothing yet," Crowley said. "We've picked up no chatter or any indication something like this was in the works, which we normally would've if they were sent by known terrorist groups."

They were spinning their wheels at this point, and Nick had heard enough. When he stood, everyone else did, too. "I'm going upstairs," he said to his chief of staff, Terry O'Connor. "Keep me in the loop on any developments."

"Yes, sir."

He left the room, feeling frustrated, disgusted and unsettled. All the systems in place to protect the nation's capital had held that day, but this was a daunting reminder of the many threats of violence against the government. As the CEO of that government, he was the main target, but a mass casualty incident on the lawn of the White House would've had the desired effect of causing chaos, even if he hadn't been one of the victims.

That one of his family members could've been killed made him sick. Scotty, Aubrey, Alden, Elijah, his little brothers, Sam's nieces and nephews and many other family members and close friends, all of them so dear to him and Sam, had been in grave danger that day because of him.

Because he held the highest office in the land. Because he'd inherited it, rather than winning it in an election. Because he was the youngest president in history. Because they didn't agree with the way he did the job.

Who knew which of those things had motivated someone to fly drones armed with semiautomatic weapons into the National Capital Region's airspace? Who knew what motivated anyone to do such a thing?

With Brant by his side, he trudged up the stairs to the residence, eager to see Sam and hopefully tuck the kids in if they were still up.

"Thank you for everything today, Brant. Please pass along my thanks to the other agents as well. We appreciate everything you do to keep us safe."

"I'll tell them, sir. We're all thankful the incident was neutralized before anyone was hurt or worse."

"I don't like the feel of this. Not one bit."

"I don't either, sir. It's unsettling, to say the least."

"Can you please let me know that we're on for normal operations tomorrow for Sam and the kids?"

"I'll confirm that and call you when I know, sir."

"After that, go home and get some rest. I have a feeling we're in for some long days around here."

"Yes, sir. I'll see you in the morning."

They parted company at the top of the stairs, where

Melinda, one of the other agents on Nick's detail, stood ready to take over.

"Evening, Mr. President."

"Hi there, Melinda."

"Are you home for the night, sir?"

"I am."

"Very good. Thank you. Have a good evening."

As if that was likely after this day. "You do the same." As he walked down the red-carpeted hallway toward "home," he tugged at his tie and released the top button of his dress shirt. He'd come upstairs to change out of the casual clothing he'd worn to the Egg Roll so he could address the nation about the day's events looking like the president rather than a dad who'd been enjoying an event with his kids and hundreds of other children until terrorists came to call.

Today was supposed to have been one of the rare "fun" days, when he was able to entertain family and friends as well as the public for an annual event everyone enjoyed. Even the fun days sucked in this place. In the nearly five months since he'd become the president, Nick had worked hard to remain positive and optimistic, even in the face of never-ending challenges, relentless scrutiny and baseless accusations that took time and energy to defuse.

But this... This was demoralizing.

He looked in on the twins, who were already asleep in the bed they still shared. At some point, they'd decide to sleep in their own rooms, but they weren't ready yet, and no one was interested in rushing them after everything they'd been through losing their parents so tragically.

The light was still on in Scotty's room, so he knocked on the door and poked his head in.

His son's smile was a balm on the wound of this day. "Hey. How's it going?"

Nick shrugged. "Nothing new. My team is on it. Try not to worry."

"What?" His tone was deceptively light. "Me worry about drones shooting my dad? And here I was afraid of plain old guns. I was so naïve."

Nick went to sit on Scotty's bed and gave Skippy the dog a scratch behind the ears that earned him a contented sigh from the dog. "I don't want you to be worried about something happening to me. As we saw today, I'm very well protected."

"They didn't mess around."

"No, they didn't, and a lot of other things went right today, such as the jets that were scrambled to shoot down the unauthorized aircraft inside the zone of protection around DC."

"Would they have shot down planes with people on them, too?"

At fourteen, he was too old for lies and deflection. "Yeah, they would've. Pilots know they're not allowed to fly over DC without prior authorization, so the military would have to send jets to figure out what they're up to and possibly shoot them down, which, thankfully, has never happened."

"I can't imagine having to do that, even if they were bad guys."

"I know. I can't either. But I don't want you awake and afraid all night, you hear me?"

"Yeah, I won't be. I'm tired."

Nick leaned in for a hug. "Knowing you're here, in the house with me, even if it's the freaking White House, makes everything easier and better for me."

"I like knowing you're just downstairs most of the time, even if you're in places I can't get to sometimes."

They held on to each other a little longer than usual after the stressful day. "Love you, buddy."

"Love you, too. I hope you can sleep."

"I'm gonna try. Don't forget to take Skippy out to pee one more time."

"She won't let me forget."

Nick gave Skippy a kiss on the head. "You're a good girl, Skip." He swore the dog smiled at him, which made him smile back. "Sleep tight, guys."

"We will."

"See you in the morning."

"Maybe I should stay home tomorrow. You know, in case there's more trouble."

"Nice try, but it's back to eighth grade for you. You already missed today."

"And I'm sure I'll pay for that tomorrow."

Nick walked away laughing. He had the best son in the whole world and would fight with anyone who said otherwise.

In their suite, Sam was curled up on the sofa, watching TV and waiting for him. She sat up when he came in, straightened her ponytail and patted the seat next to her.

He sat and put his arms around her.

She curled into his embrace and breathed him in. "How are you?"

"Better after five minutes with Scotty."

"He does have that effect."

"He thinks he should stay home tomorrow, just in case there's more trouble."

Sam snorted. "That's so something I would've tried back in the day, not that I had drones coming for my family or anything like that."

"I'm worried they're all going to be traumatized."

"They're okay. Eli and I spent a lot of time with the three of them tonight and did everything we could to reassure them. The twins have already moved on. Scotty will take a little more time to process it."

"Did Eli go back to school?" He was a junior at Princeton and had been home for the Easter weekend.

"They left about an hour ago."

Eli's detail, led by Nate, who was now dating Sam's niece Brooke, would safely see Eli and his wife back to New Jersey.

"It's a relief to me that he has a detail, and we don't have to worry about them driving."

"I had that same thought when they left." She combed her fingers through his hair, making him sigh with pleasure the way Skippy had. "What're you hearing about the investigation?"

"The drones were unmarked. No brand names or serial numbers. They were equipped with semiautomatic weapons."

"Good God."

"I know."

"So they're untraceable."

"Possibly. No claims of responsibility either, which is unusual."

"Scary shit."

"To say the least. But I don't want to talk about it anymore. What else went on around here? Tell me something cute and funny the Littles said or did."

"Aubrey is still fixated on chickens and eggs and why you don't have a baby chicken after you eat an egg. She's not sure that any of us should be eating either of those things until she gets some answers. Eli made her crazy asking which comes first, the chicken or the egg, and everyone had an opinion on that."

"I'm very sorry I missed that conversation."

"It was highly entertaining, as most things are with them."

"What did we do for entertainment around here before we had these kids to keep us on our toes?"

"We had a lot more sex."

He barked out a laugh. Leave it to her to get his mind out of the doom spiral it'd been in for hours. "That's very true, although we're not exactly hurting in that department with them around."

"We're doing just fine. Do you think you could sleep?"

"I can try." Sleep was a problem for him even on nights when he hadn't been the subject of a potential assassination attempt. It would probably be impossible tonight, but he'd lie down with her and hold her close and soak up the special comfort that came from being with her.

They got ready for bed and met in the middle of the king-sized bed. They joked that they could sleep in a twin bed because they required so little space. With her warm and fragrant and soft in his arms, he was able to truly exhale after the stressful day.

"Why does it seem that the second we deal with one thing, something else comes along to remind us not to get too comfortable?" he asked.

"I guess you could say it's the life we've chosen with two jobs that never quit."

"We should've made better life choices. What would you pick if you had it to do over?"

"Oh damn, I don't know. I've never been good at anything else."

Scoffing, he said, "Come on. That's not true."

"No, it really is. On many days, it feels more like a calling than a job. What would you pick?"

"I would've been a high school history teacher. I think I would've liked that."

"Well, anything is better than this."

He laughed. "You can say that again."

"I hate to make it about me at a time like this, but please tell me I can go to work tomorrow. We've got a new homicide, and I've been asked to attend a meeting in the afternoon to go over the new evidence in the Stahl investigation."

"Should you be in that meeting?"

"Probably not, but it's for all commanders, and I refuse to request special treatment."

"Sam..."

"Don't worry. I'll be fine as long as I'm able to get to work."

"I'm waiting to hear from Brant that you and the kids are

operating normally tomorrow. He said he'd call me when he got the word."

"I really hope I can go."

"I hope so, too. I'm sorry they kept you home today."

"That was for the best. The kids needed me. I wouldn't have felt right leaving them."

"I felt terrible about being pulled away from all of you."

"We understood."

"Still... All I wanted was to be with you guys."

"We know that, babe." She placed her hand on his face and gave a gentle tug to turn him to receive her kiss. "I know this is another awful situation after a string of them, but you'll handle this the same way you've handled the others. I have faith in you. We have faith in you."

Because her lips were warm and soft and sweet, he kept his pressed against them, breathing her in and wallowing in the comfort he drew from her.

For the longest time, they only kissed, his lips sliding over hers and nothing more, nothing demanding. This was all about relief that everyone was safe after a frightening day. It was never far from either of their minds that they could be taken from each other in an instant of madness, as both their jobs came with risks that could be deadly at any time. If they thought too much about those possibilities, neither would be able to function.

Today's events had been a reminder of how quickly everything could change.

"The thought of someone wanting to harm you..." Her voice was thick with tears and emotion. "It takes my breath away."

He wiped the tears from her face. "I'm right here. I'm not going anywhere."

Though he said what she wanted to hear, they were both painfully aware that his assurances were just words. Yes, he was surrounded by world-class security and intelligence that'd worked as designed that day—and hopefully would in the future, too. But it was nerve-racking to know that if someone wanted him dead badly enough, all it would take for them to succeed was one mistake by the human beings responsible for his security.

There were no guarantees.

She wrapped herself around him and held on tight. "It's unbearable. All of it."

"Welcome to my world, love. Every time you walk out the door, I'm terrified you won't come back."

"With Vernon and Jimmy looking out for me, I'm safer than ever."

"Still..."

She tightened her arms around him. "I know. It's a terrible way to live. I go days without actively worrying about it, and then something like this happens, and it's just a huge reminder of how you walk around with a target on your back all because of the position you hold. At least if it were to happen to me, it'd be because I arrested someone or something like that. You're just showing up to do a job that someone has to do."

"We should change the subject so we have a prayer of sleeping tonight."

The phone on the bedside table rang. He released her to pick up the call from Brant.

"Mr. President, in consultation with Director Pierce and the details for FLOTUS and the children, it's been determined that we'll proceed with normal operations tomorrow."

"Thank you for the update."

"We'll see you in the morning, sir."

"See you then." He replaced the receiver on the base of the phone. "Did you hear that?"

"Yes, and it's a relief. It'll be good to get back to normal."

"I think so, too."

She smoothed her hand over his hair and down to caress his face. "Do you think you can sleep?"

"You've got parts of me awake that have no interest whatsoever in sleep."

"What parts would those be?"

He pressed his hard cock against her soft belly.

"*Oh*, I see. What should be done about that?"

"There're several options."

"Which one most appeals to you?"

"Any of them as long as you're involved."

"I'm definitely involved." She ran her hand down his chest and over his abdomen to cup his erection in her warm hand.

Just that quickly, the horrors of the day faded into the deepest recesses of his mind to be dealt with later. Right now, he had far better things to do than wonder who'd tried to kill him and many others and whether they'd try again.

She liked to talk about his superpowers when it came to her, but that was hers. With one touch, she could take him far away from the worries that would still be waiting for him in the morning. For this moment, he could lose himself in the love of his life and forget the rest. On many a day, she and their kids were the only respite he got from the endless grind of the world's most stressful job.

He slipped a hand under her T-shirt, craving the feel of her silky skin against him. The shirt was up and over her head in a matter of seconds as his lips crashed down on hers in a kiss so hot, it made his head spin and nearly made him come in her eager hand.

"Together," he managed to say as he moved them so he was on top. He could tell he took her by surprise as he suddenly switched from fast and furious to slow and sultry, kissing her neck before worshipping each nipple, taking his time as she got more impatient by the second and tried to move things along.

That only made him more determined to go slow. His Samantha was the most impatient person on the planet, and it was his goal at moments such as this to show her the benefits of waiting.

"You're being mean, and I've already had a tough enough day."

Amused, he looked up at her from his perch at her abdomen. "How am I being mean?"

She scowled at him. "You know exactly what you're doing."

"I'm making love to my wife and giving her all the bells and whistles because it's been such a hard day." Before she had a chance to respond, he'd pushed her legs apart and pressed his tongue to the very heart of her, drawing a surprised gasp that almost made him laugh at how quickly she'd changed her tune.

He went all in, tongue, lips, fingers and suction in just the right place to make her moan from the pleasure, taking her right to the edge of release before backing off and starting over. That earned him a frustrated groan that quickly morphed into something else entirely as he pressed two fingers deep inside her and curled them just so while he sucked on her clit.

Kaboom.

She was still coming when he pressed his cock into her to ride the waves of her release.

When she finally opened her eyes, she found him gazing down at her with an expression she'd probably consider smug as he held perfectly still inside her.

"Hi," he said.

"What's up?"

He gave a thrust of his hips to answer her question, letting her know that only one of them had reached the big finish.

She ran her fingers down his back to his ass and pulled him in even deeper as she curled her legs around his hips.

Just like he knew what got to her, she knew how to return the favor.

He dipped his head to kiss her softly and sweetly before he picked up the pace. Once again, he caught her off guard when he used his fingers to draw another gasping climax from her before he let himself join her.

"So many dirty tricks," she said, breathing hard as he rested on top of her.

"You love my dirty tricks."

"For some strange reason, I do."

"Could it be because you go off like a rocket?"

He withdrew from her and rested his head on her chest.

She chuckled as she put her arms around him. "That might have something to do with it."

"Thought so."

"You're being smug."

"I believe I've earned the right."

"Mmm-hmmm." She held him close as she yawned. "Do you think you can sleep?"

"I'm going to try."

She rubbed small circles on his back. "Relax and let it go. I've got you."

Nick closed his eyes and tried to keep his mind from wandering to places that would keep him awake all night. He focused instead on the bewitching vanilla and lavender scent of his love as he drifted off to sleep.

CHAPTER THREE

T he kids were cranky and out of sorts in the morning, which made for a difficult slog through getting them dressed and fed. Nick had gone to an early security briefing and hadn't returned for breakfast the way he did some days. No doubt today wouldn't be a normal day at the office for him.

By the time the twins left with their detail, Sam was ready to go back to bed. But that wasn't an option with a new body in the morgue and the inquest in Stahl's mass murder case beginning that afternoon. At some point this week, she had to find time to meet with Assistant U.S. Attorney Faith Miller to discuss her testimony at the preliminary hearing for Harlan Peckham, charged in the murder of U.S. Attorney Tom Forrester and the shooting of FBI Agent Avery Hill.

They would also be discussing final preparations for the trial of the former president's disgraced son, Christopher Nelson, scheduled to begin in a week. He'd gone on a murderous rampage to try to push Nick, his father's popular vice president, out of the spotlight in pursuit of his own political ambitions. Among others, he'd killed Sam's ex-husband, Peter Gibson. That trial hung over her—and Nick—

as they dreaded resurrecting that horrible story and having everything about that case relitigated once again.

Nick's glory days of soaring approval numbers seemed like a long time ago now that he was the president and the subject of nonstop attacks on everything from his character to his youth to the fact that he'd never been elected.

Her day had barely begun, and she was already exhausted. Her sleep had been plagued with disturbing dreams of people coming for her and Nick, wielding guns and other weapons, including a crossbow that had her waking in a cold sweat from a dead sleep at three a.m.

"Are you okay?" Scotty asked as he put his plate in the dishwasher.

"Yeah, you know... Still processing it all."

"Same."

"Are *you* okay?"

"Trying to be, but it's hard to think about people wanting to harm my parents simply because of what they do for a living."

"When your dad and I were considering whether to bring you into our lives, that was something we talked about, whether it was fair to do that to you."

"I have no regrets about who I chose to be my parents, so don't add that to your list of worries."

"That's nice to hear, but I hope you know that we wish you weren't burdened with those concerns."

"It's worth it to have everything that goes along with you two. Except the kissing and stuff. I could definitely do with less of that."

Sam laughed as she hugged him. "Sorry, pal. That's not likely to change any time soon. Your dad is an excellent kisser."

He scowled. "Why'd you have to go there?"

"Just stating the truth. Go brush your teeth so your breath doesn't stink if you decide you want to kiss a girl."

"Ew. That's very unsanitary."

"I can't wait for your thoughts to change on that topic. Any day now."

"Whatever you say."

Scotty took off to brush his teeth and grab his backpack. When he returned, Sam was waiting to give him a hug before he left with his detail. "Have a good day. I love you."

He hugged her back, a little tighter than usual. "I love you, too. I hope you have a good day as well."

"That's the goal."

"See ya on the flip side."

As she showered and got dressed, Sam thought about Scotty and how fun it had been to watch him mature into a delightful young man. The best thing she and Nick had ever done was to take him into their home when they were barely married. Even though the timing hadn't been ideal, they had zero regrets and loved him with all their hearts. Well, the one regret she had was that they hadn't met him sooner. In four years, he'd be heading off to college, a thought that made her profoundly sad.

Thankfully, they'd have the twins to keep them entertained after Scotty left.

That reminded her that their lawyer friend Andy Simone had texted yesterday with an update on their plan to adopt Alden, Aubrey and Elijah, even though Eli was a legal adult. They hoped that would fend off any future attempts by their maternal grandparents, aunt and uncle to get at the money the kids' billionaire father had left them.

Hi there, Andy had written. *Wanted to give you an update... We've started the paperwork on the adoption, and it should be fairly straightforward since Elijah is the twins' legal guardian. As such, his approval is the only one needed, and he's completed all the initial paperwork. Will keep you posted and apprised of the future court date at which it will become official. Let me know if you have any questions!*

Sam composed a reply to him. *Hey, sorry for the delay in*

responding. As I'm sure you've heard, yesterday was a bit nuts around here. Good times. Thanks for the update. We'll all rest easier when this is done. Appreciate your help, as always!

Then she forwarded Andy's note to the secure BlackBerry she used to communicate with Nick and Eli, who'd decided to be adopted along with his siblings so they'd all belong to the same family.

As she unlocked the bedside drawer where she kept her service weapon, cuffs and other items for work, she felt weirdly off her game as she went through the rote motions of a regular day. Nothing about this day was regular, however. Hanging over everything was the reality of what'd happened yesterday and how close they'd come to disaster.

She went downstairs to meet Vernon and Jimmy, feeling the weight of it all on her shoulders and hoping she could put it aside to focus on her job after a long weekend with her family.

"Good morning," Vernon said.

"Morning."

Harold, one of the ushers, held Sam's coat for her.

"Thank you, Harold."

"My pleasure, ma'am. You have a good day."

"You do the same."

"Every day at the White House is a good day. Well, some are better than others."

That made her laugh. "Indeed."

Vernon held the door to the back seat of the SUV for her. "How're you holding up?"

"Just dandy. Anything new?"

"Nothing much. The investigation is ongoing. Yada, yada."

He closed the door and got into the driver's seat.

When they were on the way to HQ, she got a text from Andy. *Can't believe the news. Thank goodness you're all safe—and everyone else is, too.*

Thanks. Unsettling, to say the least.

"What can you tell me about what you're not supposed to tell me?" she asked Vernon and Jimmy.

"Honestly, nothing," Vernon said. "We're no closer to knowing who sent those drones than we were yesterday."

"That does nothing to calm my nerves."

"Our nerves are pretty raw, too."

"I'm sure they are. Thank you for the fast action yesterday, even if I seemed angry about the kids. I was terrified more than anything."

"We totally understand," Vernon said. "Don't give that another thought. I'd want my kids close to me during a situation like that, too."

"I can't believe how feral I can get over them."

"You're a mom. That's what moms do."

"That still takes me by surprise, though, that I'm a mother to three and a half kids." They considered Eli the half, since he was fully grown when he came into their lives, but they loved him like a son.

"It happened a little differently for you, but the feelings are universal."

"Yes, they are."

"I've been worried that I won't feel the right things for the baby," Jimmy said. His wife, Liz, was expecting their first child.

"I felt the same way before my oldest was born," Vernon said. "What if the baby comes, and I couldn't care less? But let me tell you... The second you set eyes on a child that's meant to be yours, it's all there."

Sam appreciated the way he said that—*a child that's meant to be yours.* "That's how it happened for me, too. After an hour with Scotty, I knew a million hours would never be enough. Same with the twins."

"You have a big, loving heart, Jimmy," Vernon said. "You're going to be a great dad."

"That means a lot coming from you. Your kids worship you."

"They'd better, or I'll kick their asses."

"Haha," Sam said. "As if."

"I got lucky with some pretty great daughters," Vernon said, "and you're lucky with great kids, too, Sam. You and Liz are going to be awesome parents, Jimmy. I know it. Wait till that little face is looking up at you, completely dependent upon you for everything... Even when that little face isn't an infant anymore, it's a feeling unlike any other."

"Truth," Sam said. "And that they love you despite all your faults—*many, many* faults, in my case."

"They know how much you love them, Sam," Vernon said. "You show them that every day while setting a great example of being a high-profile working mom juggling a lot of demands and doing it seamlessly."

"Right. Seamlessly. If you ask me, all the seams are showing."

"Not to them. They see a badass mom getting shit done and taking down the bad guys."

"What he said," Jimmy added. "They have the coolest mom ever, and they know it."

"Do you guys get paid extra for these therapy sessions?"

"Nah," Vernon said on a guffaw. "They're free of charge because we like you."

"Aw shucks."

"So, hey, back to business." Vernon met her gaze in the mirror. "Everyone's on edge today, as you can imagine. They want someone inside headquarters with you."

"Who do they think is coming for me inside?"

"Until we know more about who sent those drones, we're doubling down across the board."

Sam didn't like the idea of agents hovering inside HQ, but she wasn't about to cause them any trouble when they were dealing with more than enough already. "Whatever you gotta do. I know you'll stay out of the way."

"We'll do our best."

"Which one of you is coming to Take Your Agent to Work Day?"

"Vernon," Jimmy said. "I get to stay with the car."

"I'm not sure which end of that is more boring," Sam said.

"We'll compare notes at the end of the day to decide who wins that contest," Vernon said.

Sam laughed. "Knock yourselves out."

When they arrived at HQ, Vernon held the back door for her and then followed her inside through the morgue entrance.

"I stop to say hi to Lindsey every morning. Do you have to come in with me?"

"I'll wait out here."

Sam walked through the automatic glass doors to the morgue, where Chief Medical Examiner Dr. Lindsey McNamara held court. "Morning."

"Hey, how's it going?"

"Just dandy. As a result of yesterday's madness, I got me a shadow inside the building as well as outside."

"Oh joy. I'm sure they're being extra vigilant."

"Yep. Still no clue on who sent the drones."

"Jeez. That's crazy. And scary." Lindsey shivered. "To think of all those people I love being exposed to such a thing."

Lindsey was due to marry Nick's chief of staff, Terry O'Connor, in July.

"Thank God the Secret Service moved quickly to protect everyone. From what I heard, they had the whole event secured in a matter of minutes, which couldn't have been easy with a crowd of that size."

"I'm sure they have extra people and intense training for events like that."

"Definitely. We're thankful that everything worked the way it was supposed to. How was your Easter?"

"It was nice. We saw my sisters and nieces in the morning and then went out to the farm and had dinner with Terry's family. Lovely day. How was yours at Camp David?"

"Relaxing and fun. The kids enjoyed the egg hunt the staff did for them."

"Was it hard to be there?"

Her sister Angela's husband had died of a fentanyl overdose during a visit to Camp David in early February. "At first. I avoided the cabin where Spencer died."

"Understandably."

"Nick likes being at Camp David so much that I'm trying to rally for his sake, but there'll always be a bit of a dark cloud over that place now."

"Of course there will. It's still so hard to believe it happened in the first place."

"For us, too. I mean, we had no idea he was reliant on pain meds or that he'd even been injured. It was such a shock." Sam and the rest of their family had been stunned to learn that Spencer had become addicted to pain medication following a back injury. After his doctors had cut him off from the meds, he'd resorted to buying pills on the street and had gotten some laced with the deadly substance. Sam and her team had hunted down the source of the pills that'd also killed numerous other people. The perpetrators were now awaiting trial.

"How're Angela and her kids doing?"

"They're getting by. I don't know how she's going to do it with a new baby on top of everything." A GoFundMe that Freddie had started for Angela, which Nick had shared to his vast social media audience, had given Angela a way to support her children for the time being.

"You'll all rally around her and get her through it."

"I suppose so. Well, I'd better get back to work after my four-day weekend that I enjoyed far too much."

"No such thing."

"Heard we caught a new case."

"Yes, killed by a single blow to the back of the head. I'll have more info for you guys shortly."

"Thank you, and welcome back to me, where my prize is a body in the morgue waiting for me."

Lindsey laughed. "We don't want you to get lazy."

"No chance of that around here. Talk to you later."

"Have a good day."

"You do the same, Doc."

Sam joined Vernon in the hallway. "Let me ask you something."

"Anything you want."

"How many extra agents were on duty for the event yesterday?"

"We had close to a thousand of our people there, with hundreds each from multiple other agencies as well as perimeter support from the MPD."

"Wow."

"That's pretty typical for high-profile public events like that."

"It's amazing to me, even as someone under protection, how the massive presence doesn't show."

"That's the goal. We don't want to detract from the enjoyment of the event, but we want it to be safe for everyone. A lot of planning and strategy go into it ahead of time."

"Thank you for that, and please give my thanks to everyone else, too. We appreciate all you do to keep us safe, and we probably don't say that often enough."

"I'll pass that on. It'll mean a lot to everyone."

"How close to me do you have to be today?"

"I need to keep you in sight."

"Good thing we have glass walls around here." To her team, gathered in the pit, she said, "Morning, citizens. Give me five minutes and then meet me in the conference room."

"Welcome back, LT," Detective Cameron Green said. "We missed you."

"I missed you, too. Not."

CHAPTER FOUR

The others laughed as Sam went into her office to stash her jacket and fire up her computer, experiencing the familiar jolt of adrenaline that came with being in her place with her people doing the job she loved. Despite the grimness of their work, it never got old for her. Maybe that was because she loved the people she got to do that grim work with and knew they loved her right back. That made even the most unbearable days less so than they would be otherwise.

While she often wondered what the rest of their colleagues thought of having the first lady in their midst, she hadn't received much pushback and had decided no news was good news on that front. The people who mattered to her, the ones she worked most closely with, were supportive, and that was all she cared about.

Sam emerged from her office and headed for the conference room, aware of Vernon following her but keeping her focus where it belonged. The demands of the job took up all the available space in her brain on most days without worrying about what someone else was doing. He'd promised to stay out of her way, and she believed him.

"Hope everyone who wasn't working had a nice weekend and a happy Easter. Who wants to brief me on the new case?"

"I will." Gonzo clicked on the space bar of the laptop to display the image of a Black woman with short gray hair and a warm smile on the screen at the front of the room. "Lorraine Sweeny, age sixty-two, was a nurse at the Green Acres Nursing Home in Northeast, which serves a low-income population. She'd worked a three-to-eleven shift on Saturday and was attacked as she walked home from the Metro. Her husband noticed her phone had stopped moving and went to find out what was holding her up. He found her body."

Sam winced on behalf of the poor man who'd made such a dreadful discovery. "And we're sure he had nothing to do with it?"

"He was despondent," Detective Neveah Charles said. "We had him transported to the ER."

Sam nodded. "What was the cause of death for Mrs. Sweeny?"

"Blunt force trauma to the back of her head with no defensive wounds, which means she never saw it coming," Green said.

"Are we thinking it was random?"

"Hard to say," Charles said. "We're digging into her life, looking for anyone who might've had a beef and not finding anything other than that she was a kind, compassionate woman who gave of herself to her patients, her family and her church. From what we can see, she went to work, came home, spent time with friends and family, went to church, rinse and repeat. She had five young grandchildren she was very devoted to."

Sam's heart ached for people she'd never met.

"We've added to the death toll as of twenty minutes ago," Gonzo said. "Thirty-six-year-old Nate Andrews, a white, married father of two, who worked at the Department of Labor as an analyst. He was out for a run in Adams Morgan later on

Sunday evening when he, too, was struck from behind with an unidentified object. He was transported to GW Trauma and died this morning."

Sam was beginning to wish the Secret Service had forbidden her return to work.

"We started looking into him yesterday since the attack was similar to Sweeny," Green said, "but like with her, we're not finding any motivation for murder. Early days, though."

"There's one more," Gonzo said. "Twenty-two-year-old Alexa Prescott, a student at Marymount in Arlington, who worked as a waitress at a restaurant on 14th Street. She was walking to the bus stop early this morning, after working last night, when she was hit from behind. She died at the scene."

"Do we have any security footage from the scenes?"

"Archie's team is on that. He's still out tending to a personal matter."

Sam needed to check in with her friend, who was caring for a woman he'd become close to who'd been abducted, beaten and sexually assaulted but had no memory of what'd happened.

"What're we doing about an alert to the public?" Sam asked the sergeant.

"Captain Malone is working on that this morning with Public Affairs and will be issuing it shortly. He wants us to brief the media."

"I'll do that, and then I want to talk to our victims' families," Sam said as she stood.

"We spoke with each of them over the weekend," Gonzo said.

"Thank you for doing that. I'd like to see them, too, just so they know I'm here and trying to get them some answers along with my very capable team."

"Understood." Gonzo handed her the reports on all three homicides.

"Thank you for the great work this weekend. If anyone

needs to speak to Dr. Trulo, please reach out to him." She'd learned to encourage them to seek help from the department psychiatrist as needed, rather than letting the stress build up.

"Yes, ma'am," everyone said on the way out of the room.

Freddie Cruz hung back. "How're you doing?"

"I'll be better when we know who sent drones strapped with semiautomatic weapons to disrupt our event."

"They have no clue?"

"Nothing yet. They appear to be homemade devices with no traceable components."

"Jeez."

"The full power of federal law enforcement is working that case, so I'm going to stay focused on our three victims."

Freddie glanced at Vernon, positioned outside the conference room. "Your detail has moved inside."

"For now. Abundance of caution and all that."

"I'm sorry you guys are dealing with this insanity."

"We're told it comes with the butlers and the fancy digs."

"Sorry if I'm not joking about someone trying to kill my best friends yet."

"We're not joking either. Just trying to keep things real while continuing to do our jobs. That's what I need from you right now. I need you to help me keep it real. Can you do that?"

"I can try."

She placed a hand on his chest. "I know you're upset, and I know it's because you love us, and we love you, too. But I have to keep putting one foot in front of the other while this is happening. It's how I'll survive it. You know?"

"Yeah, I get it, and I'm here for whatever you need. As always."

"There's tremendous comfort in that, believe me. I've got to do the briefing and take care of a couple of other things, and then we'll go see the families, okay?"

"Sounds good. Well, except for the part about visiting the grieving families."

Sam smiled. They both hated having to do that part of the job.

"Let me know what I can do to help."

"Will do."

She went to her office and pored over the reports from the weekend incidents. They were filled with heartbreaking details, such as how Lorraine Sweeny was weeks away from retirement and Nate Andrews's wife had recently given birth to their second child. In the latest report, she learned that Alexa Prescott had grown up in foster care and was putting herself through college on a full scholarship.

Sam made note of these details so she could take them with her to the podium.

Captain Jake Malone appeared in her doorway. "Hey, welcome back. How're you doing?"

"Having the absolute time of my life. You?"

"Same. How's Nick?"

"He's coping. We're coping. What else can we do?"

"Nothing, I guess. I hear you're giving the briefing."

"As soon as I'm up to speed."

"The media is ravenous, particularly since it's cold outside."

"What's with this weather? It was seventy yesterday and forty today."

"Mother Nature is in a mood, per usual around here in the spring."

"I guess so. What's your thought on these random attacks?" she asked.

"Not sure what to make of it yet, and we're not getting much help from surveillance in the areas where the attacks occurred since they happened in poorly lit areas."

"I'll make a note of that in the briefing."

He stepped forward and handed her a sheet of paper. "Some talking points I worked up with Public Affairs."

She gave him a skeptical look. "You don't need their help with that."

"I like to make them feel needed once in a while."

Her snort of laughter was rather inelegant, if she said so herself. "Give me five minutes to review it all again, and then I'll brief. After that, Cruz and I are going to see the families."

"You don't have to do that, Sam."

"I know, but I'm going to anyway because I'm the boss around here, and they need to know I'm engaged in their cases and that I care."

"They'll appreciate your involvement."

"Even if they don't, I'm on it, and I'm going to stay on it until we get them some answers."

"I'll leave you to do your thing, but please know I'm thinking of you and Nick and your family right now. We all are."

"Thanks, Cap. We appreciate the support."

"Onward," he said with a wave as he departed.

Sam appreciated how he'd tended to business before expressing concern for her and Nick, knowing how she hated to be the story, especially at work. If she allowed herself to contemplate the level of distraction she was these days, or what some of her colleagues were probably saying behind her back, she wouldn't be able to function. Three grieving families needed her functioning at the highest level, so she doubled down on the prep work until she felt ready for the briefing.

She took her notes with her when she left the pit to head to the main entrance. The media gathered outside the doors year-round, in all kinds of weather, waiting for updates. Judging by the larger-than-average crowd, they were looking for more than just information about her new cases. Sam stood frozen for a second, trying to find the fortitude to push through the doors to face off with them—and to fend off their questions about yesterday's events.

Chief Joe Farnsworth joined her. "Morning."

"Morning."

"I'd ask how you are, but..."

Sam smiled at the man she'd called Uncle Joe growing up, as he'd been her father's best friend. "I'm just great."

"Heard you're doing the briefing."

"You heard right."

"Figured you might need some help fending off the idiots who'll be asking about yesterday."

"Judging by the size of the crowd, that's a safe assumption. Shall we?"

"After you, my friend."

"Is it weird that this feels scarier than it did before yesterday?"

"Not at all. It's totally understandable, and we do have other people who could do this."

"No," she said firmly, "it has to be me, or whoever is gunning for us will celebrate running me out of the job. I can't give them the satisfaction."

"Proud of you," the chief said quietly. "And he would be, too."

"Don't make me cry before I face the jackals."

"My apologies. Please proceed."

Having him—and Vernon—by her side made her feel better about stepping into the scrum of reporters, who began clamoring for information the second they cleared the doorway. As usual, Sam stood at the podium and stared at a spot in the distance until they quit shouting questions at her. She spotted Jimmy and two other agents she recognized but couldn't name off the top of her head positioned around the perimeter of the gathering. Vernon stood behind her.

The reporters finally realized they'd get nothing until they shut up. She found it amusing that they had to relearn that lesson every time.

"On Saturday evening at around eleven thirty, Lorraine Sweeny, age sixty-two, was walking home in Southeast after taking the Metro from her job as a nurse at Green Acres Nursing Home. While walking through a poorly lit area, she was struck in the back of her head by an assailant. When she didn't arrive home at the usual time, her husband checked her location on his phone, saw that she wasn't moving and ran to find her. She was deceased when he arrived. Lorraine was the mother of four, the grandmother of five and was weeks away from retirement."

"What are you hearing about the investigation into the drones that were set on attacking the Easter Egg Roll?"

Sam glanced at the reporter who'd asked the question and gave him a look that she hoped made his balls shrivel. "I'm briefing you on three homicides that transpired in recent days. If you're here for information about anything other than that, you'll leave disappointed. On Sunday evening, while out jogging in Adams Morgan, thirty-six-year-old Nate Andrews, an analyst at the Department of Labor, was similarly struck in the back of the head. He was transported to GW Trauma and passed away this morning. He leaves his wife and two children, one of them a newborn.

"In the early hours of this morning, after leaving work at the restaurant where she waitressed, twenty-two-year-old college student Alexa Prescott was hit from behind on 14th Street and died at the scene. After growing up in the foster system, Alexa was attending Marymount on an academic scholarship.

"The MPD is asking the public for any information you may have on any of these deadly attacks." Sam recited the number for the tip line twice. "In addition, we're urging citizens to be vigilant while walking at night, especially in poorly lit areas. I'll take a few questions about this case—and only this case."

She nodded to a TV reporter with brown hair. She didn't recognize her as one of the regulars. "As first lady, is it safe for you to be outside right now?"

"Next." She pointed to Darren Tabor, her sorta friend from *The Washington Star*, hoping he'd play by the rules.

"Are there security cameras in the areas of the attacks?"

"Our IT team is actively looking for any video that might've been captured, but the attacks took place in dark areas, which we believe was intentional to avoid camera detection. Citizens and visitors need to be extremely careful about walking outside at night while this suspect is still at large."

"Are you treating the cases as related?" another reporter asked.

"Due to the similarities of the three attacks, we're operating under that assumption until we have more information. That's all for now. We'll provide updates as we have them."

"Are you scared, Sam?" Darren asked.

She stopped, turned to look back at him. "No, I'm not scared. I'm angry that someone would threaten an event full of families and children and also thankful for the many people and systems that prevented a tragedy."

With that, she went inside, feeling resentful and resigned at the same time.

"They can't help themselves," Farnsworth said.

"They should try a little harder to follow the rules."

"What fun would that be for them?"

She hoped her scowl spoke for itself.

"People are concerned. I suppose that's to be expected with something like this."

"I wish they'd pose those questions to the White House press office rather than expecting me to speak for Nick or his administration. Has there ever been anyone less qualified to do that than I am?"

"Is that a rhetorical question?"

She laughed. "Thank you. I needed that levity."

"What's your feeling on this new case?"

"I don't have one yet, but if I did, it would probably include rage. A hardworking, soon-to-be-retired nurse, a young father, a college student working to put herself through school. It angers me that they were struck down on our streets for no good reason. My first order of business is to dig for connections between the vics, but I'm not thinking we'll find any."

"Still, we need to rule that out."

"That's the plan."

"I'll let you get to it. I'm here if you need anything."

"It helps to know that. Thank you."

"You got it, kid."

He talked to her like that only when no one else was around, and him calling her "kid" made her feel loved and supported in a way that only he and Malone could do now that her dad was gone. They'd recently told her they intended to postpone retirement to stay close to her while Nick was in office. They said it was what Skip would want them to do as his best friends. She'd wept when they said that.

Soon it would be six whole months since that dreadful day in October when Skip had failed to wake up. As Sam walked back to the pit, she tried to shake off the despondency that came with remembering that morning on Ninth Street. Some memories were forever, though, and as much as she'd prefer to forget it, that one would stay with her for the rest of her life.

"How'd it go?" Freddie asked.

"Not bad, all things considered. Massive gathering, but only a few questions that pissed me off. Do you have the addresses for the vics?"

"Yeah."

"Then let's hit the road."

CHAPTER FIVE

W hen they were settled in the back of the Secret Service SUV, Sam turned to look out the back window and saw a second SUV following them, plus the extra agents she'd spotted at the press briefing.

"This is more than a two-agent detail, Vernon."

"We hope it's temporary."

Sam closed her eyes, rested her head against the seat, took a deep breath and released it. The last thing she wanted or needed at work was a massive Secret Service detail following her around. She'd found a way to manage with her two regular agents and had even come to enjoy the time they spent together every day. But a detail of multiple cars and additional agents was a tough pill to swallow, even if she knew it was for her safety.

"Are you okay?" Freddie asked quietly.

"I'm great. Just when I think it can't get more complicated..."

"Right?"

"I'm already the hugest distraction, and now this."

"You're not distracting anyone who matters."

"You have to say that."

"No, I don't. I'd tell you if I was picking up on that vibe, and I'm not."

"That vibe would never reach you."

"Yes, it would. There're people who'd take pleasure in making sure it got to me."

"I suppose that's true."

"There's no vibe. Most of them are probably glad you keep showing up so they don't have to do what you do."

She chuckled. "That's true. Who'd want this hell job?"

"It takes a very special kind of person to do this, to go to the homes of devastated families and interrupt their grieving for the sake of an investigation."

"In case you were wondering, there's no part of me that wants to do that."

"Trust me, I know, but you'll do it because it needs to be done, and that's what makes you unique."

"Us. Our squad. We're unique. Right up there with SVU, doing work that most of the people who like to bitch about us couldn't do."

"Exactly."

"Has anyone heard from Archie?"

"Just that he extended his leave by a few days."

Sam pulled out her phone and called her close colleague, who'd once been a friend with benefits. That seemed like a million years ago now. Sam put the call on speaker so Freddie could listen, too.

"Hey," Archie said. "I was going to call you today to see how you're doing."

"I'm okay. You've got me and Cruz. How're you, and how's your friend?"

"She's still having some pain but holding up pretty well. I guess it's a blessing in disguise that she can't remember what happened."

A tingle of sensation traveled down Sam's backbone. "She was hit on the head, right?"

"Yeah, she was knocked out by a blow to the back of the head. That's probably why she doesn't remember any of it."

"We've got three new vics in the morgue who were struck in the head from behind."

"You think it's related?"

"I hadn't thought so until right now."

"Damn. What's the plan?"

"I'm on my way now to speak to the families of the other victims. When you think the time is right, I'd be very interested in seeing Harlowe."

"I'll mention it to her. When we first met, I told her I worked with you, and she geeked out. She's a fan."

"Awesome," Sam said, her tone full of sarcasm.

Archie laughed. "I knew you'd say that. I'll let you know when she's up for a chat."

"How're you holding up?"

"I'm a basket case, which is new to me. Not handling it well."

"You know why that is?"

"Please enlighten me."

"It's because she *matters*. Someone finally matters enough to get emotional over."

"If this is what that feels like, I'd like to unsubscribe."

Sam laughed. "You're getting the hard part first. I promise the good stuff is worth waiting for."

"If you say so."

"I do say so. I'm known around the world for being somewhat of an expert on this topic."

Archie and Freddie groaned at the exact same time, which made her laugh again.

"What? Am I or am I not half of an epic marriage that's envied the world over?"

"Good God," Freddie said. "She's starting to believe her own hype."

Archie lost it laughing. "I think she started believing that shit a long time ago."

"What can I say? I am a speaker of truth. I know love, boys, and trust me when I tell you that our boy Archie is on his way to the love boat. I saw it happen with my friend Cruz here. And boy oh boy was *that* messy."

Freddie scowled at her. "Shut your mouth."

"Did you or did you not get shot shortly after the first time you—"

Freddie's hand over her mouth ended that thought before she could finish it.

She turned her head to break free. "It was messy. Take my word for it. I'll expect better of you, Archie."

"I'll do my best to make you proud, oh wise one."

"I'm already proud of the way you're stepping up for her. That'll matter to her in the long run."

"Thanks. I'm trying."

"Let me know if there's anything you need. I'll send Freddie over."

"Haha," Freddie said, "but I'm here for you, too, friend."

"That means a lot. Thanks for checking in, guys. Keep me posted on the investigation."

"We'll be in touch."

Sam slapped her phone closed. "How about that? Another of my little boys is growing up."

"You have a big mouth."

"File that under things you shouldn't be allowed to say to your boss."

A snort of laughter came from the front seat.

"I can say it if it's true. Just because you know something about me doesn't mean you get to *tell* other people that stuff."

"You got shot, Freddie?" Jimmy asked.

"He sure did. Ask him how it happened. It's a good story. One of my favorites, actually, but only because he didn't die."

Freddie gave her a filthy look. "That's ancient history and not a good story at all."

"I disagree. I'll fill you guys in sometime when he's not here."

"No, you won't!"

Sam laughed so hard, she had tears in her eyes. After yesterday's fear and panic, the laughter was medicinal. There was comfort in the normal, the bickering, the banter, the day-to-day grind that was made so much more fun by having Freddie by her side.

"If you tell them, I'll know."

"No, you won't."

"Yes, I will."

"Children, behave," Vernon said with a grin for Sam in the mirror.

"What fun is that?" Sam asked.

"She loves to drive me crazy. I bet I could sue the department for workplace abuse at this point."

"Knock yourself out."

"You're the one who knocks yourself out. Regularly, in fact."

Sam chuckled. "Oh, that was a good one. Well played, grasshopper."

They pulled up to the home of Lorraine Sweeny and immediately returned to professional mode.

Vernon stayed close to Sam as they made their way to the front door of a brick-fronted rowhouse in Southeast. As they moved toward the front door, a woman approached, carrying a huge, covered platter.

"Hold up," Vernon said as he put himself between her and Sam.

"Can I take that for you?" Jimmy asked her.

"Oh, thank you," she said. "That'd be great." She handed the platter to Jimmy and shook out her arms. "I wanted to bring some food to the family. They've been our neighbors for twenty-two years. I can't believe anyone would harm Lorraine. She was just the sweetest person."

Moved by the woman's grief, Sam knocked on the door. When a young woman answered, the first thing Sam noticed was that her soft brown eyes were red and swollen.

Sam showed her badge. "I'm Lieutenant Holland with the MPD. This is my partner, Detective Cruz. We wondered if we might speak to Lorraine Sweeny's family."

The woman's eyes flooded with tears. "My mother would be honored to have you visit our home. I wish she was here to meet you."

"I do, too."

"Come in."

Sam gestured to the woman standing by the agents. "Your neighbor was hoping to deliver some food."

"Oh, hi there, Mrs. Diaz. Thank you so much."

Jimmy walked the platter to the door.

"How's your dad doing, Celeste?"

"Not well at all."

"Give him our love."

"I'll do that. Thank you for coming by and for the food."

Mrs. Diaz blew her a tearful kiss. "I'll miss your mama every day of the rest of my life."

"As will I."

Sam and Freddie followed Celeste to the back of the house, where she deposited the platter on a table. "Please add Mrs. Diaz to the thank-you-note list," she said to an older woman seated at the table.

The woman looked up, saw Sam and gasped. "As I live and breathe, is the first lady of the United States of America standing in my sister's kitchen?"

Sam gave her a small smile. "I'm also the lieutenant in charge of figuring out who killed your sister, ma'am, and I'm very sorry to be meeting you under these circumstances."

The woman stood and came to hug Sam.

She sensed Vernon go tense behind her, but thankfully, he didn't interfere.

"Come into the sitting room," Celeste said.

They stood to the side to let her go by them to lead the way.

"Can we get you anything?" Celeste asked.

"No, thank you," Sam said. "Again, I wish to convey the condolences of our entire department for the loss of your mother."

"Do you know who did this to her?"

"Not yet, but we're working on it. Speaking to the family members is where we usually begin."

"Not because you think we hurt her, I hope."

"No, even if that's the case sometimes. We aren't here to accuse anyone. We want to know more about your mother, her routine, any problems she might've been having with anyone. That kind of thing."

Lorraine's sister sat next to her niece and took her hand.

"Let's start with your full names," Sam said, notebook and pen at the ready.

"Celeste Sweeny. This is my aunt, Doris Matthews." Celeste used a tissue to wipe away tears. "I'm sorry, but we're still in shock, even with a couple of days to process this."

"Of course you are," Sam said. "We totally understand, and we're sorry to intrude at such a difficult time."

"It's no problem," Doris said. "We want you to find out who did this to our Lorraine."

"You told the responding officers that your mom was coming from work at the Green Acres Nursing Home."

"Yes, that's right. She worked the three-to-eleven shift on weekends. She used to say she'd done her share of partying on the weekends, so she took those shifts so the younger nurses could have those nights free."

Doris chuckled. "We did some partying in our time, but

we're long past that now. Give us a quiet night at home these days."

She seemed to sober all of a sudden when she realized she'd never again have a quiet night at home with her sister.

Celeste handed her aunt a tissue.

A tall man with gray hair and broad shoulders appeared in the doorway. His expression conveyed devastation and exhaustion. "I heard the first lady was paying a visit. My Lorraine would never forgive me if I didn't properly welcome you to our home."

"This is my dad, Walter Sweeny," Celeste said.

Sam stood to shake his hand. "We're so sorry for your loss."

"Thank you."

"This is my partner, Detective Cruz."

Freddie also stood to shake his hand.

Walter took a seat in one of the chairs. "It's still hard to believe, you know? Who would want to hurt Lorraine? She never did anything to anyone. All she ever did was try to help people—at work and in her off time, too."

"Often, these things never make sense," Sam said. "Celeste was saying that Lorraine took the weekend shifts so the younger nurses could have those nights off."

"She liked those shifts," Walter said. "Things were quieter. The residents didn't have as many guests that time of day, and she could get her work done quicker. She said she got quality time with the residents that she wouldn't have during the week, when the pace was much different. Plus, like Celeste said, it gave the younger nurses those nights off." He paused before he added, "She was going to retire at the end of June. We were planning to travel. See some things. Not sure what I'll do now."

"I'll go with you, Daddy. We'll see all the things."

"Thank you, sweetheart, but you have your own life to tend to. You don't need to be babysitting me."

"I want to be with you."

"We'll talk about it once we catch our breath."

"Was Lorraine having trouble with anyone?" Sam asked, even though she suspected she already knew the answer.

"No," Walter said emphatically. "She avoided trouble like the plague. She had a brother who was in all kinds of trouble back in the day. He died in prison."

"Our baby brother, Raymond," Doris said sadly. "He broke our hearts over and over again before he passed six years ago."

"Lorraine used to say she used up her lifetime's share of heartache and drama with that boy," Walter said. "As a result, she went out of her way to stay away from strife in all corners of her life."

"Do you have other children?" Freddie asked.

"We have two sons who live out of state," Walter said. "They flew in yesterday and are staying nearby. Our other daughter lives nearby and went home for a bit to take care of her kids."

Sam made a note that there were three additional adult children. "We have two other people who were killed over the weekend in similar attacks and possibly a third related victim, who survived," Sam said. "We're in the earliest stages of our investigation, but it's very possible that these were random attacks on people who were in the wrong place at the wrong time."

"Why would anyone do something like that?" Celeste asked.

"If we had an answer to that question, we'd be out of business, which would be fine with us."

"How do you do this work day in and day out?" Doris asked. "How do you sit with the heartbreak of devastated loved ones?"

Sam glanced at Freddie. "Someone has to, and I guess we see it as why not us. Does that make sense?"

"Not at all," Doris said with a small smile. "But we're grateful to those of you who work to keep us safe."

"I'm sorry we weren't able to keep your Lorraine safe."

"Y'all can't be everywhere," Walter said. "Lorraine wouldn't want you to feel bad about something you had nothing to do with. She'd say that's a pointless waste of energy."

Celeste smiled. "Yes, she would."

Sam put her business card on the coffee table. "If you think of anything that might be relevant, a dustup with a delivery driver, an argument with the mailman... Whatever. Call me."

Doris picked up the card and studied it. "You've got your phone number right there. Can you give it out like that?"

"It's how I do my job."

"Do people call you because of your other job?"

"No one has yet, but if you wanted to, you could do that any time."

"Aw, go on, I wouldn't do that."

"You could, if you needed to. Also, when you're ready, there's a grief group at MPD headquarters for victims of violent crime that you may find helpful. When the time is right."

"I read about that," Walter said. "Never imagined I might need it."

"Call me when you're ready. I'll give you the info."

Freddie took down their names and phone numbers, and then they stood to leave.

The family walked them to the door.

"Thank you for your kindness and sensitivity," Celeste said. "In the midst of the darkness, it's been a treat to meet you."

"I'm sorry to meet you under these circumstances. I'll keep you posted on any developments."

"Thank you," Walter said. "For all you do."

"I wish I could say it was a pleasure, but..."

When he gave her a small smile, that felt like a victory of sorts.

Vernon led them to the SUV, where Jimmy held the door for her.

Once they were inside the vehicle and on the way to Adams Morgan to see the Andrews family, Vernon glanced at Sam in the mirror. "That was exceptionally well done, Sam."

"What was?"

"I don't get to see that part of what you do very often, as we tend to wait outside, but how you handled that family... It was a master class in kindness, grace and compassion."

"Oh, jeez, you're going to make me cry."

"Just calling it like I see it."

"You're very good with the victims' families," Freddie said. "Always."

"Aw, does this mean you're not pissed with me anymore for telling tales out of school?"

"Nah, I'm still pissed at you for flapping your fat mouth."

"The insubordination around here! Are you guys taking note of this for when I write him up?"

"Please," Freddie said disdainfully. "Who does all the writing for you?"

"My grasshopper is out of control today." Sam sent Freddie an admiring smile. He was definitely coming along nicely, cruising toward ruination at her hands.

Despite the frivolity, her heart ached with sorrow for Lorraine's family as they began the long journey through grief and all the things that came with being victims of violent crime.

Law enforcement interactions they never asked for, a trial or trials, sentencing, appeals... That's *if* they caught the person who killed Lorraine. When the police were unsuccessful in apprehending a suspect, victims' families had to live with the question of *why* for the rest of their lives.

Answering the question posed by that three-letter word was what motivated Sam and her team to work so hard to get answers for their victims' families, so at the very least they'd know who'd taken their loved one from them. Sometimes, however, even with an arrest, they never got closure on the question of why.

"Are there any developments in the drone investigation?" Sam asked Vernon.

"Nothing new that I've heard yet."

"Let me know if you do."

"I will if I can."

As Sam pursued the *why* for her victims and their families, she hoped they'd eventually find out why armed drones were sent toward the White House with the purpose of inflicting mass carnage.

CHAPTER SIX

Nick's morning security briefing was twice its normal
length while his intelligence, national security and
defense teams covered every detail of what had occurred the
day before and updated him on what was now known, which
wasn't much. As tedious as it was to listen to them discuss the
particulars, it was much better than listening to a report on a
mass casualty incident, which was what they'd narrowly
avoided.

The thought of all those happy kids, dressed in their Easter
finery, mowed down by a terrorist attack sickened him. Not to
mention his own family, friends, staff... Sam, Scotty, the twins,
Eli... His father, stepmother, brothers... Sam's sisters, nieces,
nephews...

Life without any one of them was unthinkable. Knowing
they'd been in danger because of him was unbearable.

"Mr. President?"

Nick snapped out of his grim thoughts to realize Teresa
Howard, the national security advisor, was speaking to him.
"I'm sorry. Would you repeat the question?"

"I asked if you'd like to table this for now until we have
additional updates."

"Yes, please. Let's do that. Thank you, everyone."

After the others had filed out of the Situation Room, Terry O'Connor moved to sit next to Nick at the head of the table.

"Are you okay?"

"We don't know a single thing we didn't already know yesterday. How's that possible?"

"The case is being worked from every angle by the best people in the world."

"This was done by someone who knows how not to be found."

"It does seem that way, but the government's resources are vast. We have to give them the time to do their jobs."

"While hoping this group or individual doesn't strike again in the meantime."

"Derek is coming down to brief us on a mudslide and flooding in Juneau that's expected to result in significant casualties, including students and staff at an elementary school."

Nick's deep sigh said it all.

Deputy Chief of Staff Derek Kavanaugh arrived with two of his colleagues, who put images of the devastated area onto the screen at the front of the room.

"Oh my God," Nick said when he got his first look at the buried area.

"We're in contact with the governor of Alaska," Derek said. "He's activated the National Guard to assist in the search and rescue. We have Coast Guard in the area as well as military members being sent to aid in the recovery. Secretary Jennings is working with all the branches to get as many people there as possible with support personnel to bring in food and temporary housing."

"What about FEMA?" Terry asked.

"They're mobilizing as we speak from their Seattle office. The governor said a combination of an extra-snowy winter followed by a milder-than-average spring melted the snowpack and sparked the mudslide and flooding. It happened so fast, there was no time to evacuate. We could be looking at hundreds dead or missing in the school alone."

Derek's team had called up a feed of the local news in the area. On the screen, frantic parents were screaming for their kids outside an elementary school buried in mud while firefighters and others frantically worked to dig them out.

"We need to get you into the briefing room," Terry said to Nick. To Derek, he said, "Let's have Trevor and his team work on a statement."

"Already underway," Derek said. "Give us fifteen minutes."

He and his team left as quickly as they'd arrived.

Nick was riveted to the scene in Juneau, his heart aching for the parents and families of those trapped in the school as well as the nearby homes and businesses.

"Mr. President," Terry said.

Nick looked up at him.

"We need to get you upstairs to make a statement."

"Right. Okay."

If compassion and empathy were the two most important qualities in a leader, Nick felt them both in spades for the families dealing with the unfolding tragedy in Alaska. The way natural disasters struck out of nowhere... People never saw it coming until they were buried or stranded or shattered... And it was his job to respond to every one of them, to offer reassurance, help and support, not that any of it would matter to the parents who'd possibly lost their precious children.

As they took the elevator up to the West Wing, Nick felt hollowed out inside, his legs wooden under him as he went through the motions of walking, breathing, thinking, processing.

His communications director, Trevor Donnelly, and press secretary, Christina Billings-Gonzales, were waiting for him in the Oval Office.

"Good morning, Mr. President," Trevor said. "We've prepared a statement regarding the events in Alaska."

"Morning." Nick sat at the Resolute Desk to scan the statement, which laid out the details of the situation as well as the federal, state and local response. "Thank you for the quick work."

"Thank you, sir. We figured you'd want to add your personal thoughts as well. Shall we notify the press that you'll be making a statement in fifteen minutes?"

"Yes, please."

After they left the room, Nick looked up at Terry. "Are we having fun yet?"

"An absolute blast."

Julie, one of the admins, called on the desk phone. "Mr. President, Lieutenant Commander Rodriguez is here to see you."

Hearing Juan's name immediately raised Nick's spirits. "Please send him in."

Nick got up to meet his military attaché, who'd recently been presumed murdered until they learned he was cooperating with the Naval Criminal Investigative Service in an investigation into the former Joint Chiefs of Staff.

Juan stepped into the office, wearing his uniform and a big smile.

Nick walked over to embrace his friend and aide. "I've never been so happy to see anyone."

"That's surely not true, Mr. President."

"In this case, it is." Nick kept his hands on the younger man's arms as he stepped back to take a good look at him. Other than seeming a bit tired, he appeared no worse for wear. "How're you holding up?"

"I'm doing okay. It's nice to be back to work."

"It's nice to have you back." Nick released him. "I'd appreciate it if you didn't do that to me again."

Juan smiled. "I'll try not to, sir."

"I realize the reason you were sucked into such a situation was because of your loyalty to me, which will never be forgotten, Commander."

"Thank you, sir. I was raised to do the right thing. I have no regrets."

"Honor has gone out of style in some quarters. It's a quality I appreciate in those closest to me. I hope you've been cleared to return to full duty, as I requested."

"Yes, sir. I'm back as of today."

"I'm very glad to hear it."

"Excuse me, Mr. President," Terry said. "We're needed in the briefing room."

"Duty calls, but check in later. We have some catching up to do on important topics, such as the Caps' playoff run and the Feds' spring training."

Juan smiled. "Yes, sir, Mr. President. I'll stop by at the end of my tour."

Nick shook his hand. "Thanks again for not being murdered."

Laughing, Juan said, "I'm at your service, sir."

"Excellent."

As he walked with Terry to the briefing room, Nick said, "I wonder how much of this will be about Alaska and how much will be about the drones."

"Probably fifty-fifty."

"Which is annoying. This should all be about Alaska."

"It's never all about any one thing, is it, sir?"

"If that's not the truth, I don't know what is." A day in the White House was about everything all at once. And right when you had things somewhat under control, there was more. Such as a mudslide that struck out of nowhere.

When he stepped up to the podium, the room went quiet. "At approximately eight o'clock this morning Alaska Standard Time, a mudslide and flood struck the Valley Elementary School in

Juneau, Alaska. Located in the Mendenhall Valley neighborhood, the school serves pre-K to grade five and has three hundred and twenty-five students enrolled with twenty-three teachers plus support staff. In addition to the school, a number of nearby buildings, businesses and homes were impacted. We're in the earliest stages of determining the full scope of the disaster.

"We're working with state and local authorities to determine how many people were inside each building at the time of the incident. The governor of Alaska has deployed the National Guard to assist in the search and rescue operations, and numerous federal agencies have been activated, including the Coast Guard and other military members stationed at nearby bases, as well as FEMA and other relevant federal agencies and staff. I've directed everyone involved to deploy the full resources of the federal government to assist in this effort. Although we're in the earliest stages of this incident, it's believed that a larger-than-average snowfall followed by a warmer-than-usual spring may have contributed to this catastrophe.

"Needless to say, a heartbreaking scene is unfolding in Juneau, and our hearts are with the families of those trapped in the school as well as the greater Juneau community. I'll take a few questions."

"Mr. President, what do you know about the drones that were deployed yesterday?"

"I have no new updates to give you on that matter other than to say a massive investigation is underway at the local and federal levels."

"Mr. President, is the drone incident being treated as an assassination attempt?"

"That's all for now. We'll keep you informed on the events transpiring in Juneau."

"Mr. President!"

It seemed to him that every person in the packed briefing

room was shouting his name as he walked out. Probably because they were.

"Not one question about more than three hundred kids buried alive in their school," he said with disgust.

"To be fair, the attempted assassination of a sitting president is big news, sir."

"Understood, but at the moment, the possibility of three hundred twenty-five *children* buried alive in mud is bigger news to me."

He returned to the Oval Office to deal with the unfolding crisis with a feeling of dread hanging over him. As a father of young children himself, he wished he could go to Juneau and do something useful to help with the search without being the world's biggest distraction.

AT THE ADAMS MORGAN home of Nate Andrews, Sam and Freddie were greeted by a young blonde woman whose swollen, red eyes bugged when she saw Sam standing on the stoop of the brick-fronted townhouse.

Sam showed her badge while Freddie did the same. "Lieutenant Holland. My partner, Detective Cruz."

"Y-yes, I know who you are."

"We know this is a terrible time, but we'd like to speak to Mr. Andrews's family."

"The other police were here. We... we told them what we know."

"I understand, but I'm following up with some additional questions. May I speak to Mr. Andrews's wife?"

"She's..." The woman shook her head. "She's in very bad shape."

"We wouldn't ask if it wasn't necessary. We want to find the person who took Nate from you."

She hiccuped on a sob that seemed to take her by surprise. "He was my big brother. My hero."

"We're so very sorry for your loss."

The woman stepped back. "Please come in."

"What's your name?" Sam asked.

"Jenna Andrews."

"I'm sorry to meet you under these circumstances."

"Me, too. Normally, I'd be freaking out. Now... I'm just numb."

Jenna showed them to the living room. They could hear the low buzz of voices coming from the next room. "I'll see if Emily can talk to you."

"Please tell her we'd never disturb her unless we had to."

Jenna nodded and walked away.

Sam took a seat on the sofa. On the table was a wedding photo of a young, gorgeous couple beaming at each other on the happiest day of their lives. Next to that was a framed photo of them with a little girl with blonde curls and a new baby.

Heartbreaking.

Nate's wife was escorted into the room by an older couple, each of them gripping one of her arms as if she wouldn't remain standing if they let go. They held on to her until the three of them were seated on a sofa.

"I'm Ryan Goodman. My wife, Susan, and our daughter, Emily Andrews, Nate's wife."

"We're so very sorry for your loss."

Emily wept silently, as if she was afraid to make a sound lest she start screaming and never stop.

"It's unfathomable that anyone could hurt Nate," Ryan said. "He'd literally give you the shirt off his back. I've seen him do it. He gave his sweater to a homeless man once because the man was cold." Ryan shook his head. "How could anyone want to hurt him?"

"I wish I had the answers you need. We're doing everything we can to find the person who did this. Do you know if Nate was having any problems with anyone? At work or personally?"

"No," Susan said. "Everyone loved him. He had so many friends and was moving up quickly in his career."

"Is it possible someone he worked with was resentful of his promotions?"

"I… I don't know," Susan said.

Emily shook her head, keeping her eyes on the floor. "He was friends with his coworkers. They loved him."

"And personally, no conflicts with neighbors or extended family?"

"Nothing like that," Emily said. "We kept to ourselves mostly. We have two young children…" Her voice broke as she choked on a sob. "What're we supposed to do now? What will I do?"

Her parents wept with her as they wrapped their arms around her.

Sam put her card on the table. "If you think of anything that might be relevant, even the smallest thing, please call me. Even if you aren't sure it matters, call me anyway."

"We will," Ryan said.

"Can I please get your contact information so I can keep you updated?" She wrote down the number he gave her and stood. "Please don't get up. We can show ourselves out."

Outside, Sam took greedy breaths of the fresh, cool spring air as her eyes blurred with tears. "I fucking hate cases like this. Regular, nice people going about their lives, not bothering anyone, until they're killed for no good reason."

"You hate the cases where people get killed for a reason, too."

"True. Let's get the visit to the last vic's family taken care of so we can start figuring out who the hell did this."

"According to the reports, Alexa Prescott has no family."

"She must have someone mourning her passing. Let's go to the address we have for her and see if anyone is there."

"It's in Arlington."

"Of course it is."

CHAPTER SEVEN

Like her father, Sam had an aversion to leaving the District for any reason, but it happened more and more often lately. "What's going on at the White House?" she asked Freddie, who took out his iPhone once they were on their way to Arlington. "Anything new?"

"There was a mudslide in Juneau that buried an elementary school."

Shocked, Sam glanced at him, almost afraid to ask. "Are there survivors?"

"No info on that yet. Search and rescue underway."

"Oh God."

"Nick made a statement. Do you want to see it?"

"Yeah."

Freddie called it up and handed over his phone.

Sam fumbled with the phone, frustrated that she never knew which buttons to push.

Freddie reached over and pushed Play for her.

"Thank you." As she watched Nick give the agonizing update about the tragedy in Juneau, she ached for him. And then to only be asked questions about the drones... She could see how offended he was on behalf of the people affected by the mudslide.

She handed the phone back to Freddie. "Why does the media have to suck so bad sometimes?"

"It's a big deal that someone flew drones packing heat toward the White House."

"It's a big deal that more than three hundred babies might be *dead*, too."

"Of course it is."

"I suppose we'll have to go to Alaska."

"Maybe."

"I hope it turns out to be a great story of triumph and not another horrible tragedy."

"I hope so, too."

"But you don't think that's going to happen, do you?"

"Anything is possible, but it doesn't look good from what I've seen."

Sam couldn't allow herself to think too much about what those parents and loved ones were going through, or she wouldn't be able to function. Before she'd had children of her own, this kind of news would've hit her as sad and tragic. Now, stories like this brought a whole other level of devastation as she imagined such a thing happening to her precious kids.

A few minutes later, they arrived at the Arlington apartment building where Alexa Prescott had lived.

"Give us a minute," Vernon said as he and Jimmy got out of the vehicle.

Sam sighed with frustration. "Who do they think is lurking here to get me?"

"Maybe the person behind the drones knows exactly what you'd do after people in your city are murdered."

She gave him a perturbed look. "Quit talking sense. It pisses me off."

Freddie laughed. "Duly noted. No sense allowed."

"You don't think my case is related to the drones, do you?"

"Not really, but the agents have to proceed as if anything is possible."

"Yeah, I know that, but I don't have to like it."

"If I were you, I wouldn't like any of this bullshit."

Sam gasped. "You *swore*, young Freddie!"

"Well, what's a better word for someone attempting to send armed drones to an event full of kids?"

"'Bullshit' is a good start."

"It just makes me so angry that people treat you guys so shitty."

"That's two swears in two minutes."

"Technically, that was the same swear as the first one."

She laughed. "That's fair."

"I don't like the way you guys are treated when all he did was step up the way the Constitution intended after the president died."

"It's the nature of the office. Everything you do is under intense scrutiny. That's the number one reason why I was so glad when he said he wasn't going to run before Nelson died. I knew that would be the hardest part for me, to see people tearing him down simply because of the office he held. But knowing that would happen and living it are two very different things."

"I can't imagine what that's like for you guys."

"It sucks, but he mostly rises above it to do the job. I, on the other hand, seethe with outrage over the things people say and do. I mean, someone wanted to *kill* my husband—not to mention me and our kids and almost everyone else we know. That's tough to wrap your mind around."

"You shouldn't have to wrap your mind around such things. It's outrageous. Thank God everything worked as intended and they were stopped."

"That's only part one, though. Finding out who sent them will be a lot harder. From what I've heard, there were no

identifying marks on the drones, no recognizable parts or
components. Whoever did this intended to never be caught."

"I wouldn't want to be them today with the full weight of
federal law enforcement bearing down on them."

"We both know it's possible they might never be caught.
They went to enormous lengths to make sure the devices were
untraceable."

"Criminals often make mistakes that trip them up. Let's
hope that happened in this case."

Vernon returned to the SUV and opened the back door. "All
clear."

Sam wanted to say, *I could've told you that*, but kept the
thought to herself because he was only doing his job, which
was to protect her. "Thank you, Vernon."

"Sorry about all this. I know it's a pain in the ass."

"No worries."

They made their way into the building and climbed the
stairs to the third floor, knocking on the door for apartment
number 305. When the door opened, a young woman with
dark hair and eyes stared at Sam as if she were seeing a ghost.
Or a first lady.

Sam showed her badge. "Lieutenant Holland with the
MPD. My partner, Detective Cruz. Were you Alexa's
roommate?"

"I, uh, yes, I am. I mean, I was." She blinked back tears. "I'm
not used to talking about her in the past tense. She was just
here..."

"May we come in for a minute?"

"Um, sure."

While Vernon waited in the hallway, the woman stepped
back to admit them into the kind of place Sam would've liked
to have had if she'd been a single girl in the city. Clean,
contemporary, with big windows that let in tons of natural
light, the apartment had been decorated with colorful pillows

and artwork to offset the beige walls and furniture. Someone clearly had an eye for design.

"Your place is so nice," Sam said.

"That was all Alexa. She wanted to be an interior designer and was well on her way." She curled into a plush orange armchair. "She was so insanely talented."

"I can see that. What's your name?"

"Oh, sorry. I'm Brianna Weaver."

"We're sorry to meet you under these circumstances."

"I can't believe the first lady is here. Alexa would freak out. She had a thing for your husband."

Sam smiled. "Understandable."

"She used to say you're the luckiest woman in America."

"That, I am." While Sam normally hated talking about first lady stuff on the job, the topic seemed to bring Brianna a bit of light. "I'm so sorry you lost her this way."

"It makes no sense. She never bothered anyone. She went to work and school and came home and worked so hard."

"Where did she go to school?"

"Marymount, here in Arlington. They have a design program, and she was there on scholarship. If she wasn't doing schoolwork, she took every shift she could get at the restaurant. All she did was work because she made big money at the restaurant. That's why she went into the city to work there. I used to tease her about being all work and no play, but she'd remind me she had no safety net to catch her if she fell." Brianna looked up at them with big eyes full of devastation for her friend. "I admired her so much. We all did."

Brianna reached for a framed photo that she handed to Sam. "That's all of us with her on her birthday last year."

Dark-haired, pretty Alexa was surrounded by a group of smiling young women.

"She said we were the family she never had." Brianna wiped tears from her face. "I don't know what we're going to do without her. She was the glue that held us all together. We... we started a fundraiser to cover funeral costs."

Sam handed her notebook to Brianna. "Write down the link so we can publicize it."

"You'd do that?"

"Of course. Put down your name and number, too, so I can keep you informed."

Brianna wrote the info and then handed the notebook back to Sam.

"Was she having trouble with anyone in her life?"

"Not that I know of, and she would've told me."

"Was she dating anyone?"

"She didn't have time for men, or so she said. We teased her about that. We said she was going to die a virgin." She choked on a sob. "I hate that we said that to her, because that actually happened."

"We're so sorry for your loss, but I don't think your friend would want you to feel bad about teasing her. It's obvious from the picture that she loved you all very much."

"We loved her, too."

Sam handed her card to Brianna. "If you think of anything that might be relevant, even the smallest thing, please call me. Tell her other friends, too. We never know what might lead to a break in a case like this."

"I saw on the news that two other people were killed the same way."

"Yes."

"Are they related?"

"We're treating them as if they are, but we don't know anything for certain yet."

"Is there someone who could come and stay with you?" Freddie asked.

"My friends were here, and I asked for a little time to myself. They'll be back later. And my parents are flying in from

California. They loved Alexa, too. She was an honorary member of our family."

"We won't take any more of your time, but please reach out if there's anything we can do for you, or if you think of anything we should know."

Brianna got up to walk them to the door. "Thank you for coming by. I can't imagine how busy you must be. It means a lot that you came."

That right there was why Sam had wanted to make these visits, as hard as they were.

Sam reached out a hand to the young woman. "Alexa is mine now, and I won't rest until we get justice for her and the others."

Overcome, Brianna nodded, squeezed her hand and released it.

Sam took a feeling of outrage on behalf of Alexa and her friends with her as she went down the stairs. "I want to know who's doing this, and I want to know it right the hell now."

"Me, too."

"Call IT and find out where we are with video from the areas where the attacks took place. Sergeant Walters is covering for Archie while he's out."

He pulled out his phone and made the call.

As bad as all murders were, the ones that were seemingly random, someone killing people going about their lives just for the fun of it or whatever, were the worst.

And Sam had a sinking feeling that the person or people doing the killing probably weren't finished yet.

WHEN THEY WERE in the SUV for the return trip to the District, Sam called Malone while Freddie was on the phone with Walters.

"How's it going?" he asked.

"Dreadful few hours meeting with the victims' families. I

want a very big statement to the public about steering clear of poorly lit areas at night until we catch this person."

"We've already made that statement."

"Let's make it again. Put it on the socials. Put it everywhere. Get some media coverage. Do whatever you can to sound the alarm. I also want to publicize the GoFundMe Alexa Prescott's friends are doing to cover funeral expenses since she had no family to speak of. Cruz will send you a link."

"I'll take care of it. Are you okay?"

"I'm pissed. These people weren't doing anything wrong, and now they're dead."

"I hear you. It's terrible. Are you coming back for the Stahl meeting at three?"

"That's the plan."

"I was thinking that maybe you should sit it out, in light of your history with him and all that."

"If there's something I can do to help get justice for his other victims, I want to be part of that."

"And I totally get why you feel that way. It's just that... it might not be in your best interest. You know?"

"I do," she said with a sigh. "I still want to be there."

"As you wish, but please feel free to leave if it's too much."

"I will. Thanks, Cap, for looking out for me."

"Always. See you when you get back. Oh, and Jesse Best came by asking for you. He said to call him when you have a minute."

"Did he say why?"

"Nope."

"Got it. Okay. See you soon."

"Did who say why?" Freddie asked.

"Jesse Best was looking for me."

"Wonder what that's about."

"No idea. What did Walters say?"

"They're combing through the film but not finding anything we can use."

"Just once it would be nice to get something we can use from the cameras we have all over the place."

"I know, right?"

"Will you please send the GoFundMe info for Alexa to Roni with some context and ask her to put it on my first lady accounts?"

"Are you allowed to do that?"

"Who cares? I'm doing it."

"All righty, then."

"I'm calling Jesse." Sam flipped open her phone and found the contact for the U.S. Marshal they often worked with. "Hey," she said when he picked up. "Heard you were looking for me. What's up?"

"I need a favor."

Best was never one for small talk. "What can I do for you?"

"I've got a cold-case file that could use a second set of eyes. I heard you've had some luck with cold cases lately and thought you might be willing to give it a look. On the side."

Sam had no extra time for anything, but she'd find some for him. "Of course. Bring it by, and I'll take it home, if that's okay."

"Whatever works. Appreciate it."

He was gone before she could say goodbye.

She closed the phone.

"What's up with him?" Freddie asked.

"Cold case he wants me to look at."

"That's odd, isn't it? With all his resources, he wants your help?"

Sam shrugged. "When you need the best, you come to the best."

Moaning, Freddie said. "Oh my God, I walked straight into that woodchipper, didn't I?"

Sam, Vernon and Jimmy laughed.

"Common grasshopper mistake." Sam patted his arm. "It happens."

He scowled and pulled clear of her. "Do you ever get tired of listening to yourself?"

"Nope, not really. Everything I say and do is so interesting to me."

"And somehow, I made it worse," Freddie said.

"From one grasshopper to another," Jimmy said, "quit while you're ahead."

"He's never ahead," Sam said. "That's the problem."

"Can I quit her?" Freddie asked. "That would solve all my problems."

"You can't quit me. You'd die of boredom with anyone else as your partner."

"Whatever."

"Truth hurts, my little grasshopper."

"I'm not speaking to you at the moment."

"And yet, you're still speaking to me."

He turned toward the passenger-side window.

Sam laughed. "You'll be back. You *love* me."

Since she'd driven Freddie to silence, she took advantage of the opportunity to text Nick on the secure BlackBerry to see how he was doing after the news from Alaska. When he didn't respond right away, she assumed he was in yet another meeting.

She texted her mom to make sure she was set for after-school duty with the kids. Brenda was filling in for Sam's stepmother, Celia, while she was on a trip with her sisters.

I just got to the WH, Brenda replied, *and yes, it's still surreal to pop over to the WH to visit my grandchildren. Haha. Don't worry about a thing. See you when you get home.*

It's still surreal to live there! Thanks for your help. Very much appreciated.

Completely my pleasure. Love every minute with them.

Sam was so glad to have made amends with her mother after a twenty-year breach in their relationship following her parents' divorce. She'd taken her father's side and never looked back but had learned there were two sides to every story, and once she'd heard more about her mother's perspective, she'd realized she had been wrong about a few things.

Back at HQ, they returned to the pit where the rest of their team was hard at work.

"Anything new, citizens?" Sam asked.

Gonzo spoke for all of them. "We've gone through financials, personal, work and school for all three victims, and nothing jumps out. We're still working on the socials but not finding anything interesting there either."

"I spoke with Walters in IT, and he's got nothing for us from the cameras," Freddie said as he ran his hand through his hair, his frustration apparent.

"Did the families shed any new light?" Detective Matt O'Brien asked.

"Nothing we can use," Sam said.

"Where do we go from here, Lieutenant?" Detective Charles asked.

Sam had no idea what to tell her. "Go through it all again from the beginning. Review the reports, the autopsies, the family statements, everything."

"Yes, ma'am," Charles said, eager to please as always.

Sam loved working with her and predicted big things for her career.

CHAPTER EIGHT

S am went into her office and sat at her desk, needing a few minutes to think about next steps. She'd barely taken a breath when Jesse Best, commander of the U.S. Marshal Service's Capital Area Regional Fugitive Task Force, came in and shut the door. At six and a half feet tall, he cut an imposing figure and rarely smiled.

"Sorry to intrude."

"No worries. What can I do for you?"

He handed her a six-inch-thick file.

Sam glanced up at him, her gaze connecting with his. For the briefest of seconds, his brown eyes conveyed a level of devastation she'd never seen in him, before it was gone as fast as it'd come. "What am I looking for specifically?"

"Anything I've missed. I've looked at it too many times to be objective anymore."

"Can you give me the highlights, or lowlights, such as they are?"

He sat in one of her visitor chairs. "It's my sister Jordan's case. She went missing when I was eleven and she was seven. I've looked for her ever since and have never found a trace. It's like she vaporized into the mist or something, which of course isn't what happened. And before you say it, I know she's probably long dead. But I want to know who took her from me."

His every word was laced with agony.

"Of course you do."

"I should give it up and get on with my life, but how the hell do I do that?"

"You don't. You can't. I never would either."

"I knew you'd get it." He looked down at the floor and then back up at her. "I've never asked for help before now."

"Why now?"

"I'm out of ideas. I've tried everything I could think of, and nothing has ever panned out. So I've brought it to the best detective I've ever worked with. No pressure, though."

Sam laughed. "Not at all."

"I mean that. I'm not expecting you to pull a rabbit out of a hat for me. I just want another set of eyes."

"I'm honored that you chose me, and I'll do my best for you."

"I have no doubt. I'm sorry to add another thing to your already-full plate."

"Don't sweat it. I'm always happy to help a friend if I can. God knows you do enough to help me."

"That's work. This is personal, and we both know it."

"Regardless. I owe you a million favors I'll never be able to return."

"No, you don't."

"We'll have to agree to disagree on that one."

The left half of his face lifted into the barest hint of a smile as he got up to leave. "Thanks for your time."

"This isn't the only copy of the file, is it?"

He tipped his head. "What do you take me for? A rookie?"

She laughed. "I'll be in touch."

He gave a curt nod and headed for the door.

"Jesse."

Turning back, he cocked an eyebrow.

"I'm sorry this happened to you and your family."

"So am I."

AT THREE O'CLOCK, Sam left her team working the case and reported to the chief's conference room for the Stahl meeting. As the day had progressed, she'd experienced a growing sense of dread and queasiness that were directly related to this meeting.

The last thing in the world she wanted was to waste another minute of her life discussing the revolting Leonard Stahl, who'd twice tried to kill her. That was why she'd been offered an out on this meeting, but since the other commanders would be in attendance, she would be, too.

This session would be disturbing and upsetting for everyone involved. She was no different that way. The meeting would be led by Captain Malone and Crime Scene Unit Commander Lieutenant Max Haggerty, who'd overseen the retrieval of bodies entombed or buried at Stahl's house.

Every department commander had been asked to attend, along with Chief Farnsworth and Deputy Chief Jeannie McBride, who greeted Sam with a warm smile.

Sam missed working alongside her friend, but was so proud to see Jeannie wearing the rank that had once been her dad's. Skip Holland would so approve of Jeannie serving as deputy chief, even if the pushback from some members of the department continued unabated. Some people didn't approve of Jeannie skipping two ranks to become deputy chief, but the mayor had wanted her, so there wasn't much the grumblers could do about it.

While others filed into the room, Sam flipped her phone open to find a message from Jeannie. *Should you be here for this?*

I'm fine, but thanks for asking.

Assistant U.S. Attorney Faith Miller rushed into the room. "Sorry I'm late."

"You're not," Malone said. "We're just about to start." He stood at the head of the table. "Before we get to the agenda for this meeting, I wanted to brief you on a couple of ongoing things you may be asked about by your officers. First are the new charges filed against former Sergeant Ramsey. As a result of the scene he caused at Tom Forrester's funeral, he's been charged with disorderly conduct and disrupting an official event. That's in addition to the charges of attempted murder of federal agents and a federal official that were already pending."

Ramsey had smashed his car into Sam's Secret Service SUV. That's when she'd learned that, as first lady, she counted as a federal official. Who knew?

"The department's chief counsel, Jessica Townsend, has met with Ramsey's attorney about the wrongful-death lawsuit he filed in regard to his son's shooting by Officer Offenbach. Ms. Townsend has provided Ramsey's attorney with a detailed account of the incident that led to the fatal shooting of Shane Ramsey. She's encouraged the plaintiff's attorney to compel his client to drop the lawsuit, as they don't have a snowball's chance in hell of prevailing in court.

"As opposed to the Eric Davies lawsuit, which is proceeding with unusual speed as it's a slam dunk thanks to our good friend Stahl, who framed an innocent man for aggravated rape and sent him away for sixteen years. As you know, the body of Tiffany Jones, the woman Stahl used to fabricate the charges against Davies, who filed a complaint about the way Stahl had treated him on a routine traffic stop, was among those found at Stahl's house. Ms. Townsend expects Mr. Davies will prevail in his suit, and the department's insurer will face a significant payout that we can probably all agree Mr. Davies more than deserves."

Dr. Anthony Trulo, the department psychiatrist and also Sam's friend, came into the room and grabbed a seat. He gave

Sam an affectionate look that let her know he'd be keeping an eye on her during this meeting.

As Malone updated them on the final details of the victims found at Stahl's house, Sam contemplated the damage one man had done to so many lives as well as their department and its reputation. It would take years to fully process the impact of his actions. What Sam would never understand was how someone could raise his hand, take the oath to protect and serve and then use his position to wreak chaos rather than uphold law and order. As someone who'd been raised by a faithful public servant and tried to be one herself, she had no ability to comprehend his depravity.

Judging by the shocked, disgusted looks on the faces of many of her colleagues, she wasn't alone in that. It was an affront to everyone who worked so hard to do the job the right way, even if they failed at times. Those failures were usually not intentional.

An image of each victim was shown on the screen at the front of the room as Malone recited their names, ages and other salient facts about their lives, such as where they were from and who'd been looking for them in the years since they'd gone missing. Sam was extra sad for the two who'd never been reported missing. They'd been identified using familial DNA that'd linked them to people in the system.

All told, twenty-two young women were named, murdered over a rampage that'd spanned more than a decade during which Leonard Stahl had collected a paycheck from the District.

Bile burned the back of Sam's throat, forcing her to swallow repeatedly to keep from vomiting. When she thought of the four women who'd been entombed behind a cement wall, left to die hideous deaths, her entire body felt cold as memories of being wrapped in razor wire by Stahl, doused with gasoline and threatened with fire picked that moment to come rushing to the surface.

One minute, she was fighting back the most horrifying memories of her life, and the next, she was in a different room with people gathered around her, looking at her with concern. What the hell was going on?

"Sam," Dr. Trulo said. "Look at me. Can you speak?"

"Wh-what happened?"

"You passed out." Jeannie pressed a cold compress to Sam's forehead that felt heavenly. "Take some deep breaths."

Vernon stood behind Chief Farnsworth and Captain Malone, his brows furrowed with distress.

Son of a bitch. She'd flaked out in front of all the commanders.

"I'm okay." She started to get up and was pushed back down by numerous hands. "Let me up. I'm fine."

"We're sending you home," Malone said.

"Absolutely not. I have three new bodies in the morgue and work to do."

"You can pick it up tomorrow," Farnsworth said.

"I'm not leaving." She gently pushed Jeannie and her cold compress away and stood. She fought through a massive head rush in the effort to remain upright. "I'm sorry to have caused a scene. As you were, people."

As she walked out of Jeannie's office, a visibly upset Freddie came running down the corridor.

"Are you okay? I heard you passed out."

"I'm fine. Let's get back to work." The Stahl meeting was over for her, even if the others planned to continue it.

"What happened?"

"It was hot in there."

"And that's all it was?"

"Yep."

"I knew you shouldn't have gone to that meeting."

"Freddie... Please. I love you for caring, but I just passed out in front of a room full of mostly men who already think I'm a distraction around here. Can we please drop it and get back to work?"

"Yeah, of course. Sorry."

"Don't be. I'm sorry I worried you."

"Not the first time. Won't be the last. It's not easy being me around here."

As she laughed, she was full of appreciation for her best friend, her partner, the brother of her heart. News traveled fast at HQ, especially when a high-profile commander fainted during a meeting about the heinous crimes of a disgraced former lieutenant who'd twice tried to kill her.

Before the rest of her squad could swarm her, she held up her hands. "I'm fine. Nothing to see here. Let's get back to work."

To Freddie, she said, "I want to call Archie to see if we can talk to his friend. She may be the key to this whole thing."

"I know you don't want to talk about it, but are you sure you shouldn't go home?"

"I'm very sure. I'll call Archie, and hopefully, we can go over there today." She went into her office and shut the door, dropping into her desk chair and taking a deep breath that she hoped would help to stop the spinning in her head.

A knock sounded on her door, and before she could tell the visitor to go away, Dr. Trulo stepped inside and closed the door behind him.

"I'm fine. I'm busy. Go away."

"Is that any way to greet a friend?"

"I don't want to be fawned over. I was overheated, and now I'm not. All good in the hood."

"Then why are you pale as a ghost and your hands are shaking?"

"I just need some water." She picked up one of the half-full discarded bottles on her desk and downed the rest of the water inside. "Much better."

"Sam."

"Yes?"

"Knock it off."

"Knock what off?"

"We all know the temperature of the room isn't what took you down."

"I'm sorry to have caused a stir. The others were right when they said I shouldn't have attended that meeting, but you know how I hate to be treated like I'm special or different or whatever."

"In this case, you're the only commander in this department Stahl tried to kill. Twice."

"That's old news."

"Will it ever be old news to you?"

Sam took another deep breath and forced herself to be kind in the way she spoke to a man who'd been a tremendous friend to her. He was one of the primary reasons she was still able to do the job after what Stahl had put her through. "I appreciate you more than you'll ever know, but the last thing I want or need right now is to be psychoanalyzed. I overheated. That's all it was. I'm fine and eager to get back to work."

He could smell bullshit a mile away, and now was no exception.

But thankfully, rather than pursue the matter, he said, "You know where I am if you need me."

"I take great comfort in knowing you're nearby."

He gave her a warm smile. "Then I'll let you get back to it."

"Thanks for caring, Doc."

"Always, my friend."

After he left, Sam pulled out the BlackBerry to text Nick. *Because we have a deal... I was in a meeting about the new charges about to be filed against Stahl when I apparently passed out. It was hella hot in there. I'm fine, back to work. Nothing to worry about. What goes on there?*

Sending that text went against everything she used to believe in about pushing bad or difficult things aside and powering through. Her husband didn't like hearing news about her issues on the job through the grapevine, which was more than possible with Gonzo's wife, Christina, serving as Nick's press secretary.

The BlackBerry rang with a call from him. "Yes, dear?"

"You're sure you're all right?"

"Positive."

"Samantha... Tell me the truth."

"I swear. I'm fine. It was a weird moment, and it's over now. I'm back to work. What's the latest over there?"

"Nothing new to report on the drones, and we're working on the situation in Alaska. Hope is beginning to fade for survivors."

She appreciated that he didn't dwell on her fainting. "No."

"I know. It's awful. An entire village of children, not to mention the teachers and staff, as well as others in the area. We've sent in everyone who can help. Now it's just a waiting game."

"I can't even think about what all those parents must be going through, some of them with multiple kids in the school."

"We were just saying that."

"Do you have to go there?"

"Eventually, but not now when I'd be more of a distraction than anything."

"I'm sorry you're dealing with another upsetting thing."

"Goes with the job, or so I'm told. I'm okay as long as you are."

"All good here. I'll be home as soon as I can."

"I can't wait to hug you."

"Same, love. See you soon."

"Be careful with my wife. I love her more than anything."

"Will do. Love you more, and I already won that fight, so don't even try it."

He laughed, as she'd hoped he would. "We'll continue this fight later."

"Can't wait."

Sam hated ending calls with him, the only person she wanted to talk to all the time. Well, him and their kids. She never got tired of being around them, but there was work to be done before she could go home to them. After finding Archie's cell number in her contacts, she called him.

"Are you okay? I heard you passed out."

For fuck's sake. "I'm fine. How's your friend doing?"

"A little better."

"I'm glad to hear that. Listen… I hate to ask you this, but we've got dick on this case. Is there any way we might be able to talk to her today? If it's the same attacker, she's the only one who got out alive."

"I was thinking about that. Hers was different. After she was hit in back of the head, she was drugged and sexually assaulted. From what I've read about your other vics, they were only hit from behind."

"They were, but I'd still like to talk to her if at all possible. You know how this can go. She might remember some small thing that'll blow the whole case wide open."

"She's very fragile, Sam. I don't know if putting her through that right now is the right thing to do."

"I wouldn't ask if I didn't feel it was urgent that we stop this person before they kill someone else."

"Let me talk to her and see if she's up to it."

"Thank you, Archie."

"I'll get back to you."

The line went dead, and Sam closed her phone, feeling bad for having pressured him—and his friend—at such a difficult time. However, other lives were in danger until they caught this killer.

CHAPTER NINE

Archie gave a soft knock on the door to his rarely used guestroom, where Harlowe had been resting.

"Come in."

Her voice was a little stronger today, which he took as a reason for hope that she might bounce back from this devastating incident. He stepped into the room to find she was still as pale as the white sheet, her auburn hair like a wreath of fire surrounding her still-striking face, despite the bruises on both sides.

"How're you feeling?"

"Better."

"I'm so glad to hear that. Do you think you could eat something?"

"I'm a little hungry."

"That's great news." He'd been concerned by how little she'd eaten since he brought her home the day before. It was inching closer to dinner time, but he didn't think she was ready for anything heavy. "What sounds good to you? I can make some scrambled eggs and toast or oatmeal. Peanut butter toast is also an option. I also have soup and crackers."

"Eggs and toast sound good."

"I'll go make it."

"Would you mind if I took a shower?"

"Not at all. Make yourself completely at home."

"You're very kind. I wish I remembered meeting you before... Well... I suppose it's better that I can't remember much of anything that happened over the last week or so."

"About that... We have an incredible psychiatrist at work. Everyone loves him. I'm sure he'd stop by to talk if you feel up to that."

"I'm not sure what we'd talk about."

"There's trauma in the not remembering as well as the physical injuries. Dr. Trulo is the best."

"Why would he care about me? I don't work with you."

"He'd care if I asked him to."

"Why do you care?"

Archie shrugged. He'd been asking himself that same question for days. "I just do. We had a good time together before this happened. I want to see you back on your feet and on the road to a full recovery."

Her shy smile touched him in places he hadn't realized were there. He'd had that same reaction to her when they first met and every time he'd seen her since, even when she was in the hospital.

"Thank you for everything. I don't know what I would've done without you."

"I'm happy to help. Whatever I can do."

"Don't you have to work?"

"I took a few days off, which I never do, so I have a ton of leave."

"It's nice of you to do that for me."

"No problem at all. How about you grab that shower while I make us some breakfast?"

"That'd be great."

"Coffee?"

"I'd love some."

"You got it. Do you need a hand getting up?"

"I might."

Archie moved closer and offered her an arm to hold as she sat up, grimacing from the bruises on her ribs and abdomen. She wore one of his DC Federals T-shirts and a pair of his sweats that were far too big for her. He needed to see about getting her some clothing that fit properly.

When she was upright on the side of the bed, her feet on the floor, she took a moment to collect herself, pushing hair back from her face. "Sorry that I'm like a ninety-year-old."

"No need to be sorry. You're recovering from painful injuries. Take your time."

She took hold of his arm and stood slowly, wincing and tearing up. "This sucks."

"It totally sucks, but you're doing so much better than you were even yesterday."

"If you say so."

"I say so."

She kept a tight grip on his arm as he walked her to the bathroom.

"Let me grab a change of clothes for you. We'll see about getting something that fits you." He'd reached out to their mutual friends, Joe and Deb, to ask if Deb knew where Harlowe had been living. Deb had said she wasn't exactly sure, but she thought it had been a short-term rental or extended-stay hotel since her sales-rep assignment in the District was temporary. Erica was working on figuring out the exact location where Harlowe had been staying. Harlowe's cell phone hadn't been with her when she was found.

In the hospital, after Harlowe decided to trust him, she'd asked Archie to speak to the doctors for her because she couldn't handle hearing the details of what'd happened to her. Archie had yet to share those details with her, or the fact that the doctors had determined she'd been sexually assaulted. But he was pretty sure she knew that, based on her injuries.

"I'm sorry for all the trouble I'm causing you."

"It's no trouble. I swear. I'm happy to help you any way I can."

Her eyes filled with tears that unnerved him. They made him want to wrap his arms around her and promise he'd take care of her for as long as she needed him. He hoped that'd be a long time.

But he was afraid of scaring her, so he resisted the urge to hug her.

"Do you need anything?" He put out towels and made sure there was shampoo and body wash in the shower.

"No, thank you. I should be fine."

"Call me if you need me."

"I will."

He wasn't sure if he should leave her to fend for herself, but he also didn't feel right offering to help. Hopefully, she could get through it on her own.

In the kitchen, he poured himself another cup of coffee. His mind raced with questions, concerns and a fiercely protective feeling for a woman that was all new to him—and deeply unsettling. Archie had more questions than answers where she was concerned, and yet... He was becoming more involved with every passing hour.

In his bedroom, he found a clean T-shirt and another pair of sweats with a string around the waist that she could tighten. When he heard the shower running, he opened the bathroom door to put them on the counter.

By the time Harlowe walked into the kitchen twenty minutes later, Archie had the food ready.

She looked like a waif in his clothing.

He went to offer her an arm to hold as she made her way slowly to the small table. "Let me grab a pillow for you to sit on. Hang on."

In the living room, he grabbed one of the throw pillows his

mother had insisted he needed when he moved into the apartment and brought it to the kitchen.

"Thank you," she said as she lowered herself slowly to the now-cushioned wooden chair.

His entire body and soul ached for her. He wanted to murder the person or people who'd done this to her. Even after more than fifteen years as a law enforcement officer, he was still infuriated and saddened by the depravity he saw on—and off—the job.

Archie served plates for both of them along with coffee, creamer, sugar and sweetener, since he wasn't sure how she took her coffee. Thank goodness for grocery delivery services, or he would've had beer, beef jerky and granola bars to offer her.

"Are you okay drinking coffee later in the day?"

"I think so, but I guess we'll find out if it keeps me awake. Also, this smells delicious."

"It's one of three things I can cook most of the time."

"What are the other two?"

"Spaghetti sauce and burgers on the grill."

"Those are hard to screw up."

Smiling, he said, "That's what I've found. Do you like to cook?"

She thought about that for a second. "Yes, I think I do." A look of panic appeared in her expressive brown eyes. "What will I do if I can't remember basic things like that, things I knew how to do or who I was before?"

In addition to remembering nothing about the kidnapping or assault, she was fuzzy on other details about her life prior to the incident.

"I'm sure it'll come back to you at some point."

"But then so will the bad stuff."

"Possibly."

She took a bite of toast and a sip of black coffee. "Maybe it would be better if I didn't remember any of it."

"Do you have any memory of what happened to you?" He asked the question as gently as possible, wishing he didn't need to ask it at all.

"Even though I'm scared of the memories, I've been trying really hard to come up with anything I can, but there's just nothing before the hospital."

"You told me you're a sales rep for a food company."

Her brow furrowed.

She's adorable, he thought, *even when she's confused and upset.* The few times he'd seen her before she went missing, he'd thought she was charming, delightful and sexy, even if she was somewhat secretive about the details of her life. He'd sensed then she wasn't telling him everything, but he hadn't felt right about digging deeper.

"One of my colleagues was hoping she might talk to you about what you remember," he said tentatively.

"I've already been over it with the police. I don't remember much of anything."

"Maybe if she brought Dr. Trulo, the psychiatrist, with her, it might help."

"I'm willing to do whatever I can to assist in the investigation. I want to know what happened more than anyone. But I don't want to disappoint you."

Goddamn, but she got to him with the way she looked at him. He placed his hand on top of hers. "You couldn't disappoint me."

"Yes, I could."

"Don't worry about that. I think you're amazing, and I have since the first time we met."

"Tell me about that."

"We were at a party in Georgetown at my friend Joe's house. You knew his wife, Deb, from yoga. Joe and I play softball together. You said you're a sales rep for a national food company that services grocery stores and restaurants."

Archie's phone rang with a call from Erica Lucas. He

showed the caller ID to Harlowe and took the call on speaker. "Hey, Erica. You've got both of us. How's it going?"

"I'm making some progress on Harlowe's case. Her parents called the department, asking for a wellness check since she stopped returning their texts and calls a few days ago. They live outside of Pittsburgh, where Harlowe grew up. They said she's on a six-month assignment to DC and has been living in an extended-stay hotel. They gave me the address near Columbia Road. The parents are flying in today."

His heart sank at the thought of them swooping in and taking over caring for her.

"Archie?"

"I'm here. So she told me she came here for college and never left, but they said she's on a six-month assignment here. That doesn't add up."

"We can ask them about that."

"Can you give me the name of the place where she was staying? I'd like to get some of her things."

"Let me do that."

"Are you sure?"

"Yes, no problem. I'll go over there today and explain the situation to the management. They may want to talk to her to confirm I have permission to enter her room."

"I'm sure that'd be fine."

While he talked to Erica, Harlowe ate her breakfast and drank her coffee but was clearly tuned in to the conversation. She nodded in approval about Erica going to her hotel room.

"Did Sam tell you she's looking into a connection between her three new vics and Harlowe's case?"

"She did."

"Okay, just making sure you're in the loop. I'll get over to the hotel now and bring her a bag shortly."

"Thanks, Erica."

"Yes," Harlowe said. "Thank you so much, Erica."

"Happy to help. See you soon."

Archie ended the call and got up to refill their coffee cups. "Does Pittsburgh, Pennsylvania, ring any bells?"

Her brows furrowed as she thought about it. "I mean... Yes, of course, but the details are hazy. I remember going to school and some of my friends, but that was a long time ago. The more recent stuff isn't there."

"That's okay. You don't have to remember right now. How do you feel about your parents coming to see you?"

Her eyes filled. "For some reason, I don't like that they're coming. What's wrong with me? They're my parents."

"You took a hard knock to the head and suffered significant trauma. Losing your memory can be your brain's way of protecting you."

"From what?"

"From what happened to you."

"I don't understand any of this."

He had questions of his own. When he'd tried to find her online, he'd found no mention of a Harlowe St. John affiliated with any of the major national food companies. There'd been no social media profiles or any information at all that he could tie to the woman he'd come to know.

Which made him wonder if she'd told him the truth about herself when they first met. He hadn't wanted to ask Erica what name her parents had given while Harlowe was listening, but the first chance he got, he'd ask her that.

He hoped he got the chance to speak to her parents so he could put together more pieces of the puzzle.

While they waited for Erica to arrive, Archie texted Sam. *Harlowe is okay with you coming by, but she said again that she doesn't remember anything beyond what she's already reported.*

If you don't mind, I'd still like to talk to her.

We're here. Lucas has been in touch with her parents, and they're en route from Pittsburgh. She's going to Harlowe's hotel to get some of her things.

Glad to hear there's progress in figuring out who she is and where she's from.

Do you think Dr. Trulo might be willing/able to talk to her?

I'm sure he'd be glad to. I'll see if he's available, and we'll be there shortly.

Archie replied with a thumbs-up emoji. "My friends, Sam and Freddie, are going to stop by to talk to you, possibly with our department psychiatrist, Dr. Trulo, who's a wonderful guy. Fun fact: Not only is Sam the lieutenant of our Homicide division, but she's also the first lady."

"Samantha Cappuano."

He turned to her, surprised. "You remember her name."

Harlowe nodded. "I don't know why I do, but I remember her and her handsome husband, the president. I remember you telling me you work with her." She looked happy and worried at the same time. "Does that mean my memory is returning? How do I remember that, but I don't recall why I feel weird about my parents or any other recent things?"

"The brain is a very complicated machine. It's hard to say why you remember that but not the rest."

"It's very strange to not remember your life."

"I'm sure it is, but what's important right now is that you rest and relax and give yourself time to recover."

"It's hard to do anything else but wonder where my memories have gone."

"I know, honey, but the harder you try to force it, the longer it might take to get back to normal."

"What will normal look like after this?"

"I don't know yet, but I'm sure you'll figure it out one day at a time."

Her brows furrowed again. "That saying. One day at a time. Where does that come from?"

"I'm not sure of the original origin, but it's a recurring theme with Alcoholics Anonymous."

"That's it. I knew someone who was in that group. I can't remember who."

He took her plate to the sink. "Your memories are there, and they'll come back when you're ready for them."

"Do you really think so?"

"I can't know for certain, but I hope so, even if I wish I could protect you from memories that'll hurt you."

She gave him a curious look. "Why do you feel so protective of me?"

"I don't know. I just do."

"You said we hadn't known each other long when I went missing."

"That's right."

"And yet, you feel protective."

He shrugged. "We had a pretty immediate connection. I was looking forward to getting to know you better, and then you were gone. I thought maybe you'd decided you weren't into me after all, but I really didn't think that was the case. I'd just gone to my friend Sam—"

"The first lady?"

"Yes. I asked for her help in finding you. I wasn't sure if you were missing or what was going on. She told me Erica had a Jane Doe, which is what we call a crime victim without ID who can't remember her name. She took me to GW to find you."

"I'm sorry you were worried. That I put you through that."

"I'm just glad you were found alive, even if I wish none of this had ever happened to you."

"You're very kind." After a pause, she added shyly, "And very handsome, which I'm sure you know."

Archie felt his face flush with heat. Dear God, was she making him *blush*? What the hell was that about? "Oh, um, thank you."

"I didn't mean to embarrass you."

"You didn't. Not much, anyway."

She smiled, and his heart did a weird skipping thing that left him a little breathless.

"All I could think about after the first night we met was how pretty, funny, smart and sweet you were, and I couldn't wait to see you again."

Before she could reply to that, his phone rang with an out-of-state number he didn't recognize. "Lieutenant Archelotta."

"We... we were told to call you to speak to our daughter," a man said. "This is George Prior, Harlowe's father. Is she... Could I speak to her?"

"Hold on for one minute, please." He held the phone to the side while he updated her. "It's your father. Would you like to speak to him?"

"I... I think so. Thank you."

Archie handed her the phone.

"Hello? Yes, it's me, Harlowe."

He listened to her tell her father that she was doing a little better and that her friend Archie had taken good care of her since she left the hospital. Then her mom got on the phone, and Harlowe seemed to shut down a bit at the sound of her voice.

"I don't know what happened. I can't remember much of anything." After a long pause, she said, "Okay. I'll see you then."

She ended the call and looked at him with big eyes full of tears. "I recognized their voices, but why do I feel so hesitant about seeing them?"

A twinge of apprehension had Archie wondering if the people on the phone were really her parents or perhaps the ones who'd hurt her. "If there's a reason to be afraid of them, you'll have two cops in the room when you see them."

"That makes me feel a little better."

"We'll take care of you. Don't worry." He helped her up and got her settled on the sofa with a blanket over her. "Do you want the TV?"

"No, thanks."

"I'm going to clean up the kitchen. Let me know if you need anything."

He returned to the kitchen and grabbed his phone to text Erica. *She feels apprehensive about seeing her parents but can't say why. I'm not letting anyone near her unless they can prove they're related.*

Understood. I'll work on getting some proof.

Thanks, Erica.

He knew he didn't have to tell Erica or Sam that Harlowe needed to be handled gently. They were the best at what they did, and he trusted them implicitly. But if he had his way, no one would be anywhere near her until he knew what the hell had happened to her.

SAM WENT to find Dr. Trulo, who was eating lunch while listening to something in a foreign language. She knocked on the door. "Sorry to interrupt."

He pressed pause on his computer, seeming a bit embarrassed. "I'm trying to learn Italian before our trip next year."

"That's cool. How's it going?"

"I suck at it, but I'm soldiering on."

"Why do some people pick up other languages easily, and others can't for the life of them?"

"One of the great mysteries."

"Spanish nearly killed me in high school and college. I really wanted to learn it, but it wasn't happening."

"That sounds like me with Italian." He wiped his mouth with a napkin. "Anyway, I'm sure you didn't come by to talk about things we suck at."

Sam laughed. "Nope, but whatever you're eating smells incredible. If you made that, you don't suck at cooking."

"I can't take the credit. My lovely wife made eggplant parm over the weekend. To die for."

"It's making me hungry, and I don't even like eggplant."

"She'll send some in for you to try. I bet you'll like eggplant after you have hers."

"I'll take that challenge. When you're done, can you come with me to see a potential witness who's been through a rough ordeal?" Sam filled him in on the situation with Harlowe as well as Archie's involvement. "There's a slight possibility her case could be related to my three new homicides."

"Sure, I can do that. Give me ten minutes?"

"You got it. I'll meet you at the morgue exit."

"See you there."

Sam returned to the pit to grab her jacket and a portable radio to take with her. "Cruz, let's roll."

"Where you headed?" Gonzo asked.

"To see a possible fourth victim who survived but doesn't remember anything."

"Got it."

To Gonzo and the others, she said, "Keep me posted on any developments."

"Will do."

Sam started to walk away but turned back to her sergeant. "I'm hoping to get over to Ninth Street later this week to do a few things to make it ready for new occupants."

"Thanks, Sam. We can't wait to move in."

"No sense having it sit empty for the next few years."

"It's a huge upgrade for us. We really appreciate it."

"Glad to make it happen." Sam had another thought as she walked toward the morgue exit with Freddie—it was probably time to remove the ramp Nick had installed outside their home so her dad could visit in his wheelchair. The thought of removing that ramp and everything it stood for—especially how Nick had made their home accessible to her dad—hit her in all the feels.

She thought about the day she'd come home to find their front steps in rubble. Suspecting someone had detonated a bomb, she'd called in the bomb squad. That was when she'd found out that Nick had hired their contractor neighbor to build the ramp. Funny, endearing and mortifying all at the same time.

Those memories hit her hard.

Taking down that ramp, and the one at her dad's house, would be further proof that he was truly gone forever. Not that she needed more proof of his gaping absence. She felt that loss every single day. Sam wondered how Angela could cope with the double whammy of losing their dad and then her husband a few months later, while expecting her third child.

How could she bear it? Sam asked herself that all the time, but somehow, Angela was powering through, taking care of her children and preparing to welcome a new baby.

Later, Sam would ask Nick to reach out to the Ninth Street neighbor who'd built the ramp at their house about taking down both ramps in anticipation of new tenants.

"Everything okay?" Freddie asked as they approached the morgue, where Dr. Trulo waited for them.

"Yeah."

"I'm excited to ride in a Secret Service vehicle," Dr. Trulo said, grinning.

"It's nonstop excitement." Outside, she introduced him to Jimmy. "He's pumped for his first Secret Service adventure."

"We'll try not to make it memorable," Vernon said.

Sam laughed. "Their job is to make it boring and routine."

"I understand and approve," Trulo said. "We want to keep our favorite lieutenant safe at all times."

She told Vernon where they were going and why.

"Any chance that the people who took her know where she is?" Vernon asked.

"Archie would've been careful about that."

"We'll need to do a full sweep before you go in."

"Okay," she said, resigned to this taking way longer than it would have before Nick became president.

CHAPTER TEN

"I'm the good doctor's favorite," Sam said when they were on their way. "Did you hear that, Cruz?"

Freddie rolled his eyes. "Was that necessary, Dr. Trulo? The rest of us have to deal with her all day, every day."

Trulo laughed. "My apologies, but I only speak the truth."

Sam sent her partner a smug grin. "I'm a delight to have around."

"Sure you are."

"Ask Vernon and Jimmy. They agree with me."

"I will not ask them. They're being paid to agree with you."

"Hey now," Vernon said. "That ain't in the job description."

The tomfoolery helped to reset her emotions after her thoughts had taken a sad turn.

"How're you holding up after the chaos yesterday?" Trulo asked.

"Hanging in there. Is it weird that I'm starting to get used to stuff like that?"

"Yes, it's weird. You shouldn't have to become accustomed to that level of fear."

"No one should," Freddie added.

Sam took a few minutes to update Dr. Trulo on the situation with Harlowe.

"Nice of him to step up for her this way."

"He seems rather smitten."

"Good for him, but it's a tough situation."

"Will she get her memory back?"

"Hard to say. Amnesia can be a post-traumatic response to a brain injury. It's often temporary, but there're cases in which the memories surrounding the event never return. That can be both a blessing and a curse."

"I can see how both would apply."

Sam took a call from Roni Connolly, her communications director at the White House. "Hey, how's it going?"

"That's what I wanted to ask you. How're you doing?"

"I'm fine as long as everyone else is. That's what matters."

"So unbelievable. At an event for *children*."

"Best time to cause maximum outrage, I suppose. What're you hearing about Alaska?"

"Rescuers are making progress in getting to the school building. They're holding out hope because the structure seems to have mostly held up."

"Well, that's some good news."

"Indeed. I was also calling to remind you that we have the photo shoot scheduled for this Saturday with you and the kids."

Sam had forgotten all about that and wanted to moan at the thought of spending half a day being photographed for upcoming social media use by her first lady team. "Right."

"You're thrilled. I can tell."

"I am indeed thrilled."

"Hair and makeup at nine. Lilia and I were wondering if we can take the liberty of coordinating with Marcus on your wardrobe." He was Sam's favorite designer.

"Yes, please do. I have no time to think about that, and with you two involved, as well as Davida and Ginger, at least I won't look feral." Her hair and makeup women were top-notch.

"We figured you'd say exactly that. Kendra will be there to do your nails, too."

"Awesome."

"Your sarcasm is duly noted."

"Sorry, you're just doing your job."

"We know exactly who we work for and wouldn't have you any other way."

To the men in the SUV, Sam said, "Roni thinks I'm a delight, too, in case you were wondering."

"We weren't," Freddie said.

Roni laughed. "Do I want to know what's going on over there?"

"The usual nonsense mixed in with three new murders and a vicious assault. Other than that, just another day in paradise."

"I don't know how you do it."

"Someone's gotta. May as well be us."

"I won't keep you. I'll email you a schedule for Saturday that you can review when you have a minute."

"I won't remember to do it, so maybe leave a copy in the residence for me?"

"Will do."

"Sorry to be high maintenance."

"You're fine. See you soon."

"Thanks for all you do."

"My pleasure."

"Sure it is," Sam said with a laugh as she closed her phone. "Photo shoot with the kids this weekend."

"That'll be fun," Trulo said.

"It requires hair, makeup *and* nails. That's not fun."

"Most women would disagree," Trulo said.

"I am *not* most women."

Freddie's snort made them all laugh. "What do you think of our rolling circus so far, Doc?"

"Most fun I've had all week."

"You need to get out more," Sam said.

"That's true. Maybe you can take me out to play more often."

"Any time you want, my friend."

"I may take you up on that. Things are much more interesting out here where the action is."

"He says that now," Freddie said. "Wait until we encounter some *real* action."

"Let's hope that doesn't happen," Vernon said so sternly they all laughed.

"I keep meaning to ask if Celia decided about renting her house," Freddie said. "I don't want to bug her about it, but we have to decide what we're doing soon. Our lease is up in June."

"Oh shit, I meant to tell you yesterday that Celia texted me that she's in favor as long as it's you living there."

"Really? That's amazing. Tell her we'll take very good care of it. Did she say how much?"

"Whatever you're paying now is fine with her. I'm sorry I forgot to tell you this."

"That's not enough, and don't be sorry. You've been a little preoccupied."

"Don't look a gift horse in the mouth when it comes to rent, Detective," Trulo said.

"I don't want to take advantage."

"You're not," Sam said. "She's glad to know someone we love will be living there and looking after the place."

"That's amazing. I can't wait to tell Elin this news. She'll be so excited."

"I'm glad you guys are happy about it."

"We're thrilled."

"We'll do something about the ramps before you and Gonzo move over there."

"Don't worry about that."

"It's time." Sam saw Freddie exchange glances with Trulo. "I'm okay with it. Don't worry."

"It breaks my heart to even think about that," Freddie said.

"Mine, too, but he's not coming back, and we don't need the ramps anymore. Maybe we can donate them to another family who could use them. He'd like that."

"I'll put out some feelers, if that would help," Trulo said.

"It would. Thank you."

"I'll get back to you about it."

"I appreciate it. Thinking about helping other families in need makes it a bit easier to take them down."

"It'll never be easy to take them down," Dr. Trulo said, "but I hope that when you do, you'll remember how you and your family made it possible for your dad to have some freedom he wouldn't have had without them."

"That's true. I used to love how he'd come wheeling into our place for a visit." She teared up. "I sure do wish he could do that now. He'd be all over the White House."

"He's right there with you guys." Freddie looked a little misty, too. He'd loved Skip almost as much as Sam had. "He'd never want to miss out on that. Plus, he probably still thinks he's the boss of you from the great beyond and needs to keep an eye on things."

Sam accepted the tissue Dr. Trulo handed her, dabbing her eyes even as she laughed at the reminder of her father's supervisory skills, which never waned even after his terrible injury. "No doubt. He loved being the boss of me."

"His favorite thing," Freddie said. "That and helping on our cases. I miss his input. He always gave us ideas we wouldn't have had otherwise."

"Remember how he was the one to tell us to look at Peter on the car bomb?"

"Yes! We hadn't even thought of him yet."

"He was the best," Trulo said. "Everyone loved him, and we all miss him."

"That's nice to hear. I can't believe it's almost six months already."

"The first year is rough," Trulo said. "Especially considering the year you're having."

"It's been a year and a half, and it's only April," Sam said.

They pulled up to Archie's building a few minutes later. Vernon asked them to wait while he, Jimmy and other agents who'd been called to the scene did a quick sweep.

Dr. Trulo watched the activity through the window. "Interesting to watch them at work."

"A thrill a minute, but I appreciate what they do to keep me —and my family—safe. I just hate that we need it."

"It's a major adjustment, but unfortunately, it's the reality with which we live."

"I dislike that reality."

"I do, too."

"I dislike that it'll be our reality for the rest of our lives, but at least the agents are amazing people who've become friends."

"There is that."

"Vernon and Jimmy are like family after all the time we spend together."

"I love that for you."

"They've become my agents and my therapists."

"Hey, you're not replacing me, are you?"

"No one could replace you."

"Phew."

Vernon returned to the vehicle fifteen minutes after they'd arrived. "We're clear, Lieutenant. Right this way."

"Thank you."

Sam, Freddie and Dr. Trulo followed Vernon inside while Jimmy trailed behind them. Several other agents were positioned outside the building.

"Is this the way it'll be now?" she asked Vernon.

"For the time being, until we know more about the drones."

Sam knew she was lucky they hadn't completely sidelined her, but the added security felt like overkill to her. No one knew where she planned to be on any given day, so the possibility of being found on the job was low. At least in her mind. Who knew what they knew that she didn't?

It was probably better that she didn't have the details behind the Secret Service's various actions, or she'd never sleep at night.

Archie lived on the second floor of a nicely kept modern building that suited the IT commander—in her opinion, anyway.

She knocked.

Her friend came to the door, looking tired and maybe a little stressed.

"Come in. Welcome to my humble abode."

"We're sorry to intrude at such a difficult time," Sam said as they followed him into a well-lit, contemporary space while Vernon and Jimmy stayed outside the door.

"It's okay. Harlowe knows you're trying to help." Archie shook Dr. Trulo's hand. "Thanks for coming, Doc. This is above and beyond."

"Happy to do whatever I can to help."

"This way." Archie led them to the living room, where Harlowe was on the sofa, covered by a blanket.

Sam noticed the bruises on Harlowe's pretty face had darkened to a deep purple since Sam had seen her in the hospital.

Harlowe eyed them with trepidation.

"Harlowe, these are my colleagues Lieutenant Holland, Detective Cruz and Dr. Trulo."

"Th-thank you for coming. Archie says you're good people."

They took seats facing her.

"He says the same about you," Sam said. "We're very sorry you were hurt in our city."

"Thank you." She folded and unfolded her hands, as if she wasn't sure what to do with them. "I think, before this, I was happy, but I can't really remember."

"You were," Archie said. "You'd made some nice friends and were enjoying your job and yoga classes."

"I wish I could remember that."

"I'll bet your body would remember the yoga," Dr. Trulo said. "When you're feeling up to it."

"Will the rest of my memory ever come back?"

"I can't say for certain, but it often does when it accompanies a traumatic brain injury. I understand you suffered a concussion."

She nodded and then winced. "My head still hurts when I move around too much."

"That's to be expected after a concussion. As you heal, you're apt to remember more."

"Is it possible that I won't?"

"That happens sometimes, but it's rare."

"I'm afraid of what I might remember."

"What's the last thing you do remember?" Sam asked.

Harlowe thought about that. "I think I did something with my friend from yoga." She brightened when she seemed to recall something new. "I decided to walk home because it was the first night that wasn't freezing." She paused, frowning as she seemed to struggle to come up with more. "I don't remember anything after that until I was in the hospital."

"What part of your head was hurt?" Sam asked.

Harlowe reached up to touch the back of her head. "Here."

Sam exchanged glances with Freddie. "Do you recall where you went for dinner?"

"I... I don't remember the name of the place."

"Joe and Deb might know," Archie said. "He's my softball friend, and his wife is Harlowe's friend from yoga. We met at a party at their house."

"Do you mind asking them?" Sam said.

"I'll text them."

"Would it be possible for us to speak to Joe's wife?" Sam asked, feeling the buzz that came with a possible breakthrough on a baffling case.

"I'll ask them that, too."

"Do you mind if we speak with her, Harlowe?"

"Not if it might help to get some answers about who hurt me."

"You've been very helpful. Thank you for seeing us."

"I wish I could tell you more, but I'm sort of glad I can't remember the bad stuff."

"I understand that." Sam had her own bad stuff she wished she could forget. "You're doing great, and you're in great hands with Archie. He's one of the good guys."

"I already knew that, but thank you for confirming it."

"Would you like me to stay for a bit to chat?" Dr. Trulo asked. "You've been through a lot. It might help to talk about it with a professional."

"I... I think that would be nice. If you have time."

"I'll make time for you."

Harlowe blinked back tears. "You're all so kind to someone you don't even know."

"I know you," Archie said. "And they're my friends. It's all good."

"Can you get yourself back to HQ, Doc?"

"I'll hop on the Metro or grab an Uber. No worries."

"See you back at the house."

To Sam, Archie said, "Joe said his wife, Deb, is working from home today and to feel free to come by. They want to help if they can. I'll text you the address in Georgetown."

"Thanks, Archie. Let us know if we can do anything to help."

"Find the person or people who did this to her." His expression was fiercer than she'd ever seen it. "That's what we need."

Sam squeezed his arm. "We're on it."

Archie lowered his voice so only she could hear him. "You sure you're okay from before?"

"I'm fine. It was hot as hell in there."

Other than a raised brow, he had no comment.

"Nothing to worry about."

"I heard they're filing a boatload of new charges, and Faith intends to prosecute on every one of them," Archie said.

"Yes, that's the scuttlebutt."

"Good. Those families deserve retribution and their own justice for their loved ones."

"Couldn't agree more."

"What're you hearing about the new USA?" Archie asked.

"Catherine McDermott, former AG of Oregon. Allegedly a by-the-book ballbuster."

"Awesome. She has to be confirmed, right?"

"She does, but it's expected to go through."

"Huh."

"Don't ask me if there's anything I can do about that, because I wouldn't do it even if I could."

"I'd never ask."

"I know. Sorry. I'm just grumpy about his stuff touching mine."

Archie raised both eyebrows and smiled.

"At work, I mean. Otherwise, I love when his stuff touches mine."

He put his hands over his ears. "TMI."

Laughing, Sam headed for the door. "Thanks for the help. We'll keep you posted." She stopped and turned back to him. "I hope you're being careful with your heart in this situation, friend."

"Trying to be."

"How's that going?"

"Not so well. Or, it's going great. Depending on how you look at it."

"She'll remember that you stepped up for her this way."

"I'm worried about what else she'll remember."

"Let me know if there's anything at all I can do for you."

"Thanks, Sam. Appreciate you coming by. Let me know how you make out with Deb."

"Will do."

CHAPTER ELEVEN

Erica Lucas called to tell Archie she'd located Harlowe's efficiency apartment at a hotel near the yoga studio. "The manager wants her permission to allow me into the room to retrieve her clothes."

"Let me take the phone to her," Archie said.

He went into the living room, where she was resting on the sofa after her conversation with Dr. Trulo. "Erica has found your apartment and needs you to give your permission to the manager so she can go in and get your things."

Harlowe took the phone from him. "Hello?" She listened to Erica and then spoke to the manager. Then she handed the phone back to him.

"I'll be there shortly with a bag for her," Erica said.

Archie went into the kitchen and lowered his voice. "She feels safe with me. I want it made clear to her parents that she's not leaving here under any circumstances."

"I'll let them know not to push for that. Not now."

"Thanks, Erica."

"No problem."

"What're you hearing about the rape kit?"

"Nothing yet, but like I said before, I've requested a rush on it."

"Thanks for everything you're doing."

"It's no problem at all. Whatever we can do for her—and you."

"Means a lot."

"I'll be there within the hour."

"I'll see you when you get here."

Archie put the phone in his pocket and went into the living room to see if Harlowe needed anything.

"No, thank you. I'm good for now."

"How're you feeling?"

"A little better since I ate that delicious meal you made."

He noticed her brows were furrowed, as if she was worried. "What's on your mind?"

"Haha, not much."

Archie smiled, relieved to see her making a little joke. "Poorly worded question."

"I don't get how I understand words and situations, such as you're a police officer and Erica is and your friend Sam, too. Like, I get what that means. I knew to say your meal was delicious. Why do I know that stuff but not where I was staying or why I'm upset with my parents or anything about what happened to me?"

He took a seat on the coffee table and held out his hand to her, wanting any contact between them to be on her terms.

She wrapped her hand around his, filling him with the same overpowering sense of rightness he'd experienced with her from the start.

"I've seen this before when people suffer a serious head injury. Everything is a muddled mess while the brain is healing. Nothing makes sense."

"That about sums me up."

"I know it's hard to be patient, but your brain is on its own timeline, and there's no sense trying to rush it."

"You're so very sweet to put your life on hold to be here for me."

"I'm happy to do it."

She threaded her fingers through his. "Why does this feel... special? That's the only word I can think of to describe it, although I'm not sure what I'm basing that on."

"It was special between us. We connected right away. I couldn't wait to see you again after that first night. I actually left work right at five o'clock for the first time in longer than I can remember. I did that *three days in a row*."

Her smile lit up her pretty eyes. She looked more like the woman he'd first met than she had since before the attack. "I wish I could remember what we did."

"You wanted me to show you some of the places I like best in the city. The first night, we took a long walk in Rock Creek Park, and then we had tacos and beer. I teased you about being a beer girl, and you said you always have been. You remembered sipping from your grandfather's beer glass when you were a kid. The second night, we worked out together at my gym, and then we brought takeout back here."

"Wait. I was here before?"

"Yes, once, a few days before you stopped replying to my texts."

"Did we... you know..."

"No, we didn't, but we wanted to. There was a lot of kissing and stuff. You said we needed to save something for our third date."

"What did we do on that date?"

"I took you to Old Ebbitt Grill, a DC institution, and then we went to a bar with live music. We both thought it was too loud, so we didn't stay there for long. You had an early meeting in the morning, so you got an Uber to go home after that. You had plans to go to yoga with Deb on Friday night. We were supposed to go to a Caps game on Saturday, but I never heard from you, which was rather upsetting. I was afraid you were ghosting me."

"I'd never do that!"

"You seem very sure of that."

She appeared to give that some thought. "I think maybe I had that done to me at some point, but I'm not sure. Somehow, I know I wouldn't do it to someone else."

"I didn't think you would either. I was really worried when I didn't hear from you, but I didn't want to overreact in case something had come up."

"I'm sorry you were worried."

He shrugged. "That's my nature. Fifteen years as a police officer has made me into a worst-case-scenario thinker."

"In this case, you were right to be worried."

"I had a feeling something was wrong, but I didn't want you to think you'd been seeing a psycho, so I held off reaching out to Deb. I wish I hadn't done that."

"It's silly, isn't it? The stuff we worry about when a relationship is new and we're getting to know each other."

"Exactly. I tend to overthink everything, which is also thanks to my job. The last woman I was seeing said I was too intense for her, which was in my head when I held off on sounding the alarm on you not responding to me. I didn't think I had the right to overreact on your behalf. At least not yet."

"Please don't blame yourself for something other people did, Archie. I don't blame you."

A knock sounded at his door. "That'll be Detective Lucas." He released her hand and got up, shaken to his soul by her nearness, her sweetness, her beauty and her courage. It felt like his life was changing forever with every minute he spent with her. Did he want his life to change forever? If it meant having her in it, maybe so.

He opened the door to Erica, who held up a canvas bag. "Clothes and toiletries."

"Thanks, Erica. She'll appreciate having her own stuff."

"No problem."

"Come in."

He led Erica to the living room, where Harlowe greeted her with a smile. "Thank you so much for your help, Erica."

"Glad to do it. You're looking much better today."

"I feel a little better. I just wish I could remember things."

"That'll come." Erica sat in a chair across from Harlowe. "Archie told you that your parents are coming to town today?"

"He did."

"I'm picking them up at the airport when they arrive. Do I have your permission to speak freely with them about what to expect when they see you?"

"I... I mean, I guess so? I feel like there was some tension between us, but I can't remember why. It's all a blank."

"I've fully investigated them." She withdrew several sheets of paper from a portfolio she'd brought. "There were photos of you on their social media, which I've also provided."

Archie ached for her as she sifted through the pages, looking for clues about who she was and where she'd come from. "Does any of it look familiar?" he asked after several minutes had passed in silence.

"It does. I remember them, but not what's been going on between us lately."

"It's okay," Archie said. "It's only been a week since you suffered a serious head injury. It'll take some time."

"How much time?" she asked, her eyes full of tears. "I don't remember things about my own parents."

"It'll take as long as it takes," he said gently. "I know that's not what you want to hear, but that's the best I can do."

She wiped away tears. "I know. It's not your fault or Erica's. I'm sorry to be cranky."

"Anyone would be after what you've been through," Erica said. "You don't have to apologize."

"My parents may not understand what's wrong with me."

"I'll let them know your memory has been affected by your

injury and ask that they not push you on trying to remember things. Would that help?"

Harlowe nodded. "Thank you."

"Of course."

"There's one other thing..."

"What's that?"

"They'll want me to go with them so they can take care of me. I'm not leaving here. I want to be with Archie. I trust him."

A tsunami of emotion took him by surprise as he realized he'd kill for this woman, if it came to that. He really hoped it didn't, but if it did...

"We won't let them take you anywhere," Erica said. "You're in charge here. What you say goes, okay?"

"Thank you for understanding."

"If you need anything at all, you can ask either of us. We're here for you."

"It means so much. You didn't know me before... but you're so kind."

"We're with you for the long haul. We want to see you through this and get you back to your life as soon as possible."

"Thank you."

Erica stood to leave. "I'll be back with your parents when they land. I'm picking them up at Reagan National at five."

"See you then," Harlowe said.

"I'll walk you out," Archie said to Erica.

At the door, Erica turned to him. "How're you holding up?"

Archie rubbed the back of his neck, where all his tension seemed to gather. "I'm doing okay as long as she is. How are things at work?"

"Don't worry about that. Take care of yourself and your friend. Your very capable team is taking care of work."

"Thanks again for everything."

"No problem at all." Erica glanced toward the living room. "You two seem... committed or something like that."

"I don't know what we are. All I know is I care."

"She does, too. That's very obvious to me."

"You think so?"

Erica smiled. "I do. She wants to stay with you because you make her feel safe. That's huge, Archie. Keep doing that. It'll matter to her when she looks back on this upsetting time."

"I guess we'll see, won't we?"

"We will indeed, and frankly, I can't wait to see what this becomes."

"Don't jinx me. We're in a very strange situation here."

"Understood, and I don't mean to make light of it."

"I know. But you're right. There's a vibe for sure. There was before this happened, and there still is. For me, anyway."

"Proceed carefully."

"Will do."

"I'll text you when I'm on the way with the parents."

"And you'll tell them she's asked to stay put?"

"Absolutely."

"Thanks, Erica."

"You got it, pal."

He closed and locked the door and then went back to check on Harlowe, who'd dozed off. As he covered her with a light blanket, he wished he could stretch out next to her, wrap his arms around her and promise her that everything would be okay. But since she was in no way ready for such things, he sat across from her and tried to chill for a bit so he could get some rest and be ready for whatever came next.

CHAPTER TWELVE

S am and Freddie were in the SUV on the way to Georgetown when the BlackBerry buzzed with a text from Nick. She fished it out of her pocket.

Hey, babe, the SS wants a minute with us in the morning. Can you be available for that?

Did they say why?

Not yet.

What time?

You tell me.

Can we do it right after the kids leave for school, so I can get to work sort of on time?

I'll make that happen. Thanks. How's your day going?

It's going. Hey—I was thinking about the ramps on Ninth Street and how they should come down now that we have tenants moving in. Do you still have the number of the guy who installed ours?

I do. I'll reach out to him. I'm sure you've got feelings about taking them down...

Lots of them, but Dr. Trulo is going to find someone who can use them, so that helps to take some of the sting out of it.

I wish I could hug you. I miss him so much. I can't imagine how hard this is for you.

Skippy hated waste of any kind. He'd want someone to be using those ramps, so I'm taking comfort in that. Anything new in Alaska?

Might be cause for some optimism. The building seems to have withstood the mudslide intact. There's hope that we may find survivors. Nothing new on the drones.

So glad to hear that news from AK. How is it possible that there's nothing new on the drones?!

I don't know, but every resource is being deployed to figure it out. Someone went to great lengths to be undetectable.

So we may never know?

Possibly.

I don't like that answer.

Me either. Will you be home for dinner?

That's the plan.

OK, see you when you get here. Love you.

Love you, too.

"Vernon, why does the Secret Service want to meet with us in the morning?" Sam asked.

"I'm not in that loop yet."

"Can you venture any guesses?"

"Perhaps an update on enhanced security in light of the incident on Monday, but don't quote me on that."

"What happens in the SUV stays in the SUV," Sam said, earning a mirror grin from Vernon.

"That's right."

Sam didn't want to stew over why the Secret Service had asked for a meeting, but the pit in her stomach would stay there until she knew what it was about. She was under no illusions about the threats facing her husband and their family, but if she allowed herself to think too much about the reality of it, she'd go mad.

Monday's incident was yet another reminder that there were people out there, probably a lot of them, who'd rather see Nick dead than give him a chance to lead the country.

Sam took advantage of the opportunity to text her sisters,

her brother-in-law, Mike, her stepmother, Celia, and eldest niece, Brooke, to tell them that she and Nick were arranging for the ramps to come down on Ninth Street before tenants moved into both houses.

Dr. Trulo is trying to find new homes for them, which Dad would approve of. I wanted you guys to know so you wouldn't be shocked to see them gone if you go to Ninth.

Thanks for handling that, Sam, Celia replied. *I appreciate it, and you're right. Your dad would want them to go to someone who needs them and maybe can't afford them.*

Ugh, Tracy said. *The hits keep on coming, but you're right. It's time. Thanks for handling that for us, Sam (and Nick).*

Sam thought about how delighted her dad had been to be able to come down the ramp at his house and roll over to hers for a visit. Nick had seen to that for them, and the ramp at their house and her dad's regular visits had become such a source of joy in an otherwise difficult situation.

Her ringing phone drew her out of the rabbit hole of poignant memories she'd fallen into. She sat up a little straighter when she saw the name of the twins' school on the caller ID. They would be home by now.

"Sam Cappuano."

Freddie gave her a curious look at her use of her married name on the job.

"Mrs. Cappuano, I'm so sorry to disturb your work. This is Beatrice Reeve, head of Northwest Academy."

"Hi, Mrs. Reeve. Is everything okay?"

"Yes, the children are fine, but we're a little worried about Aubrey. She's been unusually withdrawn and fearful since the incident at the White House, and we wanted to make you aware that she's expressed some concerns for your safety and that of President Cappuano."

Sam's heart sank at the thought of her precious little girl being afraid. "Oh no. I'm so sorry to hear that. Is it possible for her to see Alden when she's upset? They take great comfort in each other."

"Yes, we're aware of that, and we brought him into her classroom today for a visit that seemed to help."

"Thank you for that."

"Perhaps a conversation at home about how well protected you both are might help."

"We'll definitely do that. Thank you for letting me know what's going on. Those poor kids have been through so much. I hate to think of them being afraid of it happening again."

"It's only natural that they'd worry. I think they would no matter who stepped up for them after their parents were murdered so senselessly."

That might be true, but Sam knew there was much more for their children to worry about because of what she and Nick did for a living. "We'll talk to them and consult with their therapist. I appreciate the heads-up."

"Let's stay in touch about this."

"Absolutely. Thank you again for calling."

"Everything okay?" Freddie asked after she closed her phone.

She filled him in on what was going on with Aubrey.

"Oh damn. That poor kid."

"Sometimes I wonder if we did the right thing taking them in."

"Why would you ever question that?"

"They'd be better off with guardians who aren't surrounded by threats and security and everything that goes with that."

"That's not true. They're better off with you and Nick and Scotty. You love them, and they know it. That's what they need more than anything."

"I agree with Freddie," Vernon said.

"Me, too," Jimmy added.

"I love them so much. We all do. But I hate to think that being with us is adding to their already considerable trauma."

"They've seen a therapist, right?" Freddie asked.

"Yes, for months after their parents died. We all agreed that we could scale back the appointments after a while because she felt they were adjusting beautifully and doing much better."

"Maybe a check-in with her would be advisable," Vernon said.

"Yes, for sure. I need to update Nick and Eli." She withdrew the BlackBerry to send the text.

Nick wrote back a few minutes later. *Sure hate to hear that.*

That's how I feel, too.

I'm sorry to hear it, too, Eli said. *I was about to text you guys that I heard from Andy this morning, and he has the adoption paperwork ready for us to review.*

Great news, Nick said.

Sam was thrilled by the idea of adopting them, but after Monday's events and this news from school, she hoped they were doing the right thing for the kids.

She dashed off a text to the twins' therapist, updating her on the latest and asking for advice on how best to handle the situation. Rebecca was good about getting back to her and would know what to do. Sam also texted her mom and Shelby to let them know Aubrey had had a tough day and might need some extra TLC. She desperately wished she could go home to be with her, but she couldn't leave work with so much left to do.

We're on it, Shelby replied a few minutes later.

Absolutely, Brenda said.

Thank you both.

When the SUV arrived at the Georgetown apartment building where Joe and Deb lived, Sam was forced to put her personal dilemma on hold after Vernon, Jimmy and the other agents concluded a sweep and declared the building safe for her to enter. The sheer madness of waiting while other law enforcement officers ensured her safety would've sent her over the edge if she didn't remind herself, every time, that she was putting up with the security because Nick had asked her to.

The delays made her crazy when there was so much ground to be covered in a given day. "I'm becoming too much of a distraction," she said to Freddie.

"What? No, you're not."

"We've burned more than thirty minutes that we don't have to waste waiting for random buildings to be declared safe for me to enter."

"No one knows that but you and me, and I'm sure as hell not saying anything about it. Don't worry about crap that doesn't matter."

"If anyone else was sitting like a princess in a fortified SUV outside a building, waiting to talk to a potential witness, we'd cry foul."

"Think about what you *bring* to the investigations. Like the fact that we're here to talk to this woman because you asked Harlowe the right questions."

"You would've gotten here eventually."

"It never would've occurred to me to ask her the last thing she remembers."

"Yes, it would have."

"I was focused on what she was doing in DC, where she's from, where she lives in the city. That kind of thing. I wasn't thinking about taking it back to the last memory. You did that."

"Well, you're very kind to say so, but I still hate the time being wasted when we have three bodies in the morgue and a traumatized young woman who may or may not be our fourth victim."

"Don't sweat the stuff you can't control. It doesn't matter in the grand scheme of things. We're working the case, doing the job, even if it takes a tiny bit longer than usual. It's no big deal."

"Thank you."

"You're welcome. Now knock it off."

Sam laughed and realized she felt a little better.

Vernon returned to the SUV, opened the back door and signaled for them to come with him.

They took an elevator to the couple's third-floor apartment, where two agents Sam didn't recognize were positioned outside the open door.

"Hey, I'm Joe. Come in." The man was tall and handsome, with sandy-brown hair, brown eyes and a lean build.

"This is my partner, Detective Cruz, and Secret Service Agent Vernon Rogers," Sam said as Vernon followed her and Freddie inside. "Sorry for all the uproar."

"No problem. It's not every day that the first lady stops by."

She showed him her badge as a formality. "I'm in detective mode right now."

"Of course. Deb is eager to help in any way she can. We can't believe what happened to Harlowe. It's terrible. Deb is finishing up a meeting. Can I get you something to drink?"

"Ice water would be great."

"For you?" he asked Freddie.

"Water is good for me, too."

Joe served the drinks to them at the island where they'd taken seats on stools.

"How long has Deb known Harlowe?" Sam asked, eager to proceed as the day got away from her.

"A couple of months now. They met in a Saturday-morning yoga class and started having coffee afterward. From there, she came to dinner with us a few times with other friends and attended a get-together we had here, where she met my friend Archie. You know him."

"Yes, I do." *Better than you can imagine.*

A pretty young woman with light tan skin and brown eyes came rushing into the room. She was fully made up, wearing a cream-colored silk blouse with sweats, and her dark hair was pulled back in a clip. "I'm so sorry I didn't have time to change out of my work-at-home getup before you arrived. I'm Deb Martland. It's such an honor to have you visit our home."

Sam shook her hand. "I love the outfit. Wish I could get away with that at work."

"It's the work-at-home mullet—business on the top, party on the bottom," Deb said.

Sam laughed. "I see how it is."

"Working from home is awesome, except for when the first lady stops by."

She showed Deb her badge. "Just a cop right now and looking for whatever you can tell me about your outing with Harlowe before she went missing."

"Let's sit over here where we can be more comfortable."

Sam and Freddie took their glasses of water with them to a comfortable sitting area with plush white sofas and a shaggy white rug that would be a red-hot mess in ten seconds with her family.

"You were the last to see Harlowe before she went missing, correct?"

"I believe so. We went out for drinks and appetizers after yoga on Friday night."

"Where did you go?"

"A taco place down the street from the yoga studio in Adams Morgan."

"Where was Harlowe living?"

"She had a place near the studio. She could walk there, which she loved."

"How did she plan to get home from the restaurant?"

"She said she was going to walk because it was so nice out. I didn't object because she said she lived close by."

"What do you know about her job?"

"She worked for Premier Foods out of Chicago. She was here to increase their presence in this city, meeting with restaurants, grocery stores and other retailers."

Sam took notes as she listened. "How much longer was she scheduled to be in town?"

"I'm not sure. I think she'd planned to stay as long as

necessary to cover as much of the market as she could. I got the sense that it was a relief to her to be away from home, but she never did say why."

"Did she like the job?"

"She loved it, especially going to conventions that were all about food and samples. She joked about doing yoga to offset her career in the food business."

"Did she share anything with you about her life before she came to DC?"

Deb thought for a second. "She graduated from American and was briefly married after college. She didn't say much about that to me. I was really excited when she seemed to connect with Joe's friend Archie when they met through us."

"Tell me about that. Was it a setup?"

"Not specifically. We had friends over on a Saturday night. They were both invited, we introduced them, and it sort of took off from there. They exchanged numbers, and I think they'd gotten together a couple of times before she went missing."

"How did you find out she was missing?"

"Archie texted Joe on Sunday, after she and I went out after yoga on Friday, to ask if I'd heard from her. He said he felt weird even asking because things were so new with them, but they'd been talking regularly, and he hadn't heard from her since Friday, and his texts to her were going unanswered."

As Sam made a note of the timing, she empathized with Archie. As a detective, he would've realized something was amiss, even with a relatively new friend. A sudden change in routine or pattern was almost always a red flag in a situation like this.

"Had you heard from her?"

"Not since we parted company Friday night, but that wasn't unusual. I didn't expect to see her again until yoga on Monday. I told her I was skipping the Saturday-morning class we went to sometimes because I've been nursing a pulled hamstring."

"Do you think you could show us where you were when you parted with her?"

She glanced at her husband, who shrugged.

"I mean, sure, if it would help."

"It would. Are you able to take a break now?"

"Let me tell work I'll be out for a bit and change really quick."

"Thank you for this."

"No problem. I want to help figure out what happened to my friend."

After she left the room, Sam turned to Freddie. "Will you let Vernon know we're heading back to Adams Morgan?" Vernon had waited inside the front door for them.

"Yep."

Deb returned less than five minutes later, which Sam appreciated.

"Would you like to come, too?" Sam asked Joe.

"If you wouldn't mind."

"Fine by me. Any friend of Archie's…"

"He speaks highly of you."

"That's nice to hear. He's an excellent cop."

"He says the same about you."

CHAPTER THIRTEEN

They left the apartment and took the elevator to the ground level, accompanied by Vernon. "Joe and Deb, this is Secret Service Agent Jimmy McFarland."

"Nice to meet you," Joe said. "I admire what you do."

"Thank you," Jimmy said as he held the door for them.

"Where're we going?" Sam asked Deb.

"Power Yoga on Columbia Road Northwest, the seventeen hundred block."

"Got it," Vernon said.

"This is so cool," Joe said when they were on the way.

"Vernon and Jimmy make it fun," Sam said.

"Is it weird to need a detail?" Joe asked.

"It wasn't something I thought I needed as a law enforcement officer myself, but I've learned to choose my battles. Vernon and Jimmy are great. We've found a nice groove, and their protection allows me to do my job without worrying about the things they're paid to worry about."

"Plus, we get a lot of work done while someone else does the driving," Freddie added.

"That, too," Sam said.

"We were sorry to hear about what happened at the egg roll," Deb said. "That sounded terrifying."

"It was, especially since we were briefly separated from our kids."

"Do they know any more about who did it?" Joe asked.

"Not that I've heard."

"My friends and I think it's really cool that you're still working now that you're the first lady," Deb said. "That includes Harlowe. She told me she's a fan of yours and your husband's. We have that in common."

"Thank you. I love the job. I wouldn't want to give it up."

"I want Joe to run for president so I can be the first lady and not work," Deb said with a grin.

"Not gonna happen," Joe said.

"He's no fun," Deb said.

Sam laughed. "Trust me, it's not as much fun as it looks." She'd no sooner uttered the words than she feared she'd said too much. "Please don't ever repeat that I said that. I'd never want to come off like I'm complaining about the extraordinary privilege of living at the White House."

"No worries," Joe said. "We'd never repeat that to anyone, and P.S., we already knew it's not as much fun as it might seem. I can't imagine having that kind of responsibility or scrutiny on me."

"That's the hard part," Sam said.

"I'm really pulling for your husband," Joe said. "He seems like a very decent sort of guy."

"Thank you for that. He cares deeply about doing the right thing and isn't more worried about reelection than he is about doing the job."

"So he's not going to run in the next election?"

"He says he's not, but I guess we'll see. Again, that's not public info."

"We understand," Deb said. "We won't repeat anything you tell us."

"We have a rule that what happens in the SUV stays in the SUV," Freddie told them.

"It's a huge honor for us to meet you," Joe said.

"Wait until you get to know her," Freddie said.

They laughed.

"He's not funny. That's a rule."

They pulled up to Power Yoga on Columbia Road about ten minutes later. As usual, Vernon asked for a minute to secure the area before they got out.

"This is the annoying part," Sam said as she watched the swarm of agents prepare a path for her that she didn't feel she needed, but no one had asked her.

"Better safe than sorry, I guess," Joe said.

Of course it was, Sam wanted to say, but the delay would always be frustrating for someone who had more to do in a day than could be done in a week.

Vernon did his best to move things along, as usual, and was back to the SUV in ten minutes. "Good to go."

"Thank you, Vernon."

The four of them got out, zipping coats against a stiff, cool breeze.

"This is the yoga studio," Deb said. "We walked two blocks that way to a taco place we like afterward."

"Show me." Sam scanned the area for cameras. To Freddie, she said, "Text Walters and see what we've got around here and have him start reviewing the film from last Friday night."

While he did that, Sam, Deb and Joe walked the two blocks to the restaurant, which was painted in colorful shades of purple and red.

"We joked about working out and then ruining it with tacos and beer," Deb said. "We made the same joke every time. Harlowe loves their chicken nachos. She said she's addicted."

"Where did you last see her?"

"Right here." Deb pointed to the curb outside the restaurant. "I was picked up by an Uber. She said she was going to walk home. I told her I'd see her at class on Monday, and she said to have a great weekend."

"Was anyone else with you, or was it just the two of you?"

"Just us. Our other two friends had plans, so they left right after class."

"Can you show me where Harlowe's place is from here?"

"I was never actually there. She said it was only a couple of blocks. I asked if she wanted us to drop her from the Uber, but she said she felt like walking because it was so nice out."

"This has been really helpful. I could call a Patrol car to get you home, if you'd like."

"No need. We'll call an Uber."

Sam shook hands with them and handed her card to Deb. "If you think of anything else that might be relevant, please give me a call."

"It's been a real thrill to meet you. I'm glad to know you're as cool as you seem from a distance."

"That's nice of you to say. Take care."

As they walked away, Sam said to Freddie, "Hear that? I'm as cool as I seem."

"Why was I *certain* that'd be the first thing you'd say?"

"Just making sure you heard it."

"What's next?"

"You've got the address for Harlowe's place?"

"I do."

"Can you put it in your phone and get us there?"

"In fact, I can."

"Let's go, then."

"Yes, ma'am."

"What's the plan?" Vernon asked.

"We're going to walk to where Harlowe was staying. It's only a few blocks from here."

She could see the internal debate he had with himself in the expressions that briefly crossed his face.

"We'd prefer to drive you."

"I'd prefer to walk so I don't miss anything."

He could insist and force her to take the ride if he chose to. If she put up a fight, that would be reported to his supervisors and would eventually get back to Nick in the form of her refusing to cooperate with her detail. That was the last thing he needed, so she held her breath while she waited for Vernon's next move.

"Let me get a couple of other people to walk with us. I need two minutes."

She could give him two minutes to keep the peace.

Jimmy stayed with them while Vernon walked away to call in reinforcements.

"I keep waiting for your head to explode," Freddie said quietly so Jimmy wouldn't overhear him.

"It's on constant boil, but they're only doing their jobs. I don't want to take it out on them, you know?"

"I get it."

"I'm sorry it slows you down, too."

"I'm with you, kid. You set the pace, and I do what I'm told."

"Right, that's all you do, along with a significant amount of backtalk and sarcasm."

"I learned from the master."

Vernon's two minutes quickly became five.

"I put up with this because Nick asked me to, but sometimes it's hard not to lose my shit and start screaming my head off in the middle of Adams Morgan."

He glanced toward a group of people with cell phones who'd spotted the first lady on the job. "Don't do that unless you want to be the lead story on the news tonight."

Sam turned her back to the phones. "It's getting harder all the time for me to do this job."

"It's intense right now because of the incident with the drones. It won't always be like this."

"What if it's like this from now on because of that? The

Secret Service director asked for a meeting with us tomorrow. What fresh hell will that bring to my life and Nick's?"

"Their only goal is to keep you and the kids safe. Whatever it is, keep that in mind."

"I tell myself that a thousand times a day, but at times like this, that doesn't make it easier."

A loud cracking sound cut through the air.

Before Sam could begin to react, Jimmy fell on top of her.

Freddie landed next to them.

"What the hell?" Sam asked, her voice compressed by Jimmy's weight.

Something warm and wet landed on her neck.

A gurgling noise came from above her.

Then Vernon was there with other agents. Someone was screaming, "Agent down."

No. No. No.

Jimmy was moved off her.

Sam was hauled to her feet and hustled to the SUV by Vernon and another agent. "Jimmy..."

"We've got people with him. We need to get you out of here."

"No! Not until we know if he's okay!"

"They'll let us know. Are you hurt?"

"I don't think so." She'd have bruises from landing hard on the pavement, but that didn't count as hurt.

Vernon slammed the door shut and jumped into the driver's seat, the other agent clambering into the passenger seat. Vernon activated the vehicle's lights and sirens, made a U-turn and punched it to get them out of there.

"What about Freddie?"

"He's with Jimmy and the others. He's okay."

"Is Jimmy... Is it bad?"

"I don't know yet."

He sounded as tense and as stressed as she'd ever heard him.

"Where are you taking me?"

"Home."

"Please take me back to headquarters. I'm on the clock, and I need to finish my shift."

"I'm under orders, Sam."

"As am I, Vernon. Take me to HQ, or they'll never let me out of the gilded palace again, and you know it. I'll take any blame that comes our way."

The young female agent in the passenger seat, Jimmy's seat, handed her a package of wipes. "You have blood on your face."

With shaking hands, Sam took the wipes from her and used them to remove a shocking amount of blood.

Jimmy's wife was expecting their first child in June.

This could not be happening.

Someone had shot at her and hit Jimmy.

This would change everything.

They'd never let her work again. The thought of that made this terrifying situation that much worse. She noticed they were heading to HQ and not the White House, which was a relief.

"What're you hearing about Jimmy?"

"He's on his way to GW. They're working to stabilize him."

"Did someone call Liz?" Sam had met his adorable wife at the Easter Egg Roll. They'd been together since high school.

"That's being handled. Don't worry."

Sam didn't want to think about Liz receiving that phone call or the terror she'd experience while she waited to hear how badly her husband was injured. Or worse.

When her phone rang, she dug it out of her pocket to take the call from Gonzo.

"What the hell happened, Sam?"

"Someone shot at us in Adams Morgan. They hit Jimmy."

"Is he okay?"

"I don't know yet. He's on the way to GW. What're you hearing?"

"Massive federal and MPD response in the area looking for the shooter."

"We were retracing the steps of a potential fourth victim in our case. I'd like to get someone over there to help Cruz finish what we started."

"I'll reach out to him and head over there myself."

"Thanks, Gonzo."

"This'll be a big deal here and at home."

"I'm painfully aware."

"I'll be back to you shortly."

"Thanks."

Sam had no sooner ended that call than the BlackBerry rang with a call from Nick.

"Hey."

"What happened?"

She tried to imagine him hearing about her being shot at in the middle of his day and how upset he must be. "We're waiting to hear about Jimmy. He was hit."

"Oh my God, Sam."

"I'm okay, and I'm praying he will be, too." Her voice wobbled ever so slightly, but he heard it. Of course he did.

"Samantha..."

The anguish she heard in that single word made her ache for him.

"I'm so sorry you were scared. I promise I'm perfectly okay, other than being shaken up and desperately worried about Jimmy. His first child is due in June... He has to be okay."

"I'll see what I can find out and let you know."

"That would help. Thank you."

"Thanks for not getting shot today."

"I do what I can for my person."

"I love you more than life itself."

"I love you more."

"Not possible."

"I already won that fight." Sam brushed away tears that

suddenly appeared as the close call came into sharper focus. "Please don't let this be another battle about what I'm going to be allowed to do until we know more about what happened."

"I hear you, babe, but I'm sure there'll be some conversations."

Those conversations were the last thing Sam wanted to have, but she'd suffer through them to keep doing her job. "It's been tough out here since Monday. Extra everything slowing me down."

"I know. I'm sorry. Hopefully, it's temporary. I've got to run to a meeting. I'll see you soon?"

"I'll try to be home for dinner."

"See you then, and stay safe. My whole life depends on you."

"Likewise."

She wiped away more tears as she dropped the BlackBerry into her coat pocket. "Pull it together," she whispered. The last thing she needed was for people at HQ to see that she'd been crying.

Another huge distraction in a long line of them was also the last thing she needed. The approach to HQ was lined with TV news trucks, and as they pulled into the parking lot at HQ, Sam noticed a larger-than-ever gaggle of reporters gathered outside the main doors.

Vernon drove around the building to the morgue entrance.

"Any word, Vernon?" She was almost afraid to ask.

"Just now. The bullet went through his arm, connected with his vest and fractured a rib, which then collapsed a lung. But the vest saved his life. He's awake and alert but in a lot of pain. He's expected to survive."

The flood of relief made her dizzy for a second. "Thank God."

Vernon came to open the back door for her. "Yes, indeed."

For a long moment, the two of them stared at each other in a shared communion over the near catastrophe.

"Are you all right?" she asked.

"If you are and Jimmy is, I am, too."

He was clearly shaken, though, which was to be expected.

"Thank you for bringing me here."

"I'm going to catch hell for it, but I'll remind them we have a deal with you and an obligation to honor it."

She reached out to him.

He took her hand.

"I hope you know how much I've come to care for you and Jimmy."

"We know, and the feeling is mutual. I'm sorry this happened today."

"It's sure as hell not your fault."

"I still feel responsible."

"Don't take that on. A wise man once told me we can only control our own actions and how we react to the actions of others."

"He was a wise man, indeed."

As she got out of the vehicle, Sam would give anything for one of that wise man's bear hugs and the reassurance that'd always come with them.

CHAPTER FOURTEEN

Vernon walked inside with her.

Lindsey came out of the morgue to hug Sam. "Thank goodness you're all right. How's Jimmy?"

"Injured, but not life-threatening."

"That's great news."

"For sure."

"Are you doing okay?"

"I'm just dandy."

Lindsey shook her head, her dismay apparent. "I can't believe someone would have the nerve to shoot at you."

"You can't? Really?"

"Well, I can, but goddamn them to hell for it."

Sam smiled at her friend. "Love you."

"Love you, too. Thanks for not getting shot."

"Nick said the same thing."

"He must be losing it."

"He is. I feel terrible about that when he's already dealing with so much crap. Just another thing."

"You're hardly just another thing to him, and you know it."

"I do, but thanks for the reminder."

"Do you have another shirt to change into?"

Sam glanced down at her blood-covered top, which she'd somehow failed to notice before Lindsey mentioned it. "Nope."

"I've got one you can borrow."

Sam followed Lindsey into a back room where staff kept personal items. Lindsey got a T-shirt out of a locker. "Best I can do."

"That'll work." Sam took off the soiled top and put on the T-shirt.

Sam hugged her friend. "Thanks for the shirt. Gotta get back to some semblance of work. Today's been a mess."

"Any progress?"

"A very little."

"Let me know if I can help."

"Will do. Thanks, Doc."

Sam and Vernon continued on to the pit, where everything came to a stop when she walked in.

"Sam," Detective Charles said on a long exhale. "It's so good to see you."

"Good to be seen."

"How's Jimmy?" Detective Green asked.

"He's expected to survive with a gunshot wound to the arm, a broken rib and a collapsed lung."

Cam winced. "Ouch."

"Thank God for the vest that saved his life." She paused before she added, "Look, I know we're all rattled by the day's events, especially after what happened yesterday, but it would help me to keep the focus on the case, so let's meet in the conference room in five to regroup. Okay?"

They nodded and murmured their agreement.

Sam went into her office, removed her jacket and sat for a second behind the desk to catch her breath.

She took a call from Freddie. "How's it going?"

"We walked the full distance to Harlowe's extended-stay hotel and nothing stood out, but we've identified all the cameras in the area and are working on figuring out who owns the ones that aren't ours and how to get access to the footage."

"Good work. Thank you for carrying on."

"I'm almost afraid to ask how Jimmy is."

Sam gave him the same update she'd given the others.

"Well, that's a freaking relief."

"Sure is."

"We'll be back in shortly."

"See you then."

"Sam..."

"I know. I'm okay. I promise. We'll talk later, okay?"

"Yeah, sure. Sounds good."

She closed her phone and exhaled, trying to find her groove, which was hard to do when she was so rattled.

Dr. Trulo appeared in her doorway. "Holy. *Shit*. Am I glad to see you."

Sam smiled at him. "You missed all the excitement."

"I heard Jimmy is expected to survive?"

"Yes, thank goodness. He's an expectant dad with his high school sweetheart."

"Is there anything I can do for you, friend?"

"Not right now, but thanks for checking. I may need you when the dust settles."

"I'm always here for you."

"Thank you. How'd you make out with Harlowe?"

"We had a good talk. She's got a long road ahead of her if her memory returns—or if it doesn't."

"What do you think the odds are that it will?"

"She's young and healthy, so it's a good possibility that it will."

"I hope she can handle what she remembers if it does."

"That's the kicker, of course. She's being very well cared for by our friend Archie."

"He's smitten."

"So it seems. I'll be checking in with both of them as things unfold."

"You're the best."

"Just doing my job."

"You do much more than that, and we all know it."

"Kind of you to say. I assume you won't make the grief group meeting tonight."

Sam had forgotten about it. "I don't think so. I should go home and touch base. They'll be upset about the day's events, and Aubrey had a tough day at school, apparently."

"Don't worry about anything. Take care of your family. I'll cover it for us."

"Thanks, Doc." Sam grabbed a notebook and pen and followed him out of the office. "See you later."

"Call if you need me. Any time."

"Will do."

She was thankful to be so well supported in all aspects of her crazy life. There was a time, not that long ago, when she would've chafed against the constant "people-ing" and nonstop conversations that came with that tremendous support. Now she took comfort in them.

In the conference room, she found Captain Malone, Deputy Chief McBride and Chief Farnsworth waiting for her.

"Who called in the brass?"

"Lieutenant..." The chief looked at her with a combination of deep-seated affection and despair over her ordeal.

"I'm fine, and thankfully Jimmy is too. I appreciate the concern. What're we hearing about the search for the shooter?"

"They believe it was another drone," Malone said. "Massive manhunt underway."

Sam's heart sank at the word *drone*. "I assume it's all over the news?"

"You assume correctly," McBride said. "We're being overrun with requests for a comment from you."

"I'll get to it. First things first, are there any updates on the case?"

"We've scoured the financials and social media of all our victims and haven't found anything that stands out or any commonalities," Charles said. "By all accounts, they seem to be regular people going about their lives, minding their own business."

"What are you hearing from Walters in IT about film in the areas of the attacks?" Sam asked.

"They're still reviewing," Green said, "but nothing useful yet. Freddie and Gonzo have been sending info about the cameras in Adams Morgan that we're forwarding to IT for review. We've offered to help if they need some extra eyes. Walters said he'd let us know."

"What's the theory about whether the Adams Morgan kidnapping and assault are related to the other three victims?" Malone asked.

"We're not sure yet," Sam said. "Other than the hallmark knock to the back of the head, the rest of that situation is very different from the others. She was kidnapped, held for multiple days and sexually assaulted, whereas our other victims were killed instantly or left for dead." Sam's shoulders and neck were tight with the tension that came from frustration at not having more information after a full day of digging. She had the starting of one hell of a headache, too.

Captain Norris from Public Affairs came to the door. "Sorry to interrupt. I heard the lieutenant was back. Are you able to make a statement before they knock down the doors?"

"Yes, I can do that." It was the last thing she felt like doing, but there was never a time when briefing the press appealed to her. Least of all when she was the story, which had happened far too often for her liking. "Give me five minutes to make myself presentable." That was another thing she'd never cared much about until she was married to a high-profile politician. They'd take far too much pleasure in her looking like a hag.

To her team, she said, "Keep pulling the threads, people, and then turn it over to Carlucci and Dominguez. We'll reconvene at zero eight hundred."

"Yes, ma'am," Green said for all of them.

Sam went into her office to brush her hair and touch up the makeup she wiped off after the shooting. She took a series of deep breaths to calm her nerves and brace herself for the onslaught.

"We need ten minutes to get our people in place," Vernon said.

"Okay."

Malone came to the door and nodded to Vernon as he stepped aside. "I can do it for you if you don't feel up to it."

"That's okay, but thanks for offering. Let's get it over with."

"We're all going out with you."

"Thanks, Cap."

"Too fucking close, LT. Too fucking close."

She grabbed her jacket and put it on. "Yeah, for sure." The day's events were also a reminder that even world-class security could do only so much to keep their family safe against people who'd do them harm. No team could cover every possible eventuality, especially when the culprits were coming at them from the air using devices that couldn't be traced.

When she was as ready as she'd ever be for a grilling by the press, she walked with Malone and Vernon to the lobby, where the chief and Jeannie waited for them.

"Are you sure you're up for this?" the chief asked.

"As much as I ever am."

"We're with you, kid," he said.

"That makes all the difference."

"Are we ready?" she asked Vernon.

"Yes, ma'am."

When they stepped outside into the crisp spring breeze, Sam zipped her jacket. She was aware of Vernon standing closer to her than he normally did at these things. His presence made her feel safer.

The reporters started shouting questions at her the second they saw her and didn't let up until she held up her hands to quiet them.

"I'll make a brief statement and then take a few questions. First things first, we're continuing to work the case involving three victims who were seemingly killed in random attacks over the weekend." She listed their names and ages. "We're further looking into a fourth incident that may or may not be related. We'll have more for you on that as our investigation continues."

"Who shot at you, Lieutenant?" a reporter asked.

"That's the question of the day," Sam said. "I was working in Adams Morgan, accompanied by my partner, Detective Cruz, and my Secret Service agents. While we were standing on the sidewalk on Columbia Road in Northwest, a bullet struck one of the agents. Thankfully, his injuries aren't life-threatening, and he's expected to make a full recovery." She paused to contend with a powerful wave of emotion. "I'll let the Secret Service take care of updating you on the agent's condition. I'll just add that he's a dedicated public servant whose first thought, upon being shot, was to protect me, leaving himself open to further gunfire. I'm deeply grateful to all the Secret Service agents and staff who work so hard each day to keep my family safe."

"What do you know about the shooter?"

"Nothing yet," Sam said. "A manhunt is underway involving federal agents working in concert with the MPD. The FBI will update you as more information becomes available." Hesitantly, she added, "I'll take a few more questions."

"Is it safe for you to continue working as a police officer?"

The question hit her right in the chest. She knew it was the subject of conversations taking place without her at this very moment. "As you know, I love this job with my whole heart. I give it everything I have every day that I spend working on behalf of the District, its citizens and the millions of annual visitors. Is the job more difficult now that my husband is the president? Absolutely. But it's also more rewarding, as it gives me a chance to continue to serve the city where I grew up and have lived my entire life while he serves the rest of the country. We take every precaution and will continue to do so going forward.

"What happened today shouldn't be taken as any kind of indictment of my ability to do the job or the abilities of the agents who work tirelessly to protect me while I'm working. That said, if you've covered me for any length of time, you know how much I despise being the story. Today's events are deeply upsetting. You can't spend eight or more hours a day with people without getting to know them and coming to care about them." She gripped the sides of the podium as she fought through overwhelming emotion. "I'm extremely thankful the injured agent will be okay."

"Have you spoken to the president since the shooting?"

"I have."

"Is there any thought that the shooting could be related to the drone attack?"

"That's a question for federal authorities."

"What do you think, though?"

"I honestly don't know. No one knew where I'd be today, even me until I was there, so there was no way this could've been some sort of planned attack. That's all I have for now. We'll update you as more information becomes available."

"Will you resign, Lieutenant?" a reporter called after she'd stepped away from the podium.

She turned back to say, "No plans for that. Have a good day."

"You did great," Jeannie said when they were back inside. "It was good to put a bit of a personal spin on it."

"I hate when the personal becomes professional."

"In this case, there's no avoiding it," Malone said. "You handled it as well as you could. The headlines will say 'First Lady Refuses to Quit MPD After Nearly Being Gunned Down.'"

"Awesome," Sam said with a grimace.

"Go home and see your family, Lieutenant," the chief said. "They'll be upset."

Judging by the way her phone vibrated nonstop in her pocket, everyone she knew was upset and checking on her.

"I will, sir. Thank you for the support out there."

"You got it."

She returned to the pit, where her day-shift detectives were turning things over to the night shift.

Dominguez, petite and dark-haired, came over to Sam and stopped short of hugging her.

"I'm okay."

Carlucci, who was tall and blonde, squeezed Sam's shoulder. "That's a fucking relief. Scared the shit out of us, LT."

"Sorry about that. If you guys are good to go, I'm getting out of here. I need to touch the grass at home."

"Go on ahead," Carlucci said. "We'll call you if there're any updates to report."

"Thank you all," she said to include the others. "See you in the morning."

Before leaving her office, she picked up the file Jesse Best had left and tucked it under her arm.

As she walked with Vernon to the morgue exit a few minutes later, she said, "I'd like to see Jimmy. Can we swing by there on the way home?"

"Probably not without causing a circus."

She stopped short of the exit door and turned to face Vernon, who looked exhausted and stressed. "I'd really like to see him—and Liz. He saved my life today. Is there a way to sneak me in?"

"That might take some time to coordinate."

"Could I go home while that happens?"

"Sure, we can do that."

"I'm sorry to ask you to stay later after such a rough day."

"No worries. I want to see him, too."

"How are you doing?"

He seemed surprised she'd ask that.

"I know how horrible it feels to have my partner get shot on the job," Sam said.

"I... I feel responsible for him, you know?"

"I do know, but he wouldn't want you to blame yourself."

"Hard not to. What was I thinking, walking away from you guys?"

"You were doing your job, even if that doesn't make you feel any better in a case like this."

"No, it doesn't. I'm also in for a grilling with my brass about how this could've happened."

"It happened in an instant, as these things do, which I'll attest to, and so will Freddie."

"I appreciate the support."

"Of course."

"They may take us off your detail."

"That'll happen over my dead body."

"Jeez, don't say that to a Secret Service agent. That's our greatest nightmare."

Sam wouldn't have expected to laugh just then, but it exploded out of her chest and had Vernon chuckling, too.

"Don't make me laugh." He attempted a stern expression. "That's not one bit funny."

"We specialize in gallows humor around here." She gestured to the morgue. "Look at where we are."

He smiled wearily. "Let's get you home, and I'll see what I can do about a visit to the hospital."

"Thank you for everything, Vernon."

"You're welcome, Sam."

He spoke into the microphone attached to his earpiece. "Are we clear?" After a pause, he said, "Let's go."

When he pushed opened the door to outside, Sam was stunned to see a swarm of agents waiting for them.

As he held the back door of the SUV for her, Sam said, "What the hell?"

"Common response to an incident in the field."

After he closed the door, Sam sat back against the seat, processing the impact of being part of an "incident in the field." A sense of weariness overtook her as it became clear she was in for yet another fight to continue doing the job she loved.

CHAPTER FIFTEEN

S urrounded by his closest advisers in his private office next to the Oval, Nick watched the live coverage of the rescue mission in Juneau that'd determine whether the people inside the building had survived the mudslide.

His emotions were all over the place after hearing that Sam had had yet another near miss on the job. He'd prefer to be watching this alone, especially if the news was bad. But Terry, Derek, Christina and Harry had asked to be with him, along with White House photographer Adrian Fenty, who'd record the moment for history.

Normally, Nick welcomed having his friends around, but he wasn't himself at the moment. All he could think about was what it would feel like to hear that Sam had been killed in the line of duty.

And while he knew it was a masochistic exercise, it was one he indulged in after every close call. Imagining the worst helped him prepare for the reality, should it ever occur, or that's what he told himself, anyway. He'd relaxed somewhat since she'd had the Secret Service detail, secure in their ability to protect the most important person in his life. But today's events had exposed vulnerabilities that would keep him awake at night for reasons that had nothing to do with his insomnia.

Those vulnerabilities fueled his nightmares.

This was the downside of loving someone so much that your very life and well-being depended upon her coming home in one piece at the end of every day.

Agent McFarland had nearly given his life for her today, and Nick would be forever grateful to him and Vernon and the others who worked so hard to keep her safe.

But the close call was yet another reminder that no system was foolproof.

"Nick?"

Terry's voice stirred him out of his dark thoughts.

"They're about to breach the door to the gym."

Nick sat up straighter and took a sip from his glass of the bourbon he'd poured for himself and the others.

Christina had declined, due to her pregnancy, but she'd joked about wanting to sniff the bottle to calm her nerves as they waited to find out if close to three hundred and fifty people had survived or perished.

"I try to imagine what this must be like for the parents," Derek said. "But I can't go there."

"It's got to be unbearable," Christina said.

The mud was so thick that cell phone signals couldn't permeate it to connect with phones inside.

An entire structure had been constructed around the main doors to the gym to protect rescuers as they burrowed their way through mud that was twenty feet deep in places.

"Here we go," Harry said as the tension in the room increased by the second.

Rescuers used a battering ram to open the door and enter the building.

Five endless minutes passed before they got the word: Everyone was alive.

His friends shouted their excitement, and Harry danced a jig with Christina, who was in tears.

"Thank God," Derek said as they watched the first of the children rush through the door and into the waiting arms of euphoric parents.

Nick wept as he watched the reunions of children and parents, aware of Fenty recording his reaction and not caring that the whole world would see him in tears over the happy conclusion to a horrific incident.

ARCHIE GOT the news about Sam's agent being shot from Sergeant Walters. He'd asked Walters to keep him in the loop about what was happening at work. He was shocked and scared for his friend after hearing that someone had taken a shot at her days after the thwarted drone attack. It was a relief to know the agent was expected to survive his injuries.

"Is everything okay?" Harlowe asked him.

She'd awakened from her nap while he checked his phone and saw the text from Walters.

"Yeah."

"I can tell you're upset about something. What is it?"

"Sam was shot at. A Secret Service agent was hit."

"Oh no. Are they okay?"

"Sam is banged up. The agent was more seriously injured but is expected to survive."

"That's a relief."

"Yes, it is."

"I can't believe someone would have the nerve to shoot at the first lady. It must be dangerous for her to do her job when everyone knows who she is."

"It was always dangerous. It's a thousand times more so now, but she's determined to keep doing the work she loves while her husband is in office."

"That's admirable."

"It is, but I worry about her."

"You guys are close?"

"We're friends." He glanced at her and caught her watching him with eyes that seemed to see right through him. "Once upon a time, it was more than that, but that was brief."

"Ah," she said, smiling, "I see how it is."

"We were never more than friends with benefits. She was hooked on the guy she's now married to, although I didn't know that at the time. I just knew she wasn't available for anything more than what it was."

"Is it hard to work with someone you used to be with?"

"Nah, we keep it real. We work together a lot, so there was no point in letting it get awkward. I consider her a good friend, and I know she feels the same about me. We both respect that the other is excellent at their job."

"So you're saying you're excellent at your job?"

"It's the one thing I'm truly good at. Sam would say the same thing about herself. It's not just what we do. It's who we are. We respect that in each other."

"What exactly is it that you do?"

"My team investigates the digital side of cases—computers, phones, networks, video. That kind of thing."

"How many people work for you?"

"Eighteen."

"Wow. That's impressive."

"I guess. I could use twice as many, but thankfully, they're all great and get the job done."

"You must be missing a lot being out of work."

"Nothing they can't handle, and I'm talking to them. Don't worry about that. I haven't taken time off in years."

"Why not?"

"Nothing better to do than work."

Her brows did that adorable furrowing thing that he was becoming addicted to. "Well, that's not good. Your life is out of balance."

"Seriously out of balance."

"You should do yoga. It helps to ground and center you."

He turned up his nose.

She laughed. "Don't knock it until you try it."

"If you say so."

"I say so. I'll take you as soon as I feel better."

"I may give it a shot if it means I get to hang out with you."

The small smile gave him was a reminder of the connection they'd formed before she went missing.

His phone vibrated with a text from Erica. "Erica is on the way from the airport with your parents. Are you feeling up to seeing them?"

"I... I guess so. I should comb my hair."

"Let me help you up."

As she gripped the hands he offered, she grimaced from the pain after being still for so long. "Ugh, everything hurts."

He wanted to do harm to the person or people who'd done this to her. He wanted them to experience every ounce of pain and discomfort that she was feeling. "Take it slow, sweetheart. There's no rush."

"I hate being so feeble."

"You're not feeble. You're injured. Big difference. Your body is working hard to heal, and you'll feel like your old self again very soon."

"I don't know who my old self was."

"You'll figure that out in due time. Don't stress about it now. Just focus on resting and healing."

"I'm scared of seeing my parents. I don't know why."

"Do you want me to tell them not to come?"

"No, I don't think so. I should probably see them. But I'm scared."

"I'll be right there with you, and Erica will be, too. Nothing will harm you on my watch. I promise you that."

She curled her hands around his arm and rested her head

on his shoulder. "You bring me so much comfort. I don't understand that either. It's just true."

"That means a lot to me. I want to help you through this."

"You are helping me. More than you know. When your memory is gone, finding someone you can trust is everything."

"I'm honored to be the one you trust."

At the door to the bathroom, she shocked the shit out of him when she went up on tiptoes to kiss his cheek. As if she hadn't just rocked his existence with one second of pure sweetness, she went into the room and closed the door.

Holy shit. A simple kiss to the cheek had completely undone him. No other woman had ever gotten to him the way she did, and it'd been like that from the start. He used to scoff when people said they took one look at another person and knew they were going to change their lives. Until it happened to him at Joe and Deb's party. One look. One smile. One word. That's all it had taken.

Every minute they'd spent together had been better than the one before. Their conversation had flowed effortlessly. They'd laughed, poked fun at each other, covered serious stuff and shared childhood memories. So many details he wished he could remember now, but they'd melded into the background of their growing connection.

How he wished he'd sounded the alarm right away when she stopped responding to him. He'd always regret that he hadn't.

The door opened, and there she was, her face glowing from whatever potion she'd used on it, the scent reminding him of when he first met her. She wore clothing that fit her and had captured her hair in a clip that put her lovely face on full display.

"How do I look?"

"You're beautiful."

She eyed him skeptically. "I did what I could to hide the bruises, but you can still see them."

"You're beautiful. That's my story, and I'm sticking to it."

She rolled her eyes. "If you say so."

He extended an arm to her. "I say so."

She curled her hand around his arm and walked slowly with him back to the sofa.

"Are you hungry? Thirsty?"

"I could eat a little something, maybe."

"Cheese, crackers, grapes?"

"That sounds yummy."

"Coming right up." He took her water glass with him to refill it and got her snack ready. In an effort to recapture some of their earlier silliness, he slung a dish towel over his arm and carried the glass and plate to the living room. "Madam, your snack."

She giggled, which pleased him greatly. "Such cute waiters you have in this place."

"Which other one do you think is cute, too?"

"Just you."

"Oh, thank goodness. I didn't want to have to fight anyone."

"Would you?" she asked. "Fight for me?"

"Hell yes, I would."

"Why?"

"Damned if I know, but I would. Every time."

She gave him a small, satisfied smile and ate a cracker with a slice of cheddar cheese. "That tastes good. Thanks."

"You're welcome."

A knock on the door roused them out of their little staring contest.

"Are you ready for this?"

"As ready as I'll ever be."

Archie went to the door and opened it to Erica and Harlowe's parents.

"Archie, this is George and Barbara Prior."

He shook hands with both of them and welcomed them into his home. George was stocky, with dark hair laced with gray, and Barbara was petite, with blonde hair and blue eyes. They both looked exhausted, as if they'd endured a difficult ordeal. In light of Harlowe's trepidation about seeing them, that was a relief to him, proof of sorts that they'd suffered over what'd happened to their daughter.

"Thank you for taking care of Harlowe," Barbara said. "We appreciate your kindness."

"It's no problem. She's in the living room and is... fragile. Please proceed with caution."

"We will," George said. "Detective Lucas has explained things to us."

If he looked at Archie with a hint of distrust in his eyes, well, Archie didn't blame the guy. He didn't know Archie from Adam, and he'd have to prove himself to him.

Barbara broke down at the sight of her daughter sitting on the sofa with a blanket over her lap. "Oh, honey. I'm so happy to see you. May I sit with you?"

Harlowe nodded.

Barbara sat carefully next to Harlowe and reached for her hand.

"They told you that my recent memory is gone, right?"

"They did," Barbara said. "That's okay. We'll remember for you."

"Was there something wrong between us? Did we argue?"

Barbara glanced at George before she nodded. "We had a terrible disagreement about you moving back here again. We didn't think it was the right thing for you after everything with Evan."

"Who's Evan?"

They seemed shocked that she'd ask that.

"He was your husband, honey."

"I'm married?" she asked, sounding slightly panicked.

"You were. You two are divorced now. You said he was unkind to you."

"Was he?"

"Not that we ever witnessed," George said. "His parents were our dearest friends. It was a difficult situation, to say the least."

"I said he was unkind to me, but you didn't believe me?"

"We were always supportive of you, but that was a tough thing for us to hear about a young man we've known all his life," George said. "We thought you two were perfect for each other. And when you said you wanted to take the transfer back to DC, we thought you might be acting rashly. That's what we argued about."

"We're so sorry, honey," Barbara said. "We felt so bad about our disagreement. We'd never gone that long without talking to you. You're our pride and joy. Having you move away was very hard for us."

"Harlowe told me she came here for college and never left, but you're saying she was back in Pittsburgh for a time?"

"For two years after she and Evan got married," Barbara said. "But when that ended, she put in for a transfer to come back here. We weren't sure she was ready to be so far from home, but there was no talking her out of it."

"Why is there nothing about Harlowe online?" Archie asked.

"She deleted all her social media during the divorce and asked her company to take her off their website. She said she did it for safety reasons, but we were never clear on what her concern was."

"I was afraid he'd kill me," Harlowe said.

Her parents gasped.

"Do you remember, honey?" Archie asked.

Her lips quivered as she nodded. "I remember Evan. He hurt me. No one believed me. They said he came from such a nice family... We grew up together. He'd never hurt me."

Archie noticed Harlowe's hands were trembling.

"Ma'am, I'd like to sit with her."

"Oh." Barbara seemed startled. Thankfully, she got up and moved to another seat.

Archie sat next to Harlowe, put his arm around her and held her close to him, infuriated by the trembling. She'd remembered something, and it had upset her greatly. He feared what else she might remember and how it would hurt her even more.

Now he knew why there was no trace of her online. In a way, that was a relief, even if he hated the reason for it.

"Where's Evan now?" Archie asked. "Could he be responsible for what happened to you?"

"I... I don't know."

"She pressed charges against him," George said, "but the case was dismissed due to a lack of evidence. We don't know where he is now."

So the son of a bitch had gotten away with it.

"Needless to say, we're not friends with his parents anymore," George said.

"Was that your choice or theirs?" Archie asked.

"Mostly theirs. We felt terrible about what happened."

"You felt terrible that their son hurt your daughter?"

"We..." Barbara looked to her husband as if she wanted him to reply.

"We felt terrible about all of it."

"I think you should go," Archie said.

"What?" Barbara said. "We just got here."

"And now you have to go."

"Is that what you want, Harlowe?" George asked.

"Archie said you should go," she said. "That's what you should do."

"Who is this man you're holding close while sending us away?"

"He's the one who stepped up for me at the darkest time in my life, and apparently, he didn't care for your answers just now. I don't remember all the details, but it's interesting to me that you didn't say you felt terrible that my husband hurt me. You felt terrible about the whole situation."

"Of course we did!" George said. "That boy practically grew up in our home."

"But *I* am your child," she said softly. "Not him."

Archie looked to his colleague for help. "Erica…"

"Mr. and Mrs. Prior, let's go. I'll drop you at your hotel."

"When will we see you again?" George asked his daughter.

"When I'm ready."

Archie was so fucking proud of her.

CHAPTER SIXTEEN

As Erica ushered the Priors out of the room, Archie felt Harlowe's body go slack with relief.

"I'm sorry you had to go through that," he said.

"I remembered something. Of course it had to be something I'd rather forget."

"That must've been a terrible thing to go through."

"I'm pretty sure it was awful."

"It's over now. In the past. Whatever it was, whatever he was, he's no one to you now."

"Yes, you're right."

"I get now why you wanted to relocate."

"I had to get out of there after the divorce. I remember feeling smothered and outraged that my own parents weren't fully supporting me. I came back to the place where I was happy before I made the mistake of marrying my childhood friend." She glanced at him. "I wish I didn't remember him." She shuddered. "He fooled me. He fooled everyone. There was a whole other side to him that no one saw until it was too late for me."

"Did he hit you?"

She nodded. "Always in places where no one would see the

evidence." Looking up at him with big eyes, she said, "I liked it better when I couldn't remember that."

"Is there any chance he followed you here and could've done this to you?"

Her shocked expression made him sorry for not asking the question in a gentler way. "I... I don't think so. He was told to stay away from me when the charges were dropped."

"That doesn't always work to stop someone with an agenda. Would he know to look for you here?"

She hesitated before nodding. "I never wanted to move back to Pittsburgh. I fell in love with DC during college and wanted to live here forever, but he had a better job than mine and wouldn't consider relocating, so I did. But he'd probably guess that I'd come back here as soon as I could."

"Would you mind if Erica looked into his whereabouts during the time you were missing and asked your parents if they told him where you were?"

"N-no. I don't mind. But they wouldn't have done that. Would they?"

Those last two words were full of hurt and bewilderment. His almost primal need to protect her from any more hurt confirmed that he'd probably fallen in love with her the minute he saw her and would do anything he could to keep her safe. "I really hope not."

"FLOTUS is on the way home, sir," Nick's lead agent, John Brantley Jr., said as he accompanied Nick for the walk "home" to the residence.

"Thanks, Brant. Let's meet her in the foyer. What're you hearing from the field?"

"Nothing other than that they're widening the net in their search for the drone that fired the shot."

"And how is Agent McFarland?"

"Out of surgery and in recovery. His wife is with him, and his parents are on the way."

"That's a relief. My wife is quite fond of him and Vernon."

"Yes, sir. They're great agents and good people. We're all happy to hear the news from the hospital."

"Today was a tough day for you guys, but I hope you know how thankful I am... How incredibly grateful..." Nick's voice failed him as he was overcome by what could've happened.

"We know, sir. Agent McFarland did everything right when it mattered."

"He sure did, but the fact that it happened in the first place will give me nightmares."

"Us, too, sir."

Hearing that his precious wife was involved in a Secret Service worst-case scenario did nothing to settle the disquiet raging within him.

"I'm not sure what to do, Brant. If I ask her to give up the thing that makes her who she is, she'll never forgive me. But if I don't, how will I live with myself if something happens to her?"

"It's a dilemma, to be certain, sir."

"Do you know what the meeting is about tomorrow?"

"I do, but I've been asked to refrain from discussing it until then."

"I'm sure there'll be additional agenda items after today."

"Yes, sir."

Nick had felt as if he had a thousand-pound weight on his shoulders since the incident on Monday. It had gotten much heavier after today's events.

When they reached the lobby area, Chief Usher Gideon Lawson was consulting with George, one of the other ushers.

"Good evening, Mr. President."

Nick nodded to them. "Evening, Gideon and George."

"We were told that Mrs. Cappuano is on her way home."

"That's why I'm here, too."

"Yes, sir. We're relieved to hear she's uninjured and that Agent McFarland is expected to make a full recovery."

"Me, too." *The understatement of my lifetime.*

Sam's SUV came rolling up the driveway five minutes later. The others moved aside so Nick was the one waiting for her when she came through the door and stepped straight into his embrace.

"Hey," she said. "Fancy meeting you here."

"Thanks for coming home."

"I do what I can for you."

"Welcome home, Mrs. Cappuano," Gideon said.

"Thank you," she said, her gaze including him, George and Brant.

Nick put his arm around her shoulders and headed for the red-carpeted stairs to the residence. "Rarely have I ever been this happy to see you."

"I can think of a few times when you were happier."

"I can't. I'm sorry this happened."

"As am I, but deeply, *deeply* thankful that Jimmy will be okay. His first baby is due in June... That was all I could think about until I heard..." She took a second to collect herself. "That he'd be okay."

"Thank God for that."

"What do the kids know?"

"Scotty texted me that he heard the news, but he said the twins don't know, and I think we should keep it that way."

"Agreed. They don't need to know, especially when Aubrey is already having a tough day."

"Eli also texted both of us to say holy shit and thank goodness you're okay. Not sure if you've seen that yet."

"I'll reply to him and a million other people later."

Though they could hear the sound of voices coming from the third-floor conservatory, Nick stopped her from heading in that direction and waylaid her into the family kitchen. "I need one minute for this." He wrapped his arms around her and held on tight. "Just this."

Sam relaxed into his warm embrace as the adrenaline she'd brought home with her seemed to leave her system in one big whoosh that left her legs feeling weak.

"Another close call," he said. "Too many of those."

"I'm sorry."

"You don't have to be sorry. It's not your fault. It's mine."

"How so?"

"I sent our already high profile into the stratosphere, and now everyone is gunning for both of us."

"Not everyone. Just today, I heard from multiple people who are very pleased to have us in the White House and think you're doing a great job. I think one of them wants to date you if the opportunity presents itself."

He scowled. "I'm off the market, and my wife has a very sharp, very rusty steak knife that she's not afraid to use."

"That's right, and don't forget it."

"I wish we could take our kids and run away somewhere that no one could find us, where we could live happily ever after without anyone wanting to kill us or run us out of town or expect us to fix everything that's wrong with the world."

"Let's go to Bora Bora tonight after the kids are in bed. We need the getaway, even if it's imaginary."

"Yes, please."

"My dad used to tell us that no matter what was bringing us down at any given moment, it wouldn't always be that way. 'This too shall pass,' he'd say. Let's remember that on days like today, okay?"

"I wish he was here to tell us that himself."

"I wish that every single day."

"So do I. I miss him like crazy. He would've loved all this, except for the drones with guns and the randos shooting at his daughter, of course."

"Of course," she said with a laugh. "Let's go check on our kids. Scotty will be anxious to see me."

Nick gave her one more tight squeeze. "More of this later, yes?"

"Absolutely."

Holding hands, they went upstairs to the conservatory, where Sam's mom, Brenda, as well as Shelby, Noah and baby Maisie were hanging out with the kids.

When he saw them coming, Scotty got up and came to hug Sam. "Thanks for not getting shot."

She clung to him, resting her face on the top of his silky head. "I do what I can for the people."

"Please don't do *that* to me again."

"I'll try not to."

She kept expecting him to release her, but he didn't, so she held on until he let go.

As he pulled back from her, she saw tears in his eyes that broke her heart. "I'm okay, buddy. I promise."

"And Jimmy is, too?"

"He will be."

"That's good."

Sam's mom came over to give her a hug. "Nice to see you."

"Nice to be seen."

"You're all right?"

"I'm fine as long as Jimmy is."

"Too close for comfort."

"Indeed."

The twins finished the show they'd been watching and came running over to see Sam and Nick, chirping about the show, their day, the snack they'd had and how funny Grandma Brenda was—all in the space of ten seconds. Sam knelt to embrace them both, breathing in the scents of shampoo and sugar that came with them. She was relieved to see Aubrey in good spirits.

Rebecca had advised they do everything in their power to

reassure Aubrey that the police were working on figuring out what happened at the Easter Egg Roll and that she should try not to worry because their family was very well protected. Sam would make a point of having a one-on-one conversation with the little girl before bedtime, and Nick had agreed to do the same. Eli planned to FaceTime with them after dinner.

Sam got about two seconds of closeness with the twins before they were squirming to bust loose. As she stood, her phone rang with a call from Freddie.

"Hey. What's up?"

"Two things. First, Walters got something on the video review from Friday night. He's got an obvious struggle between two people and a white sedan idling nearby that took off after one person pushed the other in and jumped in after. It was too dark to get any other identifying features of the car or people, but it's something."

"Sure is."

"On that same note, he's put together a list of busier locations around the city with dark areas. We've asked Patrol to give those spots some added attention."

"Great work by Walters. I'll make sure Archie hears about it."

"I thought so, too."

"What's the second thing?"

"How are you, and what're you hearing about Jimmy?"

"I'm fine, and Jimmy is out of surgery and in recovery. Liz is with him, and his parents are on the way."

"Very glad to hear that."

"I'm hoping to get over there to see him later on."

"Let me know how he is."

"I will."

"Hang on. Gonzo just came in."

Sam heard them talking in the background before Freddie came back to tell her, "We've got another victim."

. . .

"I HAVE to go back to work," Sam said to Nick and Scotty, who'd stayed close to her while the twins went back to playing.

Nick's expression was pained. "I've been asked to request you stay home until we have more information about what happened today."

"That's not possible. My team needs me, and I have to be there, especially after just having four days off."

He took her hand and drew her away from the others. "Sam, please. They were adamant that we not take any chances with you or the agents until we know more about who shot at you."

"And you agreed to that?"

"I didn't disagree. The thought of someone shooting at you while you're at work is the stuff of nightmares for me, especially since it's probably..."

"What? Your fault? As if plenty of people don't have reason to shoot at me that have nothing to do with you."

"Having this happen, one day after the drones, is too close for comfort."

"So you expect me to stay in this house and not go to work or to see the agent who nearly gave his life to protect me... *indefinitely*?"

"They've asked for some time to investigate."

"I'm sorry, but I'm not staying home. If the agents don't wish to protect me in light of today's events, that's their call, but I'm going with them or without them."

"Samantha..."

Sam raised a hand to stop him. "I love you more than anything, and you know that. I've supported you every step of the way during this unprecedented time. I said from the get-go that I'd never give up my job, and I meant it. That's my line in the sand, Nick." She went up on tiptoes to kiss his cheek. "Please make sure to spend some time with Aubrey. I'll try to be back as soon as I can."

They engaged in a visual standoff that set her already

frayed nerves further on edge. Trouble between them was so rare that she was never properly equipped to handle it, even after more than two years of marriage.

She turned to the kids. "I have to go back to work for a little while. Hopefully, I'll be home to say good night." The three of them hugged her. "Love you guys."

"Love you, too," Scotty said with unusual trepidation. "Be careful out there."

"I will. I promise."

As she headed for the stairs, she glanced at Nick, who stood with his hands on his hips, glaring at her. That he didn't tell her he loved her or to be careful with his wife left her feeling hollow inside as she continued to the first floor, calling Vernon as she went.

"I've got to go back to work."

"They've asked us to hold you here for the time being."

"I'm aware, and I'm still going, with you or without you. If you don't want to take the risk, I completely understand."

"I'm not letting you go out there by yourself."

"Then I need you ready to roll right now. We've got another murder."

"I'll meet you in the foyer."

"I'm already there."

"On the way."

"Do you need your coat, ma'am?" George asked.

"Yes, please."

He retrieved it from the closet and held it for her as she put it on.

"Thank you, George."

"Always a pleasure, ma'am."

"Could I ask you something?"

"Of course."

"If I walked out that door by myself, would you let me go?"

"Yes, ma'am, but you wouldn't get past the gate before the Secret Service stopped you."

Sam contemplated the reality that she was, in fact, a prisoner in her own home. A prisoner to safety, but a prisoner nonetheless.

Vernon arrived a minute later with Debra Nixon, the lead agent on Scotty's detail.

"Are you with us?" Sam asked her.

"I am. Scotty's in for the night, and I've handed off to his evening detail."

"Let's go."

"We're required to tell you that we advise against you leaving at this time," Vernon said.

"I hear you, and I understand the concern, but I have a job to do just like you do, and I need to go support my team. I appreciate the risk you take—always—to accompany me, especially after what's already been an upsetting few days for all of us. I'm sorry I'm putting you in a bad spot with your brass, but you can blame it all on me."

"We will, don't worry," Vernon said with a small grin as he ushered her out the door and into a waiting SUV.

As they pulled away from the White House, Sam leaned forward. "I'm sorry to ask this of you guys, especially with one of your own in the hospital. But whatever this is, I need to be out there figuring it out, not stuck in the gilded cage, walled off from real life. And yes, my position feels somewhat unreasonable to me, too, but if I give in to the fear, that'll be the end of the line for me on the job. I hope you understand."

"I do," Vernon said. "I get it."

"Believe it or not, I do, too," Debra said. "It's not easy being a woman in our line of work, and every concession we make is one step backward for all of us."

"Yes, that's it. Exactly. I understand the risk I'm taking. Hell, it keeps me awake at night worrying about how my raised profile is endangering my team as well as my detail. But I refuse to be governed by fear. I can't live that way. I can be much more useful out working on this case than sitting at home on the sidelines."

"Do you think it's all related?" Vernon asked. "The drones, the shooting, the murders?"

"I haven't thought that yet, but it bears looking into, although what would four seemingly random murders and a kidnapping/assault have to do with what happened at the Egg Roll?"

"Maybe it's about targeting you to get to the president?" Vernon asked.

"What do you mean?"

"It's a stretch. I'll admit that, but what if someone is killing these people hoping to bring you back to work? While your days vary, your actual routine after a murder doesn't. You follow a similar set of steps on each case, which makes you somewhat predictable that way."

"But what does that have to do with Nick?" Sam asked.

"The whole world knows you're his weak spot, Sam. If something were to happen to you or the children, he would resign."

"And that's what they want?"

"Like I said, it's a stretch, but it's a theory."

"Or," Debra said, "someone wants you out of the way at the MPD for whatever reason. Maybe this has nothing to do with him and everything to do with you."

Sam thought about that for a few minutes, turned it over from every angle and decided it wasn't as much of a stretch as Vernon made it out to be. And he was right—if something happened to her or one of their kids, Nick would resign.

He wouldn't be able to go forward in the job after that. People would know that because of the way he revered his family. Right before Nelson died, he'd announced that he wouldn't seek the nomination because he didn't want to be away from his young family for weeks on end to campaign.

He'd identified his weak spot before he ever assumed the

presidency, and now... Was someone gunning for her as a way of running him out of office? Or was Debra right? Were they trying to drive her and the sideshow that came with her these days out of the department?

Both scenarios sounded too preposterous to be real, but now that Vernon and Debra had introduced the possibilities, they became more plausible by the second. Vernon was right. She did follow a similar routine every time she picked up a new case. Process the scene, visit the family, track down friends, coworkers and others who knew the victim, rinse and repeat.

If X person was killed, it wouldn't be hard to determine where she was apt to turn up next and to lie in wait for her at that location.

A lump formed in her throat at realizing how easy it would be to predict her movements and those of her team. Not to mention she never should've left her family when they were upset about her being shot at, especially with Aubrey showing signs of distress at school.

"Vernon."

"Yes, Sam?"

"Take me home."

"What?"

"Please take me home."

He glanced at her in the mirror.

She met his gaze and gave a small nod.

At the next traffic light, he made a U-turn.

CHAPTER SEVENTEEN

S am texted Freddie and Gonzo. *Vernon thinks it's possible this is about luring me so someone can take me out. That, in turn, would drive Nick out of office. Or the goal is to drive me out of the MPD. I can't endanger my detail and all of you by making us an easy target. I'm sitting this one out. Gonzo, you're in charge for the time being. I'm available to consult and work the case from home. I'm sorry about this.*

Freddie wrote back first. *Holy shit, Sam. You really think either of those things is possible?*

Vernon made a good point. He said my movements are predictable any time we get a new case. It's more than possible and could be tied to the thwarted drone attack, too. Who knows at this point? But I'm not risking it—or any of the people who work with me, or the ones assigned to keeping me safe.

She texted the same information to Jeannie, the chief and Malone.

What is this world coming to? the chief responded. *Work from home, and do what you can until we know more.*

Her phone rang with a call from Archie. "Hey, how's Harlowe?"

"I was talking to Gonzo when he got your text. Do you really think this could be someone trying to get at you?"

"I don't know that it isn't, and until I do, I'm taking myself out of the game."

"So Harlowe was attacked, raped, assaulted... because someone was trying to get to *you*?"

Sam's stomach ached fiercely at the accusatory tone in his voice. She didn't blame him for being outraged. "I... I don't know, Archie. It was mentioned to me as a possibility. We still don't know if her case is related to the others."

"You were shot at while investigating *hers*."

"Yes, but..."

"Christ, Sam. If someone planned this, they know we're friends... They followed me, saw me with her... They might know she's here now."

Her mouth had gone totally dry. "I don't know, Archie. If it's true... I..."

How in the world would she ever spend another day as a member of the Metropolitan Police Department if it was true?

"I've got to go."

The line went dead before she could respond. Although what, exactly, could she say?

Back at the White House, the SUV was stopped at the gate as the agents insisted on checking the vehicle, which had never happened before.

When they saw only her and the two agents, they waved them through.

At the entrance, Vernon opened the back door for her.

Sam got out, went inside, bypassed George and went up the stairs, not stopping until she was inside their suite with the door closed. She slid down the door and into a sobbing mess on the floor, head in her hands as the horror of it fully registered with her.

People had been attacked, assaulted, *shot* because of her?

The incident at the Easter Egg Roll might've been about taking *her* out, not Nick?

Every cell in her body was rocked by this realization.

And then he was there, wrapping his arms around her, bringing the scent of home, and the warmth of his love infusing the parts of her that'd gone ice-cold.

"What happened?" he asked.

She tried to form the words, but none came.

He held her until she was somewhat calmer, until she found the ability to speak again, to say something that, once conveyed to him, could never be unsaid.

She wiped the tears from her face. "Did you talk to Aubrey?"

"I did. We had a nice chat, and I think she feels better than she did."

"I should go in there and see her."

"They were tired, so they wanted to go to sleep. It can keep until the morning. Talk to me, Samantha."

She took a deep, shuddering breath, wishing more than anything that she didn't have to tell him what'd upset her.

"It's possible... that all of this—the drones, the murders, the shooting of Jimmy, the kidnapping and assault of Archie's friend..."

"What about it?"

"Vernon suggested it might be someone coming for me because they know if something happens to me, you'd never stay in office. In another possible scenario, someone is trying to drive me out of the MPD."

"*What?*" he asked on a long exhale.

"Th-think about it. Vernon said, and it's true, my movements in new cases are predictable. I do the same things every time. If someone wanted to find me, it wouldn't take much effort to know where I'd turn up. Kill an innocent person and then watch me go through the steps. They knew I'd be on the lawn with the kids at the egg roll. What if they weren't after you but were gunning for *me*?"

"I... I can't... My God, Sam."

"I came home because I can't risk someone else I care about being hurt, or worse, because of me."

"This is unbelievable."

"But it's true... If someone killed me, that would drive you right out of public life, or if they kill someone on my detail or a member of my team, they'll run me out of the MPD. I'm not sure which of those things these sick fucks want. Maybe they want both of them."

"What're we going to do?"

"We're going to figure who's behind this, and we're going to take them down."

SAM WAS UP ALL NIGHT, making lists of people to investigate, beginning with former Sergeant Ramsey, who had a stick up his ass a mile long for her. He blamed her for his son being killed in a shootout when Shane Ramsey was holding a naked woman hostage. The disgraced former sergeant blamed her for everything that'd gone wrong in his life and career without taking any responsibility for his own actions. She wouldn't put it past him to be participating in something like this.

First on her to-do list for the morning was getting a warrant to dump his phone for the months leading up to his most recent arrest, for disrupting the funeral of U.S. Attorney Tom Forrester. He'd hated Forrester for declining to prosecute her after an altercation between them had left Ramsey at the bottom of a flight of stairs with a concussion and broken arm. He'd started it by telling her she'd gotten what she deserved from Stahl and his razor wire.

Freddie had reported in that their new victim was a twenty-four-year-old male graduate student at American University. He'd been walking home from an all-night gym when he was attacked from behind and killed with one strike to the back of his head.

As she processed that new information, she combed through the lists of people she'd helped to put away in recent years, everyone from former Lieutenant Stahl to Marquis Johnson, who'd lost his son in a shootout after Sam had been embedded with his crime organization for months.

And then she made a list of the people who had it out for Nick:

1. Former Secretary of State Martin Ruskin, fired after a scandal involving the Iranians during Nick's first week in office.
2. Former Attorney General Reginald Cox, fired for gambling on the job and blocking an investigation that would've revealed his vice.
3. Former Chairman of the Joint Chiefs of Staff, General Michael Wilson, fired for conspiring to overthrow the Cappuano administration. Charged with multiple felonies and dishonorably discharged from the military.
4. Former Vice Chairman of the Joint Chiefs of Staff, Admiral Nathan Goldstein, conspiring to overthrow the Cappuano administration and arranging for the (failed) murder of Navy Lieutenant Commander Juan Rodriguez. Charged with multiple felonies and dishonorably discharged from the military.

Any combination of the people on Nick's list and hers could've put something like this together, and she was determined to find out who was killing innocent people in an attempt to get at her—and Nick by extension. If that was even the motive. She still didn't know for sure, but the more she turned it around in her mind, the more plausible it became.

Next, she composed a text message to FBI Special Agent-in-

Charge Avery Hill, alerting him to her investigation and asking for whatever help the Bureau could provide. She'd send that message first thing in the morning, which was now a mere three hours away. He'd returned to limited duty after recently sustaining a gunshot wound to the shoulder in the Harlan Peckham case.

Nick's hands landed on her shoulders, making her startle. "You need to get some rest, babe."

"I couldn't possibly sleep right now."

"Would you try? For me?"

She was wound so tightly, she felt like she might implode at any second, but as he needed sleep even more than she did, she gave a quick nod and let him help her up.

Sam went through the motions of brushing her teeth and changing her clothes. When she got in bed, he reached for her, indicating he wanted her to curl up to him, to fall asleep with his arms around her, but she didn't want even him to touch her, so she stayed where she was.

He turned on his side to face her. "Samantha... Sweetheart, it's not your fault."

"It's not yours either."

"Neither of us has done a single thing other than our jobs. If someone is coming for you or us, that's on them, not us."

"That's damned hard to swallow when a young Secret Service agent is in the hospital tonight recovering from wounds that very easily could've been fatal. Weeks before his first child is due, no less."

"Not your fault. Not mine."

"Tell it to four innocent families mourning loved ones murdered for no good reason. Tell it to Archie's girlfriend, Harlowe, who's forever changed by what was done to her, even if she doesn't remember it yet."

"It's a terrible thing no matter how we look at it. But we don't even know yet if it's related or if it has anything to do with you or us."

"Of course it does. The second Vernon mentioned the possibility, it all snapped into focus for me."

"And while I can see the logic in it, until there's some sort of proof, that's all it is—a possibility."

"I feel it in my gut, Nick. It's related. My gut is hardly ever wrong."

"I hate to remind you of things you'd rather forget, but it was recently wrong about that woman's daughters being involved in her murder."

She huffed out a laugh. "Wow, that's a low blow."

"I don't mean it to be, but it's a reminder that sometimes the evidence leads in another direction, and before you flog yourself to within an inch of your own life, let's wait to see what the evidence shows."

"You're not entirely wrong."

"Just kinda wrong?"

"Something like that." After a long pause, she said, "Thank you for talking me down a little bit."

"I want you to know that I understand, better than anyone else ever could, how awful it feels to be responsible for something happening to someone you care about—or even people you've never met. I get it."

"You mean Juan."

"Among others. I've lost service members, too."

"It's easy to say it's not our fault, but these things strike awfully close to home."

"They do, for sure."

"It's the worst feeling."

"I know. Close your eyes and try to put it aside for a few hours. You can hit it hard in the morning with a fresh outlook."

"They killed a graduate student tonight. He was on the way home from a twenty-four-hour gym." Tears slid down her cheeks as she imagined his poor parents getting that phone call, after they'd done everything right, getting their son through college and into graduate school, thinking they were home free. That the worst of the risk was behind them and not waiting to strike him down for no good reason.

No matter what it took, she'd find the person or people who did this, and she'd ensure they spent the rest of their lives in prison. Even if it was the last thing she ever did.

SAM'S EYES opened early the next morning with a fresh thought about her working theory: If the goal was to lure her out into the open, why had people been murdered on a weekend when the whole world knew she and Nick would be at Camp David?

Maybe none of it had anything to do with her except for the shooting on the street yesterday.

If that was true, she was back to square one.

But a nagging feeling in the gut she could usually count on to steer her straight was pushing her to pursue the idea. If only her gut hadn't recently had a big failure, when she'd gone all in on pursuing a case against Elaine Myerson's teenage daughters, only to have them turn out to be innocent.

She'd been so sure they had done it.

And she'd been dead-ass wrong.

Sam reached for her phone on the charger and texted Vernon to ask about Jimmy.

He had a good night. I stopped by on the way in this morning, and I gave him your regards as well. He was glad to hear you were uninjured.

Thanks for passing that on to him. I'm glad to hear he's doing well. When will they release him?

Tomorrow, if he continues to make good progress.

Thanks for the update. I guess I'll see you in the meeting today.

I'll be there.

Nick came out of their bathroom, dressed for another day of world domination in a navy blue suit with subtle pinstripes. Sexiest man on this planet or any other.

"What?" he asked when he caught her staring at him.

"Just admiring the view."

"Stop." She loved how her commentary about his hotness mortified him. It was one of her many favorite things about him, and it infused a touch of normality into a morning that felt anything but.

"I'll never stop thinking my husband is the hottest man in the whole universe."

"You're in better spirits this morning."

"Not really, but the sight of you in a suit always gets my motor running."

Smiling, he sat next to her on the bed and took her hand. "I've got my security briefing in thirty minutes. I'll get Scotty moving. He's going in an hour early for algebra tutoring."

"He must be thrilled about that."

"He refused to discuss it last night. Can you handle the twins?"

"Yep."

"And you remember the Secret Service meeting at nine?"

"I'll be there. And speaking of the Secret Service, Vernon says Jimmy had a good night and could be released as soon as tomorrow."

"That's very good news."

"Yeah, it is." Sam slid her fingers over the silk of his royal blue tie. "At this meeting today, I want you to remember the deal we made when we started the White House phase of our journey."

"I remember."

"And you'll fight for me?"

"Always. I'm on Team Samantha."

"Even if you'd rather keep me under lock and key here where I'd be safe and protected?"

"Even if." He leaned in to kiss her. "As I've said before, I know exactly who I married and what she needs to be happy. I'll do everything in my power to make sure she gets that."

"She thinks you're very sexy when you're flexing your power muscles."

His scowl indicated what he thought of that comment.

Sam laughed. "What? It's true."

"Be prepared for significant pushback. There's always a big correction after an incident like what happened yesterday, especially on top of Monday's events."

"Still no word on where the drones came from?"

"Not that I've heard. I'm hoping for more info in the briefing this morning."

"I'm bringing Avery and his team in on my theory this morning."

"That's not a bad idea, even if it goes against everything you believe in to ask for outside help."

"There's no time for ego or pride in a situation like this."

"Aw, look at you. All evolved and stuff."

"Haha, underneath it all, I'm still the same feral beast I've always been when it comes to calling in the Feds."

"I love my little feral beast more than anything." He kissed her again and got up. "I'll see you in a couple of hours."

"Will you sit next to me at the meeting?"

"Of course I will. When do I ever pass up a chance to hold hands with my best girl?"

Sam smiled. "Well played, Mr. President."

"Love you."

"Love you, too."

CHAPTER EIGHTEEN

After Nick left, Sam sent the text to Avery and then sat back against the pillows, feeling unsettled at the thought of working from home while the rest of her team worked on the new homicide. Nothing like being the absent commander. With the distractions and interruptions to her work piling up, was it time for her to step aside to let someone else lead the Homicide division?

The very thought of it broke her heart into a million pieces. If she had her way, she'd spend at least twenty more years in this role before she contemplated retirement. But events outside her control might conspire to move up the timeline. Perhaps that was the goal of this entire thing.

With those thoughts in mind, she called Captain Malone.

"Morning," he said. "How's it going?"

"Just great. We added to the victim count overnight."

"I was just reading the report. It's tragic."

"I think all these things might be related."

"All what things?"

"The four murders, the drones, the abduction of Archie's friend, the shooting yesterday."

"What's the common thread?"

"Me."

"I don't get it."

"What if someone is killing people because they know I'll do exactly what I do every time? What if that person is using me to get at Nick with the thought being, if something happens to me, he'd resign? Or if they shoot and nearly kill an agent on my detail, it'll run me out of the MPD? I'm not sure which one of us they're after. Perhaps both."

"That's insane. There're a million other ways to run Nick out of office, if that's the goal."

"This would be the quickest. Think about all the publicity we get for our mushy marriage, from *Saturday Night Live* to political cartoons to nonstop coverage in the celebrity news of everything we do and say. The whole world knows I'm his Achilles' heel and that it wouldn't take much to get to him through me."

"It's preposterous, Sam."

"Murder often is. Think about it, Cap. From the day he took the oath, what's been the undercurrent that surrounds him? He's too young, too inexperienced, unelected, illegitimate. It goes on and on. Even the Joint Chiefs of Staff betrayed him. Why in the world is it preposterous to think someone would try to get at me to push him over the edge and out of office?"

"When you put it like that, it seems less preposterous than it was at the outset."

"Someone else whose opinion I trust put a different spin on it. What if it's someone who wants me off the job, and it has nothing at all to do with Nick?"

"You're saying someone wants that badly enough to kill four people, kidnap and assault another, send drones to the White House and shoot a Secret Service agent?"

"If there's one thing we know after all these years on the job, it's that anything is possible."

"I don't know, Sam. It still feels like a reach to me, especially the part about someone wanting to run you out of here."

"I've made a list of all the people who'd potentially be part of something like this—his people and mine. I want a dump of Ramsey's phone from the weeks leading up to his most recent arrest. He'd be an excellent consultant for filling in the blanks of how I work and what we do whenever we have a new case to investigate."

"I'll request a warrant."

"So you think this theory has merit?"

"I'm reserving judgment until you get me some proof. Until then, let's keep working the cases and putting the pieces together."

"I'll do what I can from here and consult with the others on next steps."

"Sounds good."

"Cap."

"Yeah?"

"You promised you'd tell me if I became too much of a distraction on the job."

"Yes, I did."

"Are we there yet?"

"Not as far as I'm concerned. I'd still rather have you and everything that comes with you in that role than anyone else."

"Is my presence putting people in danger? That shot Jimmy took was meant for me. It could've killed him or Freddie, who was standing right next to us."

"You were shot at before you were the first lady, and you'll be shot at again due to the nature of your job. It goes with the territory."

"Are we attempting to defend the indefensible here, Cap?"

"I'm not. Are you?"

"Sometimes I feel like I am. Jimmy getting shot on a sidewalk in Adams Morgan has me rattled. I'm not going to lie."

"This could have nothing at all to do with you or Nick or your official roles and everything to do with someone trying to get attention for God knows what. It could be someone wanting to shoot at cops for the sport of it and could have nothing do with the incident on Monday."

"It's weird that the federal government's top law enforcement officials are no closer to knowing who sent those drones than they were on Monday, isn't it?"

"Someone went to a great deal of trouble to make them untraceable."

"Don't people usually want credit for something like this? They want everyone to know they're the ones who did it."

"Not when the full weight of the federal government is poised to rain hell down upon them."

"Still... The scumbags who'd pull off something like this— or nearly pull it off—always want credit for it. Why isn't anyone saying anything? Could it be because they don't intend to stop with that? I heard the Secret Service thinks yesterday's shot came from another drone. How can it not be related to the drones that were targeting the White House?"

"Anything is possible, and I can tell your brain is exploding with all these theories. Now you have to prove them. Let's see what the dump of Ramsey's phone shows and go from there."

"Thanks for the support, Cap."

"You got it. Stay calm. We'll figure this out the way we always do—one step at a time. I'll reach out when I get the warrant."

"Sounds good."

She ended that call feeling moderately better than she had when she first woke up. Of course he was right. A theory was only that until it could be proven.

Her phone rang with a call from Avery. "Hey."

"Hey, yourself, and what the actual fuck?" Imagine those words said in the sweetest of Southern accents.

"I know. I need you, Agent Hill."

"I'm here."

"You're feeling okay? Back to full speed?"

"Not quite, but I've got you covered on this. The full

resources of the FBI are engaged in the investigation into the drones as well as yesterday's shooting, which we suspect may have also come from a drone."

"I heard that."

"We need to keep that info close to the vest until we know more."

"What do you think of my theory?"

"Normally, I'd think it was too crazy to be considered, but I'll add it to the briefing I'm due to make in an hour. Everything is on the table in a case like this, even the crazy stuff."

"Thank you and the rest of your team for what you're doing. We appreciate it."

"I'll keep you in the loop as much as I can."

"I appreciate that."

After they ended the call, she texted Gonzo to ask if they could do a phone meeting when everyone was ready.

Will call you in twenty minutes, he replied.

Sam sent a thumbs-up and used that time to shower and get dressed. In the shower, she noted huge bruises on her left hip and shoulder, which had taken the full brunt of Jimmy tackling her to the sidewalk the day before. At least she hadn't fallen on her right side, where the impact might've been enough to refracture her healing hip. The bruises were a small price to pay for not getting shot.

She'd need to get the twins up right after the meeting with her team, so she kept an eye on the clock while she waited for the call.

When the phone rang, she put it on speaker so she could multitask. In deference to the Secret Service meeting at nine, she applied some makeup while she listened to the update on the latest victim.

"Joshua Saulnier, age twenty-four, originally from San Diego. Attended undergraduate at George Mason and was pursuing a master's in public policy at American University. By all accounts, he was a hardworking young man with big dreams to work in public service after graduation. His fiancée, Mandy, had recently moved to the District to live with him while he finished school. They were due to be married in October. She was so distraught after we notified her that we had her transported to GW. One of their friends went with her."

"What about the parents?" Sam asked.

"We were able to track them down and notify them. They're on the way here now, along with Mandy's parents. Like the other victims, Joshua died of blunt force trauma from a single blow to the back of the head. Again, the assault took place in a poorly lit stretch of sidewalk, on Nebraska Avenue. Sergeant Walters is pulling film from the area, but we're not optimistic that we'll find anything that helps."

"Who went to notify the girlfriend?" Sam asked.

"Carlucci and Dominguez."

"Are they on this call?"

"We are, LT," Carlucci said.

"Did you notice anything odd or concerning in the area of the apartment when you were there?"

"Nothing that stood out."

"No lurkers or loiterers nearby?"

"Not that we saw."

"What're you thinking, LT?" Detective Charles asked.

"It's a stretch, and just a theory at this point," Sam said, before she laid out her theory—or Vernon's theory—that all the recent events could be related to some sort of campaign targeting Nick or her—or both of them.

Her commentary was met with dead silence.

"Look, I know it's a stretch, but like I said, it's a theory. Malone is pulling a warrant for Ramsey's phone to see what he was up to prior to his most recent arrest. I've got a list of others I want to look into who'd have something to gain by doing something like this."

"The blows to the back of the head... That's how Elaine

Myerson was killed," Charles said. "Maybe Ramsey got the idea for a quick easy murder technique from that case."

"That's a good thought," Sam said.

"What would he have to gain by killing innocent people?" Freddie asked.

"Sometimes it's a means to an end. We've certainly seen that before."

"I don't know, Sam," Gonzo said. "It feels a bit farfetched to me."

"I understand why, and you know how much I hate to ever be part of the story in one of our cases, but this feels personal to me. I'll be working that angle from my end."

"We'll keep you informed of any developments," Gonzo said. "Do you know how long you're going to be stuck at home?"

"I haven't heard yet, but we have a meeting with the Secret Service at nine. I hope to know more after that."

"Let us know," Freddie said.

"I will."

Gonzo handed out assignments to each of them, which included investigating Saulnier's social media and finances for any red flags and to check on the fiancée to see if she might be able to provide more information than they'd gotten from her the night before.

Sam itched to be in the middle of that but would do what she could from home. After ending the call, she stood and stretched and then went to wake up the twins to get them dressed, fed and off to school. Normally, this was one of her favorite parts of the day, as the twins were always adorable and entertaining. Today, she struggled to stay focused on them with her brain spinning in a thousand other directions.

"Are you sad, Sam?" Aubrey asked as she ate the French toast sticks Sam had made for them.

Surprised by the question, Sam forced a smile. "No, I'm fine. Why do you ask?"

"You're not teasing us like you usually do."

Was there anyone more observant than a six-year-old? Not that she'd ever seen. "I'm sorry, sweetie. I'm just thinking about what I've got to do today when I should be completely focused on you guys."

"That's okay. We know you're super busy."

Sam brought her mug of coffee with her to sit with them at the table. "I'm never, ever, ever too busy for you guys. I hope you know that."

"We do," Alden said. "You and Nick have the biggest jobs ever."

"That might be true, but you guys and Scotty and Eli are the most important people in our lives."

"We know that," Alden said.

"I heard you had a rough day yesterday," Sam said to Aubrey. "Are you feeling a little better this morning?"

She shrugged. "I guess. I'm still scared of something bad happening."

"I used to worry about that, too. You remember me telling you that my dad was a police officer, too, right?"

"Grandpa Skip?" Aubrey said.

"Yes, that's him." Sam was sad that the twins hadn't gotten the chance to know him—and vice versa. He'd have been delighted with them. "When I was a little girl, I used to worry about him getting hurt at work, but you know what he told me?"

"What?" she asked.

"That something like that was completely out of my control, and the only thing I'd accomplish by worrying about something that was most likely not going to happen was to make myself sick. That helped me. I hope it helps you, too."

"It does."

"Do you understand what it means to not have any control over something?"

"I think so. It means I can't do anything about it."

"Exactly, which means you shouldn't worry about it for that very reason. You guys know all too well that bad things can happen. But the bad things are rare, even if it seems like that isn't true sometimes."

The twins exchanged glances that had Sam wondering what was going on.

"What does it mean to be adopted?" Alden asked.

"Where did you hear that word?"

"I heard Nick talking on the phone to Elijah," Alden said.

"We were going to talk to you guys about that when we had more information, but Nick and I would like to adopt you two and Eli to make you legally our family."

"Oh." Aubrey's little brows furrowed the way they did when she was thinking about something. "Aren't we already your family?"

"Of course you are, but this makes it official and legal."

"What does that mean?" Aubrey asked.

"Our lawyer Andy will file papers with a judge, who then makes a ruling that says you and Eli are officially our family. It's really a formality. Do you know what that means?"

"I think so," Alden said.

"You know how people get married at weddings?"

They nodded.

"That's a formality. They already love each other and want to be a family, but when they go through the ceremony to get married, that makes it official."

"Will we have a wedding if we get adopted?" Aubrey asked.

Sam smiled. "No, but we'll have one heck of a party."

"I *love* parties," she said.

"I know you do. Nick and I want you to know that having you as part of our family has been one of the best things to ever happen to us, even if we know it happened because of the worst thing to ever happen to you. We can never take the place of your mommy and daddy, but we'll always love you and take care of you and be there for you."

"We know," Aubrey said. "It's very nice of you to take care of us."

"We love you so much."

"We love you, too."

"Eli will get adopted, too?" Alden asked.

"That's the plan."

Aubrey made a thoughtful face. "Isn't he a grownup, though?"

"He is, but he's choosing to be adopted so the three of you will be in the same family."

"Will we have to change our names?" Alden asked.

"Only if you want to. Eli suggested going by Armstrong-Cappuano, so you'd have both names. What do you think of that?"

"Would I have to write that on all my papers?" Alden frowned. "That's a *lot* of letters."

Sam laughed. "Maybe you could abbreviate."

"What does that mean?"

"You could do Alden A dash C for your papers."

"That would be better," he said, sounding relieved.

"I think it'd be cool for us to have the same last name," Aubrey said.

"We do, too, and I'm glad you think so." Sam glanced at the clock on the microwave. "Time to go brush your teeth and wash your faces and hands. It's almost time to go."

After they ran off, Sam took their plates to the sink to rinse them and put them in the dishwasher. Then she took the BlackBerry from her pocket and composed a text to Nick and Eli, letting them know about the conversation with the twins.

Damn, Eli wrote back, *they don't miss a thing. I was going to talk to them about it the next time I'm there, but I'm glad they know and that they approve.*

Their biggest concern was having to write Armstrong-Cappuano on all their papers. Alden said that's a LOT of letters.

LMAO, Eli said. *Too funny—and too cute.*

They were also concerned about whether you're being adopted, too, and I told them you've chosen to be so the three of you can be part of the same family. They liked that.

I like that, too! Andy says we're close. He's requesting a court date this week. He thinks they'll expedite it bc of who you guys are.

Finally some benefit to being the first couple.

LOL. Right?

When the twins returned from the bathroom, Sam was ready with backpacks and the lunchboxes Nick had packed for them the night before.

She hugged them, kissed them and wished them a good day. "Grandma Brenda and Shelby will be here when you get home, and I'll try to be home for dinner."

"Best day ever!" Aubrey said as they took off to meet their detail at the other end of the hallway.

Sam waved to the agents. "Incoming."

She loved the way their agents hugged them every morning and made them feel special. She'd be forever grateful to all the people who surrounded the twins with love in their new life. It took a village to raise kids, and they were extraordinarily blessed by theirs.

CHAPTER NINETEEN

S am was refilling her coffee when Shelby Faircloth Hill popped her head into the kitchen. "Morning."

"Hey, Tink. How's it going?"

Shelby wore a pink sweater over leggings. She was back to work very part time as the White House social secretary after giving birth to her daughter, Maisie. "Hanging in there. Just dropped the kids off with the nanny. That whole process was a lot easier when we were living here."

"I'll bet. How's the new place?"

Shelby shrugged. "It's lovely but doesn't feel like home yet."

"That can take a minute, but you'll get there."

"I really miss the townhouse where Avery, Noah and I became a family."

"I know you do, and no one should be forced to move the way you were." Shelby and Noah had been taken hostage in their home by Willy and Amber Peckham, criminals from Avery's past. The Hill family was now living behind iron gates with a top-of-the-line security system protecting them.

"That's true, and I do feel safe in the new place. It's just not home yet, but it will be."

"Have a party soon. Having your people there will make it feel more like home."

"That's a good idea. We'll do that soon."

"Don't forget to invite us."

Shelby laughed. "As if."

"We miss you around here."

"We miss being here. I'm trying to get Avery to be my butler, but he's not having it."

Laughing, Sam said, "I can't imagine why not."

"Neither can I. I'm not giving up on it just yet." She tipped her head. "Heard about what happened yesterday. How're you doing?"

"I'm okay as long as Jimmy is."

"Were you hurt at all?"

"Some bruises, aches and pains here and there, but nothing I can't handle. Could've been much worse all around."

"What the heck is going on this week?"

"I don't know, but it's got me temporarily grounded."

"For real?"

"Yep. We have a meeting with the Secret Service at nine. I'm hoping we can work something out to get me back out there."

"Gosh, this is all so upsetting. Here you two are, trying to serve the people and getting nothing but... *crap* in return."

"Was that nearly a swear out of your sweet mouth, Shelby Lynn?"

She scowled. "It makes me very angry when people are mean to my friends who are like family."

Sam hugged her friend. "Thank you for being our family and coming back to work when you should be on maternity leave. It means everything to us to have our people close by."

"I wouldn't want to be anywhere else, and honestly, being at work gives me a little bit of a break. Two kids is more than twice as much, especially when the older one is used to having me all to himself."

"I've heard that."

"How will Angela do three by herself?"

"I don't know, but we'll all pitch in and get her through it."

"Yes, we will. I'd better get to it before it's time to feed Ms. Maisie again."

"Thanks for everything, Tink."

"Love you," Shelby said as she walked away.

"Love you, too."

With thirty minutes until the Secret Service meeting, Sam went into her room to finish making herself presentable and to summon the fortitude to once again fight for the career that meant so much to her.

SECRET SERVICE DIRECTOR Ambrose Pierce had asked for a few minutes alone with Nick ahead of the nine o'clock meeting. At eight forty-five, Director Pierce was shown into the Oval Office. Nick got up to greet him with a handshake and the offer of coffee.

"Already had my allotment for the day, Mr. President." Pierce was about six foot three, with the burly build of a former college football player. He had a shock of white hair and blue eyes.

"Have a seat."

They settled on sofas facing each other.

"You asked for this meeting," Nick said. "What can I do for you?"

"It's been quite a week for all of us, and I wanted to touch base to let you know that our team has been assessing both incidents and thoroughly reviewing what went right and what went wrong in both cases. We take these things extremely seriously, as you can imagine."

"I have no doubt you all are doing everything possible to keep our family safe. I was glad to hear that Agent McFarland had a good night and is expected to make a full recovery."

"That's a huge relief to all of us. He's an excellent young agent."

"My wife speaks very highly of him and Agent Rogers."

"They speak highly of her as well. They admire the way she does the job while managing everything that goes along with being a mother and first lady."

"It's a balancing act, to be certain, but she's making it work."

"Yesterday's incident has put everyone on edge, sir. Our collective feeling is that it's becoming much more dangerous for her to be so exposed on the job."

Nick's heart sank. That the most sophisticated security organization in the world thought it was too dangerous for Sam to do her job made him want to forget all about the deal he'd made with her after becoming president. The husband who loved his wife with all his heart wanted her off the job immediately. The husband who knew what it took to make her happy would fight for what she wanted.

"Sam's job has always been dangerous. I wish this was the first time someone had taken a shot at her, but it's not, and it probably won't be the last time either."

"This is the first time it's happened on our watch, sir."

"I hear your concerns, and I respect your position, but my wife will remain on the job for the duration of my presidency. It's our job, yours and mine, to make that as safe as we possibly can without limiting her ability to move around."

Ambrose didn't like that answer. He didn't like it at all. But he only said, "Yes, sir."

"Is that all?"

"I also wanted to give you a heads-up as to why we'd originally requested this meeting with you and Mrs. Cappuano. We wanted to speak to you about your high school plans for Scotty."

"He'll attend Eastern, beginning in the fall."

"We wondered if you might consider a private school with enhanced security. Not that the District schools aren't safe, but the public schools do present some additional challenges for our team that wouldn't be present in a private school."

"I hope you're not referring to socioeconomic or racial concerns."

"Of course not. We're mostly focused on logistics versus population."

Nick wasn't sure he believed that's all it was. "Sam and I are both products of public schools, and we're big supporters of public education."

"Yes, sir, but we're looking at it from a security point of view. Having him on a campus with gates would be preferable to a more accessible location."

"I'd prefer to wait until my wife is present to discuss this any further."

"Understood. I'll return with the rest of our team in a few minutes, then."

"Thank you, Ambrose."

"My pleasure, Mr. President."

When he was alone, Nick stewed over the information Ambrose had provided. Scotty would be heartbroken if he couldn't attend high school with the friends he'd made in middle school. Through hockey and other activities, he'd made some good friends, and the thought of disrupting his life any more than it had already been by Secret Service agents and the move to the White House made Nick feel terrible.

With every passing day, his job seemed to make the lives of his family that much more complicated and dangerous, or so it seemed to him. No one would be talking about taking Sam off the job or sending Scotty to private high school if he wasn't the president.

He disliked a lot of things about this job, but the challenges for his family were right at the top of that list. Hearing Ambrose say his team was concerned about Sam's job becoming even more dangerous had hit him in his most vulnerable spot.

At his morning briefing, he'd been shown a video of the incident in Adams Morgan. Nick had braced himself for the sound of the gunshot, for Jimmy's instant reaction and how he'd saved Sam's life by diving on top of her, but nothing could've prepared him to witness just how close he'd once again come to losing her.

In some ways, he felt like they were playing a gigantic game of Russian roulette by having her working on the streets, hunting down murderers. But if he asked her to quit, he'd be asking her to stop being who she was, and he simply couldn't do that. Not to mention, she'd never forgive him.

His admin, Julie, came to the door. "Mrs. Cappuano is here, Mr. President."

Nick forced himself to rally, to smile, to welcome her with a hug. "Nice to see you, Mrs. C."

"You just saw me two hours ago."

"That feels like a long time ago."

"Has it been that kind of day?"

"Aren't they all that kind of day?"

He sat with her on the sofa, holding her hand and breathing in the distinctive lavender and vanilla scent that came with her.

"Look at us," Sam said. "Chilling in the Oval Office like it's no big deal. Just another day."

"Is it becoming routine?"

"Not quite there yet."

"Me either. It's still surreal, even almost six months later."

"We only have to do five more sets of six months, and then we're home free."

"Five more sets. I was better off not knowing that."

She laughed. "Sorry. What's the word on the street about this meeting?"

"Among other things, they want to talk about Scotty and high school."

"What about it?"

"There's a suggestion coming that we might want to consider private school with enhanced security."

"He'd hate us for that."

"That's what I told Ambrose when he gave me the heads-up about it."

"We can't do that to him. He's made such a nice group of friends, and they're all excited to stay together at Eastern next year."

Most of Scotty's closest school friends had played youth hockey with him and would be continuing into Caps Cup high school hockey next year. The thought of separating him from them at school broke Nick's heart. "That's what I said to Ambrose, and I mentioned how we're products of public school and big supporters of the public path."

"It makes me sweaty to even think about bringing this up with him."

"I know. Same."

"What'd he say about me?"

"The expected stuff. I pushed back. I think he understands our position, even if he doesn't agree with it."

"What does he want?"

"There's no point discussing that, because it's not happening."

"So that means he wants me off the streets and cocooned in the White House, doing first lady stuff."

"He wants you safe, which is our goal, too. So we'll discuss how you safely do the job you love. I made it clear to him that any other alternative is unacceptable. I told him to figure it out."

Sam waved a hand in front of her face. "*So* hot."

"What?" His annoyance was almost as sexy as him flexing his presidential muscles on her behalf.

"You. Fighting for me. Hot as *fuck*."

"You're a lunatic," he said with a huff that made her laugh.

"You knew that when you married me."

He leaned in to kiss her. "And I wouldn't change a thing about my lunatic, except for the commentary about my alleged hotness."

"Every woman in America with a heartbeat thinks you're hot."

"Stop it. You're in the Oval Office, where serious business takes place."

"Whatever you say, hottie."

"Honestly, Samantha. Will you please grow up?"

"Nah, I'm good like this."

He smiled. "Bickering with you makes my whole day worth living. I hope you know that."

"Why do you think I say things that'll cause the bickering?"

He rested his head against hers. "So you had a big morning with the Littles, huh?"

"Yep. They had questions. I had answers. I think it's all good."

"So freaking cute that Alden said it was too many letters to write on his papers."

"I almost died laughing over that. I told him he could abbreviate, and then I had to explain what that means."

"I love them so much. I'm so excited to officially adopt them."

"How soon do you think it'll be?"

"We're getting close to a court date."

"That'll be a three-ring circus."

"Whatever it takes to make them ours forever."

A knock sounded at the door. Julie had been told to wait for him to reply whenever Sam was with him. "Come in."

"Mr. President, Director Pierce and his team are here to see you."

"Send them in."

As Nick stood to welcome his guests, he hoped this meeting wouldn't become contentious as they fought for what was important to them.

. . .

AFTER HEARING from Nick that he'd laid down the law with Pierce, Sam was a little more relaxed than she'd been earlier, even if she was under no illusions about what the Secret Service director and his team would have to say.

"We've reviewed the film from yesterday's incident," Pierce said after they'd exchanged pleasantries. He sat on the sofa while Brant, Vernon and Debra stood behind him. "It's quite disturbing, to say the least. We believe you were either followed or someone was waiting for you to show up there. Either way, this presents a significant safety issue going forward."

"I believe someone may be targeting me in an attempt to intimidate my husband and possibly drive him from office—or to run me out of the department."

Pierce tilted his head as if he hadn't heard her correctly. "What do you mean?"

"Think about it. People have been in an uproar over an unelected vice president ascending to the top job. He's had defections from his secretary of State, the Joint Chiefs of Staff and the AG. It's been a rough six months, but he's put his head down and persevered, doing the job despite the bullshit. What if someone decided to take more drastic measures to get his attention by targeting me to get to him? What if the drones and the recent spate of murders are all about getting to him through me? Or what if someone wants me out of the department badly enough to go to extreme measures that'll have my husband and the Secret Service pulling me off the job?"

The director's expression was unreadable.

Sam had left out the part about the theory being Vernon's first.

"That... That's quite a stretch, ma'am."

"I realize that, and we're in the earliest stages of

investigating this possibility, which is what I'd be doing right now if I wasn't here."

The director's expression indicated he didn't appreciate her candor, but whatever. She had a job to do, and he was keeping her from it. "I'll be heading into work after this meeting."

"Have you no regard for the danger that puts your agents in, ma'am?"

She made no attempt to hide her ire. "I have all the regard in the world for Vernon, Jimmy and every other agent who protects me and my family. That you'd question my regard for them as a fellow law enforcement officer is insulting."

"I apologize, ma'am. But as the director of this agency, it's my job to assess the risk to my team as well as the people we're charged with protecting and make recommendations accordingly."

"I appreciate and respect your position, but I intend to continue to do my job with a detail or without one. If Vernon and the others feel it's too dangerous to protect me, I'll respect their wishes. I don't expect anyone to take unreasonable risks to protect me."

Ambrose held Sam's unblinking gaze when he said, "Agent Rogers."

"Yes, sir?"

"Are you willing to continue to lead Mrs. Cappuano's detail?"

"I am, sir, and Agent Quigley will be filling in while Agent McFarland is on medical leave."

Sam remembered meeting Quigley before and how he was so young, he still had acne. She felt a twinge of anxiety over asking another young agent to take her on at this dangerous moment.

"Agent Quigley has been fully briefed on the current situation?" Pierce asked.

"He has, sir."

Pierce let out a deep sigh when he realized he was

outnumbered. "I know this may go without saying, but our entire focus is on keeping you and your family alive. Anything we recommend is with that goal in mind."

"We appreciate you all more than we could ever say," Nick said. "I hope you know that, but we also have lives to live while I'm in office. I have to believe we can find a balance between your goals and ours. With that said, I want to add that we're aware of your recommendation to send Scotty to a private high school, but Sam and I are very much in agreement that he'll attend Eastern in the fall. We'd like you to do everything within your power to make that work for him."

"He should be made aware of our recommendation," Pierce said.

"He will be," Nick said with a touch of annoyance. "Neither of us has a single doubt what his reaction will be."

Pierce stood somewhat abruptly. "Then I guess we're done here. Thank you for your time, Mr. President, Mrs. Cappuano."

"Thank you, Ambrose, Brant, Vernon and Debra," Nick said.

"Yikes," Sam said after they'd closed the door behind them.

"Right?"

Sam was filled with anxiety. "I feel unsettled. I have to be honest."

"What do you mean?"

"We're going against their recommendations, which means if one of the agents is hurt—or, God forbid, killed—while protecting me or Scotty, then that's on us."

"No, it isn't. It's on the person who does the killing. What is it you're always telling me? Don't take the blame for stuff that isn't your fault."

"But if we're doing things they've deemed unsafe, then it's partially on us if one of their people is harmed."

"Pierce said they can choose not to be on your details."

"True, but it still makes me queasy to think of one of them being hurt or killed."

"That could happen at any time, regardless of current events. They know that, or they wouldn't be in those jobs."

"I guess."

"It's true, Sam. They understand they may have to take a bullet for us the way Jimmy did yesterday. And speaking of him, I want to do something for him and his wife to thank him. What should that be?"

"They're having a baby soon. Something for the baby?"

"Something big, like a college fund or something."

"That's a bit extreme."

"He saved the life of my precious wife. Nothing we do for him or them would be extreme."

Sam leaned in to kiss him. "I'll give it some thought and get back to you. In the meantime, I think I have permission to get back to work. Don't tell anyone, but I'm outta here."

"Please be careful out there. You're the sun, the moon, the stars and the whole damned world to me."

She fanned her face. "Hot. As *fuck*."

"Shut up and go to work."

Sam laughed and stood to leave.

At the door, he gave her a tight hug. "I mean it. All bravado aside. Please don't take any unnecessary chances."

"I never do, and I never would. Too damned much to live for."

"I love you."

"I love you more, and don't argue with me. I already won that fight."

Nick laughed as she opened the door to find Terry O'Connor about to knock.

"Hi, Sam. Sorry to interrupt."

"Hey, Terry. I was just leaving. See you guys later."

CHAPTER TWENTY

Nick watched her go, holding back the urgent desire to beg her not to. *Stay*, he wanted to say. *Stay with me where you're safe. Please. I need you. Don't go.*

"Mr. President."

Nick realized Terry had been speaking to him. He closed the door and turned to his chief of staff. "I'm sorry. What did you say?"

"Are you okay, sir?"

"I... ah... Yeah." He forced himself to shake off the dread of watching her walk away, headed for God only knew what. "What's up?"

"How'd the meeting with Pierce go?"

Nick returned to his seat behind the Resolute Desk. "As expected. They want Sam off the streets and for Scotty to go to private high school."

Terry sat in a chair next to his desk. "What did you say to that?"

"We told them Sam will continue in her job, and Scotty is going to Eastern with his middle school friends. Neither of those edicts was well received."

"I'm sure they weren't."

"And then, after hearing that the Secret Service has extreme concerns about Sam's safety, I had to let her walk out of here and go to work, because that's what I promised her I'd do when I became president. But everything in me wants to forbid her from leaving this place for any reason."

"Which, of course, you can't do."

"Right, so now I'm in a cold sweat about the possibility that everything from the drones to four new murders to the shooting yesterday could be a coordinated attempt to scare me so badly that I quit—or to scare her so badly she quits the force."

"*What?*"

"Sam has a theory that the goal is to get to me through her, and at first, it sounds preposterous. That is, until you dig in a little and see how effectively it would work if something were to happen to her. I'd be out of here so fast, heads would spin, and they know that. They *know* it. So they're aiming for my Achilles' heel. Or, they're aiming to scare her off the job."

"Who is it, exactly, that you're referring to?"

"We're not sure yet, but she's got a long list of possibilities to consider."

Terry sat back in his seat, seeming stunned.

"At this point, especially after the shit with the Joint Chiefs and Juan... What would've been ridiculous in another life is anything but in this one."

"Wow."

"So yeah, I just had to send my wife out to work, knowing someone could be intentionally gunning for her for any number of reasons. Good times."

"And her detail is allowing it?"

"The agents assigned to her were offered the chance to step back, but they chose to stay with her. She's become close to her lead agent, Vernon Rogers, so I'm not surprised he wants to stay." Nick rubbed at the tension in his neck. "It doesn't sit right with me to be bucking their recommendations. If something happens to Sam, Scotty or one of the agents who've become like family to us... I mean, how in the world would we ever live with that?"

Terry thought about that for a second. "The thing is, they have a say in this. Sam is willing to risk everything to continue doing the job she loves. Scotty would tell you he's willing to accept the added risk of attending a public high school with less built-in security than a private school would have. These are choices they're making for themselves."

"But the only reason they're in any danger in the first place is because of me."

"Sam was in danger on the job long before she ever met you."

"Agreed, but it's a thousand times worse now that everyone in the world recognizes her and knows what she means to me."

"Granted, but that doesn't mean she should hide out for the next two and a half years. She's got to live her life alongside you being in office with all the reasonable security measures in place."

"Pierce didn't come right out and say it, but his message was that she's a target, and that means her agents are, too."

"Again, they're choosing to accept that risk. I know it's an impossible position for you to be in, especially after someone shot at her yesterday, but everything possible is being done to protect your family, and they have to make their own choices about some of this."

"I guess." Nick fiddled with the Montblanc pen that Terry's parents, Graham and Laine, had given him for his Harvard graduation. Terry was right, and Nick knew he had to accept that he couldn't control everything his family did while he was in office. But if he had his way, Sam would work from home and the kids would be homeschooled, which would make all of them miserable.

It was truly a no-win situation.

"Moving on," Nick said. "What's next?"

"We received a phone call from your mother." He put a slip of paper on the desk. "She'd like to speak to you if you have time."

The mention of his mother detonated like a live grenade in the middle of an already stressful day. "How did she get a call through?"

"She told the switchboard she's the president's mother and that if her call wasn't put through to his office, someone would be in trouble."

He had no intention of returning that call. "Of course she did." Some things—and some people—never changed. "What else?"

"Something fun for a change."

"How refreshing."

"I thought you might say that. Every year around the Fourth of July, the president awards the Presidential Medal of Freedom to, and I'm quoting the statute here, 'any person who has made an especially meritorious contribution to the security or national interests of the United States, or world peace, or cultural or other significant public or private endeavors.'"

Terry placed a thick file on Nick's desk. "We've received numerous nominations from across the spectrum of politics and international affairs as well as business, entertainment, literary figures and so on. You can look through the nominations and also make your own choices."

"So, I could, for example, nominate your dad if I so desired?"

Terry smiled. "You could."

"You were right. This'll be fun."

Terry stood. "I'll leave you to that until the budget meeting at eleven."

"Buzzkiller."

"Haha, enjoy the fun while you can, Mr. President."

"Will do. It never lasts long around here."

Nick opened the file and began to look through the stack of

nominations, but all he could think about was Sam moving around the city like everything was normal when nothing would ever be normal again.

It would be difficult to focus on anything else until she was home safe and sound.

IN THE FOYER, Sam pulled Vernon aside. "I'm asking a lot of you."

"I'm aware of the concerns and choosing to continue as your lead agent."

"Thank you. I wouldn't want anyone else but you."

"That's nice of you to say."

"I mean it."

"I know you do."

"I hate that my work is putting you guys in danger."

"When we were assigned to your detail, Jimmy and I knew we'd be more exposed than usual due to the nature of your work, and we chose to accept the assignment anyway. You want to know why?"

"Uh, *yeah*..."

He smiled. "When your husband was the vice president, I very much admired you and your career and how you managed multiple roles. Not to mention, I enjoyed the time we spent together. You're nothing if not entertaining."

"Thank you. I do what I can for the people."

Chuckling, he continued. "Then when I heard you planned to keep the job as first lady, I was proud of you, like I'd be of one of my own daughters. I wanted to be part of it, and Jimmy felt the same way. We wanted to be able to say we were supporting the first president's wife to work outside the White House. We wanted to be part of the history you're making every day when you leave this place and go to work."

Tears filled her eyes. "Thank you, Vernon. Thank you so

much for everything—and not just the stuff you're required to do. All of it."

"It's an honor and a privilege to work with you, Sam."

She tried to contain emotions that were all over the place in light of recent events. "I don't take it lightly, you know? The risk you guys take on my behalf. I'd never want you to think…"

"We'd never think otherwise."

"And Agent Quigley?"

"He's been fully briefed and understands the mission as well as the risks."

"Okay, then. I really, really want to see Jimmy. Can you check with Liz to see if this is a good time to stop there?"

"Yes, ma'am."

When they stepped outside, Quigley was standing next to the SUV. He snapped to attention when he saw them coming and opened the door for her.

"Welcome to the party, Agent Quigley," Sam said.

"My pleasure, ma'am."

"You say that now. What's your first name?"

"Carl, but everyone calls me Q."

"We're on a first-name basis in the SUV," Sam told him.

Quigley glanced at Vernon.

"Q," Vernon said, "meet Sam."

The young, dark-haired agent blinked several times in rapid succession. "Oh, um, okay, ma'am. I mean, Sam."

Sam laughed. "It took Vernon and Jimmy a minute, too. You'll come around."

"Yes, ma'am. Er… Sam."

"There it is."

Vernon sent the text to Liz, who responded right away that they'd love to see Sam.

"I'm glad they're still speaking to me after this," Sam said as Vernon drove them through the White House gates.

"Please, they're big fans of you and your husband. We all are."

"Certainly not all of you."

"Everyone who works with you and your family are fans. Especially the agents on the kids' details. They're smitten."

"Aw, that's so nice to hear. It makes me feel good to know they're well cared for when we can't be with them."

"Trust me when I tell you their agents would give their lives for those kids."

"You're going to make me cry."

"Now don't do that!"

She laughed. "What is it with all men and female tears?"

"We can't handle it."

"It's hilarious to me."

"We live to entertain you."

"And you do. Every day."

When they arrived at the George Washington University Hospital, both agents accompanied Sam inside, working efficiently to get her through the lobby to the elevator and up to the fifth floor, where Jimmy's wife, Liz, met them with a hug for Sam. She was a pretty blonde, rounded with pregnancy.

"Thank you so much for seeing me," Sam said. "I wouldn't have blamed you for banishing me."

"Oh please, stop that. Jimmy is crazy about you and very much looking forward to seeing you."

"I'm so glad he's okay, Liz. All I could think about was you and the baby…"

"We're very thankful that he's all right—and that you are, too. Those were his first questions after he came out of surgery: Where's the first lady, and is she all right?"

"I'm fine, thanks to him."

"That's all that matters to him. While I have you, I wanted to thank you and the president for the gorgeous baby carriage you sent for our shower. I'll be the envy of all the other mommies, not to mention we adored the card signed with love from Sam and Nick, as if you're not the first lady and president."

"You've very welcome. We can't wait to meet your little one."

"Us, too." Liz linked her arm with Sam's and walked her to Jimmy's room, where a uniformed Secret Service officer stationed outside requested her ID, even though they recognized her.

Sam showed them her badge. "Thanks for keeping him safe."

One of them pushed the door open for her. "Our pleasure, ma'am."

Jimmy was sitting up in bed, his right arm in a sling and his face paler than usual. Otherwise, he looked good, considering he'd recently been shot.

"Hey, Sam," he said, smiling.

Sam went straight over to the bed to give him a gentle hug. "Thank you so much for not dying."

"I do what I can for my people."

Sam sputtered with laughter. "That saying is *trademarked* and can't be used without written permission."

He laughed and then winced. "The ribs and the lung don't approve of laughter."

"Sorry about that."

"No worries."

"Are they treating you well in here?"

"I was just telling Liz I need to get shot more often, because I've never felt more like a celebrity in my life. Needless to say, she didn't agree."

"Too soon for jokes, James," Liz said from the other side of the bed, where she held his hand.

"I'm so, so appreciative and grateful, Jimmy. I'll never have the words."

"Just doing my job, but I've been thinking about something I wanted to share with you."

"What's that?"

"Whoever did this meant to hit me and not you. I think it was intended to be a warning shot."

"Why do you say that?"

"Because you were standing to my left, and I was hit on the right side. If they were gunning for you, they missed by a lot."

"That's true, and I hadn't thought of it that way before. I'll mention that to our team and the others investigating the shooting."

"Maybe you could not mention that it came from me. I've already said the same thing to my own chain of command, and whatever happens next should come from them."

"Understood. It's a good thought, though. I don't want to tire you out. I just needed to come by to see you, to thank you..."

"I'm glad you came. I hope to be back in the most interesting SUV in town before too long."

"We'll be looking forward to having you back. It's no fun picking on my grasshopper without Vernon's grasshopper there, too."

Jimmy chuckled. "Detective Cruz needs me to help fight back."

"Yes, he does. We're going to see what we can do to ruin Agent Q while you're out."

"Go with God, Q," Jimmy said, making Quigley laugh.

Sam gave Jimmy another hug and then hugged Liz, too. "Let us know if either of you needs anything."

"Thanks for coming," Liz said. "It means a lot to us."

"Your husband means a lot to me." At some point in the last few months, Jimmy and Vernon had begun to feel like family to her. "I'll check on you later this week."

"Talk to you then," Jimmy said, smiling as he waved to them.

"I'll be back tonight," Vernon said. "You want another milkshake?"

"I'd never say no to that, boss man."
"You got it."

CHAPTER TWENTY-ONE

O n the way to HQ, Sam thought about what Vernon had said earlier, about how she made history every time she left the White House to go to work. While she'd known that was true, she'd never given it much thought because going to work was so much a part of who she was and what she did every day.

"Hey, Q?"

"Yes, Sam?"

"Thanks for stepping in for Jimmy."

"No problem, ma'am."

"It's easier to go with Sam than ma'am when it's just us," Vernon said.

"Yes, sir."

Vernon glanced at Sam in the mirror and rolled his eyes. "Another grasshopper to train."

"Excuse me, sir?"

"Inside joke," Vernon said with a smile for Sam.

"What do you guys think of Jimmy's theory about it being a warning shot?"

"It has merit," Vernon said. "Either they intended to miss,

or they're amateurs. I'm not sure which is worse or more dangerous."

When they pulled up to the morgue entrance, Vernon instructed Quigley to stay with the vehicle while he accompanied Sam inside.

She walked into the pit, feeling like a conquering emperor back from battle or some such dramatic thing. "Howdy, citizens."

They startled—she loved when that happened—and turned to her.

"Thought you were out today, LT," Gonzo said. "We were getting ready to have a party."

"Sorry to ruin your fun. What goes on here?"

"Cruz and I just got back from seeing Joshua Saulnier's fiancée, Mandy." Gonzo shook his head. "Horrific. They'd been together since the ninth grade."

"Oh damn. Does she have anyone with her?"

"One of his school friends is there, and their parents are due in from the West Coast later today."

Sam was anguished for people she might never meet. "What's our next move?"

"We're digging into Saulnier and looking for connections between our four victims but not finding anything relevant."

"Listen, I had a thought about the shooting." She shared Jimmy's take on the matter without quoting him.

"That's true," Freddie said. "If they were aiming for you, they were way off."

"So we're either looking for someone incompetent with a weapon or extremely deliberate. Let's pass this on to Agent Hill."

"I'll take care of that," Gonzo said.

"Oh, hey, LT," Green said. "Sergeant Fitzgivens from sharpshooting was looking for you."

"What'd he want?"

"Didn't say but asked you to swing by if you get a minute."

"I think I'll do that now. Be back in a few. Vernon, we're off to sharpshooting."

"Awesome. Just what every Secret Service agent wants to hear from their protectee."

Sam chuckled at his sarcastic wit. She loved that about him. "When we get there, I need to talk to the sergeant alone, okay?"

"Yes, that's fine as long as you feel comfortable being alone with him."

"I've never had any reason not to be. There's another guy in that unit, Offenbach, who hates me. If he's there, you'll probably figure out who he is right away."

"The good news just keeps on coming."

"I know it's hard for you to believe that not everyone loves me. I don't get it either."

His snort made her smile.

Talking to him helped to keep her from stressing over what the hell Fitzgivens wanted with her as they cut through the lobby on the way to the opposite side of the building. She'd worked with Fitzgivens during the sniper case but hadn't had contact with him since.

When she stepped into their office, of course the first person she saw was Offenbach, who'd been busted down to Patrol officer after Sam's sniper investigation uncovered that he wasn't at a conference in Philadelphia he was supposed to be attending. Instead, he'd been in an Atlantic City hotel room with a woman, much to the surprise of his wife, the mother of their six children. Because he was such a talented marksman, they'd kept him in sharpshooting despite the demotion.

The look he gave her was nothing short of hateful. Actually, *hateful* wasn't a strong enough word to describe it. *Sinister* might be better.

"Where do I find Fitzgivens?" she asked a young female officer, who pointed to a door at the back of the big, open space.

"Thanks." Sam felt Offenbach's gaze burning a hole in her back as she and Vernon made their way to the closed door.

Sam knocked.

"Enter."

She opened the door, stepped inside and closed it behind her, relieved to be out of Offenbach's line of sight for the moment.

"Hey, LT. Thanks for stopping by." Fitzgivens had Irish coloring, with reddish-brown hair, brown eyes and a weathered complexion.

"No problem. What's up?"

He gestured for her to have a seat in his visitor chair. "It's a touchy matter."

She sat, crossing her legs. "Aren't they all?"

"Some are more so than others." He seemed hesitant to proceed and kept his voice down when he said, "I want you to know I don't offer this info up lightly. It goes against everything I believe in as a man and a police officer to rat out a colleague."

"Okay…"

"Offenbach."

"He hates my guts."

"Yeah, that's putting it mildly."

"It's funny how he blames me for catching him in the act of fucking up at work and home but takes no ownership of his own actions."

"I've said as much to him, but it goes in one ear and out the other." Fitzgivens was clearly uncomfortable as he seemed to choose his words carefully. "You need to look out for him. He's unhinged over what went down and how his whole life blew up in his face. Because he's not self-aware enough to look in the mirror for someone to blame, he's focused on you."

A chill went down her spine.

"And…" His face twisted with a combination of agony and hesitation. "He's big into drones. In fact, I'd use the word 'obsessed' to describe his fixation. It's all he talks about."

The chill turned to horror that quickly.

"Now, I'm not accusing him of anything, but I wanted you to be aware, and whatever you do with this info is up to you. Obviously, I'm way out on a limb here, but if you could keep me out of it, I'd appreciate it."

Sam had to force herself to remain seated, to not leave the office and go beat the truth out of Offenbach. She was so outraged that she was quite certain she could beat the hell out of him, not that she ever would. "He knows I'm in here talking to you. What else would it be about?"

"I told him I have info about Stahl that I'm passing on to you and to not say a fucking word to you when you stopped by. He hates me almost as much as he hates you because they promoted me to sergeant after he was demoted. I went from being his subordinate to being his boss."

"We need a way to get people like him, Stahl and Ramsey the fuck out of here when they start becoming the problem."

"I agree, but he has rights, don't you know, and the union that protects us all also protects the bad apples."

"That's so fucking wrong." She glanced up at the sergeant. "The minute I make this info available to the Feds, he'll know you told me this."

Fitzgivens shrugged. "I don't give a flying fuck what he thinks. If he tried to assassinate a fellow police officer, not to mention the president of the United States and a lawn full of innocent kids, I could live with myself if he blames me."

"Do you honestly think he's capable of such things?"

"I wish I could say for sure he isn't, but because I can't, here we are."

"Thank you," Sam said, her voice gruff with emotion. "Thank you so much."

He nodded. "Be careful. He's unhinged and can shoot like no one I've ever seen. If by any chance it was him yesterday, he missed only because he intended to."

She swallowed hard at the idea of a fellow police officer

shooting at her on the job and injuring Jimmy, who was lucky to be alive. It was almost too big to process. "Do you know where he was at the time of the shooting?"

"I know where he told me he was—tracking down a cache of stolen weapons on Southeast."

"We can seize his phone and check his location."

"Let the Feds do that. Steer clear of this, Lieutenant. If it was him, you shouldn't be anywhere near it."

"Yes, you're right. Thank you again, Sergeant. I'll never forget the risk you took to tell me this."

"Can you go out there and walk by him and not show him a damned thing?"

She took another deep, trembling breath and blew it out slowly. "Yeah, I can do that. Let's be laughing when I open the door."

"Yeah, let's do that."

"Pettiness ranks right up there with sarcasm as among my favorite traits in a coworker."

He smiled. "Likewise. Are you ready?"

"Say something funny."

"Offenbach's wife got lucky when he cheated on her."

The laughter came naturally as she opened the door and stepped out of his office and into the grouping of cubicles where his team worked.

Sam felt the heat of Offenbach's stare on her as she nodded to two of the other officers and walked by him, chuckling, but never so much as glancing in his direction.

She kept her head down as she walked to the pit, feeling as if it would take nothing at all to shatter her composure.

"I want to know why that guy hates you, and I want to know right now," Vernon said. "He never blinked the whole time you were in that office."

"Sam," Freddie called to her.

Without acknowledging either of them, she went straight into her office, shut and locked the door and sat behind the desk. She had no idea how long she sat there, staring at the dented file cabinet before she pulled her phone out of her pocket and called Avery Hill, praying he was in a place where he could take the call right fucking now.

"Hey," Hill said. "What's up?"

"Something too big to be believed."

"Okay..."

"Avery..."

"I'm here. What's going on?"

"I'm going to tell you something that you're going to need to find out on your own. Do you understand me?"

"I do."

"Look at Officer Dylan Offenbach on the drones."

"As in MPD Officer Offenbach?"

"Yes."

"What's his deal?"

Sam filled him in on their history and how he'd been busted down from sergeant to Patrol and dumped by his wife after the sniper investigation. "Naturally, he blames me because I was charged with finding everyone who had precision shooting capability when we were working that case. It was completely my fault that he wasn't where his boss or wife thought he'd be. His new boss is the one who told me that he's obsessed with drones, and that's the word he used. Obsessed."

And then she had a bigger, even more upsetting thought. "Archie."

"What?"

"Lieutenant Archelotta is the one who tracked Offenbach's phone and determined he wasn't where he was supposed to be. Archie's girlfriend is the one who was kidnapped and assaulted..." Sam was on the verge of completely losing her shit as the words tumbled out of her mouth.

"All right. I've got this. I don't want you to tell another living soul about this, do you hear me? No one. Not Nick or Freddie or Captain Malone or anyone else."

"I hear you."

"I understand the stakes and the urgency, and I promise I'll put the full weight of the FBI behind this investigation. That's all I'll ever say to you about it."

"Thank you, Avery."

"Of course."

The line went dead, and she closed her phone without the usual satisfying slap. The full-body trembling reminded her of being wrapped in razor wire, doused with gasoline and threatened with fire.

A sharp knock at the door roused her. She took three more deep breaths, looking for a scintilla of calm so she could get through the rest of her tour. "Come in."

The knob didn't turn.

Shit, she'd locked the door. She stood and was forced to take a pause to ensure her legs would hold her before she went to unlock the door and admit Captain Malone.

"Why are you locking yourself in?" he asked. "Have we finally driven you mad?"

"Not quite, but close. What's up?"

"We've got a problem."

She wasn't sure she could handle another one. "What's that?"

He handed her a piece of paper, which had her sinking into her seat as she quickly scanned what turned out to be a lawsuit against her, Malone and the department, filed by Hector Reese. "Oh my God."

Malone sat in front of her desk and sighed. "This is bad, Sam. He's got medical reports and a witness statement from the sergeant on duty in the jail the night you interrogated him. Captain Norris said he's booked on all the big cable news shows this afternoon."

"Should we get out in front of it? Should I take the blame? Say the interrogation got out of hand?"

"The chief is consulting with the attorneys about the best way to handle it. I told him it's true and we're both complicit."

"You didn't do anything. This is on me."

"I was well aware of what you intended to do and didn't stop it because I wanted the same answers you did." After Hector's brother, Clarence, had killed his family and then taken off, detectives had found news clippings and other information about the unsolved shooting of Skip Holland.

Sam had gone into that room with Hector, wanting to know where his brother would hide out after having shot Freddie and what Clarence had to do with shooting her father. She'd taken her panic over Freddie's close call and years of frustration, emotion and grief over her dad's unsolved case into that room with her and wasn't proud of how she'd treated the man. Thank God she'd ordered him uncuffed before the interrogation.

"This will ruin me," she whispered.

"Worst-case scenario is a slap on the wrist from the department for something that happened years ago."

"You really think so? Because I can see it being a much bigger deal than that."

"Let's see what the lawyers advise before we say or do anything."

Sam felt like she might be having a heart attack as the events of the last hour landed with swift, devastating precision. "Someone is trying to take me down, Cap. Any way they can."

"It's starting to seem that way."

CHAPTER TWENTY-TWO

The Hector Reese story exploded with the force of ten tons of TNT, or that's how it seemed to Sam, who was immediately at the center of a firestorm she'd never seen coming. Reese was on the cable news shows, telling the world how she'd beaten him while he was in police custody.

"Now I don't want to say this was a racist attack, but I can't say for certain that it wasn't," he said in one interview.

"Oh my God," Freddie whispered as he stood next to her in the conference room, watching the bloodbath unfold.

"Do you know why Lieutenant Holland did this?"

"She was looking for my brother, Clarence, who'd killed his family and then ran away. She said something about her father's shooting, but I didn't know nothing about that, and neither did my brother."

"Can you detail the extent of your injuries after your encounter with her?"

"I had a bruised face from where she slapped me hard, bruised ribs, and for a time, they thought they might have to remove my spleen after she punched me in the gut twice, but that didn't end up happening. I was in a lot of pain for weeks, mostly because of the ribs."

"Did you fight back?"

"Nah."

"Why not?"

"My mama taught me to never hit a woman, even if she was a bitch cop."

Sam watched the interview in a state of disbelief. *Shit. Fuck. Damn. Hell.*

The anchor looked into the camera when she said, in the gravest possible tone, "Our requests for comment from the MPD and the White House have gone unanswered."

"Detective Cruz," Chief Farnsworth said from behind them.

They spun around to face him.

"Please give us the room."

"Yes, sir," Freddie said, casting a trepidatious glance at Sam before he walked out and closed the door.

"Well, this is a fine mess we find ourselves in," the chief said, his expression lacking the usual affection and humor she'd come to expect.

"I'm sorry, sir. This... It happened a long time ago..."

"I'm afraid I'm going to need an explanation, because it's unfathomable to me that you'd assault a man in our custody."

"It would've been unfathomable to me, too, before the Reese case. I have no defense for the indefensible other than to say that I was running on pure emotion that night. The crime scene at Reese's home was unlike anything any of us had ever experienced. Freddie had been shot by Clarence Reese, who was in the wind, and we'd found news clippings and other information about my dad's shooting in the house. I took all that into the room with Hector that night, and I own what happened. It was wrong. I knew it then, and I know it now."

"We're going to put out a statement that says exactly that and announce that you're suspended without pay for fourteen days. You're to go home and to have no contact with any member of this department until you return to work."

Sam was shocked by the length of the suspension but kept that to herself. She was lucky he wasn't firing her on the spot.

"Do you have anything you wish to say?"

"I'm deeply ashamed of my actions that night. I've thought about it a lot in the ensuing years, and I've never been able to reconcile my behavior with the code of conduct I've tried to uphold throughout my career. I lost my mind for a minute and will pay whatever price you deem appropriate. That said, I believe something bigger is going on right now, and it may be coming from inside this building."

He frowned. "What're you talking about?"

Slowly and methodically, she laid out the information she had on the working theory of how the recent murders, Harlowe's abduction and assault, the drone attack, the shooting in Adams Morgan and the resurrection of the Reese story were related. "In addition, I've been told by a reliable source that Officer Offenbach is obsessed with two things. The first is getting revenge on me for allegedly ruining his career and marriage. The second is drones. I've passed the drone thing on to Agent Hill."

"Wait. You went to *Hill* before you told me about this? *What the hell*, Sam?"

"I went to him as the first lady, not as a police officer. Those drones came for my family, sir, and the FBI is leading that investigation."

"Which you directed at one of my officers without a heads-up to me!"

"Agent Hill told me not to tell anyone so it couldn't come back around to me or the department. I was trying to protect you—and us—and to keep the investigation clean after I was given this tip. I wasn't intending to be insubordinate in any way. You know that's not how I roll."

Hands on his hips, he glared at her. "After today, I'm not sure I know you at all."

She felt as if she'd been kicked in the gut. "Please don't say that. You know me as well as anyone does, and only a lead in my dad's ice-cold case and Freddie being shot in the same couple of days could've driven me to behave the way I did with Reese. You *know* that."

"I acknowledge the extraordinary circumstances leading up to that encounter, but I cannot and will not condone violence. This is a PR disaster, Lieutenant. Not only are we guilty of assaulting an incarcerated man, but he's calling it a racially motivated attack."

"His race had nothing to do with it. He had information I wanted. That was all it was about. Not once in my entire career have I ever been accused of doing anything that was racist."

"Until now."

That hurt. "I really hope you'll fully question the timing of this news coming out in the context of everything that's happened this week. Who else knew about the incident with Reese besides me and Malone? Who told them about it? Was it the officers working in the jail that night? I'm not denying I did this, but why's it being resurrected now? It's all related, Chief."

Another thing occurred to her. "He called me a cunt cop. He'd returned to Clarence's house with his brother. They knew we were watching the place, but they came anyway, looking for ten grand in cash that we'd impounded from the basement. His sister-in-law and three little kids, including a baby, had been murdered with a baseball bat in that house, and instead of helping us get justice for them, Hector cared only about protecting the brother who killed them. You might want to add that to the statement, so people know who I was dealing with that night."

"I'll take that under advisement. In the meantime, you're to go home. Immediately. You're to speak to no one from this department, and you'll stay out of all investigations if you know what's good for you."

Not once had he ever spoken to her in that particular tone. It broke her heart.

"I have the Nelson trial starting a week from Monday, and final preparation for that with Faith Miller." Sam was one of the primary witnesses in the federal case against Christopher Nelson, son of the former president, who'd conspired to ruin Nick's chances for higher office by, among other things, torturing and killing Sam's ex-husband. The hits just kept on coming.

"Take care of that and nothing else."

"I'm sorry, sir."

"So am I."

With that, he turned and left the room to go clean up her mess.

The BlackBerry rang, and she pulled it out of her pocket to take the call from Nick.

"Babe... what the hell is going on?"

"I... I've been suspended for two weeks."

"No."

"I can't talk right now. I'll be home shortly."

"I love you."

"That helps. See you soon."

She ended the call, put the phone in her back pocket and then took a seat at the table because she didn't trust her legs to transport her to the office to get her things and then to the morgue to get out of there. The whole building would be abuzz over her downfall, many of them probably celebrating that someone had finally succeeded in cutting the cocky lieutenant down to size.

Ten full minutes passed with her staring intently at the murder board that had four new victims as well as one who'd survived a similar attack. She didn't blink or move and barely took more than a few breaths as she studied each of them, looking for something that wasn't there.

A knock on the door had her blinking and snapping out of the stupor. "Yeah?"

"Are you okay?" Freddie asked.

Sam kept her back to him. "I'm suspended for fourteen days."

"What? Sam... No way."

"I can't talk to you or the others. Let Gonzo know he's in charge. I'm going home." When he didn't move, she said, "Go, Freddie. Take care of it for me, please."

"Yes, ma'am."

Sam gave him a few minutes to put out the word and then got up to leave the room. She felt her shocked colleagues watching her as she went into her office to gather her things and as she closed the door without locking it, since Gonzo would need access. "Take care of each other," she said as she walked toward the morgue, aware of Vernon shadowing her.

"You're suspended?" he asked softly.

"Two weeks."

"I'm sorry."

She shrugged. "It's my own fault."

"I find that hard to believe."

Lindsey saw them and came to the door. "What's going on?"

"I'm out for two weeks. I'll see you on the other side. I hope."

Lindsey's pretty face registered her shock. "Sam..."

"I have to go, Linds. Take care."

Vernon waved off Quigley and held the back door of the SUV for her. "It feels horrible right now, but I have to believe this too shall pass."

Sam felt hollowed out inside, as if her very soul had been extracted. Despite her close ties to the chief, Jeannie and Malone, there was a good chance she could lose her job—and she'd probably deserve that. She couldn't imagine who she'd be without it. "I guess we'll find out if this storm will pass."

She rode home with her gaze fixed on the city she'd worked for her entire adult life. If she allowed herself to think about what might happen, she'd start crying and never stop.

And Archie... She needed to contact him about what she'd

learned and the link to Offenbach. Had he taken Harlowe and assaulted her to get back at Archie? If so, how would her friend ever live with knowing that?

She had more questions than answers.

Such as why now? Why had they chosen this moment in time to come for her? Could it be because Tom Forrester, who'd once been accused of protecting her in the case involving Ramsey, was now dead and out of their way? Or was it because they had a beef with her husband and wanted to bring them down for some reason?

She should be working on getting answers to all those questions, but she'd been forbidden to work on any case, even one that involved her. She couldn't call Freddie or Gonzo and ask them to do it for her, because she wasn't allowed to talk to her two closest friends and colleagues.

As the SUV rolled through the White House gates, it occurred to her that Nick could call Freddie if it came to that.

That scenario made her feel slightly better, that she could do something to fight back against an accusation that threatened to ruin her career and reputation. That she wasn't allowed to speak about the situation publicly, to take responsibility for her mistakes, would only make everything worse.

If that was even possible.

"Thank you, Vernon."

"I'm here if I can do anything."

"That means a lot to me."

"Sam."

She turned to him.

"Stay strong."

"I'll try."

George was working the door and had a smile for her as she came in and handed over her coat. "Afternoon, ma'am."

"Afternoon, George. Is the president in the Oval?"

"No, ma'am. I believe he's in the Situation Room."

"Okay, thank you." Bummed that he wasn't available at the moment, she went upstairs to the residence and went straight to the liquor cabinet in the kitchen to pour herself a glass of vodka straight up. When that wasn't enough, she drank straight from the bottle. She was still standing there, bottle in hand, when her mother walked in and stopped short, startled to see her there with a bottle of booze in hand.

"Sam! You scared me. What're you doing home, and why are you drinking vodka straight from the bottle?"

"I take it you haven't seen or heard any news today?"

"Not since this morning. I went right from Pilates to lunch with my friend Diana. Do you remember her? She's your old friend Caroline's mom."

"I remember her."

"Anyway, we got so caught up with chatting, I was running a little late to get here. I never took the time to turn on the radio." Brenda put water on to boil and got a tea bag from the cabinet. "What's going on?"

"I've been suspended from work for two weeks."

Brenda gasped. "What happened?"

Sam's phone rang, and she pulled it from her pocket. She signaled her mom that she needed to take the call. "Sam Holland."

"Lieutenant, this is Celeste Sweeny, Lorraine Sweeny's daughter."

"Yes, hello. What can I do for you?"

"The story on the news... They're saying you've been suspended by the department for two weeks."

"Yes, I have."

"What does that mean for my mother's case?"

"My team is actively working on the case, and they'll continue to do so in my absence."

"We want *you* on it. You're the best detective on the whole force, and everyone knows that."

Her words had tears stinging Sam's eyes. "That's so very

kind of you to say, but unfortunately, I'm not allowed to work on any cases during my suspension. The detectives on my team are outstanding, and I have every confidence they'll continue to do everything possible to find your mother's killer."

"This is so upsetting on top of everything else. I told my dad after you were here the other day that I felt better knowing you were on the case."

Sam winced. "Hopefully, I'll be back on the job soon. In the meantime, I want you and your family to think about joining our grief group at headquarters. We meet on the second Tuesday of the month, and everyone is welcome. Our members have taken great comfort in being able to talk to others who understand this journey."

"We'll get there. Eventually. We're still in the disbelief stage."

"I understand. It'll be there for you when you're ready, and I promise I'll never give up on finding your mother's killer. This is a temporary setback."

God, she hoped that was true.

"Thank you for your kindness. I appreciate you taking my call."

"Reach out any time."

"Thank you again."

"Take care of yourself and your family."

"I'm trying."

After they said their goodbyes, Sam closed her phone with a feeling of utter defeat. Those people were counting on her to get them answers, and she'd been taken off the job right when she was most needed. She didn't blame the chief for suspending her. She would've suspended herself if she were him. But the timing sucked. Not that there'd ever be a good time for a suspension.

"You're exceptionally good at your job, Sam."

She'd almost forgotten her mother was seated at the table, sipping her tea. "Thanks."

"It's what you were born to do, just like your father."

"That means a lot to me."

"You'll be back at it soon. Take this break as a moment to breathe and think about who might be trying to harm you and your career."

"I've been suspended for something I did on the job, Mom. I have only myself to blame. It's possible, though, that someone is pulling the strings on publicizing the issue in an effort to make the consequences worse."

"Why in the world would they be doing such a thing?"

"They hate me cuz they ain't me, or something like that. They hate the attention I get, the success I've had. They think the only reason I am where I am is because of my dad and his best friend. They hate me because I'm a woman doing a man's job, and they think they could do it better. One of them hates me because I caught him having an affair when he was supposed to be at a conference. He got demoted, and the mother of his six children divorced him. Apparently, that's my fault."

"That's outrageous."

"Yep, but it's nothing new. If I had to guess, several of them are in cahoots, hoping to bring me down and maybe Nick, too. I'm not sure what their ultimate goal is, but so far, they're succeeding."

"They won't succeed," Nick said when he came into the room and walked straight over to wrap his arms around her.

"I'll be downstairs to greet the kids," Brenda said as she left the room.

CHAPTER TWENTY-THREE

Sam held on tight to him, soaking in the comfort only he could provide.

"They will *not* win. Tell me you know that."

"I'm wavering after today."

"Nothing can defeat my strong, courageous, compassionate cop, especially a bunch of punk-ass men who'll never be half the detective or person you are."

"It's hot when you say things like punk-ass."

"Samantha, I'm being serious."

She pulled back so he could see her smile as she looked up at him. "So am I."

He kissed her softly and sweetly, giving her the tenderness she badly needed just then. "Where are you supposed to be right now?"

"Exactly where I am."

"That can't possibly be true."

"I cleared my afternoon when I heard you were coming home."

"Nick... You can't do that."

"I already did."

"You're giving them another reason to attack you by going silent right when this shit storm is hitting."

"I was hoping you might be able to make a statement in response to the stuff Hector Reese is saying."

"The chief has forbidden me to speak to the media or any member of my team for the next two weeks, but they're issuing a statement that I contributed to."

"So you're supposed to allow your reputation to be trashed without a single word from you? That's bullshit, babe. He needs to let you defend yourself."

"They're consulting with the lawyers because Reese's media tour also came with a lawsuit against me, Malone and the department. We'll see what they say after they've heard back from the department counsel."

"He can't prohibit you from speaking as first lady."

"That's a fine line, and we both know it."

"We have to do something."

"Back when you were first president, I stopped by Avery and Shelby's so I could ask her to be the social secretary in person. While I was there, Avery took me aside to tell me the Reese incident had come up during their investigation of the department."

"What did he say about it?"

"Just that it'd been mentioned. I asked if he thought it would turn into a big deal, and he said he didn't know yet but would warn me if he could. I'm not sure if he knew this was coming or not, but I wish I'd paid more attention to it at the time. Maybe I could've figured out where that was coming from and found a way to put a lid on it before it exploded."

"We were a little busy then. Don't be so hard on yourself."

"I was unprepared for what feels like a coordinated attack coming from inside my own house, assuming that's what this is and not Hector Reese finally getting around to filing a lawsuit." In light of current events, she believed it was far more likely an in-house hit job.

"Of course you were unprepared. You go there every day, work your ass off, try to do the right thing and have to deal with this bullshit because of a bunch of fucking jealous man babies."

"It's very sexy when you say things like 'fucking jealous man babies.'"

"I'm being serious."

"I know you are. That's why it's sexy."

"You're ridiculous."

"Ridiculously in love with you." She rested her head on his chest and took a few more minutes to soak up his special brand of comfort. "I told the chief I have the Christopher Nelson trial to prep for, which he said I could do, but that's another reminder of the many times people have come for us, trying to ruin us because they want what we have, or they're jealous or insecure or fucked-up and want someone to blame. We're so lucky to have everything we do, as well as the best security in the world, but on days like this, the downside is a lot."

"I'm sorry for my role in putting us where we are."

"You mean for putting us in the White House?"

Smiling, he said, "Yeah, that."

Hearing Scotty talking to his agents down the hall had them pulling apart to greet their son.

"Whoa," Scotty said, surprised to find them in the kitchen. "You're both here. What's wrong?"

"Nothing to worry about," Sam said. "A little dustup at work. We're handling it."

He eyed her warily. "Did you get in trouble?"

"Something like that."

"What'd you do?"

"Something I shouldn't have done two years ago that's come back to bite me in the ass."

"Is that the thing that's all over the news?"

"What did you see?"

"A thing about a guy named Hector talking shit about you."

Normally, she'd remind him about their swear jar, but this was no time for such concerns. "He's telling the truth. I roughed him up when he was in custody, and I deserve every bit of criticism I get about it."

"But why is it coming out now?"

"Possibly because someone I work with has decided they've had enough of me on the job, and they want to run me out."

"Have they succeeded?"

"For the next two weeks, anyway. We'll see after that."

"Two weeks. Damn. Are you okay?"

Sam reached out to him, and he moved into her embrace. "I'm much better now that I've seen you and Dad."

"Mostly me, though, right?"

Sam laughed. "Absolutely."

"Hey!" Nick said, making Scotty crack up.

"You're losing your touch, old man."

"I ain't losing nothing."

"Grammar, Dad. You're the president, for crying out loud."

As she held Scotty close, she finally exhaled, reminded that as long as she had them, she'd be fine no matter what happened in the outside world.

"I hate to break up this mother-son snuggle," Nick said, "but my team would like to issue a statement about the story of the moment. Would you be willing to help with that, Sam?"

Sam reluctantly released Scotty and smoothed her fingers over his dark hair. "I'm not allowed to speak publicly about it."

"What?" Scotty asked. "Why not?"

"The chief told me not to say anything."

"So you're supposed to just take an ass-kicking without fighting back?" Scotty asked, incredulous.

"Swear jar." Sam tried to make a stern face and apparently failed, because Scotty smiled. "And yes, that's what I've been ordered to do."

"He can't order you not to make a statement as first lady, can he?" Scotty asked.

"If it has to do with my work at the MPD, then yes, he can."
To Nick, she said, "I'm sorry. I know it's a huge distraction when
you have much bigger things to deal with."

"Nothing is more important to me than you are, and the
whole world knows that."

Scotty moaned. "Is there gonna be kissing and stuff?"

Nick zeroed in on Sam's lips. "Any second now."

"I'm outta here."

Smiling as Scotty headed for the door, Nick dropped a
lingering kiss on her lips and then hugged her. "It's so easy to
get rid of him."

"The very threat of kissing sends him running for his
life."

"Are we irreparably damaging him?"

"Nah, we're showing him how it should be."

"I hope he gets as lucky as we did."

"He will. He's an amazing guy. Any woman would be lucky
to have him."

"I'm trying to picture you being nice to the woman who
takes Scotty away from you. The words 'rusty steak knife' come
to mind."

"If she's not nice to him, I'll run her through with the
rustiest one I can find."

"Someone ought to warn the young women of the world to
watch out for the first lady. She's feral when it comes to her
son."

"Plural. *Sons.* I have three of them. Can you believe that?"

"I wish you could see the look of wonder on your face when
you say that. It's the sweetest thing ever."

"I love being a mom, and for the next two weeks, I get to be
one full time. And a full-time first lady, if you'll have me."

"Oh, I'll have you," he said with a dirty grin. "And P.S., that's
a great way to spin a devastating series of events."

"It's very upsetting, but not like it would've been before I
had you guys to come home to. You all make everything better

because I know that no matter what happens out there, I've got you and the kids waiting for me here."

"Works both ways, babe. We love having you as much as you love having us. I can't wait to come upstairs to you guys."

"It's important to count the blessings, especially when the shit is hitting the fan. My gut is telling me none of this is coincidental. Someone is out to get me."

"What's being done about that?"

"Avery is on it, which is another thing the chief is pissed about. I told him about Offenbach being obsessed with drones before I told the chief."

"Offenbach is obsessed with drones?"

"Yeah, I heard that on the QT."

"He's the one who was having the affair, right?"

"One and the same."

"Is this whole thing going to lead to him?"

"I'm starting to wonder, and that's what I told Avery."

"Is Joe right to be pissed?"

"I suppose, but I told him I was acting as the first lady when I passed that info on to the FBI. That didn't go over so well, as I directed a federal investigation at someone who works for him without giving him a heads-up first. I was just so shocked by what I'd heard about the drones that I didn't think. I just acted by telling Avery. But I hate feeling like I disappointed Joe with all he does for me."

"He'll get over it when he has a second to calm down and think it through."

"He was as mad as I've ever seen him."

"Because he was caught off guard, like everyone else was. Of course, that's what they wanted."

"I'm sure it was." Sam shook her head. "Imagine spending the limited time you have in this life trying to exact revenge on people you blame for screwing up your life and career when you did that all on your own."

"It's a sick way to live, and it gives me nightmares to think about people coming for you that way."

"I feel better knowing Avery is on it. If there's something to be found, he'll find it."

"I sure as hell hope so."

Gonzo called the squad into the conference room and closed the door when they were all there. He'd asked Dominguez and Carlucci to come in an hour early so they could be there for this meeting.

"What's going on, Sarge?" Detective Matt O'Brien asked. He'd been in the field with Green when Gonzo had told the others the news. "Where's the LT?"

"She's been suspended for two weeks over this uproar with the Hector Reese case."

"That's total bullshit," Detective Cameron Green said. "It happened two years ago, and it's only come to life now because someone is obviously trying to take her down."

"What's your theory?" Gonzo asked as he propped himself on the corner of the conference room table.

"Does anyone think it's a coincidence that someone pointed anonymous drones at the White House when she and everyone she loves would be fully exposed," Green said, "then shot at her on the street and resurrected a two-year-old scandal, all in the course of a few days?"

Captain Malone had come into the room while Green was speaking. "There's no way it's a coincidence."

"So why is she suspended?" Detective Neveah Charles asked.

"The chief had no choice but to suspend her as we look into the allegations raised by Reese in his lawsuit and in the media," Malone said.

"What's this got to do with our murders?" Cruz asked.

"I don't know yet," Green said, "but it's all related. Somehow."

"Lieutenant Archelotta called me," Gonzo said. "He thinks the abduction and assault of his new girlfriend could be related, too."

"I hear what you're all saying," Malone said. "But it still feels like a huge stretch to connect murders that happened when she was off duty and out of town to whatever the rest of this is."

"Think about it, Cap," Cruz said. "If you want to bring her back from wherever she is, kill three people in three days."

"That's true," Malone said.

"And we often follow the same routine with every case," Cruz said. "Check in with the victims' families, their places of business, their friends, etc. She likes to do that stuff personally, even when others have been there before her. It's not hard to predict what she'll do in pursuit of justice."

"That's what made her easy pickings on the street in Adams Morgan," Green said. "They knew she'd eventually go there to figure out if the abduction of Harlowe St. John was related."

"So someone lies in wait for days with the hope that she might show up there?" Malone asked. "That feels implausible to me."

"Unless they were following her, which isn't hard to do, even with all the Secret Service surrounding her," O'Brien said.

"Wouldn't the agents pick up on a tail?" Malone asked.

"I mean they're always vigilant, but they could've missed it," Gonzo said.

"The tail could've been way back," Charles said. "Far enough that they'd never pick it up but close enough to keep tabs on her whereabouts."

"What do we know about the bullet that hit Agent McFarland?" Gonzo asked.

"Let me make some calls on that," Malone said. "See what I can find out."

"We're going to proceed under the assumption that it's all related," Gonzo said.

"I caught a couple of Reese's interviews earlier," Carlucci said. "The cable shows are eating him up."

"Of course they are," Cruz said. "Which is exactly what these people wanted—for Sam to be on defense, defending her job and reputation."

O'Brien scrolled through his phone. "Lenore Worthington made a statement in support of Sam. 'I've known Officer Holland and later Lieutenant Holland for more than fifteen years, since my son, Calvin, was murdered, and while I can't comment on the specifics of what Mr. Reese is claiming, anyone who says she's racist doesn't know her at all. It's patently false and an egregious accusation toward someone who stridently seeks justice for all victims, regardless of race or any other factors.'"

"That'll mean a lot to Sam," Cruz said.

"Let's figure this shit out before they make it impossible for her to ever come back," Gonzo said. "Where are we with the warrant to dump Ramsey's phone?"

"He's fighting back," Malone said. "There's a hearing in the morning on it."

"What possible grounds could he have to fight back when he's facing numerous felony charges?" Cruz asked.

"That'll be my question at the hearing," Malone said. "I'm on that, and I'll let you know as soon as I have more info."

A knock on the door preceded Deputy Chief McBride coming in and looking upset. "I just heard from a reporter asking me whether Sam and her father covered up a murder and if I knew about it, too."

CHAPTER TWENTY-FOUR

"Come on," Gonzo said. "What the fuck is that about?"

Jeannie's expression was grim and maybe a bit guilty. "Remember when Skip was in the hospital with pneumonia?"

"What about it?" Malone asked.

"Because we thought he might die for a time there, Sam asked me and Tyrone to look into the one case from his career that remained open—the murder of Tyler Fitzgerald, the youngest son of Alice Fitzgerald." She was the widow of Steven Coyne, Skip's first partner, who was shot and killed on the job in a case that went unsolved until they closed Skip's case and tied the two shootings to the same people.

"I remember when you guys looked into that case," Malone said. "Nothing came of it, right?"

"It got messy. We found out Skip had sat on some crucial information that would've tied Tyler's older brother, Cameron, to the murder."

Malone's face went slack with shock. "*What?*"

Jeannie swallowed hard. "We found numerous irregularities in the original investigation, but because Skip's health was so precarious at that time, Tyrone and I told the lieutenant we hadn't come up with any new leads. We were thinking of him, and our goal was to protect his sterling reputation, especially if he died."

Jeannie crossed her arms over her pregnant belly and looked down at the floor. "We made the decision to keep this from her. We thought we were doing what was best for her and Skip under the circumstances. But then he recovered and later found out we'd reopened the case. He was furious and wanted all the info we'd uncovered. That's when she found out we'd lied to her. She suspended us for a week."

"And what did she do about the case?" Malone asked.

"Skip flipped out about it, and she did what he told her to, which was nothing. He protected Alice the way he had since Steven was murdered."

Malone stared at her, incredulous. "You're telling me that Skip Holland *knew* who killed that kid and buried it, and when Sam found out he'd done that, she *kept it buried*?"

Jeannie's expression was pained when she nodded.

"Motherfucker," Malone said. "Who else knows about this?"

"Only me and Tyrone, and he'd never breathe a word of it to anyone."

"Well, clearly, someone else found out about it, and now a reporter has it." Malone headed for the door. "This is just great." He slammed the door behind him as he left.

"What is this?" Jeannie asked, seeming devastated by the turn of events.

"I don't know," Gonzo said, "but let's get busy finding out before they ruin Sam and the rest of us, too."

JAKE MALONE WALKED toward the chief's office, avoiding several officers who wanted a word with him by raising his hand to say "not now" as he kept moving, fueled by outrage, disbelief and fear.

The fear had his full attention. Whoever was orchestrating this hit job against Sam could end up taking them all down in the process, which probably wouldn't break their hearts. If it was Ramsey, for instance, he'd be thrilled to see them all mired in scandal for the crime of doing their jobs.

He knocked on the chief's door and walked in, not waiting for an invitation.

Joe looked up at him and lifted his brows in inquiry. "What now?"

"Did you know that Skip covered up the fact that Alice Coyne's son Tyler was killed by his older brother Cameron?"

Joe stared at him, unblinking. "No, I didn't know that. How do you know?"

"A reporter called McBride, who knew because Sam had her reopen the case when Skip had pneumonia, wanting to get it settled for him if he was about to die. They found all sorts of irregularities but told Sam they'd learned nothing new in a misguided attempt to protect Skip's reputation. Then he recovered, found out about the new investigation and hit the roof because he'd told Sam before to leave that case alone."

"Oh my God."

"He demanded everything they'd found during the review, which was when Sam found out that Jeannie and Tyrone had lied to her about what they'd uncovered. She suspended them. And then she did what her father told her to and forgot about what her detectives had learned."

"No detective is perfect, but she usually plays by the rules. Now I'm wondering if that's not the case."

"There're almost always extenuating circumstances when someone like her behaves out of character. We need to find out more before we jump to conclusions."

"Yeah, you're right, but how in the hell does a reporter have this?"

"We have no idea. Tyrone is the only other person who knew, and McBride was adamant that he'd never tell anyone."

"I want every available officer working on this and only this. Any and all overtime is authorized."

"Yes, sir. We're operating on the theory that all of it—the four new murders, the kidnapping and assault of Archelotta's girlfriend, the drones, the shooting of Agent McFarland and the resurrection of the Reese and Fitzgerald cases—are somehow related to a coordinated attempt to take Sam down."

"I think that's a safe bet."

"It would help to have her input."

The chief shook his head. "We've announced that she's suspended pending an investigation into Reese's allegations."

"She did what he said she did."

"We know that, but the public doesn't need to know that yet. If we can find the people coordinating this attack, we can take the heat off her by arresting them."

"Will she be able to come back from this?"

"We'll make sure of it, but for right now, we're focused on figuring out who's doing this, and my bet is on Ramsey and Offenbach to start with. Put your focus there. I told her she couldn't talk to anyone here, but I'll lift that if you think her input will help."

"Got it."

"I want you to oversee this investigation personally, Jake. Get to the bottom of this as fast as you can."

"Yes, sir. We're on it."

"Hurry. We have a matter of days to save her career and possibly ours, too."

"Understood."

Jake left the chief's office and returned to the pit to see to his orders, determined to figure out who was trying to ruin Sam and why, before it was too late.

SAM ANSWERED the call from Jeannie McBride because Jeannie

was now one of her bosses. "Hey. I'm not allowed to talk to anyone from there."

"I know, but I wanted to give you a heads-up that a reporter called me. He asked about the Tyler Fitzgerald case."

Once again, shock hit her like she'd been electrocuted. Sam sat when her legs threatened to give out. "What did he say?"

"He said he was a reporter but wouldn't say from where, that he wanted to know what I'd found out about Tyler Fitzgerald's murder and why you never did anything with the information."

"Holy shit," Sam whispered. "How in the world would anyone know that? It was contained to you, me, Tyrone and my dad."

"Or so we thought."

"Someone is out to ruin me."

"That's how it appears to us, as well. The chief has put Malone in charge, and we're focused fully on all the associated cases. He's told us we're allowed to speak to you if it will aid the investigation."

"Well, it's a relief that he's giving it the highest priority."

"The last thing any of us wants is to see your career destroyed, especially by people who blame you for their own fuck-ups."

"Are you thinking it's Ramsey and Offenbach?"

"We've been told to focus there first."

"Why in the world would Ramsey team up with the guy who fired the shot that killed his son?"

"If I had to guess," Jeannie said, "it's because in his twisted mind, he doesn't blame Offenbach for following an order that came from you via Malone. To Ramsey, Offenbach becomes a means to an end if it results in your downfall."

"So sick and twisted, no matter how you look at it. I get why Ramsey would bother to go to the trouble, but explain Offenbach to me. He's in enough trouble as it is and still has six kids to support. Why would he risk his career and pension over petty revenge?"

"We don't know for sure that he's involved."

"I'm not supposed to tell anyone else this, but I have it on good authority that Offenbach is obsessed with drones. I've already reported it to the chief and Agent Hill."

Jeannie's gasp was audible. "That's unreal, Sam. One of our own colleagues... Does he have any idea what he could be charged with if they trace that back to him? They're treating it as a presidential assassination attempt."

"I know. Can't imagine what he was thinking, if it was him."

"I've got to run. Malone has called an all-hands meeting to discuss the various cases and how they might be related."

"Keep me in the loop if you can."

"I will, and I'm sorry this is happening to you."

"Thanks. I am, too."

"Hang in there, and I'll be back to you as soon as I know anything."

"You're the best, Deputy Chief."

"I'm only the deputy chief because of you, and I'll do everything in my power to figure this out for you. Count on that."

"Love you."

"Love you right back."

Sam closed her phone, smiling at the fierce words from her friend. She and Jeannie had been through hell together, and knowing she had Sam's back made her feel a thousand times better, as did the news that Malone would lead the investigation into the various cases that might or might not be related.

They were.

Sam had no doubt whatsoever about that or who was most likely behind it.

She just hoped her colleagues could prove it before her

career went up in smoke, along with her reputation and everything she'd worked so hard to achieve.

LATER THAT NIGHT, after the kids were in bed and Nick was in his office working on his nightly correspondence and preparations for the morning, Sam eyed the file Jesse Best had given her. Maybe it would help to dive into something new to get her mind off how her career was in major jeopardy while there wasn't a damned thing she could do about it.

When she opened the file, the first thing she saw was a photo of a beautiful blonde girl who reminded her a bit of Aubrey. And just that quickly, Sam was invested.

Jesse had included a meticulous point-by-point narrative of his investigation, from the day his sister was taken through to the present.

On July twelfth, twenty-six years prior, seven-year-old Jordan Best had been playing alone in the yard of their grandparents' Morgantown, West Virginia, backyard when she went missing. No one knew how long she'd been gone when her absence was noticed by her grandmother, who came out to tell her it was time to come inside.

Eleven-year-old Jesse had been playing with a neighborhood friend at the time and had returned to a search in progress.

At the time, their maternal grandparents had custody of Jesse and Jordan after both parents had been deemed unfit by the courts due to ongoing drug dependency. Sam learned that his parents were in and out of rehab and jail for most of Jesse's childhood, and he'd had irregular contact with them throughout his life.

His grandfather had been employed as a mechanic at a local car dealership, while his grandmother was a homemaker. In addition to Jesse's mother, who was their third child, his grandparents had four other adult children who lived nearby with their families. He had seven first cousins around his age who were regular visitors to the grandparents' home, where money was always in short supply.

Local and state police were brought in to search for Jordan, along with dogs trained to find missing people. Jesse's most vivid memory from the first hours were the dogs sniffing Jordan's precious stuffed bear to get her scent.

That heartbreaking detail stood out to Sam as the sort of thing no one would ever forget.

Hours stretched into days, which became weeks and months with no leads and no sign of Jordan, even with the FBI involved.

Jesse had pleaded with his grandparents to figure out where his parents were at the time of Jordan's disappearance, but they refused to pursue that avenue because they didn't want them involved.

"The last thing we need is them coming in here stoned out of their minds and making everything worse than it already is," his grandfather had said.

"But what if they took her?" Jesse had asked.

"They're not capable of something like this, and I don't want to hear another word about involving them."

And with that, the conversation had been shut down.

Jesse had gone around his grandparents by contacting local authorities and asking them to investigate the whereabouts of his and Jordan's parents at the time of her disappearance. He was told by a local sheriff that they'd spoken to both parents and had learned they had alibis for the time of her disappearance, thus shutting down that avenue.

I never believed they talked to our parents at the time of the initial investigation, Jesse had written. *Finding them would've taken days or even weeks, and it felt like a brush-off. I've since tracked down both my parents and attempted to determine their whereabouts at the time of the disappearance but haven't been able to confirm their alleged alibis. Both claimed to have no knowledge of what happened to Jordan.*

I don't believe them. Even if they know where she is, they'd have no reason to tell me, especially since I'm now a federal agent and could arrest them for withholding evidence in an ongoing investigation.

Other people I've investigated include some friends of my grandfather's, who were always around before Jordan disappeared and suddenly stopped hanging out afterward.

He'd made a list of the men, including their criminal records, which had been updated over the years as new crimes were added to drug dealing as well as weapons and domestic abuse charges.

I've done in-depth surveillance on all of them and uncovered no sign of a young woman in their midst who'd now be thirty-two years old.

Jesse had included time-lapse photos of what Jordan might've looked like at various points in the years since she went missing.

"What a fucking nightmare," Sam muttered as she absorbed the details of the case.

"What is?" Nick asked as he came up behind the sofa to massage shoulders that'd gone tight with tension as she read the disturbing narrative.

"My colleague, U.S. Marshal Jesse Best, has asked me to look at a cold case involving his younger sister, who went missing when she was seven and he was eleven." She showed him the photo of Jordan.

"Wow, she looks a little like Aubrey."

"I thought the same thing."

He came around to sit next to Sam. "What a heartbreaking thing."

"Jesse finds people for a living but has never been able to find his baby sister. I can't imagine how heavily that must weigh on him."

"You're going to help him carry that load, aren't you?"

"How can I not after reading all this?"

"You've got a lot on your plate as it is, babe. Should you take on more?"

"I'll do what I can to help him, in between everything else. Are you done for the evening?"

"Not quite yet. I came out for a little bourbon to fuel me to the finish line."

"In that case, I'm going to call Jesse to ask some questions."

Nick kissed her and got up. "I've got another hour or so, and then I'll meet you in bed."

"It's a date." Sam reached for her phone and called Jesse.

He took the call on the first ring. "Hey, I was just thinking about you. What a fucking shit storm today, huh?"

"Yep, and now I'm suspended for two weeks as a result."

"Come on. No way."

"The good news is I have time to read through the file you gave me, and let me just say, my God, Jesse. What a nightmare this has been for you."

"You don't know the half of it."

"What do you mean?"

"All along, I've felt that people close to me knew more than they were saying. I was just a kid when it first happened, so what right did I have to know every development? Stuff was definitely kept from me, and it haunts me to think the truth might've been staring me in the face, and I didn't recognize it."

"You were eleven, Jesse. You need to give yourself some grace."

"Trust me, that's a work in progress."

"I'm sure it is. I have a few questions. Do you have time now?"

"Absolutely."

CHAPTER TWENTY-FIVE

"I wondered about your mother's siblings and what they've had to say about it over the years. Where were they that night?"

"They were interviewed at the time and provided alibis that checked out."

"Including their spouses?"

"As far as I know. The reporting by the local police was a little spotty, as they were somewhat overwhelmed by such a huge case."

"Are you in touch with your aunts and uncles?"

"Not so much anymore. I rarely get back to Morgantown since both my grandparents have passed."

"How long ago did they die?"

"My grandmother about four years ago and my grandfather last year."

"I'm sorry for your losses. That must've been tough since they raised you."

"Are we being honest here?"

"Always."

"I appreciated them taking us in and keeping us fed and

clothed, but I've always blamed them for what happened to Jordan."

"How come?"

"Why was a seven-year-old playing outside with no one watching her? When I was home, I always went out with her and kept an eye on her. It was rare for me to hang out at someone else's house because I didn't like to leave her, and the one time I wasn't there, someone snatched her? I was outraged with them, and they knew it."

"Why were you at someone else's home that day?"

"My cousin Bryce had gotten an ATV and invited me to come check it out. That was hard to say no to. I told Jordan I'd be back in an hour, and we could go outside when I got back, but an hour became two, and when I came home, she was gone, and my grandmother had just realized it. That's why we don't know the exact time of her disappearance. I couldn't believe she'd let Jordan go out alone. I still can't believe it to this day."

"Was your neighborhood unsafe?"

"It could be sketchy at times, with people living around us that we didn't know all that well. Also, I saw the way men looked at Jordan, even when she was that young. They were dazzled by her, which was revolting to me. Six months before she went missing, I got into it with a guy at a restaurant who kept staring at her. I got in his face and told him she was *six* and to fuck off. My grandparents were angry with me for making a scene, but I didn't care. The guy was a creep."

"Did you investigate him?"

"I did. He died two months after our confrontation. I wasn't unhappy to hear that."

"Have you gone back to look for sexual offenders in your area at that time?"

"All dead ends."

"Have you thought about engaging the press? You could

publicize the age-progressed photo and tell your story to one of the true-crime shows or podcasts."

"That's something I haven't considered. Due to the nature of my job, I don't court publicity."

"I get that, but at this point, it couldn't hurt anything. Let me ask my partner, Freddie Cruz, about the podcasts. He's a fan of them and would know which ones would work best."

"I appreciate the help and the brainstorming."

"I wish there was more I could do to help."

"This was more than enough, and it's got me fired up again, which I needed."

"I'll let you know what Freddie says about the podcasts."

"Thanks again, Sam. I really appreciate it."

"Any time."

As Jesse ended the call he'd said he had to take, she watched as he plugged his phone into the bedside charger and stretched out next to her. As his girlfriend/fuck buddy/colleague/sorta friend, Memphis Rose Costello wanted to ask about the call but couldn't bear to witness the devastation that always overtook him when he talked about his missing sister.

She'd learned to tread carefully on that subject. Raised in Memphis by her grandmother and mother to be a strong, competent woman who didn't need a man, Memphis Rose had made it her mission not to become attached to the perpetually out-of-reach Jesse Best.

That mission had been an abject failure.

Her grandmother, the world's biggest Elvis fan, had cleaned Graceland for thirty years, and Memphis was born in the same hospital as Lisa Marie Presley, a point of pride for her mother and grandmother. The two strongest women she knew would be appalled by what she was putting up with in her "relationship" with Jesse if they knew about it, which they didn't.

He'd insisted on the secrecy because technically, they shouldn't be fraternizing outside of work since he was her boss. To cope with the restrictions, she'd made some rules for herself: never spend the night, never ask questions about where "this" was going and never let on that she loved him or that she hurt for him.

That last part was getting tougher all the time as she witnessed his torment over the ongoing cold case. She wanted to ask who'd called and who was helping him, but she'd learned not to stick her nose into places it wasn't welcome. Sometimes she wondered if she was nothing more than a warm body at the end of every hideous day on the job.

There would come a time when that wouldn't be enough for her. If she was being honest, that time had come and gone about two years ago. And yet, here she was, still keeping his bed warm while wondering if anything—or anyone—could permeate the barbed-wire fence he kept around his heart.

When it became clear that he had no plans to further engage with her that evening, she started to get up in deference to rule number one: never spend the night.

"Don't go."

She froze because he'd never said those words to her before. Looking over her shoulder at him, she tried to gauge his mood, but as usual, his face gave nothing away. "Why?"

"Does there need to be a reason?"

Memphis Rose swallowed hard against the lump that had appeared in her throat out of nowhere. Two little words from him invoked so many emotions in her, too many to process while she was trying to stay cool in front of him. If he had any idea how she really felt, this would be over so fast, her head would spin.

Jesse Best didn't do love. He didn't do emotional involvement. For crying out loud, he barely did sentences. He'd said more to the person on the phone than he'd said to her, collectively, in all the time she'd known him.

"I don't think I should."

She started to get up, but his hand on her shoulder stopped her.

"Please stay."

When her eyes filled with tears, she closed them, hoping that would keep the tears from spilling over and giving away her secrets. It didn't work.

"We're leaving in the morning for Shenandoah to assist the FBI." He kissed her bare shoulder. "We could leave from here and drive down together."

Wow. Two whole sentences in a row. That had to be a record. She pulled free of him and got up to find her clothes, blinded by tears that made it hard to see anything in the dimly lit room.

All at once, he was there, with his arms around her from behind and his forehead on her shoulder. "Please."

She stiffened out of sheer self-preservation.

Then he dropped the bomb. "I need you."

Memphis Rose crumpled for a second before she found her inner source of strength, although where it was coming from after he said that was anyone's guess. Did he need *her*, or would any warm body do after that phone call reopened the wound on his soul? "I have to go, Jesse. Please let me."

He held on for another long, breathless moment before he released her.

As she got dressed, she told herself he wouldn't remember in the morning that he'd needed her in the dark of night. In the morning, it would be back to business as usual, with him grunting and calling it communication, with her wondering where she stood and what it all meant, and him going on, oblivious to her until they were back in his bed, when the cycle would begin again.

Since she was the only one aware of this cycle, it was up to her to control her involvement in it.

Getting dressed had never been more of a challenge than it

was with hands that didn't want to follow the directions she was giving them. Buttons, clasps, zippers...

She grabbed her phone off the bedside table and left the room without giving him so much as a glance.

When she was in her car, driving back to her place while fighting to see through her tears, she acknowledged this situation was unsustainable. It had been from the start. Maybe it was time to request a transfer. Her mom and grandmother were always after her to come home to Memphis. That would be a step down, careerwise, from the assignment in DC, but she needed to decide which was more important—her career or her sanity.

She wiped the tears off her face, furious with herself for the emotional reaction to three simple words.

I need you.

I need you.

How long would it take for those words to stop echoing through her overcommitted heart and soul?

Probably forever.

FREDDIE CRUZ HAD RARELY BEEN angrier than he was watching the playback of the Hector Reese interviews that'd aired earlier in the day on cable news. Hector had hit all the major networks with his tale of how the first lady cop had beaten him when he was in custody.

Freddie, who'd been shot by Hector's brother, Clarence, when he'd returned to the scene of one of the worst crimes any of them had ever worked, had little sympathy for Hector. After all, Hector had enabled his brother's efforts to run from the police after he murdered his wife and children with a baseball bat—and then shot Freddie.

He still had nightmares about the murdered baby in the crib. Shuddering, Freddie quickly pushed that thought to the back of his mind, locked away with all the other horrors he'd witnessed on the job.

In addition to that, a reporter had called Jeannie McBride to ask about the Fitzgerald investigation and whether Sam—and her father—had failed to charge Cameron Fitzgerald with murdering his younger brother.

Though his tour was over, and he was free to leave work, Freddie couldn't go home when his best friend was under attack. After texting his wife, Elin, that he'd be home late, he went to find Captain Malone, who was on the phone in his office. He waved Freddie in.

He shut the door and took a seat, trying to remain calm as his entire body vibrated with the kind of tension that reminded him of the days that followed Skip Holland's death. They'd reopened the investigation into his shooting, and when the leads had begun to point to people under their own roof holding on to facts that would've closed the case years earlier, the fury had been palpable.

Thinking about that case had brought him to Malone, who was still on the phone and seemed annoyed by whomever he was speaking to. He rolled his eyes and made circular motions with his hand. "Yes, I hear you. I'll take care of it. I've got to run." He put down the receiver of his desk phone. "Some people like to hear themselves talk."

"I've been thinking about who else might've known about what Skip did for Alice Fitzgerald, and I keep coming back to one person."

"Who?"

"Conklin."

Malone stared at him for a long moment and then stood so abruptly, he startled Freddie. "Come with me."

"Where?"

"To ask him."

Holy shit. "Okay."

Malone moved as fast as Freddie had ever seen him go as

they made their way to the main entrance and outside into the cool spring evening. Neither of them said a word as Malone drove them over the 14th Street Bridge to Conklin's Northern Virginia home.

On the way, Freddie thought about how Sam hated to leave the District for any reason, especially to see the disgraced former officer who'd pretended to be a friend to her father while sitting on information that would've solved his case years earlier.

Would Freddie ever spend another day pounding the pavement with her, bickering like siblings, laughing and sharing the good, the bad and the ugly? The thought of her being forced out of the job she loved by people who were jealous of her success or threatened by her fame or God only knew what else was unfathomable to him.

"How're we playing it?" Freddie asked the captain after an interminable silence.

"I'm going to come right out and ask him if he's been telling tales out of school, and if he has, I'm going to arrest him. He can await trial in lockup rather than in the comfort of his own home."

"Never sat right with me that he wasn't locked up from the first second we learned what he'd done."

"Same, but he has rights, you see."

Malone's words dripped with sarcasm. As far as he and Freddie and many others were concerned, a man who'd pretend to serve the department as deputy chief while sitting on information that could've solved his so-called friend's attempted murder years earlier shouldn't have any rights.

"Cap."

"Yeah?"

"Um, you might want to, you know, take a breath before you go in there hot, so you don't, like, kill him or something." As a detective, he wasn't used to giving a captain advice, but in this case, he felt it was warranted.

Malone tightened his grip on the wheel as his cheek pulsed with tension. "Thank you for the concern. You're probably right that I might wring his neck if he's involved in this."

"Don't do that. Sir."

"Don't let me, okay?"

"I won't, sir."

"Stop calling me sir, for fuck's sake, Cruz."

At any other time, Freddie would've laughed. Nothing about this was funny, however.

Malone pulled into the parking lot and parked in a visitor space. He was out of the car and headed for the front door before Freddie got his seat belt off.

He ran after the captain, determined to keep his promise to not let him kill Conklin. Although he certainly understood the desire. Freddie had never had violent thoughts like the ones he'd had toward Conklin since learning of his culpability in Skip's shooting. After having a front-row seat to Sam's torturous efforts to get answers for her dad, their family and the department, knowing that Conklin could've solved the case the whole time had been hard to swallow.

Malone banged on the door with a closed fist.

"Haven't seen him around in a while," the woman next door said as she came out of her townhouse. "Not sure if he still lives there."

"Contact the parole office," Malone said to Freddie. "See if he's moved."

Freddie wasn't sure who Conklin's parole officer was, so he called Brendan Sullivan, an officer he and Sam worked with frequently. He usually took their calls, even after hours.

"Hey, Cruz, what's up?"

"Wondering if you can help me find out if Paul Conklin has moved?"

"Give me one second to boot up my laptop. I just got home."

"Thanks so much for the after-hours help."

"No problem. How's Holland? I saw the shit on the news today. Feels like a smear job, if you ask me."

"That's how we're viewing it, too."

"I don't see any updates to his residency." Sullivan rattled off the address where they currently were. "That's what we have on record."

"Thanks, man. Appreciate it."

"Any time."

"No change of residency reported to parole," Freddie told Malone.

He'd no sooner said the words than a sound from inside had them reaching for their weapons.

CHAPTER TWENTY-SIX

"What do you want?" Conklin called.

"Open the fucking door," Malone said. "Right now, or I'll kick it in."

The click of locks disengaging preceded the door opening to a man Freddie wouldn't have recognized as Conklin if he'd seen him somewhere else. He'd aged ten years and gained more than twenty pounds, if not more. In addition, he hadn't shaved or combed his hair in days.

"Again, what do you want?"

"What've you done?" Malone asked.

"What're you talking about?"

"You know exactly what I mean. Who've you been running your mouth to?"

"I haven't talked to anyone in weeks."

"If I dump your phone, will I find out that you're still a fucking liar?"

Conklin's eyes shifted ever so slightly, but Malone saw it.

"You fucking rat! *What've you done?*"

"I needed the money, Jake."

Freddie's stomach dropped to his feet.

Malone moved lightning-fast and had Conklin cuffed, the

cell phone out of his pants pocket, and was hauling him out of the house before Freddie had a second to catch up.

"*What the fuck?*" Conklin shouted. "You can't just arrest me."

"Wanna bet? You're under arrest for aiding and abetting a crime. That charge ought to be familiar to you." As Malone marched Conklin to the SUV, he recited his Miranda rights before stuffing him into the back seat and slamming the door.

"Go back and make sure the door is locked so he can't blame us if the place gets tossed."

Freddie jogged to the stairs, took them two at a time and pulled the door closed, testing the door lock to make sure. Then he returned to the SUV. "All set."

"Thanks." As they drove toward the District, Malone radiated with fury. "You know what never ceases to amaze me, Cruz?"

"What's that, Cap?"

"How people never fucking learn. They can be run out of an organization in total disgrace and still manage to make it worse. Remarkable, isn't it?"

"Truly. And disgusting."

"That, too."

A gagging sound from the back seat had Freddie spinning around and Malone looking for a place to pull over.

"He's choking, Cap!"

Malone brought the SUV to a skidding stop by the side of the road and jumped out.

Freddie got out of the passenger seat and opened the back door to find Conklin foaming at the mouth, his eyes bugging and his lips already turning blue.

"Motherfucker," Malone said. "He took something."

"When? He was cuffed!"

"Before he answered the goddamned door."

"Oh... Crap. Now what?"

"Now we drop his useless ass at the hospital so they can

declare him dead and then dump his phone to find out who paid him to tell tales out of school."

SAM WAS SITTING up in bed, sipping a glass of wine as she tried to decompress from the events of the day. After dinner earlier with Nick, the kids and her mom, her spirits were much better than they'd been when she got home. But she was still reeling from the hits she hadn't seen coming, hits that could no longer be treated as anything other than a coordinated, deadly smear campaign.

If they'd killed, attacked and assaulted innocent people in an effort to get at her, how would she ever live with that? Harlowe and the other victims' families were counting on her to get answers for them. What would they think if *she* was the cause of their agony?

The thought of that was just too big for her to process.

Her phone rang with a call from Freddie that she took because he was her best friend, and she needed him. "Hey."

"Sam, you're not going to believe what happened."

As he relayed the evening's events, Sam listened in stunned disbelief. "He said he needed the money? Those exact words."

"Yes. Exactly that."

"So someone paid him for dirt on me. My dad must've confided in him about how he'd protected Alice from further heartache by letting Cameron go into the military rather than sending him to jail. Maybe he even told him that I'd reopened the case and how he'd had to shut it down again. And now Conklin's dead. That fucking coward."

"That's what everyone here is saying, too. I'm so sorry to have to tell you this. As if he hasn't already hurt you and your family enough."

"I don't even know what to say." Her phone beeped with another call from the chief. "Hey, Farnsworth is calling. I'll call you back."

"Okay."

Sam took the call from the chief. "Hey."

"Have you heard about Conklin?"

"Yeah, just now."

"Sam, I'm so sorry. That he could've been involved in something like this after what he's already done... I lack the words to properly convey my outrage."

"It's okay. Nothing surprises me anymore. Do you believe me now that a coordinated effort is underway with a goal of ruining my career and reputation?"

"I do. Your suspension is lifted as of tomorrow morning. Come back to work and help us nail these sons of bitches."

"This doesn't change the fact that what Reese is saying about what I did is true."

"We'll deal with that later. For now, our priority is putting a case together that'll take these guys down. Avery Hill will be here at zero eight hundred. I'd like you and your team in that meeting."

"We'll be there. Thank you, sir."

"Sam..."

"I know, Uncle Joe. I know. I'll see you in the morning."

"See you then."

It broke her heart to hear him upset over something having to do with her. If she had her way, she'd be the last one on the force to cause trouble for him. Not that she was the one causing the trouble, but she was the subject of it.

She called Freddie back.

"What'd he say?"

"My suspension is lifted, and he wants us in an eight o'clock meeting with Hill. Will you text the others and tell them I want everyone there, including Carlucci and Dominguez?"

"Will do. I'm so glad the suspension is lifted."

"Me, too. But I'm not out of the woods over Reese. It's just been postponed."

"By the time we blow the lid off whatever this is, I have a feeling that no one will be talking about Hector Reese."

SAM WAS DOZING FITFULLY when Nick got into bed and curled up to her, putting his arm around her. She opened her eyes to look at the clock and saw that it was after three a.m. "What're you doing up so late?"

"Going over the briefing books for tomorrow."

"Let me turn over."

Nick raised his arm to give her room to move.

"Hi."

He kissed her. "Hi there. Sorry I woke you up."

"I'm not sorry."

"You will be in four short hours when we have to get the kids up."

She slid her leg between his and pulled him in closer with a hand on his backside.

"What is happening?"

"I just wanted you closer."

"You know I'll never object to that."

"Guess what?"

"What?"

"My suspension was lifted." Sam told him about what'd happened with Conklin and the subsequent call from the chief. "He took a fatal dose of something the minute he realized Malone and Cruz were at his door because he knew why they'd come."

"What a fucking pussy-ass bitch."

"That's quite a mouthful, Mr. President."

"It's true."

"Yes, it is. He was always a spineless coward. We just didn't know it until after my dad died."

"And he basically confessed to selling you out to someone for money."

"He did."

"Good thing he's already dead, or I might be asking to borrow your rusty steak knife."

"My hero."

"It drives me nuts that these impotent men are always coming for my wife, who's smarter, quicker, more successful and everything they'll never be but always think they could be."

"That about sums it up. It's very sexy to me when you call my enemies 'fucking pussy-ass bitches' and threaten them with violence."

"I'm dead serious, Samantha. I'd love nothing more than to stab the lot of them through the heart with the rustiest steak knife I can find. The thought of one of them taking you from me is unbearable."

"I know, love, but I'm not going anywhere. Whatever they're up to, they won't win. They never do."

"Sometimes they do."

"They haven't yet, and the good news is we're zeroing in on who might be behind all this. Let's change the subject so we can sleep."

"What should we talk about?"

Sam reached between them to cup him. "How about my favorite subject? The birds and the bees."

He sniffed out a laugh. "Only you can make me laugh when I'm primed to do violence."

She'd stroked him until he was hard and throbbing against the palm of her hand. "How about we put love before violence?"

"I'm always up for love with you."

"You're definitely up."

His lips connected with hers in a hot, sexy kiss that had her ready for more in about two seconds flat, or maybe she'd been ready since the minute he cuddled up to her.

"I love so many things about this life, but you..." He bent

his head to kiss her neck. "You're the one who makes it all happen."

"*We* make it happen. Together."

He shifted so he was on top of her.

Sam wrapped her arms and legs around him, holding him as close as she could get him.

"You've got me totally trapped in your web. Nowhere else I want to be."

"Likewise, my love."

He teased her, pressing his hard cock against her before retreating, and then doing it again and again until she was on the verge of begging. And then he gave her everything in one deep stroke that made her come so hard, she saw stars.

"Holy shit, babe," he gasped. "You almost ended me before we even got started."

"That's your fault," she said when she could speak again.

"How was it my fault?"

"You know what you did, and I loved it."

When he pushed deep inside her, she held him there by tightening her legs around him.

"Say that whole pussy-ass thing again," she whispered.

With his lips against her ear, he said, "The people who want to harm you are fucking pussy-ass bitches."

Sam came again, taking him with her this time.

He landed on top of her, panting and laughing. "Are you for real? *That* does it for you?"

"You do it for me. Your dirty talk is just the frosting on top."

"I'll have to remember that for next time."

"I'm here for my respectable president being a dirty-mouthed bad boy in bed."

"Good to know. I've got more where that came from."

"Bring it on, Mr. President."

CHAPTER TWENTY-SEVEN

Nick was right. She hadn't had enough sleep, but she wouldn't trade more sleep for the middle-of-the-night lovemaking with him. He was always worth the sacrifices, especially when he whispered dirty words in her ear and made her explode like a firecracker.

"What're you smiling about, Mom?" Scotty asked in a grumpy tone as he sipped the one cup of coffee they allowed him these days, because "a man" needed his caffeine to survive eighth-grade algebra.

"Nothing I can tell you."

"Why are you thinking about *that* stuff when there're children present?"

"I'm not allowed to even think about it? What the heck kind of rules are you making, anyway?"

"The kind that will allow us to raise halfway decent children in this house."

Sam snorted out a laugh. "Our decent children will have the example of a very loving marriage to carry with them into adulthood."

"You have to put it that way—'a very loving marriage.'" His imitation of her was spot-on, which cracked her up.

Alden and Aubrey came into the kitchen, dragging backpacks behind them. They'd managed to dress on their own, but Sam made a few adjustments to collars and buttons.

"How'd we do?" Alden asked.

"Not too bad."

"I told Nick we're old enough to dress ourselves," Alden said.

"Did you now?"

"Uh-huh. We're not babies anymore."

"No, you aren't. I made you egg sandwiches today."

"My favorite," Aubrey said as she took a seat at the table.

"I thought pancakes were your favorite," Sam said as she put plates in front of them that also included pineapple and blueberries.

"They're my *weekend* favorite."

"Oh, I see," Sam said, amused by her as always.

While they ate, Sam sipped her coffee and chatted with them about everything and nothing. She didn't care what they talked about, it was always entertaining and often comical. Thankfully, Aubrey didn't get into the recent chicken-and-egg conversation again while she ate.

"I got invited to a sleepover at Jonah's house this weekend," Scotty said. "Is that something I'm allowed to do?"

Her first impulse was to say no way because she didn't want him anywhere but with them, but she knew better than to say that. "Do we know Jonah's parents?"

"Yeah, you met them at the rink. I think their names are Denise and Mike."

"Can you get his mom's number for me, and then I'll talk to Debra and see what we can do."

"Okay. I'd really like to go."

"If we can make it happen, we will."

"Thank you."

"I'm sorry everything is a hassle."

"It's fine. There are more perks than hassles. We have our own movie theater, for crying out loud."

"This is true. Any time you want to have your friends here, you can, you know. It's easier for them to come here."

"I know, but sometimes they want to do things at their houses, too."

"I understand."

"Dad said you guys wanted to talk to me later about high school. What's up with that?"

"Nothing much. The Secret Service is starting to prepare for the transition, and they had a few questions."

"Oh, okay. As long as they aren't wanting me to go somewhere other than Eastern."

Sam tried to school her expression and must have failed, because he pounced immediately.

His brown eyes went wide. "Is that it?"

"We shut it down. Don't worry."

He gave her a wary look. "Are you sure?"

"Positive. We know exactly what you want and acted accordingly. Don't spend your day worrying about that. We'll fill you in later." Sam hugged him tightly and kissed the top of his head.

"You're sure there's nothing to worry about?"

"I'm positive. We were very clear with them."

"Thank you for that."

"Anything for you, kid. Get me that number for Jonah's mom, okay?"

"Okay."

"Love you."

"Love you, too."

Debra came to collect him, and off they went to another day of middle school.

Sam couldn't believe he'd start high school in September. They'd have only six years in total at home together, which wasn't anywhere near enough for her. She sent the twins to brush their teeth and wash their faces while she put lunch boxes in backpacks.

She met them in the hallway and helped them into their spring jackets, hooking the backpacks over their right shoulders. "You want the other strap, too?"

"That's not cool, Sam," Alden told her. "None of the kids wear both straps."

"Oh well, my bad."

Aubrey giggled. "It's okay, Sam. That's why you have us. To keep you cool."

Sam laughed as she realized she needed to start writing this stuff down because she never wanted to forget any of it.

She sent them off with hugs and kisses and love and wishes for a great day, and then she bolted into her room to unlock the bedside table where she kept her weapon and cuffs. After brushing her teeth and running a brush through her hair, she was headed down the stairs to meet Vernon and Q five minutes later.

"Let me ask you something," she said when they were on the way to HQ.

"What's up?" Vernon asked.

"Scotty wants to go to a sleepover at a friend's house this weekend. What's the feeling on that?"

"The higher-ups won't be thrilled about it," Vernon said. "We'd have to vet the parents, the family, the house... And we'd want at least one agent inside with him."

"I was afraid you might say that."

"Can he invite his friends to the White House?"

"I suggested that, but he said sometimes his friends want to host at their houses, which is a fair point."

"Yes, it is, and we've had meetings about how things will get more complicated for his detail as he gets into high school."

"There're actual meetings about that?"

"Yep."

"We have meetings about *everything*," Q added. "Meetings on top of meetings."

"When do you have time for meetings when you're with me all day?"

"A lot of them are at zero six hundred," Q said. "We meet every morning to go over the schedule for the day, to plan for backup as needed and to make sure everyone knows what everyone else is doing. Except for your detail, ma'am. They never know what you're doing on any given day."

Sam laughed. "I like to keep them guessing." She took a call from Freddie. "Morning. I'll be there in five."

"Thought you'd want to know we have a witness to the murder of Nate Andrews."

She sat up straighter when she heard that. "What'd they see?"

"The witness left the gym a minute or so after Nate and was walking about a block behind him. According to what he told Carlucci, he saw a white Nissan Altima with District plates pull up near where Nate was walking. A guy got out of the car, hit Nate and then took off. He estimates the whole thing happened in about ten seconds, start to finish."

"What did he do after the car drove away?"

"He called 911 and then took off in case they came back. He wasn't there when our people arrived on the scene."

"By all accounts, this occurred on a dark stretch of sidewalk, but the witness could ID the make and model of the car as well as the District plates?"

"He was adamant about those details."

"This is great info. A white sedan was seen on the video of Harlowe St. John's abduction, too. We need to track down every white Altima with District plates."

"Cameron is on that now, and we've put out a BOLO for Patrol to keep an eye out for the make and model."

"Good job. Let's get this meeting done so we can get to work."

. . .

CHIEF FARNSWORTH STOOD at the front of the room with Captain Malone and Agent Hill.

As Sam took a seat at the table, she noted that Avery looked exhausted, as if he hadn't slept in days. She hoped he wasn't pushing himself too hard when he was still recovering from being shot.

"Agent Hill is here to brief us on the federal response to Monday's drone incident involving the White House, as well as the shooting of one of Lieutenant Holland's Secret Service agents. Agent Hill?"

"Thanks, Chief. My team has been working around the clock since Monday to determine the origin of the drones that were dispatched into the National Capital Region's airspace during the Easter Egg Roll at the White House. We've brought in a bevy of experts on drones, and they've determined the devices were created on a 3D printer and outfitted with homemade weapons. All this to say we still don't know who sent them, but we're working on several promising leads and hope to have more information later today. I understand you're working with a theory that this, the shooting of Lieutenant Holland's agent and several recent homicides might be related? I'd like to hear more about that."

"Detective Cruz," Sam said, "would you please brief Agent Hill on what we have so far?"

"Yes, ma'am."

She enjoyed catching him off guard but also loved giving him opportunities to shine.

Freddie stood and went to the current murder board, where photos of their four victims, alive and dead, were lined up in chronological order. He went through the facts of each case, provided details about each victim and then added the possibility that Lt. Archelotta's friend Harlowe St. John might be a fifth victim due to the nature of her head injury.

"In addition to these cases, we have Hector Reese giving interviews blasting Lieutenant Holland for an incident that happened more than two years ago, as well as a reporter reaching out to Deputy Chief McBride with questions about a case that only a small number of people inside this building would know about.

"Last night, Captain Malone and I confronted Paul Conklin, the former deputy chief, about whether he'd been talking to anyone about Sam and her cases. He said he was sorry, but he'd needed the money, which led us to believe that he was one of the few people who knew about the case McBride was called about. We put him under arrest, and while we were transporting him, he began to choke and gasp for air. ER doctors have declared him deceased and he's currently with the ME. We believe that when he realized who was at his door, he took something, knowing it would kill him."

"Fucking coward," Gonzo muttered loud enough for everyone to hear him.

Avery seemed momentarily rendered speechless by the Conklin news. And then he said, "I'm struggling to piece together how the murders, the kidnapping and assault on Ms. St. John, the Reese interview and the reporter call would be related to the drones and the shooting of Agent McFarland."

"I'll take that." After taking a second to collect her thoughts, Sam said, "It's a crazy thing, being a woman on this job, especially one with a pedigree inside the department. From the day I first stepped foot inside this building, I've encountered two kinds of male colleagues. The first, including everyone in this room, is the supportive kind, the sort who lifts up everyone, regardless of gender, race, sexual orientation or any other factor outside the quality of their work.

"On the other side of the equation are the men who feel threatened by strong, capable women who outperform them on the job and in life. They simply can't handle it. Lieutenant Stahl was one such officer. Detective Ramsey was another. It's possible that Conklin was a third, although he gave off the vibe of being supportive. Who knows what he really thought?

"Another, in my opinion, is Officer Dylan Offenbach, who blames me for getting caught having an affair when he was supposed to be at a conference. His lies were uncovered during the sniper investigation last year. We investigated every person in a hundred-mile radius who had the ability to pick people off from a moving car. When we looked for him, we found he wasn't in Philadelphia at the conference he was checked out to attend, but at a hotel in Atlantic City with a woman who wasn't his wife and the mother of his soon-to-be-six children. Lieutenant Archelotta was part of that investigation. At my request, he tracked a fellow officer's phone. That's what confirmed our suspicion. Offenbach lost his rank as a sergeant. His wife filed for divorce and full custody of their children. It's come to our attention, from a source who'd know, that Offenbach is obsessed with drones. The source used the word 'obsessed.'

"I believe that the people behind this plot knew I planned to spend Easter with my family at Camp David. That was mentioned at the White House press briefing last week when the president's press secretary, Christina Gonzales, was asked what the first family had planned for Easter. So they started killing people, knowing my first priority upon returning to work would be to meet with the families. They knew I'd want to help my friend, Lieutenant Archelotta, investigate the kidnapping and assault of his friend. I did everything they expected me to, because they've been paying attention to how I do the job for years. They wanted me out of this building, working a new case, consoling family members, tracking down leads and doing what I do so they could fire the warning shot that hit Agent McFarland."

"Why do you call it a warning shot?" Avery asked.

"I was standing to the left of Agent McFarland. He was hit in his right arm. It's my belief that they missed me on purpose, knowing that having one of my agents go down protecting me would provoke a massive response. They hoped it would break me. If that young agent died protecting me while I'm out running the streets as first lady, that might be the end of me on the job. I'd also add that if Offenbach is behind this, he's considered the most accurate marksman around. There's no way he'd miss if he wanted to kill Agent McFarland."

"So the goal isn't to kill you?"

"I think they'd rather run me out of here in disgrace. They want me ruined. Killing me wouldn't be anywhere near as much fun for them."

"Why send drones to the White House?"

"They wanted me scared. They knew the drones had no chance of reaching the White House, but they wanted us freaking out about them and launching massive investigations to determine where they came from. They succeeded in that. Into that chaos came the Hector Reese interviews and the call from an alleged reporter trying to dig up more dirt from my past. Where are we with investigating Offenbach?"

"We're awaiting a warrant to raid his property in Herndon," Avery said.

"Where is he today?" the chief asked Malone.

"He took a personal day."

"Interesting timing," Gonzo said, echoing Sam's thoughts.

"And the dump on Ramsey's phone?" Sam asked.

"His attorneys are fighting the request," Malone said, "and the judge has scheduled a hearing for Monday."

"*Monday?*" Sam asked, incredulous. "No sense of urgency?"

"I mentioned the urgency to the judge's clerk, who told me it was the first available spot on the calendar."

"I still don't get why they had to kill four people," Avery said.

"The only connection we can make is that they were killed to draw me out into the field where they could continue their sick plan. We've had a break on that part of the case with a witness to the second murder coming forward to identify a white Nissan Altima with District plates as the car the murderer was riding in. He was walking behind the victim and saw the whole thing go down. We've put out the info to Patrol, and Detective Green is working on getting a full list of every white Altima registered in the District."

Cameron looked up from his phone. "My contact at the DMV said he'd have the list of owners to me within the hour."

"I don't know about you," the chief said to Hill, "but I want that warrant for Offenbach's property, and I want it right now."

Hill nodded. "You read my mind."

CHAPTER TWENTY-EIGHT

A warrant was issued for Offenbach's property in Herndon less than an hour later. To keep things clean, the FBI was handling the raid with no involvement by Offenbach's MPD colleagues. The FBI would request backup from the Herndon Police Department at the last minute, in case Offenbach had friends in that department who might tip him off to the pending raid.

"What if we're wrong about him?" Sam asked Freddie when they were alone in the conference room.

"Do you really think we are?"

"I don't know what to think."

"You do know," he said. "You just hate to realize that yet another of our fellow officers has turned out to be a criminal."

"We don't know that yet."

"Don't we?"

"You seem very sure."

"That guy has had it out for you since the minute you reported he wasn't at that conference. He thinks everything that's happened to him since then is your fault. He doesn't take one ounce of accountability in that situation. He even got away with punching you in the face when you refused to press charges."

A thought hit Sam like a bolt of lightning from above. "Freddie."

"What?"

"Remember when we were eliminating sniper suspects, and I sent you upstairs to ask Archie to track Offenbach's phone, and he objected because it didn't sit right with him to treat a fellow officer like a criminal? He said he wouldn't do it without a damned good reason."

"It's starting to come back to me."

"Archie was adamantly opposed. You brought him down to the pit to tell me that himself, and I took him to the morgue to see Vanessa Marchand's body." The six-year-old had been shot by the sniper while leaving a city park with her father. "Remember? I told him she was my damned good reason."

"I do."

"That's why he snatched Harlowe. Offenbach knew I never would've found him without Archie's help. He'd been following Archie and knew he was seeing her. This is why!" Sam pulled her phone out of her pocket and called Avery. "I'm now almost one hundred percent sure that Offenbach is involved." She filled him in on what she'd remembered. "He also has a beef with Archie, and he's waited all this time for revenge against both of us."

"This is good info, Sam. We'll add this info to the file."

"I'll let Archie know what's going on. Keep me posted."

"Will do."

She slapped the phone closed. "Can I admit to being a tiny bit relieved that there's a direct connection to Archie and that Offenbach wouldn't have grabbed his girlfriend *only* because of his connection to me?"

"That's some twisted logic there, but shockingly, I get what you're saying."

"I didn't want what happened to her to be my fault."

"Sam, none of this is your fault."

"Feels like it is, you know?"

"I get it."

"That's because you're fluent in the language known as Sam Holland."

"One of my special gifts."

Sam made the call to Archie.

"Hey."

"So, listen, I have an update, and it ties right back to Offenbach and the day you and I figured out he was in Atlantic City with his mistress when he was supposed to be in Philadelphia."

"What do you mean?"

"He's exacting revenge, Archie. That's the connection to Harlowe."

"Sam..."

"I know. It's horrible, but it's not your fault."

"Who the fuck's fault is it, then? Here I was thinking it could be her ex-husband, and you're saying this happened to her because of *me*? How in the hell am I supposed to live with that?"

Green came into her office, brows raised, expression tense.

"Hang on, Archie. What's up?"

"Ramsey's wife has a white Nissan Altima with District plates."

"Holy shit."

"Malone is requesting a warrant for their house."

"Did you hear that?" Sam asked Archie. "We've got a witness that puts a white Nissan Altima with District plates at the scene of one of the weekend homicides. We've tied that make and model to Ramsey's wife."

Understandably, Archie didn't give a shit about Ramsey. "He... He raped her, Sam."

Sam's heart broke for her friend. "I'm so sorry to have to tell you this."

"I... I don't even know what to do with this info."

"Don't do anything until we know more. I wanted you in the loop as soon as we started to put this together." When he didn't reply, she said, "Archie? Are you still there?"

"I'm here."

She could hear him weeping and wished she could hug him. "Archie, listen to me. This isn't your fault. You'd be doing yourself and Harlowe a huge disservice if you blamed yourself for what a deranged criminal did to her."

"He took her because of *me*. He *raped* her because of *me*. How do I not blame myself for that, Sam?"

"I was thinking about how you told me before all this that you weren't sure she was being straight with you about her past. Do you know any more about why you felt that way?"

He paused to catch his breath before he replied. "I think it was because she'd gotten out of a bad marriage she hadn't told me about and didn't want to talk about that in a new relationship. I know all about that now, but it has nothing to do with any of this. What's being done to find Offenbach?"

"Everything humanly possible. The FBI is about to raid his property, and we've requested a warrant for Ramsey's car and home. We suspect they're working together on the larger scheme. It'll happen fast."

"How is it possible that we work with people like this? Like these two and Stahl and Conklin?"

"I wish I had an answer for that, but all I can say is in a department of more than four thousand people, they're the minority."

"Are they, though? Or are there more of them hiding in our midst, pretending to do the job while evil lives in them?"

"I have to believe there are more of us than them."

"I'm not so sure anymore."

"What can I do for you?"

"Find the fuckers who did this and make them pay."

"We're on it. Are you going to be okay?"

"Yeah, I guess. I don't know."

"Call me if you need me? Promise?"

"I will."

"I'll check on you in a bit and will keep you posted."

"Thanks for calling, Sam."

"I'm so sorry I had to tell you this."

"I know."

"You won't do anything crazy, will you?"

"No, but I'd like to."

"That won't help anything. You know that."

"I get it. I need to check on Harlowe."

"Okay, talk to you soon."

The call ended, and Sam closed her phone with a deep feeling of apprehension overtaking her as she hoped Archie kept his promise to stand down and let the Feds apprehend the colleague who'd attacked the woman he cared about.

ARCHIE PLACED his phone on the counter and stood there, staring out the window, in complete shock that the investigation into Harlowe's kidnapping and assault had led straight back to him. He remembered that day during the sniper investigation when Sam had asked him to track Offenbach's phone. He'd told her he needed a damned good reason to investigate a fellow officer, and a hunch wasn't enough.

She'd taken him to the morgue to see the body of the six-year-old girl who'd been struck down by a sniper's bullet.

"She's my damned good reason," Sam had said. "Track the fucking phone."

He'd done it because he trusted Sam more than just about any other detective he worked with—and he worked with all of them. It'd been the right thing to rule out a possible inside job, but Offenbach had been severely punished by the department with demotion in rank and pay and by his wife, who'd filed for divorce and full custody of their children.

"Archie?"

He spun around to face Harlowe, crushed by what'd been done to her to exact revenge on him for doing his fucking job.

She studied him intently, her brow furrowing with concern. "What's wrong?"

If he told her, she'd leave. If she left, he'd never get over losing her.

Nothing said he had to tell her the truth, but how would they go forward with a lie of that magnitude standing between them? He wouldn't be able to live with himself.

All those thoughts cycled through his mind in a matter of seconds as she stood there looking at him, as if seeing a ghost or a stranger.

"You're scaring me."

"I just heard something. From work. It upset me."

"Do you want to talk about it?"

He shook his head. "I can't."

"Oh, is it confidential, then?"

"No."

She came closer to him, rested her hands on his chest and looked up at him with trust, faith and affection. He wished he deserved any of those things from her.

"You've been so kind to me, and now you're upset. I want to help you the way you've helped me."

Overwhelmed by emotions he'd never experienced before, he dropped his head to her shoulder and then startled when her hand encircled the back of his neck.

"I want to be there for you."

Agony filled his heart as tears flooded his eyes. "If I tell you, you'll hate me."

"What? No! I could never hate you."

"Yes, you really could, and you will."

She pulled back from him, forcing him to meet her gaze. "Tell me."

He shook his head as tears rolled down his face. This sweet, beautiful woman had been kidnapped, beaten and raped because of *him*. She'd never forgive him. He'd never forgive himself.

She brushed away his tears. "Is it about me?"

He diverted his gaze because he couldn't bear for her to see the truth.

"Archie... Talk to me. Please. I want to know."

While continuing to stare unseeing at the window, he said, "Last year, we had a sniper killing people randomly."

She blinked a couple of times as she thought about what he'd said. "I think I remember the news about that."

"It was horrific. The city was on edge, and we were working around the clock to stop it before more people were killed." He took a deep breath and tried to find the courage to continue, to tell her what she needed to know, to ruin the best thing to ever happen to him before it ever had the chance to truly begin. "Sam led the investigation. They were looking for people with the marksmanship abilities to hit the targets from a moving car, like this person was doing. That included investigating people within our department with that capability since it's very specialized."

Archie stepped back from her and went to pour himself a glass of cold water. After taking a drink, he said, "They now think one of the officers we investigated is tied to your case and several others."

"Why would he care about me?"

He forced himself to look directly at her. "Because I'd started to care about you."

She shook her head. "Wait... So this happened to me because..."

Grimacing, he said, "He wanted revenge for me helping prove he was off having an affair when he was supposed to be at a conference. He wasn't the sniper we were looking for, but he lost his rank, his wife and his six kids because Sam and I caught him in a lie."

She crossed her arms as if she needed to protect herself. "I feel a little lightheaded all of a sudden."

Archie moved quickly to put his arms around her and carefully guided her back to the sofa. He sat next to her but gave her room to breathe. "If you want to leave, I'll take you anywhere you wish to go."

"Do you know for sure it was him?"

"Not yet, but Sam and the others working on the case think it's highly possible he was involved in this and several other ongoing cases, along with another guy we used to work with who was already facing felony charges."

"Do you... Is there a photo of him that I could see?"

"Are you sure that's a good idea?"

"Not at all, but I remembered Evan earlier. I might remember something about the attacker if I saw his face."

Archie went to get his phone in the kitchen and then returned to the living room to find photos of Ramsey and Offenbach. He got the one of Ramsey from press coverage of his legal troubles and the one of Offenbach from the department website. Then he showed them to Harlowe.

She had no reaction to Ramsey but recoiled at the sight of Offenbach. "Oh God, that's him. That's the guy who took me and hurt me."

"I need to report this to my command. Is that all right with you?"

"Yes, of course. I want him punished for what he did to me."

"They may ask you to testify. His attorneys would rip apart how you didn't remember his face until you saw his picture."

She gave him a defiant look. "How would they know that unless we tell them?"

Archie thought about it. "Let's wait until they put his face on TV to say you recognized him."

"Can you do that?"

"I shouldn't, but I will. What does it matter? You recognized him and can attest that he's the one who attacked you. The other guy wasn't part of it?"

"I don't recall ever seeing him before, but I can't be sure. I think I might've been drugged." She covered her mouth to stifle a cry. "The memories are coming back to me. Waking up naked in a dark room, not knowing where I was. Crying out for help. And then... He came in..."

Horrified, Archie put his arms around her and held her as she cried.

Sobs shook her fragile body. "I remember what he did, how he attacked me and hurt me. I tried to fight him, but he hit me so hard..."

He didn't know what to say or how to help her. What could he say that would fix the unfixable? The sadness over realizing that any hope he had of a future with her was gone now overwhelmed him. How would she ever forgive him for being the reason for such a terrifying ordeal?

Hell, he'd never forgive himself.

"Do you want me to take you somewhere safe that isn't here? I'd totally understand if you did."

She shook her head. "I feel safe with you."

"How can you feel safe with me when I'm the reason this happened to you in the first place?"

"You're not the reason. The man who did this is to blame. Not you."

"He attacked you because he and his coconspirator were watching us. They saw that I cared about you. They wanted to hurt me by hurting you."

"And yet, here we are, holding on to each other as we get through this together."

"I don't understand."

"What don't you understand?"

"Why you're holding me closer rather than running away from me."

"Because I know in my heart that in this whole world, you're the one person I can trust."

"How do you know that?"

"Look at everything you've done for me since this happened. When I didn't remember you, you stayed anyway. I knew you were outside my door making sure no one could get to me, even after Erica told you to leave. You stayed by my side, you took time out of work, you brought me to your home and took tender care of me through the worst of days. If I can't trust you, I'll never trust anyone else again." She leaned in and placed a sweet kiss on his cheek. "This isn't your fault, and I won't let you blame yourself."

"Harlowe…"

"That's all I have to say about it, Archie. That's all I'll ever have to say about it. Don't do this to yourself. If you let them ruin us, then they win. I will not let them win. Do you hear me?"

Impressed by her guts and moved by her passionate defense of him, he said, "Yeah, I hear you."

Since she wasn't pushing him away, he held her closer, chin resting on the top of her head as he expelled a sigh of relief over realizing she wasn't going to leave him over this. With that settled, he vowed to do everything in his considerable power to ensure she got justice for what was done to her.

CHAPTER TWENTY-NINE

J ake Malone walked down the hall like a man on a mission, ducking into the sharpshooting unit and shocking the officers with his unusual presence. They sat up a little straighter when a captain walked into the room, which gave him momentary satisfaction.

"Where's Nicholson?" he asked of the captain in charge of the MPD's SWAT unit.

"At the range with the new recruits," one of the junior guys said. "He's been there all week."

"What about Fitzgivens?"

"He's in the office."

"Thanks." Malone continued to the back of the big open area and gave a knock on the door before letting himself into the sergeant's office.

"Morning, Cap. What's up?"

"Where's Offenbach?"

"Out on personal leave."

"Was that scheduled?"

"No, sir. He called out this morning and said he had something he needed to take care of."

"Did he say anything else?"

"Not to me, sir."

"Okay, thank you for the info."

"Cap."

Malone turned back to him.

"Do you think he's involved in this shit?" Fitzgivens asked.

"I do. You did the right thing passing on what you knew. Thank you for that."

"No problem. He's been unraveling since everything happened... I've tried to keep an eye on him, but he doesn't make it easy. He's sneaky, deceitful and often nasty. It wouldn't break my heart to see him gone from the job."

"All good to know. Keep me posted if you hear anything more from him."

"Yes, sir."

He headed straight to update the chief with the latest information, but was waylaid in the lobby by Gonzales, frantically waving him toward the Homicide pit.

"What's going on?"

"Ramsey and Offenbach released a video."

"Send someone to get the chief. He'll want to see it, too."

"O'Brien went to get him."

Farnsworth walked into the conference room five seconds after Malone. "What've we got?"

"Watch this," Cruz said grimly as he pressed Play on the video that appeared on the large screen at the front of the room.

Ramsey and Offenbach wore tactical gear. Night-vision goggles were propped on their heads, and their faces were painted in camo colors.

Ramsey spoke for them while Offenbach looked on gleefully. "On behalf of the thousands of men and women of the Metropolitan Police Department who don't want the fucking first lady working with us, we're here to put you on notice that she needs to go. She's only serving herself by surrounding us all with Secret Service and chaos that hampers our ability to do our jobs."

The video cut to footage of the street outside HQ, lined with satellite trucks and reporters screaming questions about the president.

"We're not sure who she thinks she is to bring this madness to our department, but we've had enough of her. We don't care what it takes or who else has to die to rid us of this menace, but we won't stop until she's gone."

Footage of Sam on the job flashed on the screen, of her leaving the homes of their murder victims and on city sidewalks, including the one in Adams Morgan where Agent McFarland was shot, played at a dizzying speed, indicating they'd been following her as she went through the motions in the cases they'd created for her to investigate. Why hadn't the Secret Service noticed they were being followed? Probably because as a cop, Offenbach knew how to evade detection.

"In addition to causing chaos in our workplace, she's gone out of her way to ruin the careers of her colleagues. She's taken the people we love from us. So we're coming after her and the people she loves."

A shot of the Easter Egg Roll on the White House lawn was shown that zeroed in on Nick, placing red crosshairs on his forehead.

Holy fuck. They were threatening the president's life.

"Ending her reign as first lady would've been child's play for us. It would've been so easy, it's laughable. Next time the opportunity presents itself, we'll be ready, but we hope she makes it a little more challenging for us." The camera zoomed in on Ramsey's and Offenbach's faces. "You fucked with the wrong people, Holland. How does it feel to have someone fucking with you, you fucking arrogant bitch? An eye for an eye, princess. We're coming for you."

"Oh my God," the chief said. "Make sure Agent Hill and the Secret Service are aware of this."

"We've notified them, sir," Gonzales said.

"And Holland?"

"She saw it, went into her office and closed the door."

"Let's go talk to her," the chief said.

SAM COULDN'T GET the sight of those red crosshairs on her husband's forehead out of her mind. That he could've been *murdered* because of two madmen she'd tangled with in the past was almost too big for her to process. Her hands refused to stop shaking, so she had them tucked under her legs as she stared blankly at the stupid filing cabinet.

Gonzo and Vernon had taken care of notifying the people who needed to know about the threat, and appropriate action would be taken to shore up security for their entire family until Ramsey and Offenbach were caught.

In the meantime, she was filled with dread and sick to her soul to know that people had been murdered and another viciously assaulted because she and Archie had done their jobs. It was almost more than she could bear to consider.

A knock on the door preceded Farnsworth and Malone walking into her office.

Malone shut the door behind them.

"Sam," the chief said, his every emotion contained in that one word.

She continued to look straight ahead at the filing cabinet, fearing that if she did anything else, she might come undone.

"You should go home," Malone said. "Be with Nick and your kids."

"No. That's what they want."

Another knock on the door.

Malone got up to admit Captain Norris from Public Affairs.

"The media is going mad over the video from Ramsey and Offenbach. They're asking for a statement from Holland."

"They want a statement?" Sam finally looked at them. "I'll

give them a fucking statement." She got up and walked past her stunned superiors as she headed out of her office and toward the lobby with purpose as they—and Vernon—ran to keep up with her.

At the main door to HQ, she stopped and turned to them. "I want to do this myself."

"We need a minute to prepare coverage," Vernon said. "We're on the highest alert after the release of that video."

"You have two minutes. Use them well."

While she waited, she stared straight ahead, preparing to do battle with the kind of evil she'd faced down once before with Stahl. They thought they could intimidate her. After Stahl wrapped her in razor wire and threatened to set her on fire, it took a lot more to scare her than it used to. Although the use of the crosshairs on Nick's forehead had been highly effective in scaring the living shit out of her. But she wouldn't ever let them see that.

"Vernon?"

"One more minute, ma'am."

"Are you sure you want to go out there alone, Sam?" the chief asked.

"I'm one hundred percent sure."

She vibrated with tension as she waited for the go-ahead from Vernon. His two minutes were long up by the time he said they were ready for her.

Sam pushed through the double doors and was briefly taken aback by the massive gathering of media—one of the largest she'd ever seen.

As usual, they shouted questions at her from the second they saw her come through the doors.

"Have you seen the video?"

"Are you going to resign?"

"Are you endangering your coworkers?"

"Have you spoken to the president?"

"Why do your coworkers hate you?"

Sam waited until they got them all out before she began to speak. "Earlier today, in a meeting with my team, we began to zero in on the two officers who released the video as being potentially responsible for the recent murders of four innocent people and for the attack on a beautiful young woman who'd begun to date one of my colleagues. We were looking at them for the thwarted drone attack on the Easter Egg Roll at the White House, as well as the shooting of Secret Service Agent McFarland in Adams Morgan this week.

"Before the video was published, questions were raised about how all those seemingly random things could be tied to two disgruntled officers. I reflected on my career within the MPD and how, from the start, I've encountered two different types of men on the job. The first kind, which includes the men on my team and many others I interact with on a daily basis, are supportive of their female colleagues. They don't treat us as less qualified to be there or as if we're taking a spot on the force that should've gone to a more qualified man."

As she spoke, she heard the door behind her open and glanced back to see Jeannie McBride and Lindsey McNamara come out to stand behind her.

The gesture filled her heart to overflowing with love for her friends.

"The other kind of man is the one who's threatened by our very presence in this building, mostly because they know they'll never be as good at the job as we are. They'll never achieve the level of success we've known or the rank I and others have earned. They'll blame my success on the fact that my last name is the same as the department's former deputy chief. They'll claim that every win I've ever had on the job is because I'm related to him, because the chief was my father's best friend. They'll go so far as to infer that I slept with the chief, a man who was a treasured uncle to me growing up, to achieve my rank. As if that's all it takes to hunt down murderers, to get justice for victims and to protect the people who live here and those who visit each year."

The door behind her opened again, and she glanced back to see Erica Lucas, Neveah Charles, Gigi Dominguez and Dani Carlucci come out.

Their show of support threatened to derail her as a huge lump formed in her throat that she cleared away so she could continue.

"Ramsey has been frustrated by his failure to be promoted beyond the rank of sergeant, which happened because he cut corners on the job. He did the bare minimum. He came at me because for every win I achieved, he seemed to notch another loss. He blamed me and others for the death of his son, who'd assaulted and brutalized numerous women and had taken another hostage in Rock Creek Park. When a department sniper took out Shane Ramsey and saved the life of his hostage, somehow his father determined that it was my fault his murdering, raping son had been killed. I understand needing someone to blame when you've raised a monster, but Shane Ramsey's sins were his and his alone.

"Ramsey told me I'd gotten what I deserved when Stahl wrapped me in razor wire and threatened to set me on fire. We got into an altercation, and he fell backward down a flight of stairs, suffering several injuries. He was outraged when the now-late U.S. Attorney Tom Forrester took the case to a grand jury, which declined to prosecute me for assault. He chalked that up to another favor being done for me because of my pedigree or my higher-than-average profile or my husband or whatever else he came up with, looking for someone to blame. He went on to threaten me numerous other times, witnessed by others, and to ransack my office. He ramped up his attacks, crashing his car into my Secret Service vehicle and interrupting Tom Forrester's funeral with his vitriol. He was out on bail, awaiting trial on numerous charges, when he apparently partnered up with Dylan Offenbach—ironically the same sharpshooter who killed Ramsey's son—to embark on a retribution tour.

"Offenbach is another case study in misogyny gone wild. A talented sharpshooting sergeant on his way to a big career in the department, he checked out of work last year to attend a law enforcement conference in Philadelphia at the same time that a series of sniper shootings terrified District residents and visitors. As we worked our way through the list of people qualified to perpetrate these heinous crimes, we looked inside our own house at the team of officers who'd been trained to shoot with devastating accuracy. That's when we discovered Offenbach was not at a conference as his boss believed. He was having a rendezvous with his mistress in Atlantic City as his wife was about to give birth to their sixth child. He was busted down to Patrol officer. His wife filed for divorce as well as full custody of their children. Offenbach was outraged that we'd investigate a fellow officer and promised to make me pay for the consequences of his actions. Another man looking for someone to blame.

"At this juncture, I want to note that despite these high-profile cases and the ones involving Stahl, Conklin and Hernandez, ninety-nine percent of the people who work in this building are dedicated public servants who have the best interests of this city and its citizens at heart when they come to work every day. They put their lives on the line by wearing the uniform and the badge, and they do so willingly in service to the public. They should not be lumped in with this band of losers who screwed up their own lives and careers and then went looking for people to blame.

"My heart is broken over the innocent loss of life associated with their reign of terror and for the woman who was kidnapped and brutally assaulted, simply because her friend aided in the investigation that determined Offenbach wasn't where he was supposed to be. These men are depraved criminals and should be treated as such. The FBI, the Secret

Service and other federal organizations are leading the investigation. They'll find these pathetic cowards and ensure they spend the rest of their miserable lives in prison."

After a beat to catch her breath, she said, "I'll take a few questions."

"Lieutenant, you're saying that four people were murdered by these men as part of their revenge against you?"

"We suspect they conducted a series of seemingly random murders knowing I'd do exactly what I did the second I returned to work from my family's Easter break. I went to each victim's home, I met with their families, I investigated the places where the murders took place and dug into their lives, looking for commonalities that didn't exist because these victims were chosen randomly. They were murdered because they were walking at night in poorly lit places where our cameras wouldn't catch the perpetrators red-handed.

"We have a witness to the second homicide who was able to identify the vehicle that was used in the crime, the same make and model as the vehicle owned by someone in Ramsey's family. They even capitalized on a terrible mistake I made two years ago when I let my emotions get the best of me while interrogating a suspect after my partner was shot. I don't deny that I stepped out of line with Hector Reese. I vehemently deny that the incident was in any way racially motivated. I desperately wanted information from Reese, and that was the only motivation for my behavior that night.

"As for the drones sent to the White House... Federal law enforcement has been stymied by the lack of elements that could be traced to a manufacturer or source."

"Officer Offenbach is known to be a drone aficionado. He was described by someone who knows him well as 'obsessed' with drones. We believe we'll find that he's the source of the drones that were sent with the intention of killing me, my husband, our children and possibly hundreds of other innocent people who were enjoying an annual event at the White House."

"In light of these events, Lieutenant, do you plan to remain on the job?" her friend Darren Tabor from *The Washington Star* asked.

"I do. I've done nothing other than the job I'm paid to do by District citizens. I come here every day and put forth my best effort in investigating the worst crimes imaginable. I seek justice for everyone touched by these crimes, going so far as to run a grief group for those impacted by violent crime. I'm good at this job. It's who I am and who I'll continue to be for as long as my superior officers are pleased with my performance. That's all I've got to say."

She turned toward her friends, who escorted her into the building and then hugged her one by one. "Thank you for that show of support. It means everything to me."

"We've got to stick together," Lindsey said. "We all know what you bring to the table here, Sam, and we won't let you go without a fight."

"Working with you has made my career," Neveah said.

"I thought we'd talked about the sucking up."

Neveah smiled as she shrugged. "I speak only the truth."

"And we agree with her," Carlucci said as Dominguez nodded.

"As do I," Jeannie said. "I wouldn't be deputy chief without your support and encouragement."

"And you're thanking me for that?" Sam asked with a grin.

Jeannie patted her expanding belly. "It's working out for the best." She'd be going on maternity leave soon. "Despite the frivolity, Lieutenant, I'm outraged over that video of two thugs playing at being tough guys. They wish they could be half the officer and person you are."

"They've certainly got my attention. I can't stop seeing those red crosshairs on Nick's forehead." She shuddered. "That's my greatest fear, as everyone certainly knows."

"Nothing will happen to him with the Secret Service watching his every move," Lindsey said. "I know that doesn't help the fear, but he's very well protected."

"I know, and the reminder helps." She turned toward Malone and the chief, who'd hung back to let her talk to her female colleagues. "What're we hearing from Hill on the raid of Offenbach's place?"

"It's imminent," Malone said.

CHAPTER THIRTY

Avery Hill had quickly organized the personnel needed for the raid of Dylan Offenbach's property and was getting impatient about how long it was taking to get everyone in place. He'd brought in numerous FBI and ATF teams as well as the U.S. Marshals and would request perimeter backup from the Herndon Police in case Offenbach was on the property and tried to escape.

He'd done everything he could think of to ensure a successful mission and was only waiting on the commander of the FBI's SWAT team to report in before Avery gave the go-ahead to proceed. He was giving that agent five more minutes before telling him he was out of time to prepare. The longer they waited, the more they risked being detected, if they hadn't been already.

Offenbach was legendary in the sharpshooting community, and Avery's greatest fear was that he'd be waiting for them, prepared to take out as many federal agents as he could. Fearing the possibility of booby traps, he'd brought in bomb technicians and had a Hostage Rescue Team on standby just in case.

Despite the fast but meticulous preparation, he feared he

was sending his people into an ambush. The SWAT team, made up of some of the FBI's ace marksmen and women, had fanned out into the dense woods that surrounded the house and barnlike structure they'd be entering. If Offenbach was hiding on the property, Avery was confident his people would find him. Hopefully, before he killed anyone.

Avery took to the radio to remind everyone involved of Offenbach's skills. "He shoots to kill and could be hiding anywhere on the property. We need to be quick and efficient. Keep your wits about you."

When the SWAT commander radioed to say his team was in place, Avery authorized them to proceed.

And then he held his breath, praying he wouldn't hear the crack of gunfire as his agents busted down doors with battering rams.

"I've got Ramsey," an agent reported. "Hog-tied in the kitchen. He's been shot in the leg and has lost a lot of blood, but he's alive."

So, Offenbach had turned on his coconspirator. Avery wondered if Ramsey would tell them why.

He didn't hear gunfire, but he did hear screaming, and it sounded an awful lot like children. Son of a bitch.

"We've got Offenbach's ex-wife and six children. They were in a locked room inside the house. Looks like they've been there for days."

Avery asked Herndon Police to summon EMS.

"We're in the barn. Looks like a massive 3D printer and homemade drone parts."

Bingo, Avery thought.

As one agent after another reported their areas were clear of the man they were looking for, Avery relaxed ever so slightly and prepared to send in crime scene and forensics technicians to process the items found.

Avery walked in from the command center and took a look for himself at the 3D printer and the items scattered on the workbenches in the barn. Then he called Jake Malone to report in. "Offenbach was holding his ex-wife and kids in a locked room, and we found Ramsey hog-tied and shot in the leg."

"Jesus," Malone said. "Are the wife and kids okay?"

"Waiting on EMS to evaluate them. Ramsey's lost a lot of blood, but he's alive. We also found a huge 3D printer that'll most likely turn out to be the source of the unmarked drones."

"It's unbelievable that he's been doing all this while showing up to work every day and collecting a paycheck from the District. Although, after what we've been through around here, nothing should surprise me anymore."

"This is a pretty sophisticated operation, Jake. If you ask me, he's been planning this since the day Sam caught him where he wasn't supposed to be."

"Seems that way."

"What do you think went down with Ramsey?"

"He probably stopped being useful to Offenbach, who's the mastermind. Ramsey isn't smart enough to pull off something like this. What's the next step in finding Offenbach?"

"We'll talk to the ex-wife and hopefully get some insight from Ramsey. I'll keep you posted. And we'll coordinate any release of information with your team."

"Thanks, Avery."

"You got it."

JAKE CALLED everyone into the conference room for an update. In addition to the Homicide squad, the chief, deputy chief and the other captains had been asked to attend as he brought them up to speed on what'd transpired at Offenbach's property.

"God, he had his wife and kids out there?" Sam asked. "How had we not heard anything about them being missing?"

"Maybe because no one had noticed yet."

"Wouldn't the schools be looking for them?" Cruz asked.

"They're homeschooled," SWAT Commander Nicholson

said. "Offenbach was adamant about them not being 'indoctrinated' by public education."

"What the hell does that mean?" Gonzo asked.

"Beats me," Nicholson said. "But he had a beef about it and insisted his ex-wife teach them from home. She taught elementary school before they were married."

"We used the pings on his cell to find him in Atlantic City," Sam said. "Can we do that again to find him now?"

"He won't have the cell with him," Nicholson said. "He'd be wise to that after Atlantic City."

"That's true," Sam said. "Does the wife have a cell he might use?"

"That's a good idea," Malone said. "I'll get a warrant for her phone, too."

"I really want to talk to the wife," Sam said. "Do you think Avery will let us be part of that?"

"He may let us be part of it," Farnsworth said, "but you will not be. Too much conflict of interest to have you anywhere near this, Lieutenant."

"Understood," she said through gritted teeth, "but someone from here should be allowed to be there when she's questioned."

"We'll send Gonzales and Cruz if Hill is amenable," Malone said.

A knock on the conference room door preceded Patrol Officer Clare sticking his head in. "Pardon the interruption. Lieutenant, there's a Ryan Goodman here to see you. He's demanding the chance to speak with you."

Sam stood as she frantically tried to remember who he was. Right. The father of Nate Andrews's wife, Emily. "Demanding, huh? He's the father-in-law of one of our murder victims."

"Cruz, go with her," Malone said.

"Yes, sir."

Sam and Freddie went with Clare to the lobby where Ryan

Goodman paced back and forth like a caged bear ready to attack someone—and apparently that someone was her.

"This was all a personal vendetta against *you*? My son-in-law is dead, my daughter is a widow, and their children are now fatherless because of bullshit that had *nothing at all to do with them*? Is this for real?"

"Mr. Goodman, come into my office," Sam said. "We're willing to answer any questions you have, but only if you calm down."

"You want me to *calm down*? This is an outrage. Do you have any care at all for the people whose lives have been devastated by your spats with fellow officers?"

"I care very deeply about everyone who's been harmed by people we considered colleagues, and we share your outrage."

"Sure you do. Your family is alive and well, while my daughter's life is ruined."

"My family was targeted by these madmen. They sent drones with guns intending to murder as many of us as they could, along with countless others."

"Yes, I know, but thank God you had the massive resources of the federal government protecting your loved ones. Who did Nate have protecting him? *No one*."

"You're absolutely right it's an outrage, and we share your anger. We've devoted our lives to keeping this city safe, and when people from our own ranks commit these crimes, please believe me, it breaks our hearts, too."

That seemed to take some of the steam out of him. "I just can't believe that beautiful young man was killed for such a stupid reason."

"Neither can we. I wish there was something I could say that would make this better for you and your family, but there isn't. The one thing I will tell you is that we'll be by your side throughout the entire process to get justice for Nate and Emily and the rest of the victims who were harmed by these men. We won't rest until they're in prison for the rest of their lives."

"You know what really gets to me? You all knew they were both bad seeds. You *knew* it, and you kept them employed anyway."

"They have the same right to due process as anyone else, whether we agree or not. If you think we didn't want Ramsey gone a long time ago, I can assure you no one wanted that more than I did. We've been fighting that battle for quite some time. Other than the lie Offenbach told his superior officers, we've had no reason whatsoever to suspect he was plotting something like this."

"He was right here. Working shoulder to shoulder with cops, and *no one* suspected him of anything?"

"We had no reason to, Mr. Goodman. I know that might seem unbelievable, but a highly trained officer like Offenbach would know how to commit these crimes and get away with them."

"That's just great. So you're effectively training criminals here. I see how it is."

"That's hardly true. We're a department of more than four thousand men and women, human beings with faults and failings. Most of us are here for all the right reasons. Please don't indict more than thirty-nine hundred hardworking, dedicated public servants for the crimes of a few."

"That few ruined my daughter's life, and you can bet we're not going to go quietly on this. You'll be hearing from our attorneys."

"I understand."

"If you're so unpopular around here that your fellow officers would resort to murdering innocent people to get you out of here, maybe you should reconsider whether you should still be working here."

After dropping that bomb, he turned and stormed toward the main doors, probably planning to share his vitriol with the media.

Awesome.

Freddie's hand on her arm made her realize she was trembling. "Sam. That's bullshit. Tell me you know that."

"He makes a good point."

"No, he doesn't. You haven't done anything wrong, and you shouldn't allow him or anyone else to blame you for what these monsters have done."

"You're hardly unbiased."

"I know better than anyone in this entire world how hard you work on behalf of every victim and every victim's family. You're relentless, focused, dedicated and determined, and, if need be, I'll go on every newscast in the world to say that publicly to anyone who'll listen."

"Thank you," she said gruffly. "You're the best."

"No, you are, and that's another thing I'll tell the world. There's no one doing this job anywhere in this freaking world better than you."

Overcome by all the emotions, she waved her hand in front of her face. "Okay, stop now before you make me cry."

"I'm not just saying it, Sam. It's the truth, and I'll tell anyone who needs to hear it. There's a whole pit full of detectives in there who'll agree with me."

"People will say they agree because I'm their boss."

"That's total bullshit, and we'd all say as much to anyone who insinuated that."

"Now you're swearing, young Freddie."

"As usual, you drive me to it."

"I heard what you said and appreciate it more than you'll ever know. Now, let's get back to work making sure Offenbach and Ramsey pay for every crime they've committed. That's how we make this as right as we possibly can. By ensuring they go to prison for the rest of their miserable lives."

SAM RETURNED TO HER OFFICE, closed the door and sat behind her desk, wounded to her soul by Goodman's accusatory words and uplifted by Freddie's vehement support. The roller-coaster ride of highs and lows was giving her whiplash.

A knock on the door came before Malone let himself in and closed the door. "What went down with the victim's father-in-law?"

"Nothing good." Sam relayed the lowlights of the conversation. "He said we'd be hearing from his attorneys, and if I'm so hated in the department that my colleagues would kill innocent people to try to get me out of here, maybe I should rethink my plan to stay on the job."

"I hope you told him you're universally liked around here, except by a few impotent men who can't deal with a powerful woman who's also good at her job."

She shrugged. "I told him we're four thousand people who have failings just like anyone else, but what does he care when two of our officers have ruined his daughter's life?"

"They did that, Sam. Not you."

"I know."

"Do you? Really?"

"Yes, but come on, Cap. It's tied to me and their hatred of me. I'm so tired of fighting this uphill battle with men who can't handle having me around. What did I ever do to deserve all this?"

"First, you were born to Skip Holland, who was a rock star around here, and then you came in and became a rock star in your own right, despite what your detractors would say. That's the part they can't handle, because if they had a million years to make it happen, they'd never be what you are."

"You humble me, Captain."

"I speak the truth."

"Cruz is raging to go outside and say something similar to the reporters."

"He should. Hell, we all should. Maybe that's how we address this, with a PR campaign of our own. I'll take it to the chief and let you know."

"I'd never want it to be said that I requested such a thing."

"We'll leave you out of it. Pretend this conversation never happened, in fact." He seemed happy to have a plan of attack to fight back against the maliciousness being hurled her way.

"Remember our deal."

"I remember. Not even close to there yet."

The BlackBerry rang with a call from Nick. "That'll be the POTUS."

He shook his head as he chuckled. "Only you, Holland."

"He'd better be calling only me."

"You know he is."

Sam took the call as Malone left, closing the door behind him. "Sam Holland's office. Sam speaking."

"Samantha."

"Yes, Nicholas, I know. It's terrible. The FBI has found a 3D printer at Officer Offenbach's home that's probably the source of the untraceable drones."

"I heard."

"We've got Ramsey. Offenbach apparently turned on him, shot him and left him hog-tied while he took off."

"Which means the more dangerous one is still on the loose."

"Yes."

"Are you okay?"

"I've been better, especially since a family member of one of their victims ripped me a new one over my colleagues hating me so much they'd kill innocent people to get rid of me."

"Sam, come on. That's not true."

"Sometimes it feels like it is. Freddie and Malone are fired up about it and want to make public statements, although I'm not sure what good that'd do."

"Let them. It can't hurt anything."

"I suppose."

"I'm sorry this is happening. You feel like it's your fault

those people are dead, and I feel like it's my fault that people there treat you this way."

"How is it your fault?"

"I had the audacity to become president, and you had the audacity to keep your job, which just gave them all new reasons to hate you."

"Don't take that on. They would've come up with other reasons simply because that's what they're about." As she tried to convince him, she realized she made a good point that she ought to take to heart as well.

"I saw your statement to the press, and I thought you did a great job. And it was an amazing visual to have your female colleagues and friends standing behind you."

"That was all their doing, but you're right. It was incredible."

"I want you to hang on to the high regard all of them have for you as well as that of your squad, your brass and so many others you work with there. I want you to remember all the families that credit you with getting justice for their loved ones and the grief group you founded with them in mind. You give so, so much, and you should never let anyone make you feel like it's not enough. Do you hear me?"

"Yes, sir, Mr. President. I hear you."

"I'm being serious, Samantha."

She smiled. "I know you are, and I appreciate the pep talk. It was just what I needed when I needed it. That's another of your many superpowers."

"I'll show you a few others when you get home."

"I'll look forward to that."

"As will I. Are you going to be all right to finish your shift?"

"Yeah, I'm fine."

"You know what we need to do very soon?"

"What's that?"

"Take that spa weekend you gave me for Christmas that's been postponed three times already."

"Yes, please. I need that, and so do you."

"Two weeks from now? I'll ask Brant to set it up."

"It's a date."

"I can't wait."

"Me either. I'll see you soon. Love you."

"Love you, too."

"Thanks for calling."

"Always a pleasure to talk to my lovely wife."

"Likewise. Now you've got to let me go."

"Never!"

"Go back to work, Nick."

"If I have to."

"You have to, and so do I, but I wish it was you and me in one of those huts over the water in Bora Bora without a problem in sight for six to eight months. With the kids next door, of course."

"Of course," he said, laughing. "We'll discuss our plans to run away when I see you."

"Okay, bye."

"Bye."

CHAPTER THIRTY-ONE

S he was still smiling when Tracy called. "Hey, what's up?"

"That's what I was going to ask you. What the hell, Sam?"

"I know. It's insane."

Tracy had recently told Sam how much she worried about her on the job—and always had—which had come as a surprise to Sam. "Are you safe from these guys?"

"I'm surrounded by Secret Service, and the department is rallying around me, too. I'm okay. Talk to me about something else, will you?"

"I was going to call you tonight to ask your advice on something."

"Wait. Stop the presses. *You* want *my* advice?"

"I'm being serious."

"So am I. This is a big moment for the baby sister. You gotta let me enjoy it. What's going on?"

"It's Ethan."

At the mention of her eleven-year-old nephew, Sam sat up out of the hunch she'd been in.

"What about him?"

"I'm not sure, to be honest. Are you sure you have time for this with everything going on?"

"Absolutely. Talk to me."

"Mike and I have noticed he's been very withdrawn lately, spending more time in his room and less time with us. He wants to be with his friends every day after school, but doesn't want me to know what they're doing, which of course doesn't fly with me."

"I should hope not. What do you know about the friends?"

"Not much. Most of them are new since he started middle school. He's more or less dropped most of his friends from elementary school. I talked to the mom of one of his old friends the other day. She said her son misses Ethan and isn't sure why they aren't friends anymore."

"Hmm. What does Mike say?"

"He thinks it's normal. Puberty is setting in, and boys tend to go silent during the teenage years."

Sam's first thought was that Scotty hadn't done that, but then again, he wasn't your average teen. He hadn't had a family for years before he joined theirs and was forever telling them how grateful he was.

"Mike asked him to go to a Caps game last week, which is something they used to do all the time."

"I remember that."

"Ethan said he didn't feel like going."

"I know you guys were talking about getting him a cell phone and debating whether it was too soon. What did you end up doing?"

"He has a phone for texts and calls. There's no internet or social media on it."

"Are you sure about that? Kids have ways around parental controls."

"They do? For real?"

"Yeah. I can have someone here check it for you if you want. They'd know where to look."

"I'd take you up on that if we could pry it out of his hands long enough. Mike told him he wanted to see what he was doing on it, and Ethan freaked out and told him he has a right to privacy."

"Not at eleven, he doesn't."

"That's what Mike told him, but he was so upset, we let it go. For now, anyway. But we're rattled by the changes in him and the way he's tied to that phone."

"You could shut it off until he's older and more responsible."

"But then I wouldn't be able to track his locations or call him if he's away from home with friends."

"That's a catch-22."

"For sure. I don't know what to do. I don't want to ignore the red flags or signs that something is going on with him, but if he won't talk to us, what are we supposed to do?"

"Have you considered family therapy? I could ask my colleague Dr. Trulo for a recommendation."

"I'd welcome that. It was such a big help after what happened with Brooke, but her therapist specializes in teenage girls."

"I'll ask him if he knows of anyone who specializes in younger kids and boys in particular."

"Thank you, Sam. I appreciate you listening when you have so much other crap going on."

"I'm never too busy for you and your family. You know that."

"I do. Thank you again. Before I let you go, I was thinking we should do a little shower for Angela before the baby comes. I think it would mean a lot to have her people around her right now."

"I totally agree. Text me your thoughts, and we'll set something up. I'll put Shelby on it. She'd love it."

"Yes, she would. I'll be in touch."

"I will, too, with the recommendations."

"Talk soon. Love you."

"Love you, too. Thanks for asking for my advice."

Tracy laughed. "You're never going to let me forget that, are you?"

"Not in this lifetime or the next."

Sam was glad that Tracy was still laughing when they ended the call. She was rattled by what Tracy had told her about Ethan, who'd always been such a happy, funny kid. In the few times she'd seen him in recent months, she hadn't noticed a change in him, but that didn't surprise her. Kids tended to save their less-savory behavior for their parents. She'd made a point of having a close relationship with her nieces and nephews—or as close as she could with the schedule she kept.

Their family had been through a lot recently. The loss of Skip had been followed closely by the passing of Angela's husband, Spencer. Both deaths had been a huge shock to Sam, a full-grown adult with coping skills. She couldn't imagine how the kids had felt or what they might still be feeling after losing two people close to them—and both of them suddenly.

Sam sent a text to Dr. Trulo, asking if he had recommendations for a therapist who specialized in middle schoolers, boys in particular.

She was catching up on the latest reports on all of her team's ongoing cases when a knock brought Dr. Trulo into her office, carrying a container and the smell of something mouthwatering.

"I was just about to come see you when I got your text." He put the container on her desk and handed her a plastic knife and fork wrapped in a napkin. "Eggplant parm from the kitchen of Anita Trulo. Be warned. It'll ruin you for all others."

"I stand warned, and I can't wait to try it. Tell her thank you for me."

"Are you kidding? She can't wait to tell everyone she knows

that she made eggplant parm for the first lady, who also happens to be my friend."

She smiled at how cute he was.

"I also wanted to see how my friend is doing in the midst of the latest nonsense."

"Oh, you know how it goes. Another day, another crisis of confidence."

"Balderdash. If anyone should be confident in what they contribute around here, it's you."

"What the hell does 'balderdash' mean?"

Trulo laughed as he sat in one of her chairs. "Go ahead and eat it while it's hot. And 'balderdash' is a fancy way to say 'nonsense.'"

"Ah, I see. Learn something new every day."

"It's all nonsense, Sam. I hope you know that."

"Try telling that to the families of the people they killed and the woman who was raped in the name of retribution against me and Archelotta."

"What's this about Archie?"

"He was the one who traced Offenbach's phone and put him in Atlantic City with his mistress when he was supposed to be in Philly. They kidnapped and assaulted his new girlfriend as part of their campaign of terror."

"Good Lord."

"How is it possible that these people walk among us as we at least *try* to uphold the law?"

"It'll never make sense, but it happens in all the big departments. We don't always hear about it, but it does happen."

"Like this?"

"Sometimes. I can give you lots of examples from many different big departments that've had criminals in their midst. Naturally, it feels more personal when it's happening to your department."

"How many more of them are there? Stahl, Conklin, Ramsey, Hernandez, Offenbach... When does it end?"

"As long as human beings are wearing the badge, it'll never end."

"That's not what I want to hear." Sam opened the lid of the container and breathed in the fragrant scents of garlic and basil. Using the silverware he'd brought her, she cut a bite of tender eggplant. The flavors exploded on her tongue and had her going back for a second bite right away. "Holy shit, that's good."

"I told you."

"Please pass along my compliments to the chef."

"She'll be delighted."

He leaned forward and put a business card on her desk. "The referral you requested."

Sam read the name on the card: CHRISTI TRULO-CARPENTER, PHD, FAMILY THERAPIST.

"One of yours?"

"My eldest daughter and the mother of my first two grandchildren. She specializes in youth and family therapy."

"Convenient."

"I thought you might say that. She's excellent, or I wouldn't refer her. Is one of your kids in need of help?"

"It's for my nephew. Tracy's son, Ethan."

"Ah, okay. I'll tell Christi to expect a call from Tracy and ask that she receive VIP treatment."

"It's nice to have friends in high places."

"I could say the same."

"For all the good that does me on days like today."

"Don't let the bullshit get to you, Sam. Focus on the job, on the cases, on the stuff that matters and try to let the rest of it go. For every Stahl, Ramsey or Offenbach, there're hundreds of others who admire and respect what you do."

"Are you sure about that?" she asked skeptically.

"I'm very sure. They get to say they work with the first lady.

How many people in the history of the country have been able to say that who didn't work in this building? I'll answer that for you—zero. Trust me. They think it's cool."

"Judging by the support I've received since their insane video went live, I'm very blessed by the friends I have here."

"Lean on us when the going gets tough and ignore the detractors."

"I'll do that. Thank you."

"Any time. In other news, I've found an organization that'd be very happy to have the ramps from Ninth Street. Would you like me to handle that for you?"

Even though she'd known it was coming, that didn't make it any easier to realize it was actually going to happen. "What the hell is wrong with me, getting choked up over a couple of ramps we don't need anymore?"

"Nothing at all is wrong with you. You've suffered a tremendous loss, and the removal of the ramps compounds the loss. It's the symbolism of what they represent that's getting to you."

"You're right. Grief is such a bitch."

"She sure is, but grief is nothing more than love."

"My dad hated waste of any kind. He'd want the ramps to go to someone who could use them. Let's make that happen. There's a guy in the Ninth Street neighborhood who could do the removal. Nick was going to call him. We'll put him in touch with you."

"That'd be great. Do you want me to keep you posted on the details?"

Sam thought about that for a second and then shook her head. "I trust you to handle it, and I very much appreciate you offering to."

"Happy to help. Now finish your lunch and get back to doing what you do best."

"Will you talk to Archie? I'm so worried about him."

"I'll reach out, and I'll check on you later, too."

"Hey, Doc?"

He turned back to her, brow raised.

"Thank you for being someone I can trust in this place. You'll never know what that means to me."

"Likewise," he said with a warm smile. "Be good to yourself, my friend."

Sam passed Christi's contact info on to Tracy. *Her dad is my good friend Dr. Anthony Trulo, the department psychiatrist. If he recommends her, it's not just because she's his daughter. He's going to tell her to expect a call from you and is requesting VIP service.*

Tracy responded a few minutes later. *Thank you so much, and of course I know about your Dr. Trulo and how much you love him. If he recommends her, that means a lot. I'll call her today. It feels good to have a plan. Thank you for the advice, baby sister. You're the best.*

Please keep me posted on how Ethan is doing, and let me know if you guys need anything at all. I'm HERE for you and your kids. Always. Love you.

Love you, too. So much.

Next, she sent a text to Celia, Tracy and Angela, telling them Dr. Trulo had found an organization that needed the ramps. *He's also offered to oversee the removal and make it easy for us. I told him to go ahead. No sense putting it off any longer when someone could be using them. I think Dad would approve.*

He would, Angela replied. *You know how he felt about waste.*

I just said that to Dr. Trulo.

Agreed, Celia said. *Let's get it done.*

Makes my heart hurt, Tracy said, *but it's time. Please thank your Dr. Trulo for us. He's a treasure.*

Indeed he is, and I will.

After she used the BlackBerry to ask Nick about the neighbor who could help take down the ramps, Sam put down the phone and glanced at the photo of her standing behind her dad in his wheelchair. She'd had it reframed after Ramsey ransacked her office and smashed the original on the floor.

She picked it up and used a tissue to wipe dust off the glass. "They can take your ramps, Skippy, but you'll live forever inside of me and the rest of us. I hope you know how much we love and miss you."

As she returned the photo to its place of honor on her desk, she yearned for him and his words of wisdom as she faced yet another crisis within the department. He'd hated how rough it had been for her to come into the place he'd loved to work so much and face strong headwinds from her male colleagues from the get-go. Most of them had been convinced the only reason she even got the job in the first place was because of her last name. Never mind the two criminal justice degrees she'd earned, with dyslexia, no less, or the years of hard work that'd brought her to the rank and role she now held.

But yeah, sure, it was all because of her dad and his best friend. It had nothing to do with her skill or tenacity or determination. To hear them tell it, it was all a big handout.

"Sam, come here," Freddie said. "You're going to want to see this."

What fresh hell would this be, she wondered as she followed her partner to the conference room. The others were gathered around the TV, which showed Lenore Worthington speaking to the media outside of HQ.

"I came over here as soon as I saw that monstrous video posted by two men who clearly suffer from sociopathy and chronic misogyny. Sam Holland wakes up in the morning with more moxie in her little finger than those two idiots will have in their entire lifetimes."

Sam's eyes flooded with tears.

Freddie handed her a tissue.

"I've known Sam for more than fifteen years. She was the first officer to arrive after my son was fatally shot in my driveway. I'll never forget her kindness or her compassion on the worst day of my life, and I'll always be thankful for everything she did to get justice for my Calvin. Thanks to the grief support group she founded for victims of violent crime, I can give you the names of thirty other people who'd say the same thing. She's the real deal, an asset to this city and this community, and anyone who says otherwise has their own agenda. The men who posted that video aren't law-abiding police officers. They're criminals and should be treated as such. And anyone who'd accuse her of being racist, on the job or otherwise, has never spent five minutes with her. That's all I have to say."

Lenore pushed through the crowd to get to the main doors and was in the pit a few minutes later.

Sam left the conference room to hug her friend. "Thank you."

"I've got no time for that nonsense, girlfriend. How're you holding up?"

"I'm finding out how many friends I have, and I'm honored to call you one of them."

"It's the least I can do for you after everything you've done for me, and don't say anything about it taking too long. You got justice for us and helped me find a community of fellow travelers through the grief group, so we're square."

Sam hugged her again. "You're the best."

"As are you. I'm sure there'll be others from the grief group speaking out before the day is over. Danita is as fired up as I am."

Danita's son, Jamal, had been shot during the sniper siege that'd led to Offenbach's downfall.

"You've helped to turn around this day, and I'll never forget it."

"We love you. We support you. We owe you. We won't forget either." Lenore kissed Sam's cheek and was gone as fast as she'd come.

Sam fanned her face. "Holy moly."

"You deserve it, Lieutenant," Cameron Green said.

"The squad has prepared a statement that I'll read on

behalf of the others," Gonzo said. "Just an FYI that I'm heading out there now."

"You guys..."

"If you expected any of us to take this lying down, you don't know us at all," Freddie said fiercely. "And you know us as well as anyone does. Come on, guys. Let's do this thing."

As they left the pit, each of them gave her a pat on the arm.

"We got you, LT," O'Brien said.

CHAPTER THIRTY-TWO

Not wanting to miss whatever was about to happen, Sam went into the conference room to watch the ongoing coverage of the explosive news story that had two MPD officers threatening the lives of their colleague, the first lady, and her husband, the president.

Though she always hated when she was the story, she sure as hell hadn't started this one.

Her team gathered behind Gonzo, who stepped up to the podium. Even Carlucci and Dominguez were there when they should've been at home sleeping.

"I'm Detective Sergeant Tommy Gonzales, second-in-command to Lieutenant Holland in the MPD Homicide division, and the people behind me make up our squad. Sam Holland is my boss and one of my best friends in this world. Everyone who reports to her would say the same thing about her being a friend, a mentor and a role model to all of us. We meet people on the worst day of their lives, when they've lost someone they love to murder. No one works harder to get justice for the victims and their families than Sam Holland.

"She's tireless, dogged, aggressive and often downright obnoxious if that's what's needed to get the job done. She's everything you'd want on the case if someone you loved was murdered. To the rest of the world, she's the first lady of the United States, but if you were to ask us or anyone else close to her, we'd tell you that she's a detective first and foremost. This is not just what she does. It's who she is, and we consider ourselves blessed to work for someone who cares as much as she does about a job that most people—including the two cowards who posted that video—could never do.

"When my partner was murdered on the job, Sam Holland was there for me through every second of the nightmare that followed, right up to and including the conviction of the man who took Detective Arnold from us. She supported me through my dependence on pain meds and never gave up on me, even when most bosses would have. I'm here today, clean, sober and living my best life in large part because of her love and support. When any of us needs help or support, she's our first call because she's always there for us—on and off the job.

"My colleagues and I are proud members of the Metropolitan Police Department, which is made up of more than four thousand men and women, human beings who make mistakes just like everyone else. A very small percentage of them are criminals hiding behind the badge. It'd be a terrible mistake to indict the hardworking members of this department or our leadership due to the sins of the few. No one wants them out of this place more than we do. And we'll work around the clock to support our federal colleagues in apprehending Dylan Offenbach and making sure he and Jim Ramsey spend the rest of their sorry lives in prison. Thank you."

Sam was mopping up tears as the news anchors returned to comment on Gonzo's statement.

"An enthusiastic endorsement from Holland's closest colleagues and further proof that Ramsey and Offenbach certainly don't speak for everyone inside MPD headquarters. We'll stay on this breaking news story with updates as they develop in the manhunt for Dylan Offenbach."

Sam went out to greet her team as they returned to the pit, giving each of them a hug as they came in. "Thank you."

"No, Lieutenant," Charles said vehemently, "thank *you*, for everything you are and everything you do. And while you'll say I'm sucking up again, I'll risk it to tell you it's an honor and a privilege to work under your command."

"Thank you, Neveah. It's an honor and a privilege to work with all of you, too. Now, let's get back to it and help the Feds find this guy."

"Yes, ma'am," they said together.

Sam went back into her office and sat behind the desk, putting her head back against the chair as she tried to catch her breath. When she'd first seen that video, she'd feared her tenure at the MPD was over. Her colleagues and Lenore had said otherwise. She was filled with gratitude for the show of support, but she wouldn't rest easy until the man who'd conspired with Ramsey to threaten her—and Nick—was behind bars.

SITTING with Harlowe on the sofa, Archie watched the ongoing coverage of the manhunt for Offenbach and the endless replay of the video released by him and Ramsey.

"I need to notify them that you recognized Offenbach," he said after they watched Gonzo's impassioned statement in support of Sam.

"Won't the DNA take care of that for us?"

"It will, but you'll still have to testify."

"Okay."

He squeezed the hand he was holding. "Your courage amazes me."

"I don't want to be a victim, and I refuse to allow him to ruin the nicest thing that's ever happened to me. So let's call Erica and do our part to put this guy where he belongs so we can get on with much more important things."

"Such as?" Archie smiled even though he was still full of turmoil since realizing her relationship with him had led to her abduction. And the reason she'd been less than forthcoming with him was due to the problems she'd had with her ex-husband and not because of any great secrets she was keeping.

She crooked her finger to bring him closer and took his breath away when she placed her hand on his face and leaned in to press her lips to his. "This, for one thing," she whispered. "Lots and lots of this."

Archie wanted to weep from the sweet pleasure of kissing her for the first time since the attack, for the way she ran her lips over his and how they curled up at the corners in a smile that reached her eyes. That she wasn't blaming him or banishing him, that she forgave him for bringing evil into her life, would go down as one of the greatest gifts he'd ever received.

"Easy, sweetheart," he whispered. "You're still recovering."

"I feel great right now, stronger than I have since it happened, and you know what I want?"

He tucked a strand of silky auburn hair behind her ear. "What's that?"

"I want to lie with you in bed and have you hold me the way you would if I wasn't injured."

"You're not ready for me to hold you that way."

"Yes, I am, and it's what I want. And need." She looked away before seeming to force herself to bring her gaze back to him. "I want to reclaim myself. Does that make sense?"

"It does, but we need to go slowly so you don't suffer any setbacks." He was as concerned about her mental health as he was about the physical.

"I'm fine with slowly. Will you hold me, Archie?"

He got up and extended a hand to help her. "With pleasure."

She winced as she straightened and walked slowly with

him to his room, proving his point that she was a long way from recovered.

When she was seated on the bed, he took out his phone and composed a text to Erica, letting her know that Harlowe recognized Dylan Offenbach as the man who attacked her. *She's willing to make a statement or whatever you need, but maybe we could do that tomorrow? It's been a lot for both of us to realize a, it was him, and b, it was tied to my work.*

Erica responded right away. *This is good to know, and I'll pass it on to the others here as well as the FBI. Yes, let's talk tomorrow about a statement of what she recalls. Her parents are settled at the Willard and asked that she get in touch if she'd like to see them.*

Thanks, Erica.

He showed the texts to Harlowe.

"Okay, good. Now, enough of that. I don't want to think about it until I have to."

Archie helped her get comfortable in his bed.

Harlowe is in my bed! He needed to enjoy this moment and let go of the distress that had gripped him for hours. If she didn't want to think about it, then he shouldn't either.

When she was settled, he went around to the other side and stretched out next to her.

"Come closer, and don't be afraid to touch me. I won't break."

Archie slid across the bed and snuggled up to her, putting his arm around her waist, below the worst of the bruising. "Is this okay?"

"You could be closer."

He moved the last few inches toward her, pressed his body to hers and smiled when she sighed.

"That's better. You're so warm. Like a furnace."

"I'm always like that—never cold even in the middle of winter. My friends make fun of me for wearing shorts in January."

"That works out well, because I'm always freezing."

"I'll keep you warm."

She pressed her cold feet to his leg, startling him. Then she laughed, warming him from the inside. He'd wondered for a time if she'd ever laugh again.

"You weren't kidding."

"Nope." To make her point, she moved carefully onto her side and put a freezing hand under his T-shirt.

"Do I need to turn up the heat?"

"Nah, I just need you to warm me up."

He gazed into her pretty brown eyes. "I'm here, and I'm not going anywhere for as long as you want me to keep you warm."

"That's apt to be a long time."

"That works for me."

Sam was reading the message from Erica Lucas about Harlowe recognizing Offenbach when Gonzo and Freddie came into her office and closed the door.

"What're we supposed to be doing now that the FBI has taken over our homicide investigations?" Gonzo asked.

"We can support their efforts by digging into Offenbach. Archie's girlfriend has identified him as the man who kidnapped and assaulted her. I want to know everything there is to know about what he's about here and outside of work. Let's do our usual drill with socials, financials, interviews, etc."

Cruz nodded. "That's a good idea. I'm sure the Feds are on that, too, but we may find something they don't due to our proximity to his colleagues."

"Exactly. In fact, I fully expect you guys will find something they don't. Let's get everyone on that, and while we're at it, look at Ramsey, too. No detail is too small in either case. I want the full rundown of what they've been up to while pretending to be law enforcement officers."

"On it," Gonzo said, seeming energized to have a new direction.

While he returned to the pit, Cruz hung back. "Are you okay?"

"Yep. How are you?"

"I'm pissed and sick of the crap around here. Like we don't have enough to deal with outside this place that we have to be fending off this bullshit, too."

She appreciated that he was swearing on her behalf. "You're right. It's ridiculous and should be the least of our concerns. But that's not the world we live in, unfortunately."

"I'm not a fan."

"Nor am I," she said, smiling. "The best thing we can do to get through this is to keep our heads down and do the job to the best of our ability. That's how we win."

He exhaled a deep breath. "You're right, as usual."

"Duh."

"Had to say that, didn't you?"

"Gotta keep it real around here. I don't want you going soft on me."

He glared at her the way she'd known he would. "It's actually a relief to me that you're busting my balls. I'll really worry if that stops."

"That'll never stop. It's one of my purest sources of daily joy."

"Glad to be of service to you."

"Work the case, Freddie. It'll make you feel better to help the cause."

"Will do. Let me know if you need anything."

"You'll be the first to know."

Before he could leave the office, Malone was in the doorway. "The chief likes the idea of having your colleagues continue to make statements of support for you and the work you do here."

"I'll go first," Freddie said.

"It's somewhat mortifying to me that it's come to this," Sam said.

"We can't leave the public with the idea that people in here want you out," Malone said, "because it's simply not true. So let's hear from the people."

"As you wish, Captain."

Malone blinked, seemingly stunned by her easy capitulation. "Do you have a fever, Holland?"

She laughed. "Nothing quite so dramatic, but if you guys want to do this, I won't try to stop you."

"We want to do it, and the statement from Gonzo was a great start. If they think they're going to ruin you on their way to life sentences, then they're sadly mistaken."

"Thank you for the support. I've gone from despair to elation in the scope of a few hours, thanks to all of you."

"We've got you the same way you'd have us." Malone's phone chimed with a text. "Hot damn, in light of the video and Ramsey being taken into custody, the judge has granted our warrant for his phone. I'll get Walters right on it and keep you posted."

"Great news. I can't wait to see what's on there."

"Me, too."

He took off to see to getting the phone to IT while Sam took a call from Nick.

"Hi there."

"I wanted to check on you again. I saw Gonzo's statement and Leonore's. I wish I could be there with you."

"I do, too, but I'm better after the massive show of support."

"Are you leaving on time today?"

"I believe so since our case has been mostly taken over by the Feds."

"Usually, you hate when that happens."

"This time, I'm all for it."

"In other news, one of my meetings today was my gun task force, and we're prepared to roll out our first major initiative—a reporting mechanism for people concerned about family members who might pose a risk. We're approaching it from a mental health standpoint rather than law enforcement. At first, anyway. The goal is to develop regional mental health task forces that would be deployed to investigate concerning situations."

"I love that so much. Send in help rather than cops."

"That's the thought, and your Dr. Trulo was instrumental in helping us craft the plan."

"He's the best."

"I'm a big fan after working with him on this."

"He told me he's found an organization to take the ramps from Ninth Street."

"How're you feeling about the ramps coming down?"

"It's time, and my dad would want them going to someone who needs them. It'll be weird to see the street without them, though."

"Yeah, it will."

"Speaking of Ninth, we need to go over there to move our stuff to the third floor."

"We can make a date night out of it."

"Gee, doesn't that sound fun?"

"Haha, but it needs to be done, so why not make it fun?"

"Why not, indeed? Let's do it this weekend, so Christina and Gonzo can start to move their stuff."

"I'll set it up with Brant for Saturday night. Woo-hoo, big night out with my best girl."

"Doesn't take much to excite you."

"Getting out of here—with you—excites me."

Jeannie McBride came to the office door and pretended to knock.

Sam waved her in. "Me, too. I've got to run. I'll be home soon."

"Can't wait. Love you."

"Love you, too."

CHAPTER THIRTY-THREE

"Just a little call with your POTUS hubby?"

"Nah, that was my side piece."

Jeannie laughed as she took a seat. "As if you'd ever cheat on the man who's so wild about you that *SNL* mocks the two of you."

"Cringe. I can't even think about *SNL* without wanting to run away."

"It's become my favorite show."

"You can't say that and be my friend, too."

"Whoops."

"What's up, Deputy Chief McBride? And yes, I still get a kick out of saying that."

"And I still get a kick out of hearing it. I wanted to check in to see how you're doing. It's been a rough day around here."

"You'd think I'd be used to the rough days after all this time. And yet..."

"This one is extra awful. Those crosshairs... My God."

"Yeah, that was the part that got to me, too, as they knew it would. And what happened to Archie's girlfriend... It's beyond horrible."

"How's she doing?"

"A little better. She recognized Offenbach as the one who attacked her when she saw his picture on the news."

"Oh wow, which means she's also remembering the assault."

"Apparently so."

"Do you think she'd be up for talking to someone who gets what she's going through?"

"I'm sure it couldn't hurt. Why don't you reach out to Archie about that?"

"I will. But I came here to talk about you. I'm hoping all this, coupled with all the crap that'd happened before this, isn't pushing you into an existential crisis about continuing on the job."

"It might have without the support of all my friends. Having you all come out to support me at the podium was amazing."

"That was Lindsey's idea, and we were all for it."

"It lifted me up when I needed it, as did the statement Gonzo made for the squad and what Lenore said. Malone is fired up, and so is the chief. That makes a difference."

"After the Deasly case, I went through it myself, wondering how I could continue to wear the badge and do the job when we'd failed that family—and so many others—for more than a decade."

Jeannie had investigated one of Stahl's unsolved cold cases involving a missing teenager and uncovered a human trafficking ring that was still being unraveled months later.

"It's taken some time with Dr. Trulo and talking it out with my family here and at home to realize that there was nothing I could've done to stop others from failing to do the right thing," Jeannie said, "and by taking on guilt that should belong to them, I was punishing myself for other people's sins. Or something like that."

"You make a very good point, and I'm glad to hear you're feeling better about things than you were."

"Dr. Trulo has helped me to see we can only do what we

can do. We can't control the actions of others. We can only control how we react to them. I choose to put good before evil and to always do the right thing rather than the expeditious thing."

"I hope you know how much I admire your courage and resilience." After Jeannie had been kidnapped and assaulted by Mitchell Sanborn, Sam had worried her friend might never come back to work. She'd not only come back, but she'd come back stronger than ever and had made an epic bust in the Deasly case.

"That means a lot to me, but I give you most of the credit for dragging me back to work."

"I wouldn't want to do this job without you."

"Same goes. Please don't quit us."

Sam laughed. "What the hell would I do with myself without this job?"

"Oh, I don't know," Jeannie said with a grin. "Maybe travel the world and give speeches?"

"That'd require far too much flying and peopling." Sam wrinkled her nose. "I'm much happier right here in this shabby office with my beat-up desk and dented file cabinet."

"I'm relieved to hear you're planning to stick it out."

"What choice do I have? It's in my blood."

"Yes, it is. While we're discussing things you dislike, my mother and sisters are planning a baby shower that you'll be invited to. You're under absolutely no obligation."

"I wouldn't miss it for anything."

"Do you have a fever or something?"

"You're the second person to ask me that in an hour!"

Jeannie laughed. "Well, it's unusual for you to respond enthusiastically to something like a baby shower."

"It's possible I could be growing up. Finally."

"Nah, don't let that happen. We like you just the way you are."

"Thanks for coming by and for all the support. Means the world to me."

"Anything for you."

"Likewise, my friend."

"Your dad said something to me once that I've always remembered," Jeannie said as she stood to leave.

"What was that?"

"When you put good out into the world, it comes back to you exponentially."

"That sounds like something he would say."

"He lived it, and so do you. Don't let anyone make you feel otherwise."

"Yes, ma'am."

"Carry on."

That was another thing Skip Holland might've said, Sam thought. When you have no choice but to carry on, that's what you should do, so that's what she *would* do, regardless of whatever challenges came her way.

BEFORE SHE COULD LEAVE for the day, Sam had to meet with Faith Miller to go over her testimony for the upcoming Christopher Nelson trial.

Faith was right on time, appearing in the door to Sam's office at the stroke of four o'clock, wearing the stiletto heels that she and her sister Charity were known for, while their triplet sister Hope had a more casual style. The Miller triplets had brown hair, green eyes, and were fiercely intelligent. Sam considered the sisters friends as well as excellent colleagues.

"Come in."

Faith closed the door and dropped into the chair. "I've been on the run all day. Feels good to sit down."

"How are things?" The murder of their boss, U.S. Attorney Tom Forrester, had devastated the sisters.

"We're finding a new normal, but I keep wanting to ask

Tom something and have to stop myself and remember once again that he's gone."

"That's grief for you."

"I hate it."

"So do I. What're you hearing about the new USA?"

"The Senate is due to take up the nomination of Catherine McDermott in the next couple of weeks. We're anticipating some significant changes when she arrives."

"I also hate change."

"Right there with you. How're you doing after everything today? And by the way, it's a freaking outrage. The whole thing."

"Yes, it is, and I'm hanging in, thanks to a ton of support from my colleagues and friends."

"I hope you know you have ours, even if we can't come out and say so."

"I do know, and it means a lot. Thank you."

"I couldn't believe the news about Conklin."

"I'm actually surprised he waited so long to punch out. The shame of it all would've been tough for him to handle after pretending to be one of us for so many years."

"That's true, but it's still so shocking. Anyway, about our old pal Christopher Nelson..."

"Do we gotta?"

"We do," Faith said with a sigh. She opened her portfolio and went through the list of questions she'd ask Sam in court, which they'd already reviewed twice before. "I want you prepared for a beating from the defense, especially pertaining to your relationship with Peter."

Nelson had murdered Sam's ex-husband after having him tortured for information about Sam and Nick that Peter had refused to divulge. In the end, he'd shown some honor despite putting her through hell for years and conspiring to keep her away from Nick after they first met.

"I'm prepared for whatever they throw my way. I've made

no secret of the fact that our relationship was terrible, but he sure as hell didn't deserve what Nelson did to him."

"No, he didn't."

"It does get old," Sam said, "fending off attacks left and right."

"I'm sure it does, especially from the old boys' club."

"Yes! Enough already." Sam gathered her stuff and walked out of the office with Faith, who promised to touch base the night before the trial began. "Talk to you then."

Vernon, who stood watch in the hallway, straightened when he saw her emerge from the office.

"Anything new?" she asked him.

"Just a much bigger detail for the time being."

"Oh joy."

"Somehow, I knew you'd say that."

"I'm worried this could drag on. Offenbach knows how to stay off the radar."

"He's made himself the most wanted man in America with that video threatening the lives of the first couple. We'll find him."

"Is Ramsey saying anything?" Sam asked as they walked toward the morgue exit.

"He was in surgery the last I heard. They're waiting for the chance to interview him."

"He won't help them find Offenbach."

"You never know what someone will do when they're facing the prospect of dying in prison."

"I guess we'll see, but I'd be surprised if he gives up anything helpful."

The lights were off in the morgue, which meant Lindsey had left for the day. Sam nodded to Agent Q, who stood inside the door. That alone was a change of procedure. Usually, Jimmy waited outside with the vehicle.

When Q pushed open the door, Sam saw that Vernon

wasn't kidding about the much larger detail. The number of cars rivaled what they used to transport Nick.

"Holy smokes."

Vernon held the back door for her as he scanned the parking lot. "Yeah, we're not taking any chances."

When they were on their way to the White House, Sam asked how Jimmy was doing.

"He's hoping to go home tomorrow," Vernon said.

"That's good news."

"He's driving Liz crazy wanting to get out of the hospital."

"I'm sure. I'd be the same way."

Vernon glanced at her in the mirror. "As I recall, you *were* the same way when you fractured your hip."

"Don't use my past against me. It's against the rules in the SUV."

Vernon's snort of laughter seemed to take Q by surprise.

"Don't worry, Q," Sam said. "The gloves are off in the SUV."

"I guess so," Q said. "I had no idea y'all were having so much fun on this detail."

"I'm a good time had by all," Sam said.

The two men cracked up.

Her work there was finished.

Sam took a call from Detective Carlucci. "Hey, what's up?"

"I was thinking about something. Not sure if it's relevant or not, but when I was in the academy with Dylan Offenbach, he organized a weekend party once at a camp his family owns in the Shenandoahs. I can't remember exactly where it is, but there were cabins, a lake, hiking trails and shooting ranges. He told us he'd first learned to shoot there when he was seven or eight, and it's where he'd honed his craft."

Sam's backbone tingled with sensation. "This is excellent info, Dani. I'll pass it on to Avery."

"I can't believe Dylan is involved in something like this. He was so by-the-book back then."

"At some point, he lost his way and made a series of bad decisions that led us to where we are today."

"I'm still trying to wrap my head around it. I would've bet he was one of the good guys."

"It's always disappointing when people we came up with prove themselves unworthy of the badge and all it represents."

"For sure."

"Thanks for the call and for passing along the info. I'll keep you posted."

"I'd appreciate that."

Sam closed her phone to end that call and reopened it to call Avery. "Hey, so I just talked to Detective Carlucci on my team. She went through the academy with Offenbach." Sam told him about the camp in the Shenandoahs that Dani had recalled visiting with him at that time. "She said his family owned it. Not sure if it was the father's family or the mother's."

"This is great info, as we're currently no closer to finding him than we were earlier. I can figure out the mother's family name. If they still own the place, we'll find it."

"Keep me posted?"

"As much as I can. Pass along my thanks to Carlucci. This could be the break we've been waiting for."

"Will do."

Sam ended the call and then texted Carlucci to pass along Avery's thanks.

I sure hope it helps.

Me, too.

"Is there a lead?" Vernon asked.

Sam filled him and Q in on what Carlucci had told her and how she'd passed it on to Hill.

"I'm picturing this guy, Offenbach, pumped up to take his new cop friends to his family's place in the mountains to show off his mad shooting skills," Vernon said.

"Yes, and wouldn't it be something if that very same outing led to his downfall?"

"Indeed it would."

THE SUV WAS MAKING the turn into the White House gates when the BlackBerry buzzed with a text from Andy to her, Nick and Elijah.

Two bits of great news to share. First, the judge has set a date of April 20 for the adoption proceeding, and second, we've succeeded in getting Elijah's juvenile record in California expunged.

Elijah answered first. *YESSSS! LET'S GO!!!!!*

Sam responded next. *I'm so, so happy to hear this news. Thank you, Andy, for everything you've done to make both things happen. We can't wait to make official what's already true: Elijah, Aubrey and Alden are our family.*

What Sam said, Nick replied. *I'm so relieved on both counts and can't wait for April 20. Thank you so much, Andy.*

A pleasure to help you all make it official, Andy said.

"Wow," Sam said to Vernon and Q. "Want a scoop that you can't tell anyone?"

"Um, yes, please," Vernon said.

"On April twentieth, Nick and I will officially adopt Elijah, Aubrey and Alden."

"That's amazing news," Vernon said. "Congratulations, Mom."

Having him call her that just made this moment that much sweeter.

"Congratulations," Q added. "I'm so happy for all of you."

"Thank you, both. Please don't tell even your significant others. I'm sure there'll be a plan for making this news public after it's official." What she left unsaid was that they didn't want to take any chances of the twins' money-hungry grandparents, aunt and uncle finding out about the plan until it was too late to change it.

"We won't breathe a word of it," Vernon said.

In just a few days, Sam would be the official mother of four children. They could stop calling Elijah their bonus son and just refer to him as their son. She who'd once believed she'd never have children now had three sons and a daughter. Not to mention a daughter-in-law!

This felt like one of the most significant days of her life, right up there with her wedding to Nick, the day they'd officially adopted Scotty and her first day on the job. She should probably count Nick becoming president as one of the most significant days, too. Funny how that was almost an afterthought compared to her four amazing children.

Vernon opened the back door of the SUV and gave her a hand out. "Happy for you, kid. You deserve a big win after this ridiculous week."

"Thank you, Vernon. I'm happy to be able to share it with you."

"Let me know the schedule for tomorrow when you have it."

"I'll do that. Thanks again for everything."

"It's a pleasure to work with you."

"You as well."

Sam wasn't surprised to find Nick waiting to greet her inside the foyer. She let out a happy shout and ran for him, mindless of who might be watching them embrace moments after learning their adoption of Elijah and the twins would soon be official.

The clicking of a camera reminded her that almost everything they did in this building was available for public consumption. "Let's go upstairs to celebrate," she whispered in his ear.

He never put her down when he headed for the steps, taking them two at a time in his haste to be alone with her. That would probably be a skit on *Saturday Night Live* in a week or two, but what did she care as her husband put her down, pressed her against the wall outside the Lincoln Bedroom and kissed her face off?

"Look at us," he said after he shifted his attention to her neck, making her want to purr with pleasure. "The parents of *four kids*."

"I can't believe it's real." And she never forgot that two special people had to die in the most horrific way imaginable to make this possible for them.

"It's very real and about to be official."

"What in the name of God is happening?" Scotty asked. "You have a whole-ass bedroom right down the hall, and you're making out like teenagers where anyone might see you?"

They lost it laughing.

"It's not funny! What if the twins had seen you instead of me?"

"I think they would've survived the shock," Nick said as he put Sam in front of him to hide the proof of his arousal. He kept his hands on her shoulders as they walked down the hallway toward their son.

"It's unseemly, even for you two, to be making out like you haven't seen each other in a month, right outside the Lincoln Bedroom."

Sam bopped him on the head and then kissed his cheek. "We got very good news."

"Must've been."

"It's the very best news. We've got a court date on April twentieth to make the adoption of Eli, Alden and Aubrey official."

"Oh wow, that is good news." He glanced up at them. "Does that mean no one can ever try to take them away from us again?"

"That's exactly what it means," Nick said.

"So I'm going to be a brother."

"You already are," Sam said. "This only makes it legal."

"I guess, in light of this amazing news, I'll give you a pass on the unseemly behavior."

"Gee, thanks, pal," Nick said. "You're a sport."

"You want to come with us to tell the twins the news?" Sam asked.

"*Hell* yes. Let's do it."

CHAPTER THIRTY-FOUR

After Sam locked up her weapon and cuffs in her bedside table, the three of them went upstairs to the third floor to share the news with the twins. Sam was annoyed to feel a twinge of pain in the hip she'd fractured, which seemed to bother her only when she climbed stairs.

The twins came running when they saw them coming. Sam scooped up Alden while Nick hugged Aubrey. Soon, they'd be too big to lift, which was a depressing thought that she pushed aside so she wouldn't ruin her celebratory mood by acknowledging that she'd gotten a late start with all four of her kids, and they would grow up far too fast.

After this week from absolute hell, the fantastic news from Andy was most welcome.

"What's the good word, my friends?" Nick asked.

"They have no idea what that means, Dad," Scotty said.

"It means, how was your day, what's new and exciting?" Nick said.

"Much better," Scotty replied.

"Thank goodness we have you around to make sure we don't mess this up," Sam said.

"I say that every day."

They were treated to a recitation of current events in first grade that, for once, included no bodily fluids. Apparently, their friend Solomon would be out of school for a whole month while his family visited their family in Germany.

"That's very cool," Scotty said. "Do we have any family in Germany that might be happy to see us?"

"Sadly for you, we don't," Nick said. "No month off for you."

"Life isn't fair."

Brenda laughed helplessly at the goings-on. "This family needs its own reality show."

"I believe we're already living one, Nana," Scotty said.

"That's true."

They sat on sofas with the twins on their laps and Scotty between them.

Sam glanced at Nick, who indicated she should be the one to update the twins.

"So we got some big news today," Sam said.

"Good news?" Aubrey asked with trepidation that tugged at Sam's heart. The poor kid had been through so much at far too young an age to handle it all.

"The best news. Remember how we told you that we applied to adopt you two and Elijah, so we'll be a family in all the ways that matter, including legally?"

"Uh-huh," Alden said. "But our mommy and daddy will always be our mommy and daddy, right?"

"Always and forever," Nick said. "Nothing will ever change that, but Sam and I will be the ones to take care of you until you're old enough to take care of yourselves."

"Right," Aubrey said. "And Scotty will be our other big brother."

"You know it," Scotty said with a fist bump for each twin.

"Today," Sam said, "we learned it'll be officially official on April twentieth when we go to court to see the judge, which is really soon."

"Can we have a party to celebrate?" Aubrey asked.

"We sure can." Sam smiled at the precious child. "You and Alden can plan it. Anything you want."

"Um, that'll mean peanut butter and Fluff for everyone," Scotty said.

"Whatever they want. It's their big day."

"You can help us plan it, Scotty," Alden said.

"I'll make sure there's something that's actually edible."

"Can we invite Jack and Ella and Ethan and Abby?" Alden asked of their cousins.

"Of course. They wouldn't want to miss it."

"And Alex and Noah and baby Maisie!" Alden said of Gonzo's son and Shelby's kids.

Sam loved how their people had become the twins' people in just a few short months. "You can invite anyone you want."

"Are we going to change our names?" Alden asked.

"We were thinking Armstrong-Cappuano if you're down with that," Nick said. "But you can use A dash C on your papers at school so you don't have to write it out every time."

"That's cool," Alden said, sounding relieved, as Aubrey nodded.

"Group hug," Sam said, pulling everyone into a big pile on the couch, which led to much laughter and screaming from tickling perpetrated by Scotty.

After they released the kids to go play, Sam's mom came over to hug her. "This makes me so happy for you and Nick, honey. Such a beautiful family."

"Thank you. It certainly didn't happen the way we thought it would, but I wouldn't trade them for anything."

The three kids had Nick pinned to the floor and were trying to keep him there while he threatened to bust loose from their hold. Sam wished the rest of the world could see him in dad mode. It would make the people who supported him love him that much more than they already did.

"Look at him," Sam said softly. "He's never had this before."

"It's wonderful," Brenda said. "He's so happy to be a dad and to have this beautiful family to come home to every night."

"You know, I used to yearn to have a baby, but I've started to realize it happened this way because my life is not at all conducive to caring for a newborn. I'd want to be with the baby all the time, and I simply can't be unless I give up my job, which I'd never want to do."

"The universe has a way of making sure we get what's meant for us."

"Indeed. I'd never have wanted Eli and the twins to go through the nightmare they did losing their parents, but if it had to happen, I'm glad they landed with us."

"They're lucky to have you."

"We're the lucky ones."

Nick let out a roar and had the three of them pinned under him so fast, they never saw it coming. Their screams of laughter made Sam and Brenda laugh, too.

"Nice move, babe," Sam said.

"He's not going to be able to pull that crap on me for much longer," Scotty said, panting from the exertion of trying to break free of Nick's hold.

"Keep talking, mister," Nick said. "I'll be waiting for you to be able to take me."

"It's coming, old man. Don't let your guard down."

Nick tightened his hold on Scotty until he yelled uncle. "That's President Uncle to you, friend."

Scotty huffed with outrage after Nick released him. "That was a dirty trick."

"I specialize in them."

"Keep your guard up, old man."

"Want us to fight him for you, Scotty?" Alden asked, flexing his muscles.

"Nah, we don't want to wear him out. He's not as young as he used to be."

"Those are fighting words, mister."

Outside the walls of this historic house, much of what Sam had spent her life working toward had been in danger of imploding during the last few horrific days, but here, at home with the family she adored, she couldn't bring herself to care about things she couldn't control.

MUCH LATER, Nick had Sam trapped under him, only she wasn't trying to break free. In fact, she was trying to bring him closer.

"Harder," she whispered in his ear before she bit his earlobe.

That seemed to spark something elemental in him as he gave her what she'd requested until they were straining against each other, chasing the epic finish that exploded within her at the same time he cried out in a moment of perfect harmony.

"Damn, babe," he said, gasping. "Way to throw gas on a fire."

Sam cackled with laughter. "Is that what I did?"

"You know exactly what that does to me."

"Which part? The demand or the biting?"

"Both. Hot as fuck."

"Good to know." She caressed his back and floated in the sea of contentment that followed lovemaking. "Funny how today was such a nightmare, but it turned out okay, all things considered. My coworkers went to bat for me, and Andy gave us the best news ever."

"For sure. I liked hearing that Eli's record in California was expunged as well. That's a huge relief. I hated the thought of that sticking to him and messing up his very promising future."

"Same. You know... We ought to throw a fancy White House wedding for him and Candace."

"That'd be awesome and would send a heck of a message to her parents that you can't get in the way of true love."

"That's true. I wonder what they think of her taking off to be with him the second she was a legal adult."

"I'm sure they're up in arms about it, but what can they do? They made the choice to prosecute the boy she loved, and now they're out of her life. It's a lesson in parenting, though. If you overreact to the natural process of growing up, you run the risk of losing them forever."

"The thought of not being close to all of them for the rest of our lives is unbearable to me."

"Let's keep that in mind when they start to test us in ways we can't begin to imagine right now."

"Our kids won't do that."

He snorted with laughter. "You just keep thinking that."

"How will we know what the right thing to do is?"

"I remember your dad saying after Scotty came to live with us that we have to remember that kids are individuals with their own ideas and opinions on things, and just because we don't agree with them, doesn't mean they're wrong. Like with Eli and Candace. If her parents had spent ten minutes with them as a couple, they might've seen what we do when they're together. That they're truly in love and devoted to each other. Were they too young to be having sex? Maybe, but what the parents did was much worse. Why not just separate them until she's older? Why call in the cops on what was a loving, consensual relationship?"

"Definitely."

"Another thing my dad always said was that it doesn't pay to be in denial as your kids grow up. They're going to drink and smoke and have sex and swear and do things we don't like. Trying to get in the way of the natural progression is like trying to stop the tide from coming in."

"Can you write all this down since I didn't have a lifetime with Skip to absorb all this wisdom?"

"It's available to you on an as-needed basis."

"Good to know. I don't want to mess this up."

"You won't. They adore you, and when you tell them something, they truly listen to you because you listen to them when they have something to say. I think we keep the lines of communication open and keep laughing with them, so when the serious stuff comes, we've set the tone in advance. Does that make sense?"

"It makes all the sense," Sam said. "I'm looking forward to everything with them. Even the hard stuff."

"Me, too, as long as you're there to keep me from messing them up."

"Oh please, who's more likely to mess them up? Me or you?"

"Am I expected to answer that question?" he asked.

"Yes!"

"Um, well, you know how much I love you, right?"

Sam smacked the back of his shoulder, making him laugh.

"I decline to further elaborate on the basis that I wish to stay married to the mother of my four children."

"Four children. It's still surreal."

"Along with you, the best thing to ever happen to me."

"Same goes, love. Same goes."

In the morning, Sam took a call from Dani Carlucci. "Morning."

"Morning, LT. I wanted to give you an update on the search for Offenbach. The FBI has located the camp in the Shenandoahs that his mother's family owns. They've asked me to provide any details of the layout that I can recall, so I'm meeting with them after my tour ends."

"Are they thinking he's there?"

"They're trying not to give away the fact that they know about the camp before they're ready. When they are, they'll send in infrared cameras to determine if he's in there."

"Which will tip him off."

"Yes, that's why they're waiting."

"Anything else new overnight?"

"We've been working on the full reports on Ramsey and Offenbach you requested, and Gigi just slipped me a note that Offenbach's ex-wife is asking to see you. She's at GW."

"What does she want?"

"She didn't say, but she said she wants to speak only to you."

"I'll go right there when I leave here."

"Sounds good. I'll let you know how it goes with the FBI."

"I hope they give you credit for pointing them in the right direction if they find him there."

"All I care about is that they get him before someone else gets hurt."

"Still... If he's there, this is all your doing."

"If you say so."

"I say so, and I'm the boss."

Dani cracked up. "We're all thankful you didn't quit this shit show with everything that's happened this week."

"I'm a sucker for punishment, apparently. I'll talk to you in a bit."

"Thank goodness and sounds good."

Sam closed her phone and went to finish getting dressed so she could get the kids off to school and then head to GW to see what Offenbach's ex-wife wanted with her.

On her way out of their suite, Nick's small office caught her eye. Feeling mischievous, she ventured in to move some things around to let him know she'd been there. Inside the desk drawer, she wrote SAM LOVES NICK MORE on a sticky note.

Smiling, she rearranged every object on the obsessively organized desktop and then walked out, whistling with satisfaction at the simple pleasure that came with messing with his anal-retentive tendencies. At a time when it felt like everything had changed, some things needed to stay the same.

The twins came bursting into the hallway, dressed in their school uniforms and dragging their backpacks behind them.

"I was just coming to get you guys up," Sam said.

"We did it ourselves," Aubrey said proudly.

"I see that," Sam said with a pout. "Does that mean you don't need me anymore?"

"Don't be silly, Sam," Alden said. "Of course we still need you."

"Oh phew. I was afraid you were going to tell me that next you were getting your own apartment."

Their giggles made her day, and it had just barely started.

"You're *so* silly," Aubrey said.

In those three little words, Sam caught a preview of what thirteen-year-old Aubrey might sound like, full of sass and sarcasm—if Sam had anything to say about it.

"What's for breakfast?" Alden asked.

"What would you like today?"

"French toast sticks!" they said as one.

"Pancakes, you say?"

"No!"

"That's not what we said."

"I heard pancakes."

The foolishness and laughter continued right up until the moment she sent them off to school with their detail. Her time with them in the mornings had become the highlight of her days. What never failed to amaze her was how every day was a little different from the one before, even if the routine was the same.

They were such a gift, and even as she had that thought, she said a silent prayer for Jameson and Cleo, who would always be close to their hearts as the twins' parents. It occurred to her that this must be how heart transplant recipients felt... Someone had to die for their dream to come true.

She took that deep thought with her as she went down the stairs to meet Vernon and Q. "Morning, gentlemen."

"Morning," Vernon said. "I got your text, and we're set to take you to GW."

"Excellent. The former Mrs. Offenbach has asked to see me."

"Is that strange?"

"Extremely. I'm looking forward to hearing what she has to say."

Vernon held the back seat door for her. "We're sending an advance team in to make sure it's not some kind of setup."

"I hadn't considered that possibility."

"Doomsday thinking is our job. Not yours."

"And thank goodness for that. Is Jimmy going home today?"

"They released him late yesterday afternoon, and he's resting comfortably, according to Liz's update this morning."

"Glad to hear it. Nick and I want to do something significant to thank him for saving my life. Any suggestions?"

"He would never expect that. He'd say he was doing his job."

"I know, but we'd still like to do something."

"I'm sure they'd appreciate anything you did, even as they said it wasn't necessary."

"I'll ask for suggestions from my brain trust—my sisters and Shelby. They'll know what to get."

"I'm sure they will."

Sam sent the three of them a text with her request for ideas.

Something monogrammed? Shelby said. *Do we know the baby's name?*

"Is there a name yet?" Sam asked Vernon.

"Austin Michael McFarland."

"Ah, I love that." Sam passed it on to Shelby.

I'll come up with some ideas for you.

You're the best.

Tracy replied just to Sam. *Wanted to tell you that Ethan met with Dr. Christi early this morning and said she wasn't terrible. Thank you again for the quick help—an appointment this soon wouldn't have happened without you. I feel a little better just knowing he's talking to someone qualified.*

Glad it's going well so far. Keep me posted!

Will do.

The George Washington University Hospital had been turned into a Secret Service fortress in anticipation of her arrival.

"Holy overkill, Batman," Sam said.

"Don't use the word 'kill' when you're with your detail," Vernon said.

Sam chuckled. "Apologies, but still... This is a lot."

"You've been threatened by a talented sharpshooter. We're not taking any chances."

"Understood."

"Our advance team has already cleared the way for you to get to the former Mrs. Offenbach's room, so we're good to go."

CHAPTER THIRTY-FIVE

S am followed Vernon inside, with Q right behind her and a bevy of other agents surrounding them. *Please, God, let them find Offenbach soon so this won't be necessary for long.* She cringed at the thought of showing up at HQ with a massive entourage.

They took the elevator up to the fourth floor, where Offenbach's ex-wife was being guarded by two FBI agents. They asked to see Sam's ID even though they recognized her. She'd have been disappointed if they hadn't asked. After they'd carefully examined her badge, one of them opened the door for her. "She's expecting you."

Inside the room, she found the woman in a hospital bed surrounded by six blond children—four boys and two girls. Sam would guess they ranged in age from a year to ten or eleven.

When she saw Sam, the woman said, "Micha, please take the kids to play."

Toys had been arranged in the corner, and the eldest child led the others to them.

"I'm Lieutenant Holland. I heard you asked to see me."

"Thank you for coming." She had washed-out blonde hair

and blue-gray eyes with dark circles under them. Her mouth was curved into a frown that involved her entire face.

"What's your name?"

"Oh, sorry. It's Laura. I'm in the process of going back to my maiden name, but legally, I'm still Offenbach. I'm going to change the children's names, too."

Sam kept her voice down in deference to the kids. "It's nice to meet you, but I'm sorry for the circumstances. Are you and the children all right?"

Laura's tone matched Sam's so they wouldn't be overheard. "We will be. Dylan kept us confined to that room for three days with no water, food or bathroom. He even put bars on the windows. We were in rough shape when they found us." She gestured to the IV in her hand. "I was dehydrated, and two of the kids were, too, but they've bounced back quickly, thank goodness."

"That must've been a terrible ordeal."

"I thought we were going to die, but of course I couldn't let the kids see how scared I was."

Sam took out her notebook and pen and sat in a chair next to her bed. "How did you end up at his place in Herndon?"

"He was due for visitation and asked if I could drive them out because he had to work late. When we got there..." Her eyes filled, and she shook her head. "He held a gun to Micha's head and threatened to kill him unless I did exactly what he told me to."

"I'm so sorry. That's horrifying."

"I'll never forget that, and neither will the older kids."

"Your children are very well behaved." The six of them played quietly in the corner, which didn't seem entirely normal. She would've expected a little commotion.

"They're good kids." Her eyes filled again. "They've been through so much over the last year with their father moving out, the divorce and now this."

"I understand that you haven't spoken to anyone from the FBI yet."

"No, I haven't, because I don't know who to trust. That's why I asked to see you."

"I'm afraid I don't understand. Your husband hates me. He blames me for all his troubles."

"Yes, he does, which is ironic. You weren't the one screwing someone else when you were supposed to be at a work conference right before your sixth child was born. Were you?"

"No, ma'am."

"I wish I had a dollar for every time I've had to remind him that there was no one to blame for the situation he found himself in but him, but he never wanted to hear that. I asked to see you because I'm worried about your safety. He's completely unhinged when it comes to you and Lieutenant Archelotta."

"Are you aware of what happened to Archie's girlfriend?"

Her eyes went wide. "What? No…"

"It might be better if you didn't know."

"Oh God. Is she… Is she dead?"

"No, he let her live so she could go back to Archie and force him to confront the fact that she got kidnapped and assaulted because of his work."

Laura shook her head. "I always knew he was intense, but I had no idea he was capable of the things they're saying he's done or that he could hold a gun to Micah's head and then lock us in a room for three days. Who does that to their own children?"

Sam didn't have an answer that would satisfy her, so she handed her a tissue and waited for her to continue. "Did he say anything before he locked you in the room or after?"

"Just that he needed to keep us out of the way. I asked him what he meant, and he wouldn't say. How were we in the way when we were at our home, minding our own business?"

"Maybe he knew you'd be the first stop law enforcement

made when we connected him to the drones and the other crimes."

"What did he do with drones?" she asked tentatively.

"He's the one who flew them toward the Easter Egg Roll at the White House. They were armed with guns."

"Oh God..."

"Fortunately, they were stopped. We found a 3D printer at his house that we believe was used to produce the drones."

"That goddamned printer." Her expression turned thunderous. "Do you *know* how much that thing cost?"

"I don't."

"Forty-five thousand dollars!"

"Where'd he get the money?"

"From a line of credit on the house I got in the divorce. He took the money before the divorce was final. That line of credit had been for emergencies. I found out about it after he'd already bought the printer, and now I'm stuck with the debt. If I'd had any idea what he planned to do with it..." Her voice caught on a sob. "I didn't know, or I would've said something."

Sam reached up to put her hand on top of Laura's. "No one blames you for any of this, Laura."

"I feel like I should've known he'd do something crazy. He was so, so angry after he got caught and demoted. He blamed you and the other lieutenant for all of it. I should've spoken up. I should've warned you. Maybe if I had, he could've been stopped before it came to this."

Sam released her to grab another tissue to hand to her.

"Are you okay, Mom?" Micha asked.

"I'm fine, honey. Thanks for watching the kids." Glancing at Sam, she said, "He's such a big help to me, and he's only eleven. I worry he's losing his childhood as a result of his father's actions."

"Kids are remarkably resilient."

"They'll need intensive therapy after what we went through in that room."

"I'll ask Dr. Trulo, our department psychiatrist, to come by to see you."

"Why would he help me when my ex-husband is causing all this chaos?"

"Because you and your children haven't done anything wrong, and he'd want to help you if he can."

"That's very kind." She dabbed at her raw eyes. "People have been so very nice to us."

"You're crime victims, Laura. And you'll be treated accordingly."

"What else has he done? I'd like to know."

"I think it's better if you don't know the details until you're feeling stronger."

She seemed to sink into the pillows when it occurred to her that it must be bad if Sam didn't think she could handle hearing about it.

"We believe he may be hiding out at his family retreat in the Shenandoahs."

Laura's gaze darted toward her. "He loves it there. It's his favorite place in the world."

"Have you spent time there?"

"A lot of time."

"Would you be willing to give the FBI as much information as you can to help them prepare to go in after him?"

"If it would help to end this nightmare, I'll do whatever I can to help."

Sam called Avery and told him where she was and what Laura had agreed to do.

"This is great, Sam. Thank you."

"Glad to be able to do something to help. How close are you?"

He'd know she was asking about going in after Offenbach. "Getting there but being methodical in light of his capabilities."

"Understood."

"My colleague Agent Colson will be there in fifteen minutes. She's great with crime victims."

"I'll wait for her and then leave them to it."

"She's excellent. You'll like her."

"I don't like anyone."

Avery grunted out a laugh before he ended the call.

"When you get out of here," Sam said to Laura, "I'd like to introduce you to my friend, Roni, who's connected with a group of young widows. They all support each other."

"I'm not a widow, though."

"You're raising your kids as a single mom. I doubt they'd quibble about the details. Would you like me to give my sister your number?"

Laura thought about that for a second. "Yes, I think I would. Thank you for your kindness. I didn't believe the things Dylan said about you."

"That's nice of you to say. The FBI is sending an agent over to take every detail you can give her about the camp. I'm sure she'll tell you this, but no detail is too small in a situation like this."

"I'll tell her everything I know."

WITH COLSON HANDLING Laura's debrief, Avery went to see Ramsey now that he was out of recovery and able to speak. He'd lost a lot of blood from the wound to his leg and faced a long recovery, which would take place in federal lockup. His days of roaming free were over for good.

The disgraced officer was shackled to the hospital bed under the watchful eyes of two of Avery's best agents.

"Take a break," Avery said to them when he entered the room.

Ramsey scowled when he realized who'd come to call. "You can fuck right off. You're in bed with Holland." He scoffed. "Living at the White House."

"My wife is close to them."

"So are you, so don't try to deny it. Everyone knows it."

Avery shrugged as he took a seat next to the bed. "I don't care what people think. Our friendship with them predates the White House. Everyone knows that, too."

"Whatever you have to tell yourself."

"I sleep just fine at night. Do you?"

Ramsey's expression turned stony. "The whole lot of you—Farnsworth, Malone, McBride, Forrester, even the fucking FBI... You're all in cahoots to protect your precious princess. People say you married her friend so you could stay close to her. Bet you didn't know that."

Avery hadn't known that people had said that, and it hurt to hear it, because it wasn't true.

"Thought people didn't know you had a thing for her, didn't you? It was the worst-kept secret in town. Your poor wife having to settle for being second-best."

Avery wanted to punch Ramsey's lights out for daring to speak of Shelby, but instead, he laughed. "Better than your wife, who lost a son and a husband to ego and hubris. That must be a bitter pill for her to swallow." He leaned in. "Do you *know* how much time you'll do for threatening to assassinate the president? You'll never see the light of day outside prison again."

Ramsey shrugged as if he didn't care, but his gaze darting around gave away his true feelings.

"That you were stupid enough to confess on that video..." Avery shook his head. "I bet you didn't see Offenbach turning on you after you recorded that. Did you? When did it happen? Right after the video? Is that when he shot you? After he got you to confess to what the two of you had done?"

Ramsey's expression became thunderous. "He shot me by accident."

Avery laughed. "Is that what you think? One of the most precise marksmen in the world doesn't make mistakes with a gun, and surely you must've realized that when you were hogtied and bleeding on his kitchen floor. What I'd like to know is how you've justified partnering up with the man who killed your kid."

The look on Ramsey's face indicated he would've murdered Avery if he could have. "Dylan was only following orders. It wasn't his fault. I blame Malone and Holland. They gave the order. And he didn't mean to shoot me. We had plans to make Ruby Ridge look like a Cub Scout meeting. He needed my help."

Avery laughed again. "What *help* could you possibly be to someone with his skills? Nah, after he'd gotten you to help him with the details, you were a liability, and that's why he shot you. But it's rich that he got you to confess on video beforehand and then let you live to face the consequences. I'll bet you were excited to make that video letting Holland know her time was running out with you two clowns coming for her."

"She's shitting a brick. The crosshairs on her husband's head was a nice touch, didn't you think?"

"She's hardly shitting a brick. She just interviewed Offenbach's ex-wife and is helping us make the case against the two of you."

"How can she do that when she's suspended?"

"Oh, you haven't heard? That was lifted almost as soon as it happened."

"She roughed up that Reese guy!"

Avery shrugged. "So what?"

Ramsey's face had gotten very flushed, and spittle collected in the corners of his mouth. "She let a murderer go free, and so did her asshole father!"

He shrugged again. "So?"

"She should be charged!"

"Do you think anyone is worried about charging her after you two idiots killed four innocent people, kidnapped and

raped a woman, sent drones to the White House and shot the
Secret Service agent protecting the first lady?"

"I never touched that woman!"

"I notice how you don't deny the rest of it." Avery stood to
leave, having gotten what he'd come for: Offenbach's plan to
make Ruby Ridge look like a Cub Scout meeting, which was
horrifying.

"I never admitted to anything."

"Sure you did." Avery patted his chest. "Glad I recorded our
conversation. I'm sure the USA will find it helpful."

"You can't record me without my permission."

"You were read your rights, and you certainly know by now
that anything you say can and will be used against you. See you
in court, Jim. Oh, and I hope you have a great time in prison.
They love ex-cops in there. I'm sure you'll be given the
treatment you richly deserve. Word to the wise: Watch your
back."

"Fuck you! Fuck Holland and the whole bunch of you!"

Avery walked out of the room while Ramsey was still
yelling at him. "He's all yours," he said to the two agents as he
pulled out his phone to call in the new info to his team, eager
to end this madness once and for all.

CHAPTER THIRTY-SIX

"I've spent the last two days trying to track down Hector Reese," Gonzo said, "hoping to find out more about who put him up to going public when he did—even though we know who did it. Interestingly, after being all over the airwaves for days, he's disappeared, which is probably intentional. I'll stay on it."

"Thanks for trying." Sam wasn't surprised to hear that Reese had made himself hard to find after putting the incident with her on blast and filing suit against her and the department. "Maybe contact the attorney who filed the lawsuit."

"I've left two messages for him."

"Per your request, Lieutenant," Detective Charles said, "we've compiled as much information as we could find on both men. Who do you want to hear about first?"

"Offenbach," Sam said when her team was seated around the conference room table.

"Detective O'Brien will brief us on him," Charles said. "Matt?"

He stood and took the video controller from Charles. A smiling photo of Offenbach from the MPD website came on the screen. "Dylan James Offenbach, age thirty-seven, a twelve-year member of the MPD until this week, when he was put on administrative leave for making threats against the president, the first family and his MPD colleagues. He's the eldest of three sons born to David and Ellen Offenbach. Incidentally, his father was a sharpshooter in the Marine Corps and retired as a colonel.

"Prior to his tenure with the MPD, Dylan did four years in the Marine Corps, where he was ranked as an expert marksman, which is the highest ranking they give. In addition, he was a certified instructor from the Armed Defense Training Association. Offenbach graduated first in his class from the police academy and holds a Distinguished Expert designation from the National Rifle Association, which is the highest rating the organization grants."

"Those were all things I didn't know about him," Sam said.

"He married his high school sweetheart, Laura Taylor, when they were twenty-one. The two had six children before divorcing last year. The kids are Micha, age 11, Mathias, 9, Miranda, 8, Madeline, 6, Maddox, 4, and Maverick, 1."

"Those poor kids," Freddie said. "Having to grow up with this tied to their name."

"They have a lovely mother," Sam said, "who's in the process of changing her name and theirs to her maiden name. I'm sure she'll protect them from their father's crimes as much as she can. Dr. Trulo will help her find therapists for herself and the kids. I think they'll be okay in time."

"I hope so," Freddie said.

Matt handed Neveah the controller and took a seat.

"James Ramsey," Neveah said, "age forty-seven, a nineteen-year veteran of the MPD, with thirteen of those years in the Special Victims Unit. Before joining the MPD, he did six years in the Army, where he drove a tank in an infantry unit. Ramsey had ten years on the job before he made detective and sixteen years in before he made sergeant.

According to several officers who entered the department around the same time as Ramsey, it was assumed he was passed over for promotions due to his aggressive communication style with colleagues and members of the public.

"One officer referred to him as the bull in the china shop of SVU, indicating he was a poor fit for the unit. An SVU colleague described him as a liability who often made bad situations worse for the victims they worked with. He'd been written up numerous times for inappropriate conduct.

"At the time of his capture at Offenbach's farm in Herndon, he was facing numerous felony charges from when he rammed the lieutenant's Secret Service SUV, as well as the disruption of Tom Forrester's funeral and other miscellaneous charges pertaining to ransacking the lieutenant's office and threatening her with assault. Until last year, he'd been married to Marlene Ramsey for thirty years. In addition to their son Shane, who was killed in a shootout with MPD after being accused of numerous crimes, including sexual assault and murder, they have a twenty-eight-year-old daughter named Kerry, a twenty-five-year-old son named William, and a twenty-two-year-old daughter named Rachel."

As Sam listened to the rundown on Ramsey, she felt for the family that'd been put through hell all because of a man who couldn't handle not succeeding at work the way he thought he should have. It was so exhausting, but thankfully, he was now permanently gone, as he'd spend the rest of his life in prison for threatening to kill the president.

If there was any silver lining to the words *assassination threat*, that was it.

"You guys did a great job with these reports. If you forward them to me, I'll send them to Avery Hill to share with his team. You never know what detail will make a difference to the investigation."

"I have a question," Charles said. "You mentioned that

Ramsey and Offenbach planned to make Ruby Ridge look like a Cub Scout meeting. What does that mean?"

"Oh God," Sam said with a groan. "Way to make me feel old."

Charles smiled. "Sorry."

"No, it's fine. We studied this in my criminal justice program in college. It refers to an eleven-day standoff in Ruby Ridge, Idaho, involving the U.S. Marshals and the FBI and a self-proclaimed white separatist named Randy Weaver. The marshals had been serving a warrant on Weaver, who was holed up with his family and a friend and refused to surrender. In the end, a marshal was killed, along with Weaver's wife and son. The agencies involved were criticized for their handling of the incident, and it set off a national debate on the use of force. That, coupled with a similar standoff in Waco, which was even worse, was cited as the motivation for the Oklahoma City Bombing."

"Jeez," Charles said.

"Aren't you glad you asked?"

"Not so much."

"Needless to say, avoiding a similar disaster has to be top of mind to Avery and the others on his team," Sam said.

"Have you heard any more about what's happening in the Shenandoahs?" Gonzo asked.

"Not yet, but Avery promised to keep me in the loop if he could."

"I don't know about you guys, but I'm glad we're not involved in this mission," Freddie said.

"Agreed," Sam said. "For once, I'm more than happy to leave it to the Feds."

AVERY HATED to admit that Ramsey had struck a nerve with his reference to Ruby Ridge. Lessons from that standoff and the one in Waco were hardwired into the DNA of every FBI agent and U.S. Marshal. The last thing any of them wanted was to be associated with something like that. But this situation was shaping up to have many of the hallmarks of those earlier events, with a target who'd been preparing for this showdown his entire life.

He'd read the detailed reports from Sam's team, and the additional things he'd learned about Offenbach and his mad skills had Avery more on edge than he'd been before. Offenbach had all the advantages, especially since he'd been visiting the Shenandoah camp since he was a child and probably knew every square inch of it.

Avery's team could prepare for a year, and they'd never catch up to the lead Offenbach had on them. Even though there were hundreds of them, including FBI and ATF agents as well as U.S. Marshals and Virginia State Police, versus one of him, that meant there were also hundreds of opportunities for something to go terribly wrong. They wanted Offenbach taken alive to stand trial, but they knew the likelihood of him emerging from this mission alive was slim. If he wasn't killed in a shootout, he was apt to take his own life rather than be arrested.

At the mobile command center located a mile from the entrance to the camp, Avery gathered his team to go over the plan one more time before they executed it early the next morning.

"What're we doing about drones?" Avery's deputy, George Terrell, asked.

Avery looked to his tactical response coordinator.

"Drone-detection technology and infrared cameras deployed over the site haven't revealed any devices."

"He knows how to keep them off the radar," George said. "Are we prepared for him to use them defensively?"

"We have our drone unit in DC on standby to deploy if needed."

"I'd say they're needed," George said. "If he'll send them to the White House, why wouldn't he use them against us?"

"George makes a good point," Avery said with a sinking feeling. What else hadn't he thought of? "Let's get them here and have them ready, just in case."

While the others disbanded to see to last-minute preparations, Avery glanced at his deputy. "Good call on the drones."

"I read the info Holland's team sent over. He scares the shit out of me, Avery."

"Yeah, me, too."

Avery returned to his hotel room shortly after midnight, exhausted and as stressed as he'd been in a long time. The first thing he did was text Shelby to see if she was still awake since he hadn't talked to her all day. He hated missing a whole day with his family and would give anything to be tucked in at home with them rather than preparing for a mission that felt doomed from the start.

He wasn't sure why he felt that way. Offenbach was one guy. Avery was bringing an army. It was that one guy's extraordinary skills that made this the most dangerous thing he'd ever be a part of, and that was saying something, considering the things he'd done in his career.

Shelby responded a few minutes later while Avery was splashing cold water on his face and trying to shake the feeling of dread that'd followed him through the long day. *I'm feeding Miss Maisie.*

Avery called her.

"Hi, honey," she said softly. "How's it going?"

"It's going. Hoping to be home sometime tomorrow if all goes according to plan." He hadn't told her anything about where he was going or why so she wouldn't worry, but after that video had gone public, she'd known what he was working on and who he was after. The thought of a protracted standoff wasn't one he could bear to entertain. "How're things there?"

"We had a good day. Noah got to play with the twins this afternoon, which always makes him happy, but he was missing his dada tonight."

"I miss him, too, and you ladies as well. How's Maisie?"

"She's delightful as always."

"Just like her mama."

"Aw, thanks. You sound tired, love."

"I'm beat." And so wired, he doubted he'd sleep at all. He was beginning to look forward to the day when this shit wasn't his problem anymore. And that was new—ever since the scumbag Peckhams had broken into his home, threatened his pregnant wife and son and made him question every choice he'd ever made for his life.

"Why don't you try to get some rest while you can?"

"Yeah, I will. I wish I was there with you guys."

"We do, too."

"You set the alarm, right?"

"The second we got home."

The horror of the Peckhams terrorizing Shelby and Noah would stay with him forever. Leaving them home alone certainly felt different now than it had before that happened, even with them behind a gate inside a secure house. Was anything really secure in this crazy world?

"I love you, darlin'."

"I love you, too."

"Kiss our babies for me."

"I will. Be safe, Avery. We love you so much."

"Love you just as much. I'll call you tomorrow when I can."

"I'll look forward to that. Good night."

"Night."

He set the alarm in case he fell asleep, stretched out on top of the bed and tried to calm the storm raging inside him. But the only thing that would settle him would be the sight of Dylan Offenbach in shackles. Until that happened, there'd be no rest for the weary.

· · ·

WHILE SHE WAITED for news from Avery, Sam went ahead with the planned photo shoot at the White House on Saturday morning. She had hair and makeup with Davida and Ginger and nails with Kendra at eight a.m.

Nick would be joining her and the kids for some family photos later in the morning and had left for his security briefing right before Sam reported to the ladies for primping.

Sam felt discombobulated with the FBI preparing to raid Offenbach's camp, as if she should be briefing someone or plotting worst-case scenarios or doing something other than sitting still while the hair, makeup and nail wizards made her look good for photos that would be used by her communications team throughout the coming year as she pretended to be an engaged first lady when she was anything but.

She said a silent prayer for Avery and his team that they would capture Offenbach with no injuries or loss of life.

When her cell rang, she said, "I have to take this."

The ladies stepped back to give her space to take the call from an unknown number. "Holland."

"I, um..." a woman said. "I... I called your office, and they gave me your number..."

"What's your name, and what can I do for you?"

"It's Savannah, and I'm Dylan Offenbach's girlfriend."

Sam sat up straighter and signaled to the women that she needed a minute.

On the phone, Savannah began to cry.

"Have you spoken to him?"

"Yes. And I'm so afraid for him. He said the FBI is trying to kill him."

"They're not looking to kill him. They want to take him into custody before he hurts someone else."

"He's... He's not a bad person. His wife took his kids from him. Something in him snapped."

Sam wanted to tell her that his ex-wife getting custody of their kids didn't give him the right to kill four innocent people and terrorize another—or to direct armed drones at the White House or shoot a Secret Service agent. Not to mention what he'd done to the kids he supposedly loved.

"What can I do for you, Savannah?"

"I think he might listen to me. He... He loves me. If he thought my life was in danger, or something like that, he might be willing to surrender. I don't want him to die."

She was crying so hard that Sam could barely understand her.

"I'll reach out to the FBI agent in charge and ask him to call you. Will you be at this number?"

"Yes."

"Stand by."

Sam ended that call and made one to Avery, hoping he'd pick up when he saw it was her calling.

"Hill."

"Offenbach's girlfriend has reached out. She thinks she might be able to help because he loves her and listens to her."

"You got her number?"

Sam recited it. "Her name is Savannah, and she's worried he's going to die."

"Got it. Thanks."

Having done what she could, Sam put her phone back on the counter and signaled to the ladies that they could proceed. Her stomach was in knots, however, as she waited to hear that this nightmare had ended with no further casualties.

"Mrs. Cappuano," Ginger said. "Adrian is here. Can he have a minute while we finish up?"

"Sure."

The White House photographer came in, wearing a vest with

pockets over a denim shirt and faded jeans. His shoulder-length brown hair was pulled back from his handsome, arresting face, and his green eyes twinkled when he smiled at her. In her former single days, he would've turned her head in circles.

Now, she simply appreciated a beautiful man and got on with the business at hand.

"Adrian Fenty, ma'am," he said with a nod, since Kendra was painting the nails on her right hand a rich rose color.

"Please, call me Sam since we're spending the day together."

"Of course. I wanted to go over the schedule with you, if that's all right."

"You're the boss, my friend. Whatever you think we should do is fine by me."

"Excellent. We'll start outside with some casual photos of you playing with the kids on the play set and then move into the residence for some 'at home' shots. Maybe you helping them with homework or cooking together or coloring. That kind of thing."

Sam was ashamed at how infrequently she did any of those things with her kids, but she nodded in agreement anyway.

"Very well. I'll let you finish up in here, and I'll meet you outside when you're ready."

"See you there."

Scotty had been left in charge of getting himself ready and making sure the twins were wearing the first of three outfits Shelby had arranged for them.

When her hands were free, she called Scotty to tell him where to meet her in fifteen minutes.

"We'll be there. They look so cute."

"I can't wait to see you guys."

"You say that like you've been away for a month."

Sam laughed. "Having to sit still for an hour feels like a month."

The women tending to her laughed.

"See you soon." She slapped the phone closed. "Sorry, ladies. Patience is not my strong suit."

"No worries," Davida said. "We understand that sitting still doesn't come naturally to you."

"Thank you for making me look good."

"You don't need much help from us to look beautiful," Ginger said as she stood back to inspect her work. "I declare you good to go. Have a wonderful time with your kids."

"Thank you." Sam was thrilled to get to spend the day with them, even if there were photos involved. "I'll do that."

CHAPTER THIRTY-SEVEN

A s Sam walked back toward the residence, she was surprised to see Shelby coming toward her with Roni.

"What're you guys doing here on a Saturday?" Sam asked them.

"Supervising you," Shelby said as Roni laughed.

"Those are her words, not mine," Roni said.

"Oh please, if anyone needs supervision, it's me. You've really popped since I saw you last, Roni."

She patted her pregnant belly. "Six weeks to go, if I make it that far."

"I can't wait to meet your little one," Sam said.

"Me, too."

Sam's heart broke at the thought of Roni giving birth without her late husband by her side. She hoped that Angela reached out to Roni at some point, because the two of them had far too much in common. Roni and Angela were living Sam's worst nightmare, and she admired them both more than she could say for their courage, resilience and fortitude in facing the future without their loves.

She'd been delighted to hear that Roni had been spending

time with their sweet friend Derek Kavanaugh, who'd lost his wife, Victoria, to murder almost two years ago.

Sometimes the universe brought the right people together, she thought as she walked with her friends and Vernon, who'd come in for the day, to meet the kids outside.

They'd scored a gorgeous, sunny spring day with tulips in full bloom and a fragrant, floral scent in the air.

Armed guards were positioned around the perimeter of the White House grounds for the first time that she'd noticed. They'd be on high alert until Offenbach was in custody.

Scotty and the twins emerged through a different door, along with their Secret Service details and Skippy the dog in hot pursuit. Seeing Sam by their swing set had the twins running for her in adorable navy blue outfits. Aubrey wore a V-neck sweater with a skirt, and Alden had on a matching sweater with shorts.

"You guys look so cute," Sam said as she hugged and kissed them.

"Shelby said we can't get dirty," Alden said, "because we gotta take pictures." His wrinkled nose indicated his thoughts on the matter.

"You can get dirty after the pictures," Sam said.

"We'll get out the squirt guns," Scotty said.

Alden brightened at that.

"Adrian, we're all yours," Sam said. "How do you want us?"

SAM FOCUSED on the kids and was almost able to forget they were being photographed as she pushed swings, waited at the bottom of the slide and supervised the monkey bars. Playing with them was the most fun she'd had in ages, and the laughter brought by Skippy trying to catch the kids only added to the comedy of it all.

She couldn't wait to see what Adrian had captured.

When they moved inside, they changed into new outfits for

photos in the residence. Adrian took group shots along with individual photos of Sam with each of the kids, reading, coloring, cooking and cuddling. They'd bring in Eli and Candace for photos the next time they were home.

At one point, she smiled at something Scotty said just as he grinned up at her. She had a feeling that one might end up in a frame. Adrian also got some of Scotty and Skippy that she couldn't wait to see. They'd be a huge hit on Skippy's Instagram account.

Nick joined them right before lunch for family shots and a few of just the two of them in casual poses.

"Are you ready to stab someone with your rusty steak knife?" he asked her while Adrian switched lenses.

"It hasn't been terrible. I just wish I'd hear something from Avery."

"I was told in the morning briefing that the raid is on for today."

"Yes, I talked to Avery earlier." She rested her hand over her abdomen. "I have a pit in my stomach a mile wide waiting to hear that he and his team are okay, and Offenbach has been neutralized."

"I want this over for everyone involved."

"I feel guilty sitting in my gilded palace surrounded by security while my colleagues are in danger."

He pulled her in closer and kissed the top of her head. "I get that, but I'm so glad you're in the gilded palace and not out there in danger."

"Yeah, I know. It just feels wrong to me, though."

With every minute that went by, she became more anxious about hearing something from Avery.

AVERY GAVE the order at eleven eleven, hoping that would bring some kind of luck to an operation that needed all the luck it could get.

Agents stormed the perimeter of the twenty-acre property, coming in from all sides simultaneously as choppers flew overhead, tracking the location of the body heat coming from deep in the woods.

Everything was going according to plan when a frantic message came over the radio indicating the presence of hundreds of drones. "They're everywhere," the agent cried, "and they're shooting at us."

Motherfucker.

The commander in charge of the drone unit replied in a calm tone that went a long way toward reassuring Avery. "We're on it. Shooting them down."

Avery held his breath as the crackle of gunfire echoed loudly through the radio.

"Agent down."

"Marshal down."

"Holy shit."

Fuck.

Screams.

Groans.

Sharp cries.

Nonstop gunfire.

Avery glanced at George, who was monitoring the progress with him. The situation was too volatile to send in EMTs to assist the people who'd been shot, which only added to his anxiety.

"Fucking hell," George said. "This is going sideways fast."

"Get the girlfriend."

They'd waited for her to arrive before sending in their people.

Savannah was about five feet three inches, curvy, young and beautiful, with light brown hair, brown eyes and a flawless complexion.

George escorted her into the command vehicle.

"We need you to talk to him, Savannah," Avery said. "Call the number he used to contact you. Ask him to surrender."

She made the call and put the phone on speaker.

It rang eight times before he picked up.

"I'm busy."

"Dylan, honey, please... I'm so scared for you."

"You ought to be scared for *them*."

"I thought you said you loved me," she said between sobs.

"I do love you. I'm doing this for us so we'll have a future."

Avery glanced at George, raising a brow. In what world did he think he had a future with anything other than a cell on death row?

George shook his head in disbelief.

"What about your kids? You said you love them, too. If you come out now, they might let you see them—and me."

"She'll never let me see them."

Over the receiver in his ear, Avery heard one of his guys say, "Keep her talking to him. We can hear him."

Avery waved his hand to encourage her to continue the conversation with Dylan.

"The kids will want to see you. She'll honor their wishes. I'll make sure you see them, and me, too. I'll never give up on you, Dylan. Please... If you keep fighting, they'll kill you. I don't want to lose you."

"I don't want to lose you either," he said, sounding tearful, "but they're never going to let me out of here alive."

Avery wrote quickly on a piece of paper. TELL HIM THAT'S NOT TRUE. WE DON'T WANT ANYONE TO DIE. BUT HE MUST SURRENDER.

Savannah repeated the message. "Dylan? Did you hear me?"

"Yeah, I heard you."

"Will you surrender? Please? Do it for me and your kids... We need you."

"I don't know. I need to think."

"Drop your weapon and put your hands up!"

"Dylan! Do what they tell you to! Please!"

"Put down your weapon! You're surrounded on all sides!"

Avery barely took a breath or blinked or did anything other than listen until one of his agents said, "The subject is in custody."

Savannah broke down.

George smiled and pumped his fist.

Avery closed his eyes and exhaled. "Send in the EMTs."

EPILOGUE

S am got the full report from Avery as he drove back to the District. "He had a huge arsenal of weapons and drones, as well as enough MREs and water to last for weeks. He'd prepared for a long siege."

"Thank God it didn't turn into one. How are your injured agents?"

"One of our guys was hit in the vest and has a broken rib. The other, Marshal Memphis Rose Costello, is in surgery for a gunshot wound to the thigh. She's expected to survive, but it was touch and go for a minute there."

"Does she work with Best?"

"Yeah, one of his deputies."

"It's great news that no one was killed."

"Yeah, this could've turned out much worse than it did."

"I'm so relieved it's over."

"Me, too," Avery said. "Are we on the news?"

"Nonstop coverage, most of it positive toward you and your team, and a rehash of all the shit about me and my history with him and Ramsey. The department is taking another beating."

There'd been a tearful interview with Lorraine Sweeny's family, who expressed appreciation to the FBI for apprehending the man who'd taken their loved one from them and continued disgust over the motive for her murder.

"It'll never make sense to us why our wife, mother and grandmother was killed in such a senseless crime," Celeste Sweeny said. "We're extremely disappointed that Metropolitan Police officers who should've been keeping us safe were instead murdering innocent people."

The department had issued a statement praising the work of the federal agents who'd brought Offenbach and Ramsey to justice. *Our department will be devoted to ensuring that these lawless men spend the rest of their lives in prison,* the statement had read.

"Thank you for all you and your team did to end this thing," Sam said to Avery. "We owe you one."

"All in a day's work."

"Hardly."

"I gotta be honest. The fucking drones freaked me out, but our team was all over it and shot them down as fast as he deployed them. I'm afraid this case will serve as a how-to manual on using drones to commit crimes."

"They'll become a much bigger problem after this, for sure."

"Just what we need is more big problems."

"Don't think about that now. Go home and be with your family, with thanks from me and my family for getting the people who threatened us."

"I'm sorry the trail led to people you worked with."

"As am I, but maybe this'll be the end of the nightmare inside our house, and we can get back to fighting criminals outside our walls."

"I hope so, for all your sakes."

"Talk soon, Avery."

"Take care."

"What a fucking relief," Nick said when she closed her phone.

"Is the Secret Service standing down?"

"Somewhat. They're concerned about copycats after something like this."

That wasn't what she wanted to hear. "I need to call Archie, and then I'm all yours for date night."

Sam's mom was coming to spend the night and hang out with the kids while they were at the Ninth Street house. Due to the ongoing situation with Offenbach, Scotty had been asked to sit out the sleepover at Jonah's that weekend, with promises that the agents would make it happen when things returned to normal.

He'd been disappointed but had understood in light of current events.

Technically, he was old enough to hang at home with the twins for an evening, surrounded as they were by security, but Sam had still asked her mom to come since her nerves were raw from the last few days.

Sam made the call to Archie, hoping he'd talk to her after everything that'd happened.

"Hey," he said after the fourth ring.

"You heard the news?"

"Yeah."

"Fucking relief."

"Yep."

"How's Harlowe?"

"Much better today. Moving around without as much pain."

"I'm so glad to hear that. And what about you?"

"It's gonna take me a minute to process this."

"I'm so very sorry someone you care about was hurt because we did our jobs."

"I am, too. It's got me rethinking my life choices."

"We need you on the job, Archie. There's no one like you."

"Sure there is. There're plenty of people on my team who could step up."

"I don't want them. I want you. You're the best of the best, and we all think so."

"This has shaken me, Sam. That someone was watching me, and I had no idea. That someone I worked with could do what was done to her..."

Sam sighed. "I know, but take some time and talk to Dr. Trulo, and... well, talk to me, your friends, the people who care. There're way more of us than there are of them. You know that."

"We'd like to think so, but I'm beginning to wonder if that's true."

"It is. Of course it is."

"Thanks for calling, Sam, and for all the support this week. Means a lot."

"Call me if you need to talk. Promise."

"Yeah, okay."

"I'll check on you tomorrow. Tell Harlowe I'm so glad to hear she's feeling better."

"I will."

Sam closed her phone, feeling overwhelmed with sadness for her friend and Harlowe. What'd been done to her—and to him by extension—was outrageous. She hoped they'd be able to rise above to continue what'd begun to seem like a significant relationship for both of them.

She got a text from Freddie. *Check your email. All-hands message from the chief that you'll want to see before it's released to the media.*

Will do. Thanks for the heads-up.

She sat on the bed and opened her laptop to read the email from the chief.

To all,

Today, FBI and ATF agents as well as U.S. Marshals arrested Dylan Offenbach with the assistance of the Virginia State Police and our MPD team. Needless to say, I'm disgusted and disheartened by the role two now-former members of this department played in a series of unspeakable crimes, the latest in a series of unspeakable crimes committed by current and former members of this department.

The disgrace of Stahl, Conklin, Hernandez, Ramsey and Offenbach belongs to me and to all of us to a certain extent. They were on our team and were supposed to be defending the law, not breaking it. It sickens me to have worked with people capable of these crimes.

Let me be clear: The Metropolitan Police Department has zero tolerance for criminals in our midst. Anyone found to be violating the law or their oath to protect the citizens of this great city will be prosecuted to the fullest extent possible. I've had enough of people hiding behind the badge and collecting a paycheck from the city while living as criminals.

That ends right here and now. In consultation with union leadership, we've reached an agreement that anyone accused of a crime—misdemeanor or felony—will be suspended without pay until the matter is adjudicated. If you're found guilty, you'll be fired, and any accrued pension/benefits will be donated to charity. I will not rest until the pensions of the above-named officers are revoked and redirected to their victims' families.

Working here is a privilege, not a right. Please treat it as such. If you're incapable of serving this department and this city with honor and distinction, find another line of work. You're not wanted here.

Joseph Farnsworth

Chief of Police

Sam wanted to stand up and cheer after reading the chief's statement. Let that be a lesson to anyone who'd dare to commit crimes while wearing the badge.

Amazing, she said in a text to Freddie.

Agreed. Well done.

Let's hope we've seen the last of this shit.

Yes, please. Also, they tied Offenbach's DNA to Harlowe's rape kit, and the bullet taken from Jimmy was a match for others they found in his possession.

Horrifying all around. It's hard to believe he went to these lengths to get retribution for something HE caused. Did he honestly think he wouldn't be caught?

I think he fully expected to get away with it.

Yeah, probably. Go enjoy the rest of your weekend. Thanks for everything. Love you.

Back atcha.

She also sent a message to the chief. *Your statement was perfect. Thank you for your tremendous support and leadership.*

After stashing her laptop, Sam went into the closet to pick out stretchy black pants and a peach silk blouse to wear on her date with Nick and was dressed by the time he emerged from the shower.

He gave an appreciative whistle. "My date is the hottest gal in town."

"If you say so."

"I say so, and I'm the president."

"I love how you trot that out when it's convenient for you."

"That's the only time it's useful to me."

Smiling, she said, "I'm going to check on the kids while you finish getting ready."

"I'll be quick."

Sam kissed him and left him to get dressed. The kids were upstairs in the conservatory, watching a movie. They'd requested pizza for dinner that would be delivered to them in half an hour.

"You look pretty, Sam," Aubrey said when Sam sat next to them on the sofa.

"That's left over from the photo shoot."

"No, it isn't. You always look pretty."

Sam kissed the top of her head. "You're very nice to have around, my love."

Aubrey's sweetness filled her heart.

"You look relieved," Scotty said.

"*So* relieved. Thank goodness that's over, and everyone is okay."

"Another week, another nightmare—or two—handled by my parents."

"That about sums things up around here. We're headed to Ninth Street. Is there anything you want from over there before we pack it up?"

"Not that I can think of. Nana said if I've lived without it for six months, I probably don't need it."

"Nana is very wise. All right, kiddos. Scotty's in charge until Nana gets here."

"And then I'm still in charge," Scotty said.

Alden snickered at the muscles Scotty made.

She kissed each of them. "We'll see you in the morning, and we love you."

"Love you, too," Aubrey said for all of them.

Nick came up for hugs and kisses.

"Hey, you guys," Scotty said. "We never talked about the school thing."

"I told you," Sam said. "It's handled. They wanted you in private school. We said no, you're going to Eastern and to please make it work."

"Best parents ever," Scotty said, looking relieved. "I would've hated that."

"You think we don't know that, pal?" Nick asked. "We've got your back."

"Thank you. You know... for everything. All of it."

"We're the ones who should be thanking you," Sam said, giving him a squeeze. "Having you around has made our lives complete."

"That's nice to hear."

"Don't act like you didn't already know that."

"Well, I wouldn't want to be cocky or anything."

As always, he made them laugh.

"Be good, everyone."

"We're always good, Sam," Aubrey said.

"Yes, you sure are. We'll see you in the morning."

Nick took hold of her hand as they went downstairs together. "Greatest kids ever and date night with my best girl. Life is good."

"Sure is, except for the part about having to clean out our old house." She made a frowny face. "The fun never ends."

"It'll be fun because we get to do it together."

"Yes, it will. Thank you for the reminder that all we need is each other to have fun."

He patted her ass. "Since when do you need a reminder of that?"

"After this week, my brain is barely functioning."

The media coverage of the whole mess had been relentless, and they weren't letting go of the Hector Reese story. They'd determined that the so-called reporter who'd reached out with questions about the Fitzgerald case was probably either Offenbach or Ramsey, disguising their voice. Thankfully, the media hadn't caught wind of that story. Not yet, anyway. The fact that Ramsey and Offenbach knew about it thanks to that fucking rat Conklin meant it might still become public, which meant she'd also continue to worry about it. That was probably their goal.

In consultation with Jeannie, the chief and Malone, they'd agreed to "play dumb" if that happened. "We have no idea what you're talking about. That never happened." Or something to that effect.

Malone believed if the two men had the full details, they would've taken it to the media the way they'd done with the Reese case. Conklin must've told them only that Skip—and later Sam and Jeannie—had cut someone a break in a murder case and hadn't tied it to the Tyler Fitzgerald case, Steven Coyne's widow, Alice Fitzgerald, or the family she'd had with her second husband. The last thing in the world Sam wanted was for Alice to be put through another ordeal when she'd already had more than her share after losing her first husband and then her young son to murder.

As they were loaded into The Beast for the ride to Ninth Street, Sam was determined to push the crap out of her mind to enjoy a few hours alone with her love.

WHEN MEMPHIS ROSE opened her eyes, she had no idea where she was and was surprised to see Jesse sitting by her side, looking distraught. When she tried to move, her right leg wasn't having it. A blast of pain made her gasp.

"Easy," he said. "Don't try to move around. They want you to stay still."

"What happened?" Her mouth was so dry, it was hard to speak.

"You got shot in the thigh."

She had no memory of anything after being in the woods with Jesse and their team, looking for Offenbach. "Hurts."

He smoothed the hair back from her forehead. "I know, baby."

Did he call me baby? *What is happening?* "Is there water?"

"Yeah, right here." He held the straw for the best sip of cold water she'd ever taken.

"Did we get him?"

"We did."

"Anyone killed?"

He shook his head. "An FBI agent got hit in the vest. Busted a rib, but he's okay."

"What about the perp?"

"Taken alive."

"Good."

"Yeah, he deserves to rot in prison for the rest of his life, especially for shooting you."

"You look rough. Are you okay?"

"I'm better now."

"How come?"

He dropped his head to rest on their joined hands. "Because you didn't die."

"Did you think I would?"

"It was possible. You lost a lot of blood. Took forever to get you out of there, or so it seemed."

"I'm sorry."

When his head whipped up, she was shocked to see tears in his eyes. "You have nothing to be sorry about."

"I made you worry."

"You scared the shit out of me."

"I'll try not to do that again."

"That'd be good. I didn't enjoy this experience one bit."

"Are you being funny, Jesse?"

"No, I'm not being funny. Today was one of the worst days I've ever had, thinking I was going to lose... well... you."

"And that would've been bad?"

"Yeah. Woulda been a ton of paperwork."

Her mouth fell open in the second before he laughed. Jesse Best *laughed*.

"Are you drunk or something?"

"No, but I'd like to be. Anything to forget how close we came to disaster."

"I'm okay."

"No, you're not, but you will be. Your mom and grandmother are on the way."

"What? You called them? Why?"

"It's what we do when someone gets hurt on the job. We notify the next of kin."

"Did you call them yourself?"

"Yes, I called them myself. What kind of jerk do you take me for?"

"Am I allowed to answer that question honestly?"

Scowling, he said, "No, you're not."

"More water, please."

He held the cup and the straw while she took greedy sips of the best-tasting thing she'd ever had.

"When are they coming?"

"They land at DCA at nine."

"What time is it now?"

"Seven thirty."

"You might want to get out of here before they arrive. They'll drive you batshit crazy."

"It's fine."

Her eyelids were too heavy to stay open. "Seriously, Jesse. Get out while you can."

"I'm not going anywhere, so quit trying to get rid of me."

They were the best words he'd ever said to her. Maybe her getting shot in the leg would turn out to be the best thing to ever happen to them. Wouldn't that be something?

"WHAT SHOULD WE DO FOR DINNER?" Sam asked on the ride to Ninth Street. "Takeout?"

Nick curled his fingers around hers. "We'll think of something, I'm sure." Leaning forward in his seat, he looked out the window. "So this is what the outside world looks like. I asked them to take us the long way so I could catch a glimpse of the cherry blossoms."

"Oh, good call. I haven't seen them yet either."

"I always think of our wedding day when they bloom."

"We got lucky that they came early that year," Sam said, remembering one of the best days of her life.

"We got lucky in more ways than one that day."

"Best day ever. Right up there with Scotty's adoption and April twentieth of this year."

"Five more days until they're ours forever," he said. "I can't wait."

"I know. Aubrey is so excited about the party that night."

"Cutest daughter ever."

"We have four kids!"

Nick gave her a squeeze. "Look at us."

"Sometimes when I think about how it all happened... It's still surreal. When I offered to care for Alden and Aubrey, I never imagined it'd be forever."

"Or that we'd get Elijah out of it, too."

"Right. And a daughter-in-law."

"We have a *daughter-in-law*."

His giddiness touched her heart. All she'd ever wanted for him was the family he'd never had before. Seeing him in dad mode was one of her favorite things.

"I'd like to go on the record saying if they make me a grandmother before I'm forty, I'll never forgive them."

His laughter sparked hers. "Can you even imagine?"

"Absolutely not. *SNL* would have a blast with that."

"They'd be ruthless. Hopefully, they'll wait a while before they have children. They're still so young."

"God, I hadn't even thought about grandkids. This expedited parenthood thing isn't for the faint of heart."

"No kidding."

"I hope Jameson and Cleo would approve of us," Sam said.

"I'd like to think they would. If they're watching, they're seeing their babies being very well loved by our entire village."

"For sure, although they might not have chosen for them to grow up in the White House village."

"But what a cool and unique childhood it'll be for them. They'll tell stories about it for the rest of their lives."

"Yeah, probably."

"Speaking of cool and unique, I received an invitation to meet the king and queen of England at Buckingham Palace."

Sam sat up so she could see him. "Shut. Right. *Up*."

"I wondered if you might like to come with me."

"Duh."

Chuckling, he said, "I thought we might also swing a trip to

Paris to see the French president, since we'll be in the neighborhood."

"*London and Paris?* Am I dreaming? When?"

"June."

"It's later in June, so we might get lucky and have the new babies before we go."

"That'd be good. Can we bring the kids, since they'll be out of school?"

"Absolutely."

"I want to do high tea with Aubrey."

"We'll do it all, babe."

"Do you think the Littles will like that kind of trip?"

"They're usually up for whatever we want to do, especially if Eli and Scotty are there and excited about it."

"That's true. They tend to follow their lead. Wow, this just gets more interesting all the time. London and Paris! Sign me up!"

"I'm glad you're excited about it."

"It's even better if we bring the kids and don't have to miss them."

"What'll we do with the terrorist puppy?"

"I'm sure my mom would take her. She loves Miss Skippy."

"That'd be great. Scotty would feel good leaving Skippy with Nana."

When they took the turn onto Ninth Street, Sam ran her fingers through her hair. As the car stopped in front of their home, the first thing Sam noticed was the ramp was gone, and the concrete stairs had been rebuilt. For a second, all she could do was stare at the vastly different landscape outside their former home. Then Brant opened the door for them, and Nick took her hand to lead her out of the car.

"That was fast," she said when they were on the sidewalk. She couldn't stop staring at the spot where the ramp had once been.

"Craig was able to fit it in yesterday. I should've told you that."

"No, it's fine. I knew it was imminent." She glanced to her right to see the one in front of her dad's home was gone, too. "Everything is different now."

Nick put his arm around her. "Not everything. Some things are exactly the same, including his overwhelming love for you and the rest of us. He's so much a part of us, Sam. He always will be."

Moved by his sweet words, she nodded and went with him up the stairs and into the house they used to call home.

The place was completely empty.

"What the heck?" Sam asked as she spun around to face him.

"It turns out that when the president asks the White House staff for a little help, they're happy to oblige."

"So we don't have to do it?"

"Nope."

"Best news I've had all day."

With the furniture having been moved to the third floor, their footsteps echoed through the empty rooms. "Amazing, isn't it?" she said. "The president asks for a little help, and it's done. Just like that."

"The White House staff is outstanding that way."

"They sure are. What's left for us to do?"

"The closets in our room and the kids' rooms. Gideon said they left boxes for us."

"Do I smell food?"

Nick gave her a mysterious look. "Maybe."

"Where will I find it?"

Using his chin, he pointed to the stairs.

Intrigued, Sam went up to the second floor, where the scent was strong enough to make her mouth water. When she opened the door to their bedroom, she was greeted by the glow of candlelight. A table set for two with a bouquet of red roses on it was positioned in the middle of the otherwise empty room. Her delighted squeal made him laugh.

"Did you know," he said as he wrapped his arms around her from behind, "that the president comes with a personal chef who delivers?"

"Look at you, working the perks."

"There's gotta be something in this for me, and I couldn't take my best girl on a date and not feed her."

"I see you got your florist involved, too."

"I wouldn't have wanted her to feel left out of date night."

"What's for dinner?"

"The salmon and risotto you love, along with some filet mignon and vegetables. I asked for all our favorites. I bet he sent the cookies, too."

"The cookies are to die for." Sam turned to him and gave him a big hug and then a kiss. "This is awesome. Thank you for planning it."

"My pleasure, love. Thank you for everything."

"Haha, by 'everything,' do you mean the whole White House/first lady thing?"

"That as well as your unwavering love and support, our four beautiful kids—and our daughter-in-law—for Skippy, the first dog I've ever had, too, and the extended family you've given me. I have nieces and nephews! All of it. Every single thing."

"Your joy is my joy."

"I'm filled with it, thanks to you and the kids and the family we've created for ourselves with them and everyone else we've kept close to us during this crazy ride. But first and foremost, I'm thankful for you, the one who makes all the rest of it happen. Thank you also for not getting shot this week. I very much appreciate that."

"Whatever I can do for you."

He kissed her softly, sweetly, and had her knees going weak in a matter of seconds. "More of that after dinner."

"Yes, please."

"We can't forget that we do have to pack some stuff," he said, attempting a stern tone that was comical.

"We won't forget."

He nuzzled her neck. "We might forget when there're so many better things to do besides pack."

"What do you have in mind, Mr. President?"

"You'll see. First, dinner." He guided her to the table and held the chair until she was settled. Then he uncorked a bottle of rosé for her and cabernet for him, pouring for them like he was a sommelier and not the leader of the free world.

That thought made her giggle.

"What's so funny?"

"I was thinking that you've changed jobs and are now a sommelier."

"Is that an option? I think I'd like it better than the job I have."

"Anything is better than the job you have. Hell, the one I have, too. Why'd we pick such awful careers, anyway?"

"That's a very good question and one a shrink would have a field day with."

"The historians will wonder what brought two career masochists like us together."

"We know what brought us together."

"Hot sex, according to *SNL*."

Laughing, he said, "Yep, that's it exactly."

"It's weird to me that everything about us will be examined by historians and recorded for all of time."

"You'll have dresses in the Smithsonian."

"Stop it. No way."

"Yes way. They have a first lady exhibit. They've probably already requested the gown you wore to the inaugural ball when I was VP."

"That's so bizarre to me. Like, who cares what I wore?"

"History cares, love."

"History is a weirdo."

He nearly choked on his sip of wine. "That's something only you would say."

"I don't think much of nature either, if you must know. All that violence of animals eating each other." She shuddered. "I *cannot* with that."

"How come I've never heard about this aversion to nature before, he asks as she digs into her salmon, which comes from nature?"

She aimed her fork at him. "Do *not* talk about where the food comes from. I've got enough trouble with Aubrey's questions about chickens and eggs. Wait until someone tells her chickens have feelings. And I've told you before that I don't do nature."

"I don't believe you have."

"Is this a deal breaker?"

"Only if you refuse to go walking with me at Camp David out of fear of seeing something that can't be unseen."

"Would you protect me if an antelope was attacked by a cheetah?"

He laughed so hard, he had tears in his eyes. "There're so many things wrong with that question that I don't even know where to start."

"There's only one correct answer to the question," she said with feigned indignation.

"Of course I'd protect you from the antelope and the cheetah, but if we see them at Camp David, we have bigger problems than them attacking us or each other since neither of them is native to the mountains of Maryland."

"How do you know that?"

"Um, everyone knows that."

"Shut up. That's not true."

He rolled his lips as if trying not to laugh in her face.

"I said to shut up."

"Yes, dear."

"It's annoying how smart you are."

"And I'm not even the one who grew up right next to Maryland."

"You're pushing your luck, mister."

"Then I'll quit while I'm ahead and say I'd protect you from anything that might want to eat you. Except me, of course."

Sam choked on her mouthful of wine as she sputtered with laughter. "That's disgusting."

"You don't really think that. In fact, if I recall correctly—"

She gave him a look that ended that thought before he could finish it.

He responded with a look that would melt the panties off any straight woman with a pulse, including her. "I could always refresh your memory after dinner."

That was all it took to get her motor running for whatever he had in mind for dessert.

"We're here to pack."

"Among other things. Finish your dinner. We have an agenda."

"What agenda do we have?"

"That's for me to know and you to find out."

NICK HAD NEEDED this night away from the White House with her far more than he'd realized until they were sitting in the place they'd first called home together, bantering over cheetahs and antelopes. He recalled how she'd resisted moving in with him when he first bought this place down the street from her dad's house, because she'd felt their relationship was moving too fast. Once they'd reconnected six endless years after they first met, it'd happened at the speed of light, and he wouldn't change a thing about it.

Funny how silly that seemed now that they were married more than two years and about to be the parents of four kids. Everything they were, though, had begun in this place, and it was sad to think about not living there anymore. He doubted they'd come back there after the White House, since the Secret Service would want them somewhere more secure. They'd allowed them to live there when he was the VP only because of its close proximity to Sam's injured father. But it hadn't been ideal then, and it wouldn't be an option later.

"What're you thinking about over there?" she asked as she took a bite of the chocolate cake he'd requested because she loved it so much. He'd saved the cookies for later.

"I'm thinking about how this was the first real home I ever had and how we probably won't live here again."

"Does that make you sad?"

"More reflective than sad. Home is wherever you and the kids are, but this place will always have a special place in my heart because it's where we began—after I finally talked you into moving in with me, that is."

"Haha, I had to put up some resistance, or you might've thought I was too easy."

He laughed like he always did when she talked about being easy. "That's one word no one is *ever* going to use to describe you."

"I'm pretty easy where you're concerned."

"In some ways. In others, you keep me on my toes."

"Stop it. That's not true. I've never been easier with anyone in my life than I am with you—in every possible way it's possible to be easy."

"If you say so, dear."

"I do say so, and if you want me to continue to be easy, you'd better say so, too."

"If you were any easier, you'd melt like butter on my tongue. Better?"

"Kind of a gross way to put it, but okay."

"What's gross about butter melting in my mouth?"

She cringed. "Quit saying that."

Laughing, he said, "You know what's one of the many things I love best about you?"

"I can't wait to hear this."

"How I never, ever, *ever* know what you're going to say or do next."

"That's also not true. I'm the most boringly predictable person ever."

His eyes went wide. "Are you serious? Do you honestly think that's true? Because no one who knows you would *ever* say that about you."

"Please. What do I do but get up, go to work, come home, be with you guys, go to bed, rinse and repeat? Day after day after day."

"Oh, babe, you may follow a routine, but nothing about you is boring *or* predictable. Take my word on that. And if you don't believe me, I'm happy to take a survey of our people to ask their opinions. It's safe to say they'll all agree with me."

"Because you're the president."

"No, because I'm right." He reached across the table for her hand. "You're the most endlessly fascinating, sexy, funny, complicated, passionate, clumsy, delightful person any of us has ever met, and you keep everyone in your life highly entertained."

"You just had to toss in clumsy, didn't you?"

"Did you hear anything else I said?"

"I heard it, and most of it was nice, but the clumsy thing sort of ruined it for me."

"Is there any way I can redeem myself?"

She shrugged. "We'll see."

"Have you had enough of the cake?"

"I might have some more after we pack."

He stood and held out a hand to help her up. "Dance with me."

"To what?"

He could tell he surprised her when he pulled his iPhone from his pocket and used the music app to pick a song.

"I thought you had to give that up when they gave you the BlackBerry."

"There's no phone or internet service on it. But the music app still works." He drew her into his arms as the Bon Jovi song "Make a Memory" came on. "Remember the night I came home from making the 'welcome to Virginia' video as a senator to this song blasting through the house while you read *Congress for Dummies*?"

"How could I ever forget? That was the night I learned about Seersucker Thursday and when our favorite saying—fill her buster—was born."

"That's one of my best memories from here. What are some of yours?"

"The time I told you not to pee on me to mark me when you were afraid Avery Hill was going to steal me from you."

He scoffed. "I was never afraid of that."

"Sure you weren't."

He spanked her ass and made her laugh. "What else?"

"The first time Scotty came to stay with us for the baseball camp, and we were so freaked out about what kind of mac 'n cheese to buy for him."

"As I recall, we got it just right where he was concerned."

"Because he's the perfect kid for us."

"That, he is. I'll always remember your dad coming busting through the door in his chair, smiling from ear to ear because he could go somewhere on his own."

"Thanks to you and the ramp, which ranks right up at the top of my reasons why I love Nick C."

"Remember how you thought someone had bombed the place and called in the bomb squad?"

Sam laughed. "Mortifying."

"This is where you brought the twins to stay the first night they were with us."

"And then Miss Picklestein came to determine whether our home, which was fortified by the Secret Service, was safe for them while trying not to stare at your hotness. When you came out of the gym all sweaty with no shirt on, I swear she spontaneously combusted. She is, after all, only human."

"Shush with that."

"All those glistening muscles and rippling abs." Sam gave an exaggerated shiver. "The poor thing was lost."

"Lalala, I can't hear you."

She laughed at his usual resistance to talking about his hotness. "Harry and Lilia met here, and we staged that get-together to bring down Melissa Woodmansee. That was a night to remember."

"I'd prefer to forget how crazy that got."

"All in a day's work."

The next song was their wedding song, "Thank You For Loving Me."

"Ah, I love this song," she said. "It's so perfect for us."

"Sure is."

"We really ought to do some packing."

"If we have to."

Nick released her but only because he knew she'd be back in his arms in a few short minutes. As he followed her across the hall to her closet, he was right there when she opened the door to an empty room except for a few things that'd been left at his request.

She spun around. "What the hell?"

He put his hands on her hips and kissed her. "Did you honestly think I was going to waste precious time alone with you packing boxes? It's all done."

"This is a full-on hoodwink."

"Nah, it's just a night alone together. Look in the box."

She bent to flip open the flaps and found the pillows and blanket he'd asked them to leave behind.

"I was thinking we could re-create our first night here, when we made a camp in front of the fireplace. I think we even used that blanket."

"We did." She smiled up at him. "This is perfect. I hate to pack, and I hate to move."

"You think I don't know that?"

"What about the kids' stuff?"

"It's already been moved. It'll be brought up to the residence tomorrow for them to go through what they want to keep and what can be donated."

"You think of everything."

"I didn't want to waste any time with you. Shall we go make a camp?"

"Yes, please."

They carried the pillows and blanket into their room. Nick lit the electric fireplace while she arranged the pillows on the floor.

"I remember thinking that having a fireplace in the bedroom was the most bougie thing I'd ever have in my life, but of course you had to go and top that a million times over with butlers and ushers and chefs."

Smiling, he unbuttoned the peach silk blouse that he'd been dying to get his hands on since the moment she appeared in it earlier. Her stretchy black pants landed next to it on the floor a minute later, followed by his sweater and jeans. "I do what I can for my person."

"Trademarked."

"That's not the exact phrase, so the trademark doesn't cover it."

"Quit being a smarty-pants if you want to get laid tonight. I already know you're the smartest person in every room you're in. You don't have to keep proving it to me."

"I'm just saying…"

"Clearly, there's only one way to shut you up." She went on tiptoes to kiss his face off. "Thank you for this, by the way."

"Anything for you."

With the music still playing in the background, he spun her around and into a dip to lower her to their setup on the floor.

"Wow, smooth move, babe," Sam said as he came down on top of her to nuzzle her breasts.

"I practiced that in my head before I did it."

"I'd give it a ten out of ten for execution—and you didn't throw your back out. That's impressive."

"Oh please, you're lighter than a feather."

"Sure I am."

"I love every delicious curve." He released the front clasp of her bra and pushed it out of his way. "I love your soft skin and the sexy scent of your skin and the way you taste. Everything about you does it for me."

"I feel like I've said this before, but you know I'm a sure thing, right?"

Smiling, he said, "Don't interrupt me when I'm on a roll telling you all the things I love about you." He sat back to help her out of her panties and his boxer briefs before coming back to kiss her.

"I love being here all by ourselves."

"With agents outside."

"Shhh, we're as alone as it gets these days."

With her arms and legs holding him hostage, he kissed her as he joined his body to hers and felt himself completely relax even as the blood pumped through his veins the way it always did when they were together this way. She was the only one who could make him forget the relentless demands he lived with every other waking moment.

"Mmm, Samantha... How does this get better all the time?"

"I don't know, but I never get enough."

Her phone rang, and they groaned.

"Don't stop. I'll get it after."

He wished the whole world would leave them alone for a few hours so they could wallow in the time to themselves.

The phone rang again.

"Fuck," he muttered as he withdrew from her and flopped

onto his back, knowing she could no more ignore a ringing phone than he could.

She got up to retrieve her phone from her coat pocket. "Sorry."

"It's okay." He took advantage of the opportunity to watch her walk around naked.

"Hey, Trace? What's up?"

Sam went completely still. "For how long?" After another second, she said, "I'm coming."

"What's wrong?" Nick asked, alarmed by her tone and expression.

"Ethan is missing."

∼

Oops, I did it again! LOL! Come on, you know you love my baby cliffhangers that have you demanding the next book *right now*!

Thank you for reading STATE OF RETRIBUTION, the TWENTY-FIFTH full-length book in Sam and Nick's ongoing story. I never cease to be amazed by how fun these characters are to write after all this time, and how they continue to be the gift that keeps on giving in the way they inspire me with new stories and banter and all the rest. I'm super excited for STATE OF PRESERVATION, which will be out in late December to give you something to do during your holiday break! Preorder STATE OF PRESERVATION right now at marieforce.com/stateofpreservation.

June 20th marked the 15th anniversary of FATAL AFFAIR's release. Thank you to everyone who's been on this ride with me, Sam and Nick for the last fifteen years. Without all of you, I wouldn't still be writing their story or living my dream come true every day as I get to lose myself in these stories. Best "job" ever, and it's all thanks to you, the readers.

Discuss STATE OF RETRIBUTION with spoilers allowed

here: *www.facebook.com/groups/stateofretribution/* and make sure you're a member of the Fatal/First Family Group (no spoilers please) here: *www.facebook.com/groups/FatalSeries*. If you're not receiving weekly emails from me, please join my list at *https://marieforce.com/subscribe* and make sure you indicate where you prefer to get your books, so we can keep you informed of books coming and going from your favorite retailer.

As always, a huge thank you to the amazing team that supports me behind the scenes, including my husband, Dan, and my tremendous HTJB crew: Julie Cupp, Lisa Cafferty, Jean Mello, Nikki Haley and Ashley Lopez, as well as my daughter and sidekick, Emily Force. A HUGE thank you to Captain Russell Hayes, Newport Police Department (retired), for being my cop on call for all these years. I couldn't and wouldn't write one of these books without his help with the law enforcement aspects of the story.

To my editors, Linda Ingmanson and Joyce Lamb, thank you for always being ready to help me whip a new book into shape, and to my primary beta readers, Anne Woodall and Kara Conrad, thank you for your many contributions. Gwen Neff reads for continuity, which is a huge help as this series becomes ridiculously long! Keeping track of all the details makes my addled brain go muzzy, so I'm thankful for all the help that Gwen and the other Fatal/First Family betas provide, including: Kelly, Kelley, Jennifer, Ellen, Sarah, Karina, Elizabeth, Viki, Maricar and Gina.

Thank you so much for fifteen years of Sam and Nick. I'll be forever grateful to everyone who loves them as much as I do.

Much love,

Marie

ALSO BY MARIE FORCE

Romantic Suspense Novels Available from Marie Force

The First Family Series

Book 1: State of Affairs

Book 2: State of Grace

Book 3: State of the Union

Book 4: State of Shock

Book 5: State of Denial

Book 6: State of Bliss

Book 7: State of Suspense

Book 8: State of Alert

Book 9: State of Retribution

Book 10: State of Preservation *(Dec. 2025)*

Read Sam and Nick's earlier stories in the Fatal Series!

The Fatal Series*

One Night With You, *A Fatal Series Prequel Novella*

Book 1: Fatal Affair

Book 2: Fatal Justice

Book 3: Fatal Consequences

Book 3.5: Fatal Destiny, *the Wedding Novella*

Book 4: Fatal Flaw

Book 5: Fatal Deception

Book 6: Fatal Mistake

Book 7: Fatal Jeopardy

Book 8: Fatal Scandal

Book 9: Fatal Frenzy

Book 10: Fatal Identity

Book 11: Fatal Threat

Book 12: Fatal Chaos

Book 13: Fatal Invasion

Book 14: Fatal Reckoning

Book 15: Fatal Accusation

Book 16: Fatal Fraud

Contemporary Romances Available from Marie Force

The Wild Widows Series—a Fatal Series Spin-Off

Book 1: Someone Like You *(Roni & Derek)*

Book 2: Someone to Hold *(Iris & Gage)*

Book 3: Someone to Love *(Winter & Adrian)*

Book 4: Someone to Watch Over Me *(Lexi & Tom)*

Book 5: Someone to Remember *(Nov. 2025)*

The Gansett Island Series

Book 1: Maid for Love *(Mac & Maddie)*

Book 2: Fool for Love *(Joe & Janey)*

Book 3: Ready for Love *(Luke & Sydney)*

Book 4: Falling for Love *(Grant & Stephanie)*

Book 5: Hoping for Love *(Evan & Grace)*

Book 6: Season for Love *(Owen & Laura)*

Book 7: Longing for Love *(Blaine & Tiffany)*

Book 8: Waiting for Love *(Adam & Abby)*

Book 9: Time for Love *(David & Daisy)*

Book 10: Meant for Love *(Jenny & Alex)*

Book 10.5: Chance for Love, *A Gansett Island Novella (Jared & Lizzie)*

Downeast

*The Treading Water Series**

The Butler, Vermont Series*

(Continuation of Green Mountain)

Book 1: Every Little Thing *(Grayson & Emma)*

Book 2: Can't Buy Me Love *(Mary & Patrick)*

Book 3: Here Comes the Sun *(Wade & Mia)*

Book 4: Till There Was You *(Lucas & Dani)*

Book 5: All My Loving *(Landon & Amanda)*

Book 6: Let It Be *(Lincoln & Molly)*

Book 7: Come Together *(Noah & Brianna)*

Book 8: Here, There & Everywhere *(Izzy & Cabot)*

Book 9: The Long and Winding Road *(Max & Lexi)*

Single Titles

In the Air Tonight

Five Years Gone

One Year Home

Sex Machine

Sex God

Georgia on My Mind

True North

The Fall

The Wreck

Love at First Flight

Everyone Loves a Hero

Line of Scrimmage

Historical Romance Available from Marie Force

*The Gilded Series**

Book 1: Duchess by Deception

Book 2: Deceived by Desire

* Completed Series

ABOUT THE AUTHOR

Marie Force is the #1 *Wall Street Journal* bestselling author of more than 100 contemporary romance, romantic suspense and erotic romance novels. Her series include Fatal, First Family, Gansett Island, Butler Vermont, Quantum, Treading Water, Miami Nights and Wild  Widows. Watch for her all-new Remington Family Law Series coming in 2026!

Her books have sold 15 million copies worldwide, have been translated into more than a dozen languages and have appeared on the *New York Times* bestseller list more than 30 times. She is also a *USA Today* bestseller, as well as a Spiegel bestseller in Germany.

Her goals in life are simple—to spend as much time as she can with her "kids" who are now adults, to keep writing books for as long as she possibly can and to never be on a flight that makes the news.

Join Marie's mailing list on her website at *marieforce.com* for news about new books and upcoming appearances in your area. Follow her on Facebook, at *www.Facebook.com/MarieForceAuthor*, Instagram @marieforceauthor and TikTok @marieforceauthor. Contact Marie at *marie@marieforce.com*.

Made in the USA
Coppell, TX
22 July 2025

52141126R10246